Eva

Kevin C. Popp

Copyright

ISBN: 978-1-7323211-3-7
Written by Kevin C. Popp

www.TheGarrisonSeries.com
Instagram www.instagram.com/popp.kevin
or Facebook at www.facebook.com/TheGarrisonSeries

Editing and Interior Design by Nita Robinson, *Nita Helping Hand?* NitaHelpingHand.com
Cover by Kelly Martin, KAM Designs www.KAM.design

Chapter One

*I*s attaining nearly complete perfection, like no human has ever achieved, enough to satisfy my innermost passions? Would my Marci ever grow tired of her new body and appearance? Would the future progenies that I was to have with my sister be as perfect as us?

Life is a strange adventure. The longer you live, the more eccentric life becomes. This part of my existence on earth, my life, was at a good juncture. I finally had a family that respected and at times loved me. It was pleasant not to have family members or other humans running around my house who were afraid of me.

My Marci, the love of my life, wanted to have children, many of them, but I was afraid she would die during pregnancy or childbirth. I couldn't live with myself if I were the cause of her death. That wasn't a possibility. In my past experiments with animals and humans, the mother died giving birth. The formula produced multiple kids in the womb, and it seemed that four fetuses was the popular number.

I believe one of the main reasons why Marci wanted children was because all her life she had felt unwanted. No one even came close to adopting her. She naturally felt the urge to nurture and protect little ones. She wanted to be sure she would offer her future children a life filled with the love that she had never experienced. I feared that someday reality would set in for her and she might not want to have children for one reason or another. She is a very loving person, but she also can be ruthless and unfeeling. She has a quite a demonic side to her personality when she is angered.

I often wondered if my sister, Eva, ever came to total acceptance of having a child with me in the future, and I wondered how that would affect the relationship with my Marci and my sister?

My sister was a beautiful and perfect being. She was the finest example of perfection that was created from the purest version of Formula L, which I share with her. We are one and the same physically and metabolically.

I had so much to teach her. I was the only one in the world that understood what she was experiencing. I was the only one that could guide her the proper way. I wished I'd had someone in my life guiding me when I was her age. I wished I'd had someone that loved me for who I was and not out of fear of me or a sense of duty. I grew tired of always being looked at as the freak of the family when actually I was the one that was pure and perfect. Little did they know, I was better than all of them. They couldn't understand who I was and even to this day, that lack of knowledge was buried in their coffins with them. To think that at one time I mourned their deaths and waited for them to show me love or the slightest bit of attention. I even blamed myself for their lives being terminated. Today I know better, thanks to my parents and Marci. I have them to thank for my mental freedom and for them giving me that personal revolution.

I worried about my parents and Marci constantly. I worried about my parents fully adapting to this new world, and feared that any day someone might discover their existence and call the authorities. That would have been very difficult to explain. I then had concern over my sister. She was young and unafraid. What if someday she made a mistake and tipped her hat to our way of life? I was also troubled with the fear that one day I would wake up and something might happen to my love, like Marci might start to experience a secondary metamorphic change. From all accounts and from the vast array of experiments I didn't believe that would happen, but one never really knew. I wondered if someday the formula might start to change Marci. I thought she was perfect the way she looked now, but what if her body started to transform further? Worse yet, what if that possible transformation ended up killing her? I knew Marci feared this as well. I sensed her thinking about it from time to time.

There were so many facets to the formula, so much that we didn't know or understand. These aspects of the formula tended to lay dormant in the innermost hidden parts of our DNA. No one could predict with certainty that her form would stay true to this original transformed state. I pondered these thoughts every day of my life.

Many years had passed and Eva was now in grade school. Because of her high level of intellect, she skipped kindergarten and the first three grades. For grades four and five, as well as middle school, I sent her to

Louisville Collegiate School. Collegiate was regarded as the top grade, middle and high school; not only in the state of Kentucky but in the southeast region of the country.

Eva made many friends and was well liked in the beginning. I wanted Eva to attend a better school because she was far more advanced than any other students, as well as her teachers. Wolfgang kept insisting we keep her at her current school. He thought she was too young to attend another school in a different state or at a more advanced school with much older students. My father was correct in his assertion. We needed Eva to grow emotionally and to be able to get along with people that looked like her. Every day was a challenge because we didn't want her to tell others about the way our family looked. Her 'sister-in-law' and her parents would be perceived as monsters to anyone that would lay eyes on them. We could never allow that to happen. Not a day passed that Eva was not aware of the responsibility she shouldered. We needed to keep her close to home because if we sent her off to a school out of state, there was no one that we could trust to take care of and look after her.

Eva continued her education at Louisville Collegiate. She was widely known throughout the city as the most impressive of young prodigies. We had numerous tutors for her that were experts in an array of subject matters and we participated in many online courses. It was a struggle keeping her attention because she wasn't challenged academically in any way.

Every instructor that we met was impressed with Eva. We had many colleges sending us literature and attempting to contact us through social media and phone. All the major schools wanted Eva to attend their university, not only because of her notoriety but also because of our family money and prestige.

The most important element in Eva's education at this point in her life was her social development. Because of my parents and Marci's physical appearance, we rarely had any of her friends over to our house. The only way Eva could spend time with her friends was at school. Time was of little consequence to any of us so spending a few years here and there was not an issue.

Early life was a fun time for Eva. She loved her cat, Midnight. She would play with her for hours on end. Our father kept a close eye on the cat and Eva whenever she played with her. He never wanted the cat to escape into the wild. She would be impossible to catch and it would only be a matter of time before she bit another animal. In so doing, she would cause that animal to mutate, thus an entirely new species would develop that the world had never seen.

During her days at Collegiate, Eva played soccer and was far advanced with the sport. She was, by far, the best player on her team, and her hand-eye coordination was unworldly. She never missed a kick. Her ability to dribble the ball with her feet was uncanny to watch. Everyone marveled at her abilities. After a year of playing for her grade school team, she quickly grew tired of the sport.

In the winter months she played basketball and excelled beyond any of her coaches' expectations. She was the tallest and most physically developed student in her class and, for that matter, most developed in the school. I videotaped all her games and many of her practices for my parents and Marci to watch. Since they couldn't go to the practices or games, that was the only option for them to see her in action. She was an athletic marvel.

Eva also took up karate and dance during her grade school years, excelling in both, and became a black belt in a remarkably short period of time. Eva loved to dance. I suggested ballet to her and in a few months she was dancing like a professional. I was told by all her instructors that her balance was something they had never seen before. She had such command of the predetermined choreographic movements that many at the ballet school were afraid of her.

Eva quickly grew bored and frustrated with the fact that no one could keep up with her. Everyone kept making mistakes and it slowed her down. She quickly lost interest and abandoned the ballet practices as well as karate. I received so many calls from her many instructors, begging me to encourage her not to give up ballet. I sat down with Eva on many occasions and told her she was very special and that her many skills were so far advanced compared to others. She knew she was different, but in her mind she couldn't understand why sports, dance, playing musical instruments and academics came so difficult to others. It frustrated her not to have competition. She quickly viewed her peers as subservient and unworthy of her time. Her superior attitude showed at school and many of her classmates began to ignore her.

Eva got depressed a few times during these years. To use her own words, she felt like "a freak of nature" compared to everyone else. I couldn't argue that fact because she was an oddity of humankind. She wanted to be with people that were just as good as her. It was very difficult to convince such a prodigy of life that there were just a handful of people in this world that had her skills, and all of them lived under the same roof.

Eva struggled with her friends' imperfections and quickly grew annoyed by their simplistic minds. To further complicate matters, she became even more aggravated when I told her that her friends were some of the smartest kids in the city. Louisville Collegiate was for highly advanced children, and she had the hardest time understanding that there were slower and lesser developed kids her age. She couldn't believe that so many "ignorant" people existed in this world. I understood what she was going through. I tried as hard as I could to explain what it was like to be a normal human and the difficulties that existed for them. For example, they had trouble remembering formulas and facts, and had difficulty figuring out mathematical equations. Trying to understand others' shortcomings was by far the most difficult part for me as a child. It was more difficult than my teenage years. This depressed Eva often and would haunt her throughout her young life.

Eva's interests were wide and varied. When I was a child, my interest was geared toward the violin and experimenting with my hand-eye coordination. I didn't have someone in my life that understood who I was when I was Eva's age so I took it upon myself to help my sister in any way possible throughout this most difficult juncture of her long life. When I was Eva's age, my passion toward chemistry and biology grew exponentially. If I'd had someone that would have helped guide me at that time, I would have gotten through school quicker than what I did. I felt that it was my duty as an older brother to help Eva find her passion in life. For that to happen, I wanted to expose her to as many interests as possible so she could make her own decisions on what she wanted to do with her life.

One of Eva's hidden passions was her love of opera. For years, Eva was used to Zelda singing throughout the house or listening to Marci play her violin while Zelda sang an aria. I remember studying her when she listened to our mother sing. Her eyes would fill up with tears and I sensed the depth of her passion for singing. She loved the sound that the voice created. I had that same passion when I played the violin. I believe it was the creation portion that drove our longing for that particular vehicle of musical expression. I understood more than most about the after-effects of the formula. For Eva, it was the attention that she derived from performing that drove her passion.

This revelation came to light one afternoon while Eva stood in the great room listening to our mother sing. Without warning, Eva started singing along with Zelda. The sound that came out of her mouth was pure, strong and so delightful that it brought tears to my eyes. Eva demonstrated that her operatic voice was one of her greatest talents, besides her ability to play the violin. Zelda stopped after a few bars. She was overcome with joy that her daughter had a great gift, but this was not a gift that was only created by the formula. Formula L only enhances the host's innate talents; therefore, if the host is naturally skilled in a certain area, the formula only improves that gift.

Eva's voice was more advanced than at the beginning stages of her learning to play the violin. Singing came naturally for her. Zelda taught her many nuances of voice. Eva took her instructions very seriously and never wavered from Zelda's direction. In the beginning stages of her voice training, we treated the experience as something fun for Eva and Zelda to share together. As time progressed, Eva's voice morphed into a stunning display of incredible control of a wide range of pitches. Through the many years of Zelda's structured past, including majoring in voice during her college years, she quickly took notice of Eva's incredible talent. Zelda trained Eva to the best of her ability and in a short time Eva was singing with the best of voices. They would listen to recorded concert arias and parts of selected operas. Many times, they would act out the selected parts they heard.

Over the years we fed Eva's desire to play her violin with some of the greatest orchestras around. Over the previous five to seven years she played in London, England, Rome, Italy and Amsterdam, Holland, not to mention orchestras from New York, Boston, Seattle, Louisville and Cincinnati. At times, I would perform with her or play a separate work on the same night. Now she had another avenue for adventure. Now Eva greatly desired to sing in front of people.

Eva was about to graduate from the eighth grade, thus the next step for her was high school. Every local high school wanted Eva to attend their school. We had numerous offers from performing arts schools from across the country inquiring about Eva's future and current interests. Few of these schools offered her an immediate opportunity all because of her young age, although Eva was far advanced. Eva knew what she wanted to study when it came to her schoolwork. She had many interests and excelled in all subjects, but she didn't have an interest in pursuing any traditional areas of education. She didn't have an inkling of what she wanted to major in when it came time for college, but she knew she wanted to pursue a life in music.

Although Eva received tons of offers from the best performing arts schools in the world, Wolfgang and I again thought Eva going to school away from home at such a young age was not a possibility. Of course, this greatly upset Eva. She wanted to get out from under her dad's thumb, but she understood her situation and knew why she wasn't allowed to leave home.

We decided Eva would continue her education at Louisville Collegiate High School. Eva grew into a beautiful and talented young high school student. She was a towering nearly six-foot-tall, blonde-haired goddess. She was consistently getting into trouble at school, partly because she was so bored, partly because she was just rude to others. She became so bored with school simply because it was so easy for her. Again, because of her youth I wanted her to stay in school as long as she could. The administration was patient with us because having her at Collegiate gave them an even better reputation.

Eva passed the time by playing in most of the sporting events the school had to offer. She was the best at lacrosse, basketball and soccer. She was the leader of the debate, robotics and quick recall teams. Every college in America and abroad knew of the great Eva Seawick. She was offered a fully paid scholarship to every Ivy League school, including Notre Dame, Stanford, Oxford, MIT, Julliard, and Northwestern, plus over a hundred other schools.

We could have pushed her along at a faster rate, but we wanted her to stay home as long as possible. When it came time for college choices, all of the best schools were trying to court her and Eva was becoming very upset with our father. She wanted to attend Juilliard, mostly due to prestige and vanity issues. I sat down with my sister countless times and told her that Juilliard couldn't really teach her anything she didn't already know, but that didn't make a difference to her. She wanted to attend Juilliard, her dream school. She was concerned that if she didn't take their offer now, it wouldn't be there in the future. Of course, she knew that we would be able to get her in at any time because of her talent and our money, but the concern still lingered in the back of her mind.

I made a deal with Eva. I told her if she received her undergraduate degree from one of our local colleges in Louisville, I would see what I could do about Juilliard. Eva was very receptive of the idea. Without any hesitation, Eva enrolled at Bellarmine University, a small Catholic college that rests in the suburbs of Louisville. Bellarmine was largely known as a nursing and business school. Years ago, it was a small college, but through the years the college developed into a university. After the depression hit, Bellarmine was one of the few universities in the Commonwealth that received public funding to keep it growing. Bellarmine developed into one of the leading educational intuitions in the southern part of the United States, quickly becoming known as the Notre Dame of the south.

The administration people were overcome with joy when they heard that we had decided on Bellarmine. Eva was growing so fast both physically and mentally that I was concerned she was going to be bored out of her mind. Eva was so advanced, well beyond her years. Wolfgang and I were concerned about her going to college by herself so we pondered the idea of hiring someone to at least drive her to school, but Eva flatly refused. She wanted to drive to school but she was too young to drive legally. Marci and I talked with Eva about the issue. After several long discussions, we reluctantly decided to take the chance and allow her to drive herself to school. Eva was thrilled beyond belief and wanted to pick out her own car.

Eva and I went car shopping and she decided on a fire red Porsche. Eva always wanted to make a statement and this sports car certainly did that. Eva didn't have to learn to drive. It came naturally to her after five minutes behind the wheel of her new toy. She could sense what others were going to do in front of her. Whenever I drove with her, she handled the car with great ease and precision.

Eva's first year was a productive one. She majored in Music, with an emphasis on the violin and Business Finance. Eva didn't make many friends and didn't join the clubs or sororities that were offered. Most of the students wanted her to sign up but when some of the students got to know her, word quickly spread that she was a very difficult and unfriendly person.

One club that Eva thought she would like was the Debate Club. When she joined, the members were honored, but they wondered how good of a debater she would be. After the first practice, Eva was noted to be Bellarmine's best debater. Her physical beauty and size mixed with supreme intellect made her one of the best debaters in the Commonwealth. She would go to other local campuses and debate, and she never lost. Her quick recall of facts and figures set her apart from all the rest.

Eva was a rock star on campus. Everyone knew who she was and how famous she had become. Half of the women on campus wanted to be her best friend while the other half hated her, mostly because they were jealous of her. Eva dated a few guys but they all knew she was under eighteen. This was very frustrating for Eva because her body was screaming for sexual adventure, but no boy wanted to fuck her because of her youth. Many of the guys on campus were totally infatuated with her. Her beauty was so difficult to clearly define.

Her long blonde hair was her staple. When she walked, her head never bounced. She walked in perfect rhythm and harmony every step that she took. She had a flawless complexion, perfect teeth, and wore the most expensive clothes at the school.

Marci and Eva would spend hours online buying clothes for young Eva. I paid the bill and they did the shopping. Eva never wore any underwear at any time of the day. She hated the feeling of anything on her private areas. This little fetish she had against bras and panties was quickly noticed by the students and the professors.

Eva never made less than an A in all her classes, and only missed three test questions throughout her undergraduate classes. Against the administration's policy and rules, she doubled her class load and took as many summer classes as possible. Due to some rather large donations that I made, the administrators allowed Eva to take as many courses as she wanted. In a short two years, Eva graduated from Bellarmine with the highest of honors. She was the talk of the city and the Commonwealth. She received many national honors and acclaims for her accomplishments. Eva was a fast study who could read something once and have the content committed to memory.

Not only was she a brilliant violinist, she was one of the smartest people to ever attend Bellarmine University. Eva later decided to get her Master's Degree in Finance.

Eva was cocky and not all the professors liked her. She was argumentative and degrading to others, which came naturally to her. She often had no clue how rude and obnoxious she was to both students and professors.

During these years at Bellarmine, Eva wanted to pursue a more professional avenue with her voice instead of just singing in the house with her mother. Eva knew that because of her voice talents, she could perform in front of people. Like her talent with the violin that had afforded her so much national attention, she knew the same could be done with her voice. Eva would sing at small afternoon concerts where music students got the chance to show off their talents.

The first day, Eva showed up and walked to the microphone while most in attendance quietly mocked her. They thought she was just making fun of the situation. From the moment Eva sung the first note, the entire group of fifty or so students were transfixed in a state of marvel. When Eva was finished, she walked out quietly with just a smile on her face. The Dean of Music chased Eva down as she was making her way out of the building. The Dean, José Kussing, said, "Eva, I had no idea that you could sing like that. Your voice is purely magnificent."

Eva said, "I know. I practice at home occasionally and my father tells me all the time that I have a wonderful voice. But I don't need him to tell me that. I know I have a great voice."

José asked, "Have you ever considered working with someone at the university?"

Eva laughed and said, "You mean someone like you?"

José smiled and said, "Yes. Do you like performing in front of people?"

Eva looked the other way and smiled. "Yes I do."

José said, "Stop by tomorrow around noon and we can talk more about your vocal talent."

Part of Eva's personality was the desire to perform for an audience. Eva wanted to sing in front of people because it made her feel alive. Eva's personality pushed her to be an adrenaline junkie of sorts. The pressure and thrill of performing made her senses more alive than at any other time and that is what she craved. She needed to feel that experience. Her soul required this adrenaline rush.

During Eva's time at Bellarmine, Eva met with José numerous times and he did teach her a few things about voice. Toward the end of Eva's time at college, whenever she would practice in the voice room, Eva had a rather large contingency of students that wanted to hear her sing. Eva enjoyed the attention that her voice demanded. Word traveled throughout the city about this talented violin prodigy who could also sing at a very high level.

After Eva graduated, she wanted to explore her vocal talents. Through my numerous contacts, Eva was able to audition in front of some of the voice experts with the Louisville Opera. They were impressed with how advanced she was with her newly found expertise. The Louisville Opera arranged for her to try her hand at singing for churches and small concerts that were in association with the Louisville Opera. Eva didn't like going into churches, but she swallowed her pride and performed.

Eva's voice improved dramatically during this juncture. Zelda, our mother, wanted to be her only voice coach, but Eva had other thoughts in mind for her future. Zelda could sense her wanting to stray in other directions with a potentially new voice coach. Zelda understood that she couldn't be there for her because of her physical appearance and could only do so much for Eva. Over time, Zelda backed off the notion of being her sole voice coach. Zelda knew she needed to let go of Eva and allow someone else to venerate her passions, although it was difficult for Zelda. It was, for her, like losing a part of her daughter to someone else. Because of her great love for Eva, Zelda gave her permission to seek out new people to teach her and nurture her in the future.

Eva and I interviewed several voice coaches at the Louisville Opera and the University of Louisville's Performing Arts. I was there with her every step of the way and assisted her with any help that she might have needed. Eva really enjoyed the company of Brittany Knights, a lady that worked and taught at the Performing Arts School at the University of Louisville. Brittany was a middle-aged brunette whose personality fit Eva's very well. She had a nurturing personality with a brilliant smile to match. I asked Brittany if she would like to be Eva's voice coach and she was delighted to accept the challenge.

Brittany was most impressed with Eva's voice and within no time had made many calls to people she knew in the industry. Eva was going to numerous auditions and each time she impressed them beyond belief. Before we knew it, the Louisville Orchestra wanted Eva to sing an aria and play a violin piece on the same night. Eva accepted and completed the challenge without making a mistake. The local and national print and radio media all witnessed the recording of her work. Within days, Eva was a renowned child prodigy twice over. Every major concert hall was calling to reserve a place for her to perform. Eva was beyond happy. This type of attention is what she craved. It made her feel so alive and fresh. Over the many months, Eva performed numerous times in front of her desired group of fans.

I spoke with Brittany about Eva's future. She told me that she had some pull and might be able to work something out that would benefit Eva greatly. I knew what she was working on, but I kept it to myself for a few days. I was sitting with Marci in our great room and Eva was in the kitchen with our parents. Early that afternoon, out of the blue the phone rang. I checked the caller ID and a smile developed on my face. I answered the phone and a gentleman was on the other end of the line. His name was Walter Goins. He told me he was the headmaster of one of the most esteemed arts and music schools in America. He wanted to interview Eva for a spot at the institution. I called for Eva to see if she wanted an interview. Knowing full well that she would have done anything to get an invitation for an interview, I wanted to surprise her. When Eva came into the room, her senses told her that I had some wonderful news. I said to Eva, "I have Juilliard on the phone. They are requesting an interview. Are you interested?"

Eva screamed loudly and started jumping around. Walter was laughing on the other end of the phone and said, "I take it that is a yes?"

I said, "I believe so."

When I hung up the phone, Eva ran into my arms and hugged me tight. She was so excited. Juilliard is one of the best performing arts schools in the world. Eva had dreamt of attending this institution and this was the school she wanted on her resume. It fed her vanity. Juilliard was one of the few schools that accepted very young students, so this was the perfect opportunity for young Eva to really excel.

Eva was jumping and running around the house with excitement. She went up to our father and suddenly Wolfgang said, "You are not going. It's too risky, too dangerous for you."

Zelda, nodding her head in agreement, said, "Yes. You are too young, Eva, and it is too risky."

Eva stood still, listening to the most awful news that she had ever heard in her life. She was speechless. I will never forget the horrid expression Eva made as she heard those dreaded words coming out of her parents' mouths. Of course, I was concerned myself, but I had felt this was a great opportunity for her, like my Harvard experience was for me when I was young. Eva's eyes started to fill up with tears. She quickly placed her hands over her face and wept harshly. Eva struggled to gain control over her emotions. After several moments she wiped the tears from her eyes and said sternly, "I want to go to Juilliard!"

Wolfgang said, "I said NO!" and banged his large hand on the table.

Normally Eva would have backed down, but this time she stood firm and didn't move a muscle. She again said, "I said, I want to go to Juilliard!" As the words ran out of her mouth, she stomped her foot as hard as she could on the hardwood floor of our great room. Wolfgang's breath started to increase, and you could hear the beat of his heart and feel the anger in his soul as he sat there looking at the defiant one.

Eva's facial expression didn't waver. She was angry. Wolfgang slowly rose to his feet. Zelda stepped over and placed her hand on his forearm. She was concerned about what Wolfgang might do to their daughter. Eva spoke, "I am mature enough to handle Juilliard. I have been all over the world with Garrison. At Juilliard they have people that will take care of me. You know I would never do anything that would hurt you, Father. I have never said anything about you or Mother to any of my friends." Wolfgang looked at me and I nodded in agreement. Eva continued to make her plea. "You want me to mate with my own brother. I told you that was fine with me so the least you can do for me is allow me to attend Juilliard."

Wolfgang looked at Zelda. Eva sensed something was different, but she couldn't place her finger on it so she asked, "You are keeping something from me. What is it?" Wolfgang's anger had greatly subsided. He turned his back and walked out of the great room and into the kitchen. Zelda looked at her daughter with tears flowing down her hairy cheek. Eva started to get very emotional and asked, "What are you not telling me?"

Zelda said, "My dear Eva. We love you so much. We just worry about you being alone and such a far distance from your home."

I felt that I had to say something. I had to come to the aid of my sister. I said, "I can make some phone calls, and probably after making a substantial donation to Juilliard, I could pull some strings to make sure Eva will be taken care of during her boarding."

Eva looked back at me and smiled as if to say, *Thanks for the help*. She then turned back to her mother and said in a calm voice, "I sense there is something you're not telling me. Please tell me what it is."

Wolfgang cleared his throat and said, "When your brother visited us the first time in Germany, I knew he would come back. At that time, I was more interested in what he had uncovered and what direction he might take the formula. I also thought about Garrison mating with his future sister, and wondered how the baby would turn out. From a scientific point of view, it was an experiment that had to be conducted. So, I had sex with your mother and she bore three children. I killed two and kept you alive for the sole purpose of the future experiment. Then over time I got… closer to you. When Garrison came to Germany for the second time with Marci, I knew I had to go back to The States with him. We did and we brought you with us." Wolfgang stepped closer to Eva, then witnessed something I never thought I would have ever seen. My father knelt on one knee before his daughter and said, "The moment I saw you, I fell in love with you. I vowed to myself that nothing bad would ever happen to you as long as I am alive. When you agreed to have your brother's child, my heart went out to you even more. What a selfless act you will demonstrate in due time. I love you, Eva. I love you as much as I love Zelda and Garrison, my only living son. I spared your life in the name of a scientific experiment, but little did I know at the time, I would fall in love with the people involved in the experiment. I spent most of my adult life killing people and have killed many of my own offspring. I am an evil man. I know this, but when it comes to this family, I will do anything to keep the members safe. If this Juilliard is what you want, then I will let you attend the school." Eva raced into the arm of her father and cried hard.

I looked over my shoulder and there was Marci, listening and standing with her arms folded. She didn't say a word. Her eyes caught mine and she licked her lips with her long tongue. That was her way of saying that Eva got her way.

Wolfgang said, "Now we must find a suitable caregiver for Eva. I know you are advanced for your age, but I would feel better if someone that we knew could look out for you. I am concerned that you may lose control at some point and time. If you bite someone, they will transform and that is the last thing we need."

Eva said, "Dad, I'm not going to bite someone."

Wolfgang said, "I want someone with you."

Marci broke her silence and said, "I would love to take care of her, but I cannot. My Garrison cannot go because I need him here."

Wolfgang sharply said, "You just want him for sexual pleasure."

Marci stomped her large foot on the floor and exclaimed, "Wolfgang!"

Eva laughed. I broke the awkwardness by saying, "I will find someone to help Eva. Juilliard is basically a boarding school. If anyone is mature enough to handle this situation, it is certainly Eva. She is mature beyond her years. She will flourish at Juilliard and that was our original goal for her from day one. We need her to have her own life. It is not healthy for her to stay at the estate for the rest of her life. I think we are all in agreement with that assertion."

A few days passed and before we knew it, Eva and I were on a plane headed for her audition with Juilliard. We stepped off the plane, got in our rental car, and went to our hotel room. Later that evening, Eva and I dined at one of New York City's finest restaurants, located in The Majestic Towers. We had a wonderful night out. We were greeted by a few people that knew who we were through their interest in classical music.

The next day we went for Eva's audition. We met the headmaster at Juilliard, John Van Kessler. We also met with two instructors, Jerome Malone, the head of the violin department, and Cecilia Bartimorela, the head of the voice department. After introductions, Eva and I were escorted to the auditorium. I sat with the headmaster and the two instructors. Eva was asked to play the violin first.

I sensed that Eva was nervous. I knew this was a good thing for her because she would play perfectly because of her nervousness. Eva looked at me and I heard her thoughts, *Wish me luck.*

I sent my thought to her saying, *You don't need any luck. Just play with passion.* Eva gave me a wink to say she would.

One of the current students came walking across the stage. Eva looked at him with the strangest look. He was carrying a stand and some sheet music. Eva said, "What is this?"

The student stopped in his tracks and looked confused. Mr. Van Kessler said, "This is Ken. He is here to turn the pages of the music you will play for us."

Eva quickly said, "But you told us that I could play my own selections."

Van Kessler said, "That is correct, but we thought Ken might be of some service to you."

Eva said, "I have no need for any assistance. Thank you."

Ken looked puzzled and Van Kessler waved him off the stage. Jerome and Cecilia both smiled and laughed under their breath. Eva noticed their actions and grew angry, sensing that they thought of her as a joke. Eva looked at the three strangers as a wicked smile came upon her face. She said, "I love Mozart. Shall I play any particular piece or is that up to me to decide?" She raised the violin to her chin and positioned her violin, bow and feet. She looked at them cockily as she threw most of her weight onto one hip.

Jerome stopped smiling and said, "Why don't you start with something you know. Something simple." Eva frowned. Jerome didn't mean to make little of her, but Eva didn't take that as a nonchalant comment. Eva quickly stood up straight and started playing. I had no clue what Eva would play. The only instruction that I was given before we left Louisville was to bring her violin and the music scores would be provided. Eva started playing the overture to "The Marriage of Figaro." She played the melody to the best of her ability. After several minutes she stopped and glared at her onlookers.

Suddenly, Cecilia said, "How about Mozart's third Violin Concerto, the second movement." Eva immediately started playing the entire piece. I watched the three gentlemen and Cecilia as they sat there in amazement. They didn't move a muscle.

After she concluded the work she asked, "Shall I continue?"

Jerome forced a cough to make sure his throat was clear then said, "I would like for you to play this piece." He pulled out some sheet music and motioned for Ken to come over and help turn the pages for Eva. Jerome said, "You will need some help from Ken on this one, unless you have Beethoven memorized."

Eva looked at Jerome, not liking his sarcasm. As Ken positioned the metal podium in front of Eva, he looked at her with a smirk. As he placed the sheet music on the podium he said softly, "Don't mess up. This is a complicated piece."

I felt Eva's hatred toward Ken and even Jerome. I thought, *Eva, control your anger. Channel it to the Beethoven piece.*

Eva glanced over at me and smiled then looked over at Ken and gave him a smirk. She started the Beethoven piece, which she had never seen, played or heard before. I watched as her eyes danced flawlessly across the notes on the sheet music. While I didn't have knowledge of this piece of music, from my standpoint she was playing the piece perfectly. Eva's performance was immaculate. Her bow balance, finger placement and tonality were unworldly. I glanced over at the three most annoyingly imperfect people – and not one of them moved. The look on their faces was priceless. I knew that look well because I had seen it countless times in my own life. Now my sister was experiencing the same lookfr.

After five minutes, Jerome slowly raised his hand. After several moments, Eva caught his motion and abruptly stopped playing and stared at Jerome. Her uncanny stare made Jerome uncomfortable as he repositioned his body in the chair. I was concerned that Eva might say something that would hurt her interview. I told her through my thoughts to keep her comments civil. She quickly glanced in my direction and batted her eyes toward me in acknowledgment of my request.

Jerome bent down and pulled out another sheet of music from his haversack. He slowly raised the sheet music in the direction of Ken. Ken quickly walked over and took the music. Without looking at Eva, he placed the sheet of music in front of her. Eva had this bizarre but intoxicating smile on her face. Her expression lit up the room with an uncanny aura of confidence and supreme command of her environment. I was so proud of my sister. This was a special moment for both of us. For the first time, I was witnessing something unworldly. I was experiencing something that I had not witnessed before in a group of people outside of my family. I was observing perfection being achieved. I was undergoing feelings of what others experienced when they first listened to my virtuosity.

Eva looked down at the music sheet before her and smiled. She said, "Brahms... too easy." She didn't even wait for the room to grow silent, she just quickly started the piece. Like the Beethoven piece before, she played the Brahms work perfectly. There was a moment when Ken was late in turning the page. Eva abruptly stopped playing and looked at him with an aggravated gaze as he nervously turned the page. Just before the sheet rested after Ken's turning of the page, Eva started on the first note that she saw.

After demonstrating her supreme skill for almost five minutes, Jerome slowly raised his hand again and this time he had a huge smile on his face. Jerome said, "I have been the director of the violin department here at Juilliard for over twenty years. I have seen the best the world has to offer. Young lady, you are... by far... the best I have ever heard play. Not only during an audition, but ever. I have watched tapes of you and heard your skills but had to see this for myself. I have never seen anything like this before in my life. It would be my honor to have you attend Juilliard's Master's Degree Violin program." Eva smiled, giggled and bounced a little on the tips of her toes. She loved to be praised, especially from someone outside of her family.

The next challenge came from Cecilia. Cecilia was a beautiful older lady from Verona, Italy with salt and pepper colored hair. She said, "Eva, you play beautifully. Now are you ready to do some singing for us?"

Eva said as she smiled, "Yes, Madam."

Cecilia smiled back, and as they were conversing, Ken walked behind a large grand piano that was onstage. Cecilia reached into her files and gave the selected music to Eva. Eva looked down and smiled. It was an aria from Mozart's "The Marriage of Figaro." As Eva quickly paged through the sheets, she noticed many of the arias that she had sung before during her young career. She playfully looked at Cecilia and walked over to the piano. Eva laid the sheet music down next to Ken. Eva whispered, "Don't fuck this up, bitch boy."

Eva walked over to her designated spot on the floor. She was ready to go as she playfully bounced on her toes. Cecilia said, "What are you doing? Are you not going to sing for us?"

Eva looked confused as she said, "I'm sorry. I don't understand. I am ready to sing now."

The professors laughed at Eva's comments and even Cecilia chuckled some. She said, "But your sheet music is over there. You need that to sing the arias."

Eva looked over her shoulder at the sheets lying next to Ken, smiled and said, "Oh, no, I don't need them. I have sung all of these arias before."

Cecilia was perplexed. She just shook her head and said, "Okay. Let's begin... I guess."

Eva waited for Ken to hit the first key on the piano. Ken paused for a few seconds because of the confusion. Eva abruptly said, "Well aren't you going to start? We're all waiting on you." Eva shook her head in a disgusted manner.

The first piece of music was "Non so piu cosa son." Eva impatiently waited for Ken to hit the first tone. The moment Ken's fingers hit the ivory keys, Eva's attitude immediately changed. She closed her eyes momentarily and her arrogance, facial expression and total demeanor changed. I was filled with anticipation because I knew the listeners were in for a treat. As soon as Eva sung the first word, the entire theater stood still. Not a word or sound was made. It was as if we were in a vacuum devoid of any outside sound, the way music should be heard and experienced.

Eva sung like never before. Her voice cascaded down upon everyone in attendance. Eva's voice caused Cecilia to be rapidly escorted into a place that she had never visited. A place where perfect pitch, pronunciation of words, and the composer's pure initial feeling of that particular aria come together as one. When she finished the piece, everyone remained silent for an awkward but treasurable moment.

Without warning, an abrupt applause reverberated throughout the auditorium. Cecilia sat there with her mouth pursed. She didn't utter a word and her hands remained grasped tightly to her sheets of music and notes.

The next aria was "Voi che sapete," followed by "E Susanna non Vien... Dove Sono" aria, which Eva might have sung the most perfectly executed version anyone had ever heard. The multitude of minutes that passed seemed like only seconds. Eva's voice graced every inch of that auditorium and they, as pure mortals, were truly the most fortunate people to listen to such beauty. Every ear was starving for more pleasure.

Cecilia and the other professors didn't want her to stop her audition. She continued by singing the "Queen of the Night" aria from "The Magic Flute" then the next aria was Bellini's "Costa Diva" from his opera "Norma." Thunderous applause poured down, around and through everyone present. All were expressing their approval and the pure honor of hearing such perfection.

Cecilia had to force herself to break away from her trance-like state in order to continue Eva's already successful audition. Cecilia had a student, Christina Emerlee, come out to sing alongside Eva, and she requested Eva and Christina sing "Sull'aria...che soave zeffiretto" from Mozart's "Figaro." Ken again started the aria with the piano and the two sung one of the most delightful duets in all of opera. It was a beautiful sight to behold.

When the duet was finished, I looked over at Cecilia who had tears flowing down her cheeks. Cecilia said, "Eva, that was stunning. I have never heard such beauty from such a young lady. How long have you been playing the violin?"

Eva said, "I have been playing the violin for several years."

Cecilia looked over to the gentlemen that were in the auditorium and she said, "Several years! What were we doing at this young age?"

John Van Kessler laughed and said, "Not playing the violin and singing at many of the world's greatest orchestra and opera houses!"

John came over to me and motioned Eva to join our conversation. John said, "Mr. Seawick, it is obvious that Eva is talented, and we would be most honored if Miss Eva Seawick would accept our offer to attend Juilliard."

Eva jumped around with joy. I shook hands with John and said, "We accept your scholarship offer." Ken walked over and congratulated Eva, of which she was most grateful. Cecilia and Jerome also congratulated us.

Eva did have some concerns. She asked John, "Mr. Van Kessler, I am torn between the violin and voice. I would prefer to major in both. Can that be done?"

John said, "Eva, with your talents, we would be disappointed if you didn't major in both disciplines. Yes, you can major in both fields. If one of the majors becomes too much on you, you may feel free to change to just one discipline for your studies. I will have to remind you that Juilliard is also a school for more than just the Arts. We teach all subject matters so we do except you to excel in the other fields of endeavor. I don't think that will be a problem for you considering your grades throughout your academic career. To be very blunt with you, Miss Seawick, we have never seen anyone like you here at Juilliard. We have all seen the finest students from some of the paramount families around the world that have walked through the door of this institution. You, my lovely young lady, might be the best I have ever seen." Eva was thrilled to hear the compliments and was looking forward to taking Juilliard, and the world for that matter, by storm.

Eva and I spent the next two nights in New York City's famous Majestic Towers. We visited the campus and some of the areas surrounding the city then left for Louisville on the third day. I had never seen Eva so excited about anything. When we landed in Louisville, we drove home and were greeted by our parents and my lovely Marci. Eva was talking a mile a minute and the three couldn't get a word in edgewise. She told everyone about what we had experienced and how the audition went, as well as the scholarship offer.

Wolfgang was a little impatient. He said to Eva, "All of this is nice, but you are not going there alone. Someone must stay with you." Wolfgang looked at me.

I suddenly sensed Marci was getting upset. I said, "I cannot go with Eva. I need to stay here with Marci." Marci smiled at me with great pleasure. I continued, "I know when I was off to Harvard, Carolyn was with me during all of those years, but this is just not possible with Eva."

Wolfgang said, "I don't like her being by herself. She's too young."

Eva spoke up loudly, "You mean you don't like it because you can't control me being that far away."

Wolfgang snorted, "Shut up, Eva. Mind what you say to me. I am your father."

Eva said, "Yes, Father, I know, but I really want this. It will be so much fun. I won't speak of you or Mother or even Marci. I haven't told anyone about you all during my school years, why would I start now?"

Zelda said, "Eva, we are just concerned about you staying by yourself."

Eva said, "But I would have a roommate."

Wolfgang walked away from the conversation saying, "Roommate!"

I had to act quickly. Since I knew this was going to be an issue I said, "Okay, I knew you would have some issue with this, Father. Let me make some calls and see if I can arrange a suitable roommate, one that we can trust for Eva."

Eva said, "Yes, Father, let Garrison find me a suitable roommate. Then I can go, right?"

Wolfgang looked at me and rolled his eyes. At that moment he and I both knew that Eva was going, no matter what. Wolfgang knew that sooner or later he had to let her go. Even Zelda was coming to that conclusion. Marci, who was like a sister to Eva, was bouncing on her tiptoes in excitement for Eva. I knew Marci wanted Eva out of the house so she could spend more time with me, but at the same time she would miss her not being at the estate.

I understood Wolfgang's feelings. He didn't want his family to be discovered if Eva were to tell people about them. It took everything my father had in him not to force Eva to stay, even if that meant the possibility of enslaving her. Over the years he had fallen in love with his only daughter, much like he learned to have feelings for me. There was good in the man that had killed thousands of people almost a century ago. In reality, he couldn't hurt his daughter so with that thought in mind, he knew she would run away if he didn't let her go. If that were to happen, he would lose all control over her.

I made a phone call to Van Kessler, the headmaster at Juilliard. I told him I would prefer for Eva to be roomed with a responsible roommate, one that would look after and protect her. I told him that I would make a sizeable donation for this arrangement. He told me he would see what he could do and assured me that she would come from a stable family that would be beyond reproach.

The next day, Van Kessler called me and said he had the perfect student in mind. He had spoken with the student and her parents and they were thrilled to help Eva adjust to Juilliard. John was kind enough to introduce us on the phone in a three-way conversation. Eva's new roommate would be Miriam Staples, the daughter of former Secretary of State Eric Staples. Eric and I conversed for several minutes and felt comfortable with each other. Eva and I sensed that either Miriam was a little shy or that she might not be totally on board with her being an overseer for Eva. After the phone conversation was over, I spoke with Eva and we shared our feelings about the situation. Eva seemed confident that she would be taken care of and would be fine. I told her if she needed anything to just call me and I would pick her up as soon as I could get there. Eva reassured again me she would be fine.

I told my parents about the living arrangements and they seemed somewhat pleased. Wolfgang repeatedly grilled Eva about keeping the family secret close to her heart. Eva understood the gravity of the situation. The issue I worried about even more was not that my parents or my love would be discovered but that people would think Eva was crazy. In all reality, who would believe her in the first place?

We packed Eva's belongings and bought what we thought she needed. I told Eva that if she needed anything else to charge it on her credit card.

When the time came for departure, Eva told everyone in the house her goodbyes. She didn't shed a tear, nor did she hug anyone except Marci, who promised Eva that she would look after Midnight while she was gone.

I drove Eva to the airport. While going through security, Eva was incensed with their lack of intelligence. After an hour of waiting amongst the dreed of society, Eva and I were on the plane headed back to New York. We landed in New York City, collected our luggage and took a taxi to the hotel. We had a wonderful dinner at the hotel and stayed up late watching TV. The next day, we went to The Juilliard School. We met with John Van Kessler who welcomed Eva to the school. Eva was so excited it was hard for her to stand still. She wanted to learn more about the violin and voice, but she mostly just wanted to be on her own. She wanted to make friends with people that had similar interests and talents. Of course, her talents would probably not be matched, but Juilliard would push her more than her previous school or former tutors.

As timing would have it, that weekend was the start of the fall semester. Many parents were with their child, trying to get them acquainted with the new school. They were putting clothes and supplies in their dorm rooms for the semester.

John received a message that Mr. Staples and his daughter Miriam were on campus and wanted to meet us in their dorm room. Eva and I followed John to the dorm area. The door was open and there stood Mr. and Mrs. Staples with Miriam. John introduced everyone.

Eric Staples was a tall, thin man with jet black hair. His skin was a bit dark gray in color. His wife, Joyce, was a short, overweight redhead that seemed very stiff in nature, and I sensed her to be very nervous. Eric, on the other hand, couldn't wait to get out of the room. He was an ambitious man with a tremendous political future ahead of him. I knew that he had jumped at the opportunity for his daughter to shadow Eva. He hinted, in a very subtle way, of needing political contributions. He, at that time, wasn't aware of his secret intentions, but I sensed them. Eva sensed them as well.

Miriam all but ignored Eva and I. Eric and Joyce were embarrassed by her behavior toward us and excessively apologized for her attitude. Eric told Miriam of Eva's unique talents with the violin and voice. He also praised me for my violin playing. Nothing Eric was saying impressed Miriam. She actually rolled her eyes more than she had at the beginning of our introduction. This embarrassed Eric and Joyce but most especially John. I sensed that John knew he had made a huge mistake in putting Eva with Miriam. John was only out for Juilliard, and Eva was only a pawn in his grand scheme of having another great prodigy on campus.

Eva and I were uncomfortable with Miriam from the start. Miriam was an entitled little bitch and she wore that label for all to see. She cared little of what others thought of her. I had done some research on her before we left home and she was quite the talent. Miriam majored in the violin and was contemplating a minor in voice. Miriam was an older girl of twenty years of age. She was thin and tall with long, jet black hair and a pale complexion. She had a haunting expression and air about her. She didn't want to be at Juilliard because she felt her parents only used her as a pawn in her father's political career.

Miriam had never felt love from her father, which was probably the reason why she was hateful and resentful to everyone she met. She was the type of person that felt threatened whenever someone of equal or better status was around. Most of her life she had been the best at what she excelled in and rarely did she ever meet someone of equal ability, which could also be said for the students at Juilliard. She was highly put off at having the responsibility of looking after Eva and she showed it from the start.

I looked at Eva and thought to her in order to get her attention. Eva immediately looked at me and smiled. She could hear my thoughts in this situation. I thought, *I do not feel comfortable with this Miriam. I do not like this set up.*

Eva nodded to me and thought, *I have this. Don't worry. I'm not scared of the bitch. I will be okay. I'll call you if there's a problem.*

Miriam noticed our staring at each other during our silent conversation. She was the type of person that studied people thoroughly and didn't miss picking up any odd behavior in others. She knew something wasn't quite right about our relationship and suspected that we communicated to each other with our minds. She remained slumped in her chair with her mouth open, wondering what we were thinking. It troubled Miriam that Eva wasn't overwhelmed by her. Most of the girls that Miriam met were intimidated, and some even scared of her, but not Eva. This baffled Miriam. Both Eva and I sensed all of this within a matter of moments.

After a couple of hours, it was time for me to leave. Miriam's parents left to go back to Washington, DC and Miriam was out socializing, which left Eva and I alone. I reconfirmed everything with Eva and made sure she remembered that if she had any issues to call me or John, the headmaster. I knew Eva was scared. This was the first time in her young life that she was going to be left alone. She had looked forward to this opportunity so that made this moment easier for her. I said my goodbyes without any tears being shed.

Eva seemed relieved as I walked toward the door. When I opened it she said, "Thank you for this new life, Garrison." I turned around and smiled. As I closed the door behind me, I heard her run and jump on her new bed. She laughed and allowed a small scream to slip out.

It took everything I had to walk away, but I couldn't go back. I had to move forward and leave my sister. It was for her own good. This was a huge risk for us to take, but I always knew this was going to happen some day. It had to happen. You cannot control what is not controllable.

I walked out of Juilliard and went to my hotel room then took a taxi to the airport. After several hours of waiting, I boarded my plane. Before I knew it, I was back home in Louisville. I drove home and when I got out of my car, I was greeted by my family. It was a rare occasion to see my mother cry, but this time I witnessed her emotional meltdown. Wolfgang was strong and didn't make any attempt to comfort Zelda in her mournful time of need. Marci came to her aid and told her that Eva was going to be fine. I told them of our experiences and made sure everyone was up to speed.

Chapter Two

Eva pulled herself together and familiarized herself with her new surroundings. She was concerned but at the same time excited to embark on the new era of her long life. Before she could get out of her dorm room, Miriam returned. Miriam looked at Eva and rolled her eyes. She walked quickly past her, slightly brushing her shoulder against Eva's. Eva turned angrily and said, "So what's your problem?"

Miriam turned around with a wicked smile and said, "I don't like spoiled little girls and I especially don't like having to babysit one. I mean for fuck's sake, you are what, old enough to drive a car?"

Eva said, "You don't have to babysit me, and I am not a spoiled little girl."

Miriam laughed and said, "Oh… you're a spoiled little girl alright. I've heard stories about you. Asking Daddy to have someone take care of you in the big bad New York City." Miriam placed her hands on the sides of her face saying, "Oh… I am all alone, I am so scared. I had to get my daddy to pay someone to look after me."

Eva stood there without moving a muscle, staring through Miriam. Miriam stopped laughing, stared back at Eva, lifted her arms up high and said, "Fuck you!" Eva remained motionless. Her eyes didn't leave Miriam's. Miriam put her arms down at her side and folded them. Her tongue was pressed against her cheek as she tapped her foot on the floor.

Eva blinked slowly and said, "Really?"

Miriam reacted by saying, "You're such a little girl, bitch!" and moved toward Eva in a threatening matter. Eva quickly jumped back in a karate stance, positioning her arms and hands in an attack mode. Miriam laughed and said, "Oh look what we have here, a little bitch ninja baby girl." Eva stayed focused and didn't move. Miriam said, "Don't let me hurt you, whore."

Eva said nothing. She just stared and was ready to react. Miriam said, "This is fucking ridiculous." Miriam moved toward Eva and was going to push her away. As soon as she came dangerously close, Eva grabbed Miriam's left wrist and with her free hand, quickly moved it behind Miriam's elbow. Eva could have dislocated it, but she only put enough pressure on the elbow to keep the arm semi-hyperextended. This move caused enough pain to get Miriam's attention.

Eva quickly seized Miriam's index finger and pulled it back, causing extreme pain and forcing Miriam to her knees. Eva grabbed a fistful of Miriam's long black hair, pulled her head back awkwardly and said, "I don't like brunettes. It's a sign of an inferior race of people." Eva let go of Miriam's finger and hair. As she released her hold, Eva took her right foot and pushed roughly into Miriam's side, causing her body to slam into the cement floor of the room. Eva slowly walked to her bed and sat in a ladylike manner. She said in a matter-of-fact way, "I also don't like being called a little bitch. I am nearly six foot tall. Don't be stupid. I don't like stupid cunts, especially when uneducated sluts like you make inaccurate statements. So, don't be a fat cunt to me and we will get along just fine."

Miriam slowly rose as she pressed her index finger to her side while she held the back of her head. Miriam thought, *What amazing strength this girl has, and she is so quick with her movements.* Miriam said, "You just wait. When you're asleep one night, you will get yours."

Eva looked at her with the steeliest blue eyes Miriam had ever seen. Eva said, "I don't sleep much. Maybe an hour or two a night. Don't worry. I will sense when you will be coming after me. I will stop you before you even start, my inferior, fat bitch. In fact, let's play a little game, shall we? The first one to fall asleep loses and the loser must do anything that she is told to do. Anything."

Miriam nervously laughed but quickly noticed Eva wasn't. Miriam felt she was losing control of the situation as well as feeling emasculated by this strange girl that had invaded her life. She had underestimated this "little girl." Miriam was very angry, but she knew she couldn't fight back because she knew she couldn't cause a scene that might bring national attention to her father.

Miriam saw a lot of herself in this beautiful young woman. Eva continued to stare at her for an answer so Miriam, without thinking the situation through, reluctantly agreed to Eva's bet by nodding her head. Eva said, "Good! The game begins now." Eva bounced on the bed in order to position herself to be in the middle of the bed. Suddenly, she laid down, lying straight as a poker with her eyes closed. Miriam was furious and stormed out of the dorm, only hearing Eva's wicked laugh.

Hours passed, and Eva turned out all the lights in the room and sat on the floor between Miriam's bed and dresser. The room was pitch black although Eva could see perfectly in the dark. Eva put clothes and pillows under the blankets, making it look like someone was sleeping. Eva then waited for Miriam to enter the dorm. Suddenly, Eva heard someone at the door and it slowly opened. It was Miriam. Eva saw everything perfectly in the shadowy dorm, but Miriam struggled to get her eyes to adjust to the darkness. Miriam quietly walked over to Eva's bed and quickly jumped on the hidden clothes and pillows. As she did, she screamed, not expecting to feel what she touched. Eva said nothing. Miriam was so upset that she punched the fake body of folded up blankets as she struggled to get off the bed.

Eva sat watching the entertaining show, and when Miriam was on her feet, Eva spoke, "Hello, Miriam." Miriam, startled, looked around and fell back on the bed from fright. She got up again and quickly went over to the light switch to turn the lights on. At first, the sudden light bothered Miriam's eyes. She looked around and couldn't see Eva because she was crouched down between Miriam's bed and dresser.

Miriam, in somewhat of a panicked voice said, "Where the fuck are you?" Eva got up as quickly as she could, bouncing up with all her massive blonde curls flowing around her perfect face. Her breasts, which were fully developed, bounced with each movement of her body. Eva walked over to her side of the bed and looked at Miriam out of the corner of her eye. A confident smile came across her face as she said, "Now, you couldn't have thought it would be that easy, could you?"

Miriam's heart was racing and her breathing was fast. This "spoiled little girl" had an unworldly aura about her. Miriam said, "You're a weird little freak!"

Eva turned to her and said, "I don't like to be called little. Are you really so stupid that you cannot comprehend something as elementary as a simple command?"

Miriam looked at her in bewilderment. All she could muster was, "Whatever!"

Eva turned her back and picked her clothes off the bed, put them away, and quietly made her bed. She then picked up the chemistry book that was on Miriam's desk and walked over to her bed and sat quietly. Eva looked through the pages rather quickly.

Miriam asked, "What are you doing with my chemistry book?"

Eva said, "I'm just looking through the pages."

Miriam was dumbfounded. She said, "But that's Advanced Chemistry."

Eva rolled her eyes. "Yes it is. That was an incredible deduction."

Miriam was confused and said, "But you're not... whatever."

Eva said, "Would you like me to teach you a thing or two about chemistry? I studied the subject in my spare time."

Miriam was shocked. She struggled to sit down and as she looked at Eva she said, "So what are you, a genius or something?"

Eva didn't raise her eyes from the pages as her long fingers flipped through the first chapter. She said, "Aren't we all geniuses here?" Eva stopped, looked up and said, "Look, I know that you don't like me. I really don't like you either, but we must make the best of this situation. Right? I won't bother you if you don't bother me. See, I don't need you. You don't have to escort me around campus. I will figure this out for myself. Is that understood?" Miriam slowly nodded in agreement. Eva said, "Good. Now don't forget about our little bet."

Miriam's emotions went from anger to being scared. She thought, *There is something not right about this girl.* Eva had so much confidence and command of her emotions. Normally Miriam intimidated everyone she met, but not Eva. Eva had turned the tables on her and she didn't know how to react to the newest development.

That night, Miriam struggled to stay up the entire night whereas Eva had no trouble staying awake. In fact, Eva, for the fun of it, taught Miriam the entire first five chapters of the chemistry book. Miriam sat there, even though she was exhausted, in amazement at Eva's recollection of the numerous pages of difficult information being regurgitated, and in some cases word by word. Miriam even pulled up a copy of the book and attempted to follow along. She was speechless. After the long night turned into morning, Eva got ready to go to class while Miriam struggled to get to her feet.

As the ladies exited their room together, Eva continued to intimidate Miriam by telling her that she was going to graduate from graduate school at Juilliard in about a year to a year and a half, which was true. She also told her she would probably test out of most of her classes. Miriam just walked alongside Eva in total awe and silence. Miriam didn't know what to believe, but she knew this was no ordinary roommate. Down deep inside, she knew she had met her match. She already knew she had lost the bet and was very concerned about what Eva might ask her to do.

Miriam stayed awake for about two days before she accidently fell asleep on her bed during the night, waking just before sunrise. She was very alarmed to find Eva kneeling at the side of her bed, stroking her forehead with her long finger saying, "Miriam... oh, Miriam... wake up, my sleeping beauty." Miriam quickly sat up, looking at Eva's smiling face.

Eva remained on her knees at the edge of the bed. Her eyes stared a hole into Miriam's soul, and Miriam knew she had just lost the bet. Miriam said, "Okay! Okay! Okay! You win. You won the bet. So, what is it? What do you want from me?"

Eva continued to smile at Miriam. She slowly rose to her feet, walked to her bed and sat down. She pulled her legs up to lie down on her side. Eva felt so alive. She loved the control that she felt over Miriam. She craved that controlled feeling unlike any of the vast array of sensations that she possessed. Her smile remained on her perfectly formed face as she stared at Miriam, which caused her great unrest.

Eva pushed back a mass of her curly blonde hair to reveal her long, perfectly sculpted neck. Eva wore a long, loose fitting blouse that came up to the highest point of her thigh. Although she never wore panties at any time, especially not to bed, this night was different. Eva's large breasts were firm but flowed with the movements from her strong shoulders. She made sure her movements on the bed drew attention to her large breasts. Eva sensed Miriam's uneasiness with the situation. Eva moved her right knee up and exposed her small, clothed womanly part. Eva said, "What I want from you, Miriam, is..." Eva paused as she took her fingers and snaked them around and between her well-developed breasts. Eva had learned a lot of her sexuality from Marci. Now, for the first time in her young life, she was experiencing a sexually arousing moment. Eva had no interest in Miriam sexually, but she wanted to play with Miriam's mind for a brief moment.

Miriam looked down at Eva's breasts and pleaded, "No! Please. Not that." Eva laughed as she allowed her head to fall back on the bed as she laughed harder. She quickly sprung up and sat on the edge of the bed with her front teeth over her lower lip. She laughed at Miriam and said, "Come on, bitch, don't you want to touch my sexy little girl body? You never know, you might like it." Eva laughed loudly.

Miriam was scared out of her mind, but a part of her was aroused. She was confused. She naturally looked away because she was embarrassed. She moved her body around on the bed as that warm, fuzzy feeling was developing in the pit of her stomach. Eva could sense that at any time she could have Miriam if she wanted, but she quickly said to her, "No, silly. I don't want you, but one day, I might want... someone... you know... sexually. So, what I want from you is to help me get what I want. It won't be anytime soon, but just keep it in the back of your mind. Remember, a bet is a bet, right?"

Miriam was somewhat relieved but at the same time disappointed. She got caught up in the game and, truth be told, she enjoyed the teasing in a twisted way. Miriam quickly agreed, but she was uneasy with the commitment. She didn't know Eva well enough to play along with any sexual adventures. Miriam didn't want to be a part of anything illegal and she feared Eva. Eva had a way about her that made many feel uneasy in her presence. Miriam was afraid for her life because she didn't know what Eva was capable of; therefore, she feared the worst. She had to agree to Eva's terms, but down deep, Miriam knew she just might have gone through with a sexual encounter with Eva, which further deepened Miriam's discomfort.

Miriam knew she had overstepped her boundaries with Eva at the start of their relationship. She knew she didn't treat Eva with the respect that she commanded, and now she was living in fear of what the "little girl" might do to her physically or to her reputation. Being the daughter of the Secretary of State of the United States carried an awesome responsibility, and Miriam knew she had to conduct herself as a young lady so she wouldn't embarrass her father and his lofty executive office.

Eva caught everyone's attention from the moment she stepped foot on campus. In no time at all, word got out that she was a new student. On her first day of class, she was fully awake and bouncing down the hallways. She captured every boy's attention and many couldn't keep their eyes off her. Countless students knew of her by the numerous concerts she had performed over the past few years, as well as her economic and social status.

Privately, Eva was concerned and scared of her unfamiliar world since all of this was new to her. The new city, people and teachers; everything felt strange. She heard sounds and smelt aromas that she had never heard or experienced before. She sensed so much talent in everyone that she met, although she wasn't concerned with the competition she had met. In fact, she loved being surrounded by so many with such great talents and intellect. It was a welcomed feeling for her. What she struggled with the most was dealing with people's attitudes. Many of her classmates loved the idea of Eva's greatness but were not in love with her as a person. This was somewhat new to Eva. When she met these people, they treated her as if she was just an object to be admired. Although this is what Eva's personality craved, it was a different treatment than what she was used to. In the past, she had been protected by her family, namely me. I always spun the attention as love. Now she was experiencing these strangers' attention as just that – attention, not love. The attention came in all form of disguises, including jealousy, hatred, and being treated as an inanimate object and not as a person. The vast array of attitudes was difficult for Eva to accept. She missed my guidance and, to some degree, my ability to deflect the attacks on her person and her skillset. While she was at Juilliard, she knew I couldn't be there for her and serve as her protector.

Eva quickly made friends. She sensed the people that were friends out of potential career advancements as well as the people who truly wanted to be friends, which were few and far between. She made up her mind, early on in this process, not to get close to anyone. She knew she had to keep her private life a mystery to all to protect her family. It was difficult for her to keep her family life to herself.

Eva had always been a beautiful young woman. Even at the age of ten, she was tall, thin and her body was perfectly proportioned in size. She was physically well-developed and radiated a sophisticated womanliness air about her that was trapped inside of a young body. Her hair was long and blonde with curls that ran down the middle of her back, which many times she pulled back into a long ponytail. Her complexion was flawless, without a blemish on any part of her body. Her skin tone was fair but not pale, her eyes were the bluest you would ever see, and they sparkled with confidence and self-assurance. Her personality was a blend of controlled aggressiveness and a touch of aloofness but most of all, she possessed extreme confidence in her many skills. Throughout the years, she had such a command of her talents in voice, violin and, of course, her schoolwork. At times, her aura was unnerving to many, thus some people felt uneasy around her. Many people that met her thought she was full of herself because of her overconfidence and brashness. It wasn't actually Eva's fault that she had this type of personality. She carried herself way beyond her years, which added to her perceived cocky attitude.

Eva's first day at Juilliard was very successful. She had many students come up and welcome her. Although Eva sensed that many of the greetings were just halfhearted salutations, she appreciated the attempts by her fellow students. Eva knew she was better than everyone she met and that didn't sit well with others, especially when she proved just how great she was at almost everything she touched.

When the time came for Eva's violin and voice lessons, the students created a buzz around the anticipated events. Eva thought this was very strange and was astounded by the fact that others were so interested in her abilities. Many people isolated themselves from her, either out of jealousy or by being intimidated by her skills and status. People knew her only by her vast performances onstage throughout the world and her father's reputation. Many called her the greatest child prodigy of our time, and some thought she was even greater than me, her 'father.'

Everyone at Juilliard knew she was special. Because of the students' competitive nature, many of them were more jealous of Eva than excited to watch and listen to her perform. Rumors quickly ran rampant throughout the university to the fact that not only was Eva majoring in violin but in voice as well. Many didn't believe the rumors, but after hearing confirmation from Eva that this was indeed the case, this alienated Eva even more from many of the students.

One must understand that Eva was what many of the Juilliard students wanted so desperately to be from the start of their lives. Eva had already performed with a multitude of the best orchestras and opera houses throughout the United States and Europe. These facts created an even bigger barrier between Eva and her fellow students. The jealousy was monumental, but at the same time, there was also respect for her.

When Eva walked into the auditorium for the first time, you could have cut the tension with a knife. Eva calmly walked over to her seat and laid the violin case down on the floor. She bent down, opened the case, and pulled out her violin and bow. She sat calmly and quietly in her chair and waited for further instructions.

After several moments, Jerome Malone, the head of the violin department, walked into the auditorium. The only sound that could be heard was his fast steps across the wooden floor. Jerome was a short, overweight gay man whose effervescent personality was insufferable to many. Eva didn't like him very much from the first time they had met although he was excited to hear her playing skills compared to the others in the class.

Miriam made sure she was in attendance. She, like many others, wanted to see Eva's skills in person and she, as well as most of the non-violin students that were there, were sitting quietly, waiting for Eva's turn to play. Many students were there out of sheer curiosity, to see the superior prodigy in action. They wanted to hear Eva for the first time in person. They wanted to see just how special she was on the violin.

In Miriam's private thoughts, she believed she possessed the best talent at Juilliard, especially at violin. She knew Eva was also a voice major, and Miriam's competitive nature wanted to show Eva that she was the most talented student there. It had been widely known that Miriam was the most talented at the famed school, especially at the violin. She secretively didn't want Eva to succeed at the violin, or at voice for that matter. Miriam was hoping Eva would completely fall on her face at her first violin practice.

Miriam was obviously jealous of Eva's many talents, but this was where Miriam knew she could dominate Eva. Miriam wanted to take back some of the student and teacher admiration that Eva had taken from her since her arrival. Miriam had to play it safe because down deep in her soul she was afraid of Eva and she didn't want to upset her to a point where she would take revenge on her.

Jerome made his way up to the stage and addressed sixteen violinists that were seated at attention in front of him. He introduced Eva and she received a lukewarm response from the jealous students in attendance. Jerome had a couple students stand up and play sections of selected parts of works from several different composers. Eva was the third one that was called to the podium. She made her way up to the stand and waited for Jerome to give her the go ahead to begin playing. When Eva got the signal from her teacher, she began to play. She didn't miss a single note during the few minutes of her performance. The bow slid across the strings effortlessly, the pressure on the strings was perfect, and her finger placement and bow balance was unworldly. But what made Eva's playing even more special was the passion that she possessed for the instrument and the work. That passion showed through during her performance.

Eva didn't have to concentrate on if her fingers were on the correct strings nor if she created enough tension on the draw of the bow. All Eva needed to do was concentrate on the music that she was creating and how the composer wanted the piece to be played. Few musicians possessed this command of the violin. She played longer than her fellow violin students, and after she was finished, she smiled at Jerome and walked back to her chair. There was a buzz in the air by everyone in attendance. Eva looked around, and out of the corner of her eye she spotted Miriam. Eva just glanced at her, nothing more. After several moments, a smile appeared on Eva's face. Miriam knew Eva saw her and at that moment, incredible jealousy swelled up in Miriam's soul. The envy was so great it forced her out of her seat and she hurried out of the auditorium. As she was walking, she knew she had just admitted defeat to herself, to Eva and to everyone in that auditorium, which upset her even more. At that moment, Miriam's actions showed everyone at Juilliard that she was impressed and jealous of Eva's ability. Funny how there is such a fine line between jealousy and admiration.

The students that followed Eva played as well as they could, and after they finished their selection of music, they would ask Eva her opinion. Eva obliged and commented on each of her fellow student's traits. For the students that were lucky enough to be in attendance, many of them asked her a ton of questions on the proper way to either hold the instrument or how to draw the bow properly.

Jerome felt a little out of place since he was the one that taught most of them these basic rules. He allowed this conversation to take place, and at the end he was very pleased that he had Eva in his class. In Jerome's mind, she was going to make him famous, but Eva's fame had already taken shape years ago.

Later that day, Eva went to Cecilia Bartimorela's voice class. Cecilia was a beautiful, shapely woman from a small town just outside of Rome, Italy. She was also a former graduate of Juilliard. Cecilia had sung in many opera houses in Europe before she took a teaching position at Harvard then made her way to her current position. Eva liked Cecilia the first time she performed for her.

Miriam was already in the class when Eva entered. Miriam was well known at Juilliard and she could attend any class as long as she was not disruptive. She wanted to see just how talented this prodigy was. Miriam sat with one of her few friends on campus, Evelyn Cupett. Evelyn was regarded as one of the most talented and certainly one of the newest up and coming voice talents in the business. Miriam wanted Eva to notice that she was in attendance.

Eva was coming off the natural high from her violin class and was so busy trying to find the class that she didn't pay any attention to sensing what she might encounter. As Eva entered the large auditorium setting, you could have heard a pin drop. The silence and people's reaction somewhat surprised and slightly unnerved her as she entered. In her mind, all she wanted to do was sing, have fun, meet people, and create new friendships.

Miriam had other things in mind. To gain Eva's attention, she raised her hand and waved. Miriam was prepared for this classroom confrontation. Even Miriam's classmates knew this was going to be an intense moment.

When the class started, Eva was introduced by the teacher. Cecilia said, "It gives me great pleasure to introduce a wonderful talent that has just started here at Juilliard, Ms. Eva Seawick. Ms. Eva has performed at the Metropolitan Opera, as well as in Louisville, Boston, L.A. and throughout some of Europe's finest opera houses. So please welcome Eva to our class." The rest of the students gave a soft clap and Eva was instantly upset at another lukewarm response.

As the class continued, Cecilia was demonstrating certain techniques and wanted her students to use them during the arias they sung. After several singers attempted to follow Cecilia's instructions, not one did what they were instructed to do. When it came to Eva's turn, she quietly walked up to the podium and waited for the music to start. As soon as the first note came out of Eva's mouth, everyone in the auditorium knew she was going to demonstrate exactly what the teacher wanted. Eva sang extremely well. She hit every note per the teacher's instruction. After the first aria was completed, Cecilia gave Eva more sheet music. Again, Eva sung the aria perfectly. Cecilia was beaming with joy. What a pleasure it was to have such a gifted student in her class, which was really something special since her students were some of the best in the world.

Cecilia said to Eva, "Eva, I would like for you to sing any aria you wish to the best of your ability. Sing it the way the composer wanted it to be sung." Eva nodded her head, accepting the challenge. Eva began one of the most challenging arias, "The Queen of the Night" in Mozart's "The Magic Flute." Eva started the aria in German. German was her second language and it was spoken often in the Seawick house. Her accent was perfect and she hit every note with extreme precision. Eva sung so well that not a sound was made throughout the cozy concert hall.

Miriam and Evelyn sat there listening to this marvel of perfection. Evelyn was thinking to herself that never in her lifetime could she hit every note perfectly like Eva demonstrated. What made matters even more extraordinary was the way Eva sung. She sung so effortlessly throughout all her arias, like it wasn't even a struggle to hit the most difficult notes ever written. It was as if she was born to sing, like it was as effortless as her heartbeat and as natural as it could possibly be. Nothing was forced or seemed difficult. Eva's voice was so powerful that it soared throughout the concert hall. At times the chairs would seemly have a slight rumble as certain notes were reached.

When Eva completed the aria, the students sat motionless, then moved in their chairs as the talking started. Some of the students had never taken the time to hear Eva sing before Juilliard, but now they would never forget that moment.

Eva knew she had sung well and stood there smiling. She glanced over at Miriam sitting amongst her friends who were all talking about the performance. Evelyn was in awe as she was commenting on Eva's beautiful voice; however, Miriam didn't say a word. All she could muster was a slight movement of her lips as if to start to mouth the word "what." Miriam had known Eva was good, but not this good. Miriam's jealousy was present in her heart, but it was turning into more of an admiration of Eva's skills, in her ability to sing as well as to play the violin with such precision, such excellence that defied all human reason. The moment Eva started singing, Miriam knew she was no longer the best. The bitter defeat was hard for her to accept.

Cecilia broke the whispering by clapping her hands, acknowledging approval. No one had ever seen Cecilia clap for any student in her class. The room grew silent when Cecilia finished clapping. She turned and said to the class, "That is true beauty." Cecilia turned to Eva and said, "Eva, God has certainly blessed you. You should be very proud of yourself and thankful that God has blessed you with such a great gift. The gift of boundless talent."

Eva's emotions were stirred into a twisted knot at the words that Cecilia had bestowed upon her. Eva momentarily lost control over her emotions and said, "God gave me nothing! My parents are the ones that created me. Not a god. My voice is not a gift, it was always there at my disposal. It is my possession. I was the one that developed it. I created those notes without any help from this god you speak of so reverently."

When Eva was finished, she looked around the room and everyone was looking at her. She knew she had just fallen short of saying that her parents created a formula and she was the byproduct of that creation, thus the formula created her talents.

Cecilia was shocked at first then quickly grew angered. She said, "You might not believe in God, but in my opinion, He does exist."

Eva said, "Only in your mind, Professor Bartimorela, but I appreciate the kind words. Just leave god out of it please."

Cecilia said with a slight attitude, "Okay... fair enough."

Eva confidently walked across the stage and sat down. Not a word was said to her about her views. At that point, Eva was almost feared around campus and looked at somewhat differently because of her apparent dislike of religion and God. This was a tactical error on Eva's part and she knew it, but what was done was done and it couldn't be reversed.

In less than a day, the entire campus was buzzing about Eva's performances. Miriam's mixture of jealousy and admiration grew by the hour. She knew Eva had taken over her crown as being the best at Juilliard. Miriam knew she had met her match. She thought the best way to deal with the Eva situation was to join forces with her. In her mind, it was her only chance for popularity survival.

As the week passed, Miriam grew nicer to Eva. She guided Eva to help her out socially by introducing her to many of her friends. These kind acts didn't fool Eva. She knew Miriam's strategy. She knew she was a fraud, but Eva wanted Miriam as a pawn more than anything else. Eva knew how to work people, and this was one of those times where she was playing Miriam for a larger role in the future.

Eva was known to have a cocky attitude, but she was just so talented that many thought it couldn't be helped. Eva's vast array of boundless talent had created this opinion of herself. What annoyed many was that Eva's talents came so easy to her. Many were jealous of her because of that. Eva rarely made fun or belittled anyone, but she would often, either verbally or physically, demonstrate that she was vastly superior to all others, not only in voice or musical instrument but in academics as well.

Eva's school work was easy for her. She was so far advanced that she never studied. If Eva was not practicing the violin or voice, she would be found in the library, reading her chosen book at breakneck speed. Eva loved to learn and at this point in her life, she was having the best time that she had ever experienced.

Miriam began to appreciate Eva as the weeks passed. Miriam's popularity increased during this time because of her close relationship with Eva, and people often associated one with the other. Eva was now viewed as the best at Juilliard, not Miriam. This is not what Miriam wanted, but she had no choice but to accept her new status. Miriam's friends treated Eva like a rock star, and this pleased young Eva significantly. Eva desired and longed for attention, which was one of the many reasons she performed in concert halls.

One of the few drawbacks the formula possessed was that it can apparently make some of your obsessions increase in sensitivity. The formula highlights your natural ability and perfects that area more than other zones of your being. For Eva, the obsession in her world was attention and an excessive desire for praise. That was her weakness. My weakness is the desire to love someone and for that love to be returned to me.

Eva, like our parents and I, holds a grudge toward any possibility that a greater being exists, a being that no one has seen, heard or spoken with the entire history of mankind. Eva was much like me. We tend to get very angry when others talk about god and his gifts to us, especially when it concerns our talents. Our parents created us, not god. Humans create humans. God, if he ever existed, never created anyone.

We don't believe that god gives you gifts or talents. Your talents are innate; buried deep into your being or your mind. It is your responsibility to find those gifts and once they are found, it is up to you how they are developed.

Maybe there is a god or some force out there that oversees everything we do day in and day out, but I have never met this said being. I also don't believe that some god created man. Human beings create other human beings. People create, not god. People and animals evolve through time. People, animals and plants all develop their size, structure and cell makeup over millenniums. Time is what governs and guides certain mutations of living organisms. When you change the variables, you effectively change the outcome of events. God is not involved in this process.

Allow me to explain using a family reunion as an example. Which people come to a reunion affects what type of party it will eventually transform into as the party progresses. If a large group of fun-loving people show up, the reunion will probably follow suit. Different people have different personalities. Thus, depending on whether certain people come, that will change the multitude of variables that will adversely affect the outcome. If a controversial figure comes and disrupts the reunion, that variable changes the end result.

This goes for breeding in humans as well. For example, if a family breeds poorly — say they start out breeding unintelligent people — the chances for continued unintelligence to be present in the multitude of generations will continue to be at high risk unless someone changes the intelligence quotation.

The above example is why my father and I believe the formula is so important to the future of the human race. The formula will help correct the shortcomings of a human subject and will, at the same time, enhance the subject's strongest areas. But any change by other outside forces will have alternating results. In addition, those alternating results will dilute the basic, original version of the subject.

This fact has been well documented throughout history. As time passes, some cultures aspire to keep their natural traits while other cultures let their natural traits fall by the wayside. If you take the Chinese or Japanese cultures as a whole, from the very beginning of time they tended to marry their own kind of people, thus preserving the natural traits of what makes a Chinese person, Chinese and a Japanese person, Japanese. The basic origin of those traits is handed down from generation to generation. Those traits are what identifies a particular race or culture of people from a proud and specific part of the world.

You see this in other areas of the world, from the depths of the Congo in the continent of Africa to the vast cultures of Europe. The problem with this practice is that not one of these cultures is the ultimate example of the human species. They are all imperfect. They, for the most part, may represent that culture well, but there are still imperfections. Why? Because that culture has allowed other cultures into their race, diluting the natural fiber of the traits which made that culture different or unique from others. Many times, many cultures breed incorrectly. For any society to stand the test of time, war or plagues, its best representation of their species must breed with a similar species. If not, the race will never improve over time or, in some cases, will eradicate themselves.

The greatest problem with the vast specific species of man, throughout centuries and millenniums, is that there is no master race. The inhabitants of those different species have nothing to aspire to throughout history of its particular culture. Mixed breeding, on all levels, dilutes the human family into a lesser human. You can see that no one species has dominated from the start of the human race until now. Why? This proves my point that instead of a master society focusing on proper breeding, all cultures tend to interbreed with each other, thus never allowing nature to improve its class of species.

When I walk outside and make my way into the forest area on my property, I see many animals roaming around. When I stop and think of a squirrel, I typically have a concrete idea of what a squirrel is supposed to resemble and how they are supposed to naturally act. Why does the squirrel resemble a squirrel over decades, if not centuries? Because they breed with other squirrels. Their race also learns to adapt to their society. They learn from the other species they meet throughout the many centuries of their existence.

Every animal is different and has a unique place and purpose in this world. Thus, various animals vary in size, speed or their natural, physical make up. All animals adopt the positive traits that they need for survival. They slowly discard the traits that they don't need in their current living state and they hold onto the traits that they need for survival and improvement.

This process applies to all animals in their kingdom. For example, take a horse in the wild. That horse wouldn't mate with an elephant or a cheetah. That horse will mate with other horses because that is their inherent nature. Nature guides them to mate with another animal that is similar to them and their species.

Horses will mate with other horses from their commonly shared area until they eventually dominate their region. They may, through time, share that land with a few others if there are enough resources for all the species' needs. They may move to other foreign regions for additional food sources or for weather purposes but most likely they will stay with their group of like species. Now comes the interesting part. As time passes, some of those horses will get sick and die and the stronger horses will live. The natural selection continues, and the strong, healthy horses will mate with each other. This process will produce offspring that are like their parents.

I use this rudimentary example to demonstrate how important selective breeding is to all species. Throughout time, we have witnessed this process play out to be widely successful. The natural traits of one species will seek out their own species for mating purposes. What is problematic is that wild animals don't differentiate the better selections from the lesser selections when it comes to their mating sample. Humans tend to copy this same process. The natural selection is the only catalyst in that species lineage. This dramatically impedes the process of developing the close as possible purist example of that species. Thus, the species only develops on a limited basis. The goal for the species' survival is not for the development of its species' complete characteristics, instead its goal is strictly for survival of their species. If those characteristics were properly developed, it would enhance the species to levels that have never been obtained. The species would thrive and possibly dominate not only their territory but territories that exist around them. This practice, in the long term, would cause this species to develop faster, and become stronger and perhaps more intelligent.

What if only the best of that particular species would only mate with the best of its own kind? We see this in the practice of breeding dogs. It is the practice for a breeder of a specific breed to take two of the best and almost perfectly pedigreed dogs and force them to mate, creating the purest of a particular dog breed as one so desires. If you want a short muzzle and long ears, you mate the dogs with these characteristics repetitively until the desired result is achieved. The inadequacy of that selected breed will lessen over time and the desired enhancements will dominate, making the dog purer in the eyes of the breeder. The dogs will separate themselves from the other dogs that don't practice this selection process. Over time, this breed of dog would be so different from the other breeds that don't practice this process. The result would be an independent breed both in their physical make up and their personality development.

The driving force behind this process is an entity or a leader that is more intelligent and is powerful enough to force this breeding process to take place. In this case it would be a human. A human's intelligence is greater than the dog. A human can force two dogs to mate at will.

Hence, the human has created, over time, a more pure and desired result.

Humans even do this to their own species, as previously mentioned, and the Japanese and Chinese have been practicing this behavior for centuries. From Indian tribes to even people of certain religious beliefs, man has quarantined their people by race or beliefs with others that have the same interests. This practice is found in all cultures, but like my father has said since he first started in genetics, humans tend to stray from their culture's principal beliefs or beginnings. Wolfgang called this principal belief, the core. The core is what your family is made up of from the earliest genesis of your family's lineage. My core is made up of Aryan, German speaking, white ancestry. For generations, the people in my lineage have come from this area of Europe and are made up of the characteristics that I mentioned.

Millions of people tend to crossbreed. Those people have children, their children procreate and so on. Some people in these kinds of families might attempt to return to their core, the original basis of a family's lineage, but most do not. The problem is that over a few generations, the pureness of the core is obviously diluted. In many cases, the current state of the core is unrecognizable to the original core. The end result, the current family's DNA, is not part of that because they are so far removed from the basis of what made up the original culture.

One could argue that through crossbreeding, you pick up the better traits of the 'other' culture. While this is true, you could also argue that you could inherit the lesser qualities as well, but the end result is you lose your basic core traits, thus your line of species are in a constant state of evolution. During this process, you aren't developing your basic core; you are spread too thin. Your traits become a slave to many and a master of none.

If you could find a culture or a tribe of people that are relatively pure and the best participants in that group only mate with the better people, over centuries of time you will develop a nearly pure race of that selected group. I bring this up in accordance with my father's lifelong goal and work with the Nazi party. They wanted the best of the best in their carefully chosen group of people to mate with each other to create the closest possible form of the perfect human.

Cultures have practiced this since the beginning of time. We all tend to think we are better than other cultures. The cultures or groups that continue to venerate this practice are the most fortunate of people.

We desire to possess what we feel is most comfortable to us personally by associating with others that we perceive to share our physical and emotional echelons. It is man's basic desire to have children that are more like their parents than different from them. That is why most couples have babies of their own instead of adopting a strange human from a different culture. I understand this more than most.

Most people dismiss these ideas or are outraged when this subject is discussed. This subject matter needs to be explored. If there were a way to have a culture that is disease free, why would that culture want to procreate with a less subculture? All of us desire to be perfect or pure. We desire those features or traits in our looks, our personality, and our intellect, amongst a host of other areas.

This all leads up to my sister, Eva. She is perfect in almost every way. Her lineage is strong and pure. The same goes for me. When we mate, we should produce the perfect child; the perfect human would be created by us. Our creators are our parents, Wolfgang and Zelda. They are the modern-day Adam and Eve. Their only flaw is their physical appearance. If my baby with Eva would produce a human child void of all physical abnormalities, then Eva and I will have started the perfect human race. A race that is completely healthy, has superior intelligence, and will never die. What an opportunity for man's continued domination of all the animal species. What an honor it is for me and for my sister to be able to participate in a controlled, evolutionary process that will change the human species forever.

Chapter Three

My relationship with Marc intensified after her transformation. Marci was at her apex of happiness in either of her lives. Her skills at the violin were at the highest level she had ever experienced, and she read and comprehended books and textbooks as easily as drinking water on a hot summer day. Once I mentally accepted her newly shaped body, our lovemaking was superior. Wolfgang, Zelda and I taught her a vast number of subjects such as chemistry, biology, and the entire history of Formula L. The formula was Marci's greatest interest when it came to her studying. She wanted to know how she changed physically and what caused that change to take place.

Wolfgang and I had taped everything, and Marci watched every second of those infinite recordings. She studied the tapes of Trevor, Adam, Adelle, and the multitude of our experiments on human and animal subjects. The process was so very difficult to comprehend, and there were so many moving parts to the transformation process. The factors included changes in the temperature of the blood, the amount of the formula being introduced to the host, the amount of the host's adrenaline, and even the transferor of the formula; all must be taken into account to the degree of the receiving host's physical transformation.

For example, if Person A would inject Formula L into Person B, those physical changes would be different than if the infected Person B would inject the formula into Person C. The formula is constantly changing and it mutates with each host. The formula works differently on each of the vast array of genes that make up the host's natural state. In other words, the same formula will mutate a horse differently than it would mutate a mouse, cat, dog or chicken. The formula enhances the desired traits of any certain species and at the same time eliminates the undesired traits.

Marci wanted so badly to be a part of our family and our culture that she worked hard to fit in at every angle. Marci helped around the house with cleaning and tried to assist Zelda with the cooking and even hunted small animals for dinner. She also kept her promise of taking care of Eva's cat, Midnight. Every other day, Marci would take Midnight out for a walk, and they got along rather well. In fact, Midnight didn't like anyone in the house besides Eva and Marci.

My parents learned to treat Marci like their daughter. We sometimes fought and had our moments, but at the end of the fights, we came back to care for each other because all we had was the five of us and one was off to college.

My parents missed Germany, but they were more willing to accept the American way of life through exploring the multitude of media outlets. I sometimes forgot that, for them, so much had changed in the world. It was difficult for me to remember just how much their new way of life was so different from just a few years ago when they were living in a cave. They had been separated from society for over a hundred years. Sometimes that was hard to acknowledge and easy to forget.

Wolfgang and Zelda constantly worried about Eva. Wolfgang knew that Eva was very young, and he feared that she might slip up someday and expose her identity, but he knew he had no choice but to let her go free. Eva was going to do what she wanted, and no one was going to stop her.

One day, Marci came to me with a very disturbing yet thought-provoking idea. She wanted us to have a baby. She wanted to experience motherhood and wanted to bear children with me. She said, "Seeing you with Eva and how you interact with her so well, I just know you would be a great father. It is so hot seeing you take charge and help with Eva and her needs. I want what your parents have… children."

Of course, we both knew the risks were great. I feared this process might kill Marci before, during or after the birth. Also, there was no way to tell what type of baby or babies would be created inside of her womb. My thoughts went straight to our experiment with the homeless female named Mary. During her pregnancy, the babies tore through and exited her abdomen, instantly killing her. I was very concerned that something like that might happen to Marci. We talked at length about this issue and to be honest with you, the thought had crossed my mind. I wanted to start a family. That was something I never felt I'd had and, of course, Marci never experienced having a mother or father watching out for her.

I told Marci that we needed to discuss this issue with Wolfgang. I told her of my fears and she admitted that she also had great concerns about her wellbeing.

When we approached Wolfgang with the idea, he was sitting in the great room watching a documentary on his Fuhrer. He knew immediately what we had in mind before we could speak a word. "You want to have babies, right?"

I smiled as I lowered my head and uttered, "Yes, sir."

Wolfgang looked at Marci and smiled. He said, "Do you know the risks, young lady?"

Marci said, "I do, Wolfgang. I do. I could die from it and that makes me very concerned. That's why we are coming to you. Do you think having a child with Garrison would kill me?"

Wolfgang's smile left his face and he looked down at the floor. "I don't know what would happen. It didn't work out well for the bitch that Garrison found on the streets, but your situation is much different from hers. You possess the formula as well as Garrison. Your body could, in theory, correct any issues that would develop during the pregnancy. Your little homeless woman had no chance, but it was enjoyable, no... the experience? I rather much enjoy watching your experiments, Garrison. You remind me so much of myself when I was younger." He just sat there and smiled at me. I felt at the time that he was making fun of me and my experimental ideas, but all I had were questions and very little answers at that time.

I looked at my father and said, "Maybe with your help we ought to perform another experiment to help us gauge whether Marci is able to survive a pregnancy with me."

Wolfgang caught my eye and said, "So what are you suggesting?"

I said, "Well, in honor of my love, I am willing to find a woman, kill her, bring her back to life, wait for her transformation to be complete, then impregnate her and see if she could survive the birth. If she survives then we will know that Marci could survive a pregnancy with me as the father."

Marci spoke with great excitement and said, "Yes. Yes. It will be a trial run. Then if it's successful, you can become a grandfather, Wolfgang." Marci laughed at her own joke. Wolfgang didn't find the joke to be funny, although I sensed he was intrigued with the idea.

Wolfgang said, "So where do we find this woman? We must be as discrete as possible. We don't need the authorities knocking on your door."

I said, "No. I understand. Believe me, we need to be careful. I have a place in mind, but I do not know how to go about capturing a living woman from this settlement. I want as pure a specimen as I can find, free from both physical and mental deformities. Therefore, any homeless women are out of the question. I know the formula will correct any abnormalities, but I want a purer specimen. There is a small Amish community in the southern part of Indiana. They keep to themselves, have been at this settlement for decades, and are very strict in their beliefs. They are very religious people and they have little contact with the mainstream world. If somehow we could capture a specimen from this village, I do not think they would cause issues for us."

Wolfgang stood up and walked over to the window in the great room. Each step created a thud that resonated throughout the room. I continued aloud with my thoughts, "I think it would be wise for you to be the one to capture the specimen. I cannot afford to be caught. If I get caught, this game is over and maybe for good. I need to stay out of the scene."

Marci spoke, "I can do it. Oh, please let me do it. I am strong enough to capture this fucking bitch."

Wolfgang quickly said, "No! I will go with you, Garrison. I will choose. I have more experience at this sort of thing than you, Marci." Marci nodded and backed down, knowing that she was getting closer to the family that she always wanted. She had to be wise and not have Wolfgang change his mind.

Marci listened to many of our conversations and never spoke a word as Wolfgang and I planned out our mission. I took a drive out to the small community. These people lived in a very rural area of Indiana. Some of the roads were made of dirt, a fair number of trees covered the area, and there were a lot of hills. Many of the male Amish worked as carpenters, making cabinets, stools and other pieces of furniture in their community. They would accept work on a jobsite outside of town, as requested by their clients who wanted something made or a house constructed. This was their primary source of income. The other source was farming vegetables and, in many cases, raising farm animals for their eggs, milk or meat, or whatever a family would raise on their farm.

A while back I had bought a large SUV with all the windows tinted to a point where you couldn't see inside. There were times that I would take the family out and show them different parts of the city. Wolfgang was always nervous about these small outings, but when all was said and done, he enjoyed being out and away from the confines of the estate.

As I drove around the area, I wanted to make sure I wasn't spotted. I parked my car on a lonely dirt road off the main highway. This dirt road ended abruptly, just past a large area of thick trees that seemed to have sprung out of nowhere in this large hilly field of hay next to a field of corn. I parked the car while my father stayed in the backseat, shielded by the dark windows of my Mercedes SUV. I got out and started to explore. The first thought that came to mind was that we couldn't attempt this capture in wet or snowy weather. I used all my senses to help me scope out the area. I was as quiet as I could be, and I made sure that I wasn't seen by anyone. I traveled through the thick hay and came upon a large treed area that rested high on a steep, massive hill. Just below this hill was the Amish community. I saw numerous small houses that were spaced rather far from each other. Each house had a barn on the property. Some of the barns housed tools and were used as workshops while others were used for farm animals.

The community was made up of many men who all dressed the same and looked alike, and the same could be said about the women. There were a few dogs but no cats were seen. The number of animals in this community concerned Wolfgang and me. Animals have an extreme reaction whenever we're around them. Most of the animals want to run away from us but many tend to growl, snort or lash out at us. This was obviously not a good development if we were trying to go unnoticed while abducting a young woman.

I quickly studied the landscape and community. I now had a game plan set in my mind. I needed to take my father to the community so he could scope out the individual that would cause the least amount of trouble during the abduction.

Early the next morning, I again took my father out to the community. We traveled early so we wouldn't cause any suspicion. I pointed to where he needed to walk so he wouldn't be seen. It was still dark outside, which didn't affect my father in any way. The ground was dry except for the dew resting on the grass and trees. Wolfgang took a cellphone with him just in case he got himself into trouble. He never actually used the cellphone because his hands and fingers were so large it made it difficult for him to use.

Wolfgang left the SUV and I watched him glide across the fields of hay. He passed some tall brush areas of the field and hid in the cluster of trees on top of the large hill just overlooking the Amish community. Traveling at night through a field or heavily laden forest of trees and brush came second nature to my father. For decades he had hunted in such environments. On many occasions, Wolfgang visited the small community that was near his forest area in Germany and had rarely been seen.

Wolfgang settled in the thick trees on top of the hill. He listened for and watched everything, waiting until the locals got up from their beds. He paid special attention to the one house that I had earmarked for him. Wolfgang was prepared to just scope the community out first and come back the next several days to make his capture.

Not long before the sun rose, he watched the light come on in the small house below. A young lady of childrearing age walked out of the small house carrying a lantern which was so out of date for the time but seemed to fit into the culture of this community. The woman had long black hair that was rolled up under a bonnet. She was very light skinned with a pudgy stomach and rather thick legs. Her arms and head were proportionate to the size of her body.

It was an hour before dawn, and the darkness still dominated the setting of this community. A slight wind came out of the northwest which was the opposite direction of where Wolfgang was headed. He was very concerned about any animals in the community catching wind of his scent. Wolfgang used all his senses while watching for anyone else to emerge from the house. He listened as intently as he could to hear if anyone was walking outside either with her or doing some other chore. He also attempted to assess the other houses in the distance. At that time, the only person outside was this young woman. Wolfgang watched her as she walked slowly down the hill toward the barn. The distance from the house to the barn was about three hundred feet. In between the barn and the house was a toolshed which looked to be about eight-foot wide and ten-foot long.

Wolfgang heard cows in the large barn making noise and stomping around on the dirt floor of the barn. Apparently, milking the cows was one of the girl's chores. Wolfgang had every intention of coming back another day for the abduction, but he sensed this might be the best time to capture the human. He swiftly but quietly hurried down the hill and as he came to the toolshed, he stopped and looked back at the house. He saw no one outside or anyone looking out. The cows inside of the barn started to make more noise and their movement increased. Wolfgang remained as still as he could. His heart leapt somewhat when he heard the human come out of the barn to look around to see what was making the cows so nervous. After a few seconds, which seemed like minutes to Wolfgang, the human spoke to the cows, "Come on now, stop making such a fuss." The human's verbal pronunciation was strange to Wolfgang's ears. He was not familiar with such an accent.

Wolfgang waited for the human to emerge from the barn. He was on constant alert to be sure he was not seen or heard. He had devised an escape route through the small forest on the hill and calculated how long it would take to make his way back to my car. Wolfgang knew the human would probably scream, but he wanted to limit that time to the best of his ability. He looked down and noticed a large rock close to where he was standing. He dug his large, thick fingers into the soil and pulled out the rock. He thought throwing the rock in the opposite direction of where he was coming from would buy him some time before she screamed.

Wolfgang was used to stalking and attacking prey, from animals to human beings. When he was in Germany he took a fair number of humans from the village just outside of the forest where he lived.

Wolfgang's ears perked up when he heard the human walking toward the barn door. He heard every step on the dirt floor of the barn. He heard and smelt the fresh milk that sloshed back and forth in the metal bucket that his specimen was carrying. He allowed her to make her way out of the barn, place the bucket down on the ground, and close the barn door. She reached down and picked up the milk bucket then turned to walk away. She nonchalantly started her way up to the house.

Wolfgang's grip on the dirty rock tightened as he quietly raised it to his side. He kept moving the rock around in his large, furry hand, attempting to remove as much of the dirt on it as possible. He glanced at his target and began to raise the rock over his head. He released the rock from his hand with almost flawless execution. The rock sailed high in the air and after what seemed like an eternity, it made its way down. Wolfgang waited patiently for it to hit on the other side of his prey.

The specimen was making her way along the dirt-covered trail up to the house. It was the same trail she had walked every day for years, doing the same laborious morning chore. Like a human robot, she habitually never paid any attention to the picturesque scene that filled her unconscious senses. This place was her home, probably since the day she was born. The area from the house to the barn was lined with wildflowers, a few lonely shrubs, and several small fruit trees that sprang up over the years.

The rock came down about ten feet from where the prey was walking. When the large rock found its way to the ground, it hit hard, causing a thud. The woman turned toward the unexpected sound and simultaneously sucked in a deep breath. Wolfgang, as quietly as he could, raced toward his prey as her back was turned toward him. His prey twisted her head around and saw a large beast-like figure coming at her. She gasped in anticipation of being attacked and before she had time to react, she felt two large hands on her, one on her back and the other across her chest. She dropped the bucket of milk on the hard ground as it spilled everywhere below her feet. She let out a loud scream, but it only lasted a couple of seconds as Wolfgang quickly spun her around while his large, furry hand reached up and clasped over her mouth. Meanwhile, his other arm reached across her body. He moved to his right and picked up the specimen by her waist while still holding her mouth shut. He started running as fast as he could, looking over his shoulder as he ran. He was looking for anyone that might have heard her scream. As Wolfgang ran up the hill, he heard the cows in the background moving around in the stalls and making a fair amount of noise.

Wolfgang ran as fast as he could and after several moments, he found himself at the top of the hill. He only saw one person out, but they didn't seem to know what had happened. Wolfgang ran into the forest area, all the while his prey was kicking and attempting to scream through her capturer's hand. Her heart had never beat that fast in her life. Her body was being bounced around like an old rag doll that she'd had when she was a little girl. She kicked and kicked, trying to escape, but Wolfgang's legs took the blows from the back of her thick heeled boots without ever slowing down. Wolfgang stopped, looked around while in the middle of the treed area, and threw her down on the ground, being careful not to injure her permanently. She was trying to recover from her rough journey and attempting to catch her breath from her back slamming into the hard ground.

Wolfgang took his right leg and placed it over her body to hold her in place. He grabbed a rope from his pocket and with a lot of force, gagged his victim then quickly tied the rope to the back of her head. The victim was trying to scream and kicked in an attempt to get away from her assailant. Wolfgang picked her up and repositioned her with her legs dangling on the side of his body.

I could see Wolfgang running out of the forest area and across the field. I quickly exited the car and opened the back door. I looked around but didn't see a soul. My father was carrying his prey as his heavy footsteps made his way to me. The closer my father got to me, the more I felt the thudding of his large feet as they confronted the ground. When he approached me, I said, "Get her in the back seat." Wolfgang roughly moved his prey and released his hand from her mouth. She screamed as loud as she could but her screams were cracking from pure fear due to her vocal cords being under great stress over the past couple of minutes. Wolfgang threw her into the back seat and gave her a push with his large hand as he got into the SUV with her.

I quickly shut the door and got in the driver's seat. I started the car and made my way down the dirt road. We looked in all directions to see if anyone had either followed or seen us from a distance. Wolfgang grabbed his prey by the wrist as she screamed louder, looking at her as he pulled her closer to his face. The lady was about to go out of her mind from fear alone. He brought her face just inches from his and said to her, "Shut the fuck up, bitch!" She looked at him in silence then started screaming again. She kicked the back of the seat and was twisting and turning around, trying to get away. The gag muffled her screams, but she was still annoyingly loud.

I drove away from the community and after several moments, we finally reached the main road. I made sure not to speed but traveled as fast as I could down the road and onto the expressway back home. I noticed in my rearview mirror that the sun was coming up in the distance. Meanwhile, Wolfgang had blindfolded his target so she wouldn't be able to see where we were going. He said, "Shut up... quit screaming. I will take the gag out of your mouth, but you have to stop screaming."

The young woman stopped screaming but she was crying uncontrollably. She could hardly catch her breath but when she did, she smelt something foul, the smell of rotting meat coming from her assailant's mouth. She inhaled an animalistic smell that excreted from the pores of this large, hairy beast that she was convinced was the devil himself. Wolfgang removed the gag and in moments the prey was screaming, "Help me!" The outburst angered Wolfgang and his instincts caused him to react. He grabbed her throat with his strong hand and pushed her head up against the headrest. The woman stopped screaming, unable to speak because of the pressure that Wolfgang used on her throat. He squeezed harder, placed his mouth just inches from her ear, and yelled with his large, booming voice, "I told you to shut the fuck up!"

The victim closed her eyes from the pain that she felt in her throat and ear. Suddenly, Wolfgang released his grip from her throat and the prey gasped for much needed air. She continued sobbing uncontrollably, trying to the best of her ability not to speak. She tried to gather her emotions. Wolfgang said, "That's right... Gooood girl. Try and calm yourself. We are just going for a ride." The woman was so scared that she forgot to swallow. Her saliva was dripping from her mouth and liquid was running from her nose. She wanted to speak but she thought it would be in her best interest to follow the devil's instructions.

I drove home with the sobbing sounds of a scared woman's cries ringing in my ears. I pulled into the driveway and after several moments, I reached the back of the estate where the garage was located. I stopped the car, and Wolfgang said to his blindfolded victim, "Come." Wolfgang and the girl got out of the car and walked toward the house. She stumbled several times, which got on my father's nerves. Out of frustration, he reached down, picked her up and placed her over his shoulder. She let out a small scream, but quickly stopped because of my father's strong encouragement to keep quiet. We entered the house and my mother was in the kitchen. She glanced over without saying a word. In fact, she had no expression on her face. My love was sitting in the great room playing her violin, but stopped as soon as we entered. Marci looked at the woman being carried by Wolfgang. Our eyes met and she unexpectedly blew me a kiss.

I followed Wolfgang downstairs to the landing in the basement. He unlocked his lab located on the right of the landing, stomping his way to the cell that would now house our latest experiment. Wolfgang roughly placed her on the cot, ripped off the blindfold, and untied the gag from her mouth. Suddenly, our victim started to scream loudly and uncontrollably while drawing her legs up onto the cot.

Wolfgang slowly walked out of the room and closed and locked the cell door. The girl started to violently shake and finally spoke in a panic-stricken voice, "Why are you doing this to me? What is this place?" She looked around at her new environment, seeing the large barred cell with a small bathroom attached. She quickly glanced out across the cell and saw Wolfgang's laboratory. She said, "Where am I? What do you want from me?" Wolfgang nor I answered her questions. She asked again, "Why are you doing this to me? Answer me!" She continued to look around the cell then suddenly slid down onto the floor in front of her cot, got on her knees and started to pray.

The woman prayed, "Oh God, oh God, please help me. Take this cup of suffering from me. I beg you to forgive my evildoers for they do not know what they do."

This praying upset my father greatly. He shouted, "Shut up. Stop that fucking rhetoric!"

The woman continued to pray. Her voice cracked saying, "May God have mercy on their souls, for the damned think that life is hopeless…"

Wolfgang shouted again saying, "Shut up! Shut the fuck up, you god damned bible freak!"

The woman raised her voice to where she was almost yelling, "May God forgive the beast, for the devil is blind to his own selfish ambition…"

Wolfgang stormed toward the cell door, unlocked it and within seconds was in front of his chatty specimen. Wolfgang reached down and pulled her up by the arm. She continued to pray in a very hurried prayer, "May God forgive the devil…"

Wolfgang raised his specimen toward his mouth and shouted in a thunderous voice, "I told you to shut the fuck up or I will pull your tongue out of your head."

I was worried about the woman's safety. I said, "Father… please… ignore her. We need her. Let her go." Wolfgang angrily looked at me and without taking his eyes from mine, he aggressively threw her onto the cot. Her right shoulder hit the cot with such force that the front of the cot bent in about an inch. She screamed from the pain. Wolfgang walked out of the cell and secured the lock behind him.

He walked past me and sneered. I said, "I understand. The prayers to her imaginary god bother me as well, but we need her alive."

Wolfgang continued to walk past me as he said, "Understood."

I looked at the woman in the cell and asked her if she was okay. She muttered, "Yes, yes..."

She started to desperately cry harder. She asked, "What is this place? Who is he? What is he? Who are you?"

I put my finger to my mouth and said, "Shhhhh. Everything is going to be okay."

The woman said, "Is that your father? Real father? Are you the devil's son?"

I said to her, "That man is my father and he is not the devil. Please, stop praying because it will only upset him, and me for that matter. I need for you to be calm. I understand that you are confused right now, but we just need you for an experiment. Do not worry. Everything is going to be fine."

The woman looked around and said, "Experiment! What kind of experiment? I want to go home. I want out of this place. This is hell, isn't it? I know you are the devil's son and I will not succumb to your evil tongue or evil ways."

I interrupted her saying, "Oh, would you please shut up about the devil shit."

Without warning I heard someone walking down the hallway. Before I knew it, my Marci walked into the laboratory. Marci's appearance had to be quite disturbing, to say the least, especially to a human who was not prepared to see her for the first time.

I glanced over at the woman in the cell and her eyes got very large and her complexion was as white as snow. I sensed not only fear in her, but I felt the madness that engulfed her entire soul. Her body started to shake uncontrollably. There before her stood a monster. Her thoughts of the devil and his followers, who come in all forms, shapes and sizes, dominated her attention. The most unthinkable act the woman could imagine happened. The monster smiled at her and said, "Hello. What do we have here?"

The woman took a quick, deep breath then let out the most blood curdling scream I had ever heard in my life. She started to run away from Marci and went toward the furthermost part of the cell. She was shaking and hysterical. She wanted to speak but the words couldn't come out due to fear. This behavior lasted for several minutes. Marci walked along the outside of the cell, pacing back and forth like a wild animal stalking their prey. She was enjoying the fear and suffering the woman was experiencing. The woman couldn't keep her eyes off Marci who playfully hissed at her while showing her long, sharp teeth, causing the woman to go back into hysterics. I attempted to calm the woman down, but wasn't having any success.

Marci walked over to Midnight's crate. The woman, although hysterical, kept her eyes on my love. I knew what she was thinking. *How can this be happening? How can something that looks like that be alive?* She was in disbelief that something so in-human could be allowed to live. Her God wouldn't create such a creature.

Marci bent down and unlocked the crate. She reached in and pulled out Midnight. The all white, hairless cat that looked like it could glow in the dark was alternating its hissing and purring. Marci picked up Midnight and brought the cat over to the cell. The religious bitch again started to scream as she ran around the cell trying to escape from this madness. She saw these two creatures that had skin the color of pure white snow, one a cat that had large blue veins running throughout its body. This was something unworldly. Marci then walked away from the cell and put Midnight back in its crate.

Finally, the woman started to speak. She said in a breathless voice, "What kind of people are you? What kind of place is this?" She looked at Marci, pointed to her and said, "Is... is she the devil's mistress?" Marci laughed as she put her long arm across my shoulders. At this time, Wolfgang entered the woman's line of sight. With Marci lurking next to me, the woman felt as if she was the freak. Her mind was racing with all kinds of thoughts. All she wanted was for this experience to end as soon as humanly possible.

I politely asked Marci and Wolfgang to leave the lab. I wanted to speak to the woman by myself. Marci and my father left the lab as I pulled up a chair and sat in front of the cell. I watched the woman cry, scream and sob. Her mumbled, incoherent words proved to me that she was scared like no other time in her young life.

After several minutes had passed, the woman controlled her emotions. She looked around at her surroundings and tried to take in where she was and why she was in the cell, but nothing made sense to her. She got up from the floor where she had been curled up, and slowly made her way to the middle bars of the cell. She placed her hands around the bars that were before her, looked at me and said in a pleading voice, "Sir. Sir. Please help me. Please help me. I beg you, please don't hurt me. I have done nothing to anyone."

I slowly got up from the chair and walked up to her. I placed my hand on her hands that gripped the bar tightly. When my hand touched hers, she jumped back. I asked, "What is your name?"

She looked at me and her eyes quickly scanned the room without seeing the other abnormalities. I sensed that I was gaining her trust, albeit slowly. She took a couple of steps toward me and said, "Please! Please help me. Get me out of this prison of sin."

I said again, "Please tell me your name."

The question disturbed the woman. She spoke in a trembling voice, Sssssarah, Sarah Hershberger. I am from an Amish community in Indiana. I... I was born and raised there. I have never been away from the community. Please... please... you must help me. I must get back to my community of Christ-loving people. I have done nothing wrong."

I smiled and said, "Hello, Sarah. My name is Garrison. I know this is a lot for you to take in so please forgive us. The wolf-like creature is Wolfgang and the beautiful tall lady with the white hair is Marci."

Sarah looked at me with a bewildered look and said, "Beautiful lady? She... she is a monster, or the devil's mistress, is she not? Is the wolf man Lucifer? Why are you with them? Why do they not attack you?" She looked at me, her eyes widened and she asked, "Are you their leader? Yes... yes, you are their leader. That is why you are talking to me. Who are you?"

I interrupted her and said, "I know this sounds crazy and is very difficult for you to accept. I realize this is a lot of information to process but Wolfgang, the wolf-like creature, is my father." Sarah looked at me as if I was crazy. I continued, "He experimented with injecting a formula into his body and the formula changed him physically. The same goes for Marci. Marci is my mate, my girlfriend, my wife-to-be. The formula was used to make them a more perfect person, both physically and mentally. They can perform tasks that no one can duplicate, and their intelligence level is extreme. They possess great knowledge on any subject matter. I also have a mother that looks like Wolfgang. Her name is Zelda. Now, I know what you are thinking... *What does all of this have to do with me?* Well, we need you to help us with an experiment and once that experiment is over, you will be free to go."

Sarah looked at me in disbelief. I sensed her fear was increasing to a maximum level and she was starting to panic. She said, "Oh God... oh my sweet Jesus… please help me." She started to cry violently as she fell to her knees in front of me. Wolfgang suddenly appeared, and Sarah lost control over her emotions again. She tried to get up but fell a couple of times in her attempt to rise. When she got to her feet, she ran over to the furthest part of the cell, standing next to her cot with her back against the wall.

Marci entered the laboratory and asked, "So… what's going on in here? Is she still crying?"

I said to Wolfgang and Marci, "I told her why she is here, that she will be assisting in an experiment for us."

Marci quickly interrupted and said, "Did you tell her everything? Did you tell her exactly what she will be assisting with?"

I smiled and said, "No, my love, I was just trying to calm her down. Please, let us keep her calm."

Marci smiled at me. This was enjoyment to her. She looked at the captured little teenager who was scared out of her mind. Sarah stared at Marci while she was being studied by this large, seven-foot white creature that dominated her sight. The pale white skin and hair with those large, lifeless eyes of pure darkness sent shivers down Sarah's spine. Marci asked, "Did you ever get her to speak?"

I said, "Yes, her name is Sarah."

Marci nodded and walked up to the cell. Sarah's back inched ever so slowly up the cement wall. Marci said, "Hello, Sarah. I'm Marci. Don't be afraid of me." Marci moved her sexy, long body along the front of the cell as she never lost sight of Sarah. Her eyes burned deep into Sarah's soul.

Sarah muttered the words, "P-pla-please stay away from me."

Marci repeated, "Oh, don't be afraid of me." Marci took two long fingers and stroked both sides of one of the bars of the cell. "You just don't know how lucky you are to be chosen for such a magnificent experiment."

Sarah slightly interrupted in a fearful voice, "Experiment? What is this experiment? Why do you… and he keep talking about an experiment? What is going on here?"

Marci laughed as she grasped two bars of the cell with her large, pearly white hands. She said in a matter of fact voice, "My dear, I was once like you. Human. But these gentlemen changed me into something wonderful… powerful… special. I feel amazing. I think on a different level than before. See, my Sarah, I am going to live forever. Yes, that's right, I am going to live forever. I will never die, thanks to them." Marci turned her large head and smiled at me. She moved her tail up toward my hand and curled her tail around my wrist.

Sarah looked down and started screaming again. Sarah said, "You... you... have a tail. What is this place? What are you? Tell me, what are you?" Sarah again cried uncontrollably.

Marci started to act disgusted and said, "Would you please stop that fucking crying? It serves no purpose. Just fucking stop." Sarah sobbed and tried to follow Marci's demand. Marci said, "That's better. Now, I want children. I want children with my love, Garrison. But I am worried that if we mate and I get pregnant, I might not survive the pregnancy. We conducted an experiment years ago where the pregnant bitch didn't survive. So, we can't have that happen to me, now can we? So that is where you come into play."

Sarah started saying, "No. No. This is not happening. This is blasphemy."

Marci shouted back angrily, "Shut up, bitch. Stop with the fucking god and bible shit or I will make this so painful for you that you will die from the pain alone."

Sarah started screaming as she ran into the bathroom area of the cell, trying to find a way out. Marci screamed at her, "There is no way out of this cell! Come back here! I am not through talking to you!"

Sarah ran out of the bathroom and went to the other side of the cell. Marci said, "Listen to me! Listen to me, bitch!" Sarah turned and looked at her worst nightmare standing in front of her. Marci said, "We are going to kill you, and Garrison will bring you back to life just like he did with me. You will then transform into a better being and before you know it, we will impregnate you and see if you survive the pregnancy. If you do, which we all hope this is successful, we will let you go."

Sarah just stood there trying to process all of what was happening to her and what was being said. She felt saliva running down the left corner of her mouth. She quickly wiped it away as she started to shake her head and fidget. She walked quickly back and forth saying, "No! No! This is not happening. This is not going to happen. You cannot do this to me."

Marci laughed and said, "Oh, it's happening, and yes, we are going to do this to you. But, my dear, it will feel so good in the end. But I cannot lie to you; it's going to hurt like a bitch."

Marci started to laugh as Sarah screamed, "Nooooooo!" Sarah quickly fell to her knees. She clasped her hands together and started praying, "God, we pray for those who suffer injustice and..."

Marci started to scream and said, "Shut the fuck up."

Sarah continued without missing a beat, "...those who suffer senseless violence."

Marci turned her large, sexy body toward Wolfgang's lab. She opened a drawer and pulled out a large ten-inch skinning knife that Wolfgang sometimes used on his prey. In the cell, Sarah continued to pray, "We pray that your justice will reign."

Marci went to the cell door and said, "Wolfgang, would you mind opening this door?" Wolfgang went to his drawer and retrieved his key. He tossed the key to Marci from across the lab. She cleanly grabbed it and quickly opened the cell door.

Sarah was nervous and kept repeating the same words from the prayer; "We pray that your justice will reign. We pray that your justice will reign..." Marci ran over to Sarah with her mouth just inches from Sarah's ear. Suddenly, Sarah stopped praying. Her eyes were tightly clinched and she could feel Marci's warm breath on the side of her face. Sarah, still sobbing, said, "Oh please God, please, please spare me."

Marci hissed and said loudly in her ear, "God is not the one you need to pray to. It doesn't exist. I exist. You need to pray to me and ask me for mercy, not some imaginary genie."

Sarah, so visibly upset, said, "God exists. He is my savior. He is good."

Marci's anger swelled inside of her soul. She was getting more upset with each passing second. Marci moved the knife up under Sarah's throat. Sarah gasped for air. She felt the cool steel blade on her warm, sweaty neck as Marci slowly ran the sharp side of the knife up her throat. Marci said in her sexual, hissing voice, "Denounce your god to me. Condemn his false image to hell before everyone in this room and I will see that your suffering is limited."

Sarah swallowed hard and in so doing, felt the knife slightly break her skin then a small bead of warm blood ran down her neck. She cried hard while not moving an inch. She said, "I will never condemn my Lord. I will never denounce Him. My God is my savior. He is your savior. Savior of all animals and all things living."

Marci reared her large head back and let out a blood curdling scream. She raised her leg and pushed Sarah down onto the floor of the cell. Marci looked at her and said, "You stupid, self-centered bitch."

Sarah was lying on the floor clasping her hands together tightly, her fingers intertwined. She continued to pray, "God, we pray... for those who suffer... injustice... suffer senseless violence. Oh God, we pray that Your justice will reign."

Marci walked toward her victim and quickly straddled Sarah's legs, making movement an impossibility. Marci grabbed Sarah's right forearm and said, "Stop that mumbling."

Sarah continued praying, "We also pray for the gift of grace... and mercy in these situations. And we..." Marci quickly twisted the large, sharp knife in her massive hand so the sharp end of the blade faced up. Without notice, my love moved the knife between Sarah's forearms.

Sarah continued to pray, "...pray that victims will... find wisdom they need... in every situation... oh, Jesus, help me."

Marci said, "When I tell you to stop with the praying, I mean... stop praying." With one swift stoke, Marci pulled the knife upward while still holding onto Sarah's right forearm. The knife quickly dug into Sarah's thumb and with great force Marci pulled the knife upward as fast and strong as she could. The knife severed most of Sarah's fingers, with the exception of the last two on her hand. The fingers that were severed were cut off in the proximal phalange area of the finger. One of the partial fingers fell onto Sarah's chest while the others hit the floor around her head.

Sarah immediately shrieked the loveliest sound from her very virtuous lips. At first, she had trouble breathing. The pain immediately settled into her partial fingers then quickly made its way up the hand and forearm. Sarah looked at her lost fingers and lie there, not able to move Marci off of her. Marci said, "Now shut the fuck up. You will never clasp your fingers in prayer again as long as you are a human."

Marci looked down at a few of the disengaged fingers lying on Sarah's chest and the ones close to her head. At that moment, I knew Marci would do something that, at least to my knowledge, had never been endeavored by our species. Marci slowly picked up two of Sarah's detached fingers and without hesitation, placed both in her mouth. Her massive and extremely sharp teeth cut through the bone and cartilage. Sarah remained on the floor, watching Marci chew. At this point, Sarah couldn't make a sound. The combination of the pain and shock of what had just transpired was too much for Sarah's simple brain to process, even though the pain and the veracity of the situation was crystal clear in her mind. I sensed that for her, it was like this was happening to someone else, but the burning pain and shock of what had happened soon brought her simplistic mind back to reality.

Marci looked over her shoulder at me and said, "Have you ever tasted human before? It actually tastes good. Not like an animal, but they are rather tasty."

I looked at my love in disbelief. Wolfgang broke the awkwardness by shouting, "Marci! We don't eat humans. I never ate human flesh."

Marci said, "You ought to try it. Here." She reached down, picked up half of a finger, and tossed it through the cell wall. Wolfgang caught it and said, "Fuck, Marci."

Marci said, "Come on, try it."

Wolfgang shook his head in disbelief as he placed the finger in his mouth. To my surprise, he liked the taste. Marci laughed and said, "Imagine all of the great tasting meals you have missed over the years."

I stood there watching this scene. During my father's and my love's newfound feast lay Sarah, who was now screaming on the floor. She had found her voice. When Marci released her hold on her wrist, Sarah held her severed fingers close to her chest. She attempted to move and escape from Marci, but her efforts were futile. Marci looked down at Sarah as her smile slowly disappeared from her face. Marci quickly bent down and came within inches of Sarah's face.

Marci looked at Sarah with her large black eyes. "You will condemn your god before me and to everyone in this room, and for your efforts I will spare you great pain."

Sarah moved her head from side to side and uttered, "Noooo... I can't."

Marci said, "You will, my little bitch. You will." Marci took her knife and held it to Sarah's forehead. Marci said, "Condemn it! Condemn it to hell!" Sarah said nothing. Marci let out a small growl from the back of her throat. With one quick movement, she grabbed hold of Sarah's face with her free hand, took the knife, and skated the sharp blade up the forehead then imbedded the blade just before Sarah's hairline. Marci moved the knife back, and with a quick stroke, peeled the scalp back to the crown of her head. Marci then made another run of the blade and peeled another strip of the scalp back to the middle of her head.

Sarah was in intense pain. She instinctively grabbed for Marci's arm. Marci quickly took her knife and made a gentle cut on the back of Sarah's hand before she could touch her. Sarah found it almost impossible to scream with Marci's death grip on her jaw. She was finally at her breaking point.

Marci looked down at her victim and loosened the grip on her jaw, "Condemn it to hell. Use its name and denounce your god. I will ease your pain."

Sarah cried out, "Oh, God, forgive me! It... it... hurts so bad."

With those words said, Marci shouted, "Just fucking do it, bitch!"

Sarah cried out and said, "I am so sorry, my Lord... he is not my savior."

Marci yelled, "Go on... who is not your savior? Say it!"

Sarah said, "Oh, God... God is not my savior, Jesus Christ is not my God." Sarah cried hard for it was the toughest words she had ever uttered.

Marci continued, "Do you denounce this Jesus as your god, lord and savior?"

Sarah uttered, "Yes... yes. Please make the pain go away... please."

Marci said, "Damn him to hell. Say it."

Sarah cried louder, "I condemn him to hell and all who believe. Please help me."

Marci smiled and said, "That wasn't that hard now was it, bitch?

Marci looked down, took the knife, and cut open Sarah's buttoned up blouse. Marci quickly took her long finger and pulled Sarah's bra up from between her breasts, took the knife and cut the bra in two, exposing her blood-covered breasts. Marci placed her large hand between Sarah's breasts, her long fingernails scraping along her soft, white skin. Marci placed her hand on Sarah's left breast, rubbing and squeezing it, mixing Sarah's sweat and blood together. Sarah, still crying and in so much pain, said, "Wha... what are you doing? I know not woman or man."

Marci laughed as she took the long knife by the handle and held it in her fist with the blade pointed down. Marci moved the point of the knife over Sarah's heart. She bent over, inches from Sarah's blood-filled face. Marci said, "Oh, bitch, that's not going to last for long." Marci smiled and her long, snake-like tongue escaped from her mouth and licked Sarah's chin. Her tongue went over Sarah's lips and before Sarah knew it, Marci's mouth was kissing hers. Suddenly, a sharp pain developed in the middle of her chest. Sarah exhaled because of the pain and she couldn't catch her breath. Marci slowly pushed the knife deep inside of Sarah's heart. Marci continued to kiss Sarah until she expired. After several moments, Marci ceased her passionate kiss. She got up, slowly pulling the knife out of Sarah's chest. Sarah's eyes were still open and her body fell helplessly to her side.

Marci looked over at me and said, "Now it's your turn, my love." I walked into the cell and made my way to Sarah's body. I knelt before Sarah's body and raised her upper body into my arms. Her head fell sideways, exposing her neck. I moved down toward her and quickly placed my teeth on her skin. I waited for a few moments in the attempt to time the bite in accordance with the time of death of my Marci. I then proceeded to bite into her neck.

My adrenaline was flowing fast, my heart rate was up, and all of my senses were sharp. I felt the formula flowing from the inside of my gums and through my teeth. As I bit this innocent woman, all I could think about was my future kids with Marci. I hoped this experiment would be a success so we could have children together. All I wanted was for Sarah to deliver my offspring during her delivery. Once that was completed, I would have no use for her or her children.

Chapter Four

Wolfgang and Zelda, as they did with Marci after she died, helped clean up Sarah's body. We placed her on a hospital bed and strapped her in place. Wolfgang recorded every moment and all we had to do was to wait for the formula to start working. We had very little experience with bringing humans back to life since we had only tried with Marci. We predicted that she would come back to life in a couple days or so. While we waited for the event to occur, I texted Eva with the news. She was excited for Marci. Eva was very close to Marci and wanted her to have children.

This was a stressful time for everyone in the household. We were all nervous about the experiment. Sarah took about a day longer to come back to life than it took for Marci, although the way Sarah came back was similar. The formula first worked on the nervous system, stimulating the brain, then it worked on the heart and blood. The heartbeat pumped the blood, which is the carrier of the formula, through the body. As the blood flows through the veins, the formula 'corrects' any abnormalities that would differ from the original DNA. The formula repairs or reconstructs the cells. After so long of a time, the subject slowly starts to regain movement. The first movement is breathing, then the neck, and from there the arms. The last area of the body to regain movement is the upper legs and feet.

Marci recalled that after the second or so day of coming back from the dead is when she started to remember things. Her mind was in a world all its own, but she remembered where she was and what had happened to her. I wanted to keep Sarah's mind intact, a very important part of this experiment. One could easily go mad or have one's imagination run wild during this time because the body cannot move but the mind still works. Marci said the most difficult time was when she was not able to move or have the ability to communicate. She said she had an extreme sense of being abandoned.

I kept Wolfgang, Zelda and Marci away from Sarah as much as I could since I was the only one in the house with a similar face and body as hers. As the weeks progressed, so did Sarah's abilities. Similar to

Marci's experience, she slowly started to gain control over her body, and her wounds began to heal quickly. The entry wound to her heart closed and her scalp began to grow back. As the scabs quickly healed, some of Sarah's hair started to grow around the areas that Marci had scalped. During this time, I got to know Sarah well. I could sense her feelings, so our communication didn't have to be too elaborate.

The weeks passed quickly and soon Sarah was able to speak. I worked with her many hours during the day to get her speech back. It was important for me to be able to communicate with her during this transformation so we could compare her experiences with Marci's. At this point, Sarah's experiences were mirroring Marci's at every juncture. Within no time, Sarah started to walk from one side of the cell to the other. Her hand-eye coordination improved rapidly, and after about eight weeks she was completely normal and functioning.

Sarah asked me many questions about the experiment that was taking place. She was shocked that she had come back from the dead. At first she thought it was an act of the devil, but I convinced her it was a great thing. I could sense that Sarah was starting to doubt her god more and more each passing day. Sarah knew what we did to her was evil and wrong, and bringing her back to life was beyond her reasoning. On one hand, she was somewhat grateful, but on the other hand she thought, *Why me?* She had never done anything wrong in her life then suddenly her whole life was turned upside down, without any sensible reason. She knew her body was going to change. I didn't tell her how much, but she had heard enough of our conversations to know that her physical looks would be altered. She knew she must bare my children, which she was very uncomfortable with.

I was always honest with Sarah. One day, Wolfgang told me to place a loose-fitting collar around her neck. On the back of the collar was a strong link of thick chain. Sarah was scared and couldn't understand why this was on her. I told her that her body was going to change and she was going to feel strange at times. After hearing this, her fears increased.

Truth be told, Wolfgang and I had been afraid she might attempt to kill herself. The formula needed time to completely learn her cell and DNA structure for it to be able to repair any damage that might have occurred. As the weeks progressed, the start of her transformation was almost the carbon copy of Marci's alteration from human to the most unique species known to man. The joints in her arms and legs hurt, and she had extreme pain in her back, neck and head. I attempted to calm her down, but as the days progressed, she became more and more nervous and scared.

Sarah asked me repeatedly how much her body was going to change. At some point, I had to be honest with her, but I didn't want her to freak out too much. I ended up telling her what I thought might happen to her physically and mentally. This confused her, but mostly it frightened her. She didn't want to look like Marci. I told her that a whole new life would open up for her and that the one area that would develop beyond understanding was her mental capabilities. I attempted to tell her that she would never grow old or fear the threat of disease. I told her that her body would be constantly self-correcting its cells and DNA. I further explained that her mental status would be elevated to levels that were previously not attainable.

Sarah was afraid of her ever-pending change and she didn't want to experience this alteration. She pleaded with me on a multitude of occasions to stop this from happening to her. I told her that I couldn't.

Sarah and I became rather good friends during this process. She was a simple-minded person with limited worldly experience. The more we spoke, the more comfortable she became with me. She told me that this was God's way of punishing her for her sins. That was the only way, in her mind, she could rationalize what was happening to her. I allowed her to think along these lines. I needed her mind to stay sharp.

Each day created a new pain in areas throughout her body. As the weeks turned into another month, her physical body started to change. Her schedule continued to be on par with Marci's. As her pain increased, I had to use the straps on her. I moved the hospital bed in her cell, placed her in the bed and bound her ankles, torso and wrists to the bed. Sarah's pain increased each week and her transformation went the same way and rate as Marci's.

Sarah's legs and arms grew rapidly, to a point where the skin and muscles were stretched so much that it looked as if they were going to rip open. Sarah screamed in pain and begged for me to take her suffering away from her, to kill her to put her out of her misery. She prayed aloud as best she could. Over time, her head swelled to the size of a basketball, to a point where she could no longer speak. Her neck, hands, feet and back grew. At times I could hear her vertebra pop and crack, which was quickly followed by loud groans of pain.

Over the next several weeks, Sarah's body continued to change. Her metamorphosis was almost identical to what Marci had experienced; from the pain to the swelling to the increased size of her body. Finally, at the end of eight weeks from the day her changes started, the transformation was complete. The body grew to almost seven and a half feet in length, and the skin tone was bleached white. Her hair was dark black and long. Like Marci, the length of the hair went down to the small of her back. Her tail was shaped and the approximate length as my love's. The length of her teeth and the size of her eyes, gum line, ears, nose and mouth were all similar. There was a slight difference though in the color of Sarah's eyes as compared to Marci's. Sarah's eyes were a few shades lighter in color and her pupils were more noticeable. Sarah was very pudgy in her waist and had a rather thick torso.

Sarah endured a great amount of suffering. I sensed that she continually wanted to die through the process. I kept trying to speak to her and warn her of what was coming next in the transformation process. At times, I believe that might have scared her more. She knew she was changing into something unholy, in her way of thinking. She felt so different, not only physically but mentally. She couldn't express her thoughts, but from what Marci told me, the mental changes were the most difficult part. Your mind is in pain during the process. You have trouble thinking and processing your thoughts. Some of that is due to the pain you feel, but most of the problem is the formula changing the way you think and how your body processes information.

During this transformation, Sarah had many emotional meltdowns. She would scream and cry out saying, "What is happening to me?" Her whole system was in shock. Many times I had to calm her by talking to her — asking her about her family or doing whatever I had to do to get her mind off of what was happening to her. I continued to keep Wolfgang and Marci out of her line of sight. As the days went by, Sarah adjusted rather well to what was happening to her. I was surprised.

When Sarah's transformation was complete, her road back to total recovery was a long one. It took Sarah a week to regain complete control over her new body. Walking and talking was extremely difficult, as one could imagine, but after several days of training and working, Sarah mastered those tasks. The most difficult part of her body to master was her tail. Like Marci, Sarah had a lot of trouble controlling its movements. Many times she was bothered by its existence. After several weeks, Sarah got used to her tail and was using it like a third hand.

We kept the neck brace with the chain attached throughout this time. Sarah probably could have pulled on the chain and might have ripped one of the links of the chain if she had wanted to, but I sensed that she was too scared. All she wanted was to be released, but as the formula stewed in her system and took control of her senses, she quickly began to understand that she was never going to leave. At some point, she was at peace with the idea of never going back to her old life. She couldn't even if we had allowed her to go. She knew beyond a shadow of a doubt that this was her new home, but she also knew it was not going to last forever. She personally wanted to die and be with her dear god in that fabricated, imaginary world called the afterlife. She felt that it was her earthly punishment, sent by her god, that she had to endure his will. She felt that she had sinned, that she had disappointed her god, and this was her penance.

Over the next week, Sarah began to experience the full effects of the formula. She was amazed at what her senses were picking up from her environment. I worked with her hand-eye coordination and she found it fascinating what she could do with a tennis ball. She wasn't the most athletic creature, but she could throw the ball against the wall and catch it with her eyes closed. She became so good at this that she could throw the ball at any bar of the cell, have it bounce directly back to her, and catch it behind her back. I let her read books, and she read at an astounding pace. She was able to retain information like she had never done before. She was enjoying her new gift, but as soon as she felt happy, she would have this incredible sense of guilt that fell upon her soul. She thought it was a sin to enjoy a gift from the 'devil.' She viewed my father and Marci as the primary devil but viewed me as a disciple. Sarah would constantly attempt to sway me over to the 'good' side. Little did she know, I WAS the 'good' side, but she quickly dismissed any of these notions when those thoughts developed.

The one area that disturbed Sarah the most was her strange desire for animals. I forgot how that might be difficult for someone to overcome. I was so young when I first had my taste of a live, warm-blooded animal, I thought it was something that I should do because it felt so natural for me. Marci had the desire from the very start after her transformation, so for some strange reason, we were caught off-guard when Sarah was struggling with her newly discovered obsession. We attempted to help her get past her issue with eating live animals, but she violently refused. Therefore, we had to cut the live animal's meat up and serve it to her raw before she would even entertain the thought of eating it. It was still difficult for her to process the desire of raw meat verses what she was taught her entire life.

Eva came home for a couple of weeks around this time while Juilliard was on spring break. She loved Juilliard. Even though she was more advanced than her classmates, at least they were better than anyone she had met at her previous schools. Eva was developing further, both physically and mentally, and got stronger in both areas each day. Even at her young age, she was a young adult, and her sexual urges were robust. We all sensed this and did our best to have her control them. We all knew that at some point she needed to explore sexually. It was going to be a challenge for her to control her desires.

Wolfgang and I always explained to Marci and Eva about being able to control your emotions from within. Not being able to control your anger, happiness, thoughts and even your sexual desires could lead to your personal downfall. That is our demon; ourselves and how we handle situations, learning to balance aggressiveness with self-control, to balance anger, sadness and happiness. What gives us so much power is having the ability to process thoughts quickly, the ability to analyze all facets of a problem, and being able to come to a logical conclusion after all possibilities are examined thoroughly.

When Eva first met Sarah in her cell, Eva was very impressed. She said, "So, you created another Marci. She is not as pretty as Marci, now is she?"

I said to Eva, "Now, Eva. That is not nice."

Eva said, "Of course not. It's not meant to be nice. It's meant to be the truth, a statement of fact."

Sarah looked down and was very sad. Sarah said, "This is not my choosing."

Eva said, "Don't worry, girl, you are better off this way than how you were before."

As Eva walked away, Sarah watched and said, "I am not better. The devil is inside me now and I cannot rid him of his possession." Eva stopped walking and turned toward Sarah. She said, "There is no devil. The devil is not reality. You are reality. My father made you into what you are. He is your god, not that imaginary figure you so blindly pray to. You ought to pray to my father for he is the one that created you."

Sarah looked at us and asked, "What are you?"

Eva pointed to Wolfgang who was standing next to his lab. Eva said, "He is my father. Garrison is my brother. Garrison gave you life, but he received that power from our father."

Sarah was shocked. For the first time she finally understood the complicated angles to our family. Sarah backed away from the bars of the cell. She was trying to process all this information. She looked down at herself and saw her long, white legs. She moved her tail across her legs in place of her hand and started to cry. I quickly said, "Sarah, you need to control your emotions. Don't worry about what she said."

Sarah continued to cry and said, "I am a monster. I am ugly."

I said, "No. No, you are not a monster. You are not ugly. I find my Marci very attractive. You know that. You know how much I worship her."

When Eva left the lab, she passed Marci. Marci had a suspicion that Eva had said something to Sarah by the way Eva smiled and carried herself. Marci entered the lab and stood next to Wolfgang. She looked over at me and motioned for me to come over to where they were standing. Marci said, "I think it is time that we progress to the next phase of this experiment."

Sarah, who could now hear as well as we could sasked, "What phase? What are you people talking about?"

Marci, totally ignoring Sarah, continued, "I think it's time."

Wolfgang nodded and said, "When do you want to proceed?"

Marci looked at me and said, "Now. Let's do this thing today. Why not?" Marci looked deeply into my eyes and I sensed her feeling sorry for me. She knew I didn't want to fuck Sarah. She was also becoming jealous. Marci was always the jealous and possessive type, but she knew this had to be done. She knew the whole purpose of this experiment was to see if her species and mine could safely have children together.

We turned and looked at Sarah. There she stood, looking at us in disbelief. Wolfgang said, "We need to strap her down. Marci, help me!" Sarah started shifting around in the cell, trying to find a way out, but she knew there was no escape. She took her large hands and placed them around the chain, attempting to break them. Before she knew it, Wolfgang had made his way over to the pulley and had started to retract the chain toward the wall. Marci opened the cell door and walked inside, never taking her eyes off Sarah. I knew down deep that this was turning Marci's sexual inhibition into overdrive. Wolfgang quickly went inside the cell and moved the hospital bed over toward Sarah then he and Marci grabbed Sarah. She tried to get away, but they were too strong for Sarah to overcome.

Wolfgang roughly manhandled Sarah onto the bed. Marci took control of her ankles and helped position Sarah in the bed. Wolfgang strapped Sarah's torso with long, thick leather straps. Sarah was screaming, "No! No! What are you doing? Why are you doing this?"

Marci hissed, "Shut up, bitch."

Wolfgang took each arm, one at time, and secured them to the head of the cot. Sarah's arms were over her head to a point where she could hardly move her arms. Wolfgang took one of her legs and bent her knee about ninety degrees. He adjusted the strap coming from the bottom of the bed and secured her ankle. Wolfgang did the same with the other leg. He wanted her legs to be open, but wanted her to have just enough freedom to move her legs out.

I noticed Sarah fighting every step of the way. Her massively strong legs moved around, and every time she moved them, the straps would resist her moving any further. This scared her, and each time the straps resisted her movement to get up or to straighten her legs, she cried out for help. Sarah wore a few of Marci's clothes which consisted of a large tee-shirt and a rather short skirt with no panties. Marci wouldn't allow her to wear her better clothes, especially her dresses because Sarah was thicker in her stomach area than Marci and the dresses wouldn't have fit anyway.

Sarah screamed, "Help me! Let me go! Oh, please let me go! No more, please, no more! No more pain! Please don't hurt me!"

Marci looked at Wolfgang and smiled then walked over to Sarah. She looked at her and said, "Oh, my ugly slut, we are not going to hurt you, my love. We are going to fuck you. We are going to give you pleasure, my dear."

Sarah shook her head from side to side. She said, "No. No! I am a virgin. I know no man!"

Marci laughed and said, "You will know man today... and maybe you will get to know a woman as well."

Sarah screamed, "No! No! Oh please, God... No!"

I finally made my way inside the cell as Marci walked over to me. As our eyes met, I said, "So, how are we going to do this? I do not think I can do this by myself. I hate this."

Marci smiled and said, "I will assist."

Wolfgang smiled and walked out of the cell. He said, "I will be upstairs. Carry on."

We watched my father walk out of the lab. Marci looked lovingly into my eyes and said, "I love you. I will never hold this against you, my love. This is for us." Marci reached down and unzipped my pants then unbuckled my belt and slowly pulled my pants down. She reached up and took off my shirt then walked along the side of me, sliding her long fingers across my chest. She stood behind me and with her strong hands she ripped my underwear in two. I stood in the cell and before Sarah, naked as the day I was born. Marci proceeded to remove her top then her skirt.

Sarah was twisting around on the bed, trying to get loose from her restraints which caused her skirt to ride up, exposing her vagina. All she said was, "Oh, God, no! No!" She watched Marci's hands running up and down my stomach, chest and thighs. For the first time in Sarah's life, she saw a male's penis. At her first glance, she looked away, but a small part of her wanted to see it. She was naturally drawn to my manhood.

Marci quickly spun me around and started kissing me. Her long tail was sliding up the back of my leg and over my ass. Then, without any hesitation, it wrapped itself around the base of my manhood and curled around my shaft and the back of my scrotum. It was a firm yet gentle squeezing motion as she fondled my penis. Before I knew it, I was fully aroused.

My mind was racing and my heart was pounding. I was so confused. I didn't want to do this, but nature was controlling my desires. Marci sensed all of this and wanted to encourage me to have sex with Sarah. It was for our future. It was for Marci's wellbeing. We wanted children together and this was the only way to test if it was safe for my Marci.

Sarah was scared. She was trying to accept what was happening to her. The idea of having someone else's baby, plus the solid possibility that she might die from giving birth to her babies, was a lot for her to process. What made this so confusing for Sarah was that a part of her wanted to have sex and this disturbed her even more. She didn't want to have the 'devil's' children, but a small part of her was turned on to the fact of engaging in the sexual act. These thoughts haunted her from the start and now her pending rape confronted her with the reality of the situation. She was feeling guilty, dirty and liberated all at the same time. The combination of these thoughts and the act that was about to happen caused great division in her soul.

Marci turned my body toward Sarah while still holding me with her tail. She bent down and said in my ear, "I want you to fuck this bitch hard and don't be gentle. Come on, I will feed your cock into her." She pushed me toward Sarah. I could feel her large breasts on my shoulders then her hard nipples running across my back. Marci continued to talk in my ear, "Come on. I want to see you with another woman. Come on, baby. Fuck her."

Marci moved her sexy body to my right side. Her large breast gently brushed my arm while her long fingers softly drug across my shoulders. Her long tail still had control of my manhood as she pulled me closer to Sarah's vagina. Sarah's legs were still bound and she was trying to free them from the restraints. Marci looked down at the struggling victim and suddenly grabbed Sarah's tee-shirt dress that was once hers. She ripped it from Sarah's body, exposing her breasts and rather thick stomach. Sarah screamed for help. Marci said to her, "Scream louder, bitch. It makes fucking more enjoyable." Marci took her large left hand and cupped Sarah's breast then took her long thumb and rubbed Sarah's nipple until it was hard. Sarah continued to scream and tried with all her power to free herself from the restraints. Marci bent down, her large mouth inches from Sarah's ear. Marci said, "You are going to get fucked now. Enjoy it, bitch, because you will never fuck my man again. He is going to impregnate you then we'll see if you survive the pregnancy."

Marci proceeded to use her tail to push the head of my penis next to the lips of Sarah's vagina. She moved me up and down the length of her lips. Marci went to Sarah's exposed breast and started sucking on her nipple. Sarah arched her neck back saying, "No! Oh, God... please, no!" Slowly, Marci put my manhood inside of her. Sarah gasped and yelled, "Nooooooo! Oh... Goooood... Noooooo!" Marci kept her tail on me and continued to slide my cock into Sarah until I was completely inside her. Marci continued to suck and lick on Sarah's nipple.

Sarah was in a strange and different world. A part of her was enjoying this moment while the other half of her was completely experiencing the feeling of being violated.

Marci removed her mouth from Sarah's breast and licked her way up to her neck. She looked into her eyes and said, "I bet your father never did this to you. He only played with you. Right?" Sarah started to cry and shake her head as best she could. Marci said, "Don't worry. Just enjoy it, bitch."

Marci moved me back until I was almost completely out then pushed me deep inside again. She repeated this several times until I got Marci's rhythm down. I looked down and saw Marci masturbating with her right hand. She was so sexy it was difficult for me to control myself. Marci's tail would occasionally squeeze with just enough pressure around the base of my penis. I continued to rock back and forth, and held onto the stirrups as hard as I could. Marci had full control over both of us. Sarah was starting to enjoy her forced sexual encounter and was now moaning. Marci looked at me and said, "I know you are going to come. Come in her hard, baby. I want us both to come together." Within seconds I lost it. I couldn't control myself any longer. All I heard was Marci saying, "That's right, baby. Fuck her good. Fill her up. Come on... do it." Marci lost it as well. Sarah was moaning, yelling out incoherent words while crying.

Marci took me out of Sarah slowly. Sarah said, "No. No. Please don't take him out."

Marci laughed at her and said, "Are you still horny? You want more pleasure?"

Sarah nodded yes, and Marci began to laugh. She moved around to the back of the bed and moved it slightly. She adjusted the head of the hospital bed down to where Sarah's head was lower than her shoulders. Marci turned around and exposed her vagina to Sarah. She took a fist full of Sarah's hair and pushed her head down hard onto the mattress then lowered her ass to just inches from Sarah's face and told her to lick her. Sarah didn't at first, but after some additional harsh demands and a hard slap to Sarah's face, Sarah's tongue made its way to my Marci's vagina. Sarah was repulsed at first but as the moments rushed by, she started to like the feel and taste of my love. After several minutes, Marci was finished. She lifted the head of the bed into a straight position and left Sarah in the bed.

Sarah screamed and begged for us not to leave her, but we went upstairs after we dressed ourselves. Wolfgang then went into the cell and started to unpack his equipment. He wanted to test everything so if any mistakes were to happen we would have it on file. Wolfgang said, "Now we wait and see if you will be with child."

The stark reality of the words now hit home, and Sarah began to weep violently. In her mind, she was going to have the devil's children and she had totally turned from her god, but what made her more upset was that she had actually enjoyed being violated.

The next morning, Eva sensed what we had done. When she came down to the breakfast table she looked over at Marci and smiled. Eva looked at me and started laughing. She said, "You evil little bastards."

Marci laughed with her, but Wolfgang and Zelda were not amused. Wolfgang shouted, "Silence! Enough laughter. This is not a laughing matter. It is a matter of science. Your brother wants children. This is the only way to see if someone like Marci could have children with someone like Garrison."

Eva nodded and said, "I understand, Dad." Wolfgang looked at me and I knew what he wanted me to say to her. Eva, of course, quickly picked up the unspoken conversation between me and our father. Eva said with a smirk and using her hands as air quotes, "Oh great, are we going to have... the talk? You guys know that I know all about sex, right? I mean, god damn it, guys, you can't be that fucking stupid."

I said to Eva, "We know. We just want you to be careful. I cannot tell you not to have sex, but just be careful. You can get someone in lots of trouble, plus it will ruin your singing career."

Eva said, "I know that."

Wolfgang interrupted by saying, "Do you? Do you know the consequences of you having sex at your age or at any age for that matter? Don't have sex. No sex. Zero. Understood?" Eva looked at our father and smiled. Wolfgang was very irritated and said, "You know I can take this Juilliard away from you in a second. Show me some respect."

Eva's heart dropped and she said, "Yes, sir. I will not have sex at Juilliard or anytime soon. Okay! I understand what is ahead of me." Eva was good at masking her feelings. She had so much control over her emotions and hiding them from others. Even as acutely aware as my father was, she could even fool him at times. Before Eva, I knew of not one man or woman that could hide their thoughts or feelings from my father. He was an expert at reading people and, of course, the formula made it so easy for his senses to detect the slightest mistruths.

Eva's body was growing fast, just like mine did at her age. She had the benefit that I didn't have with someone helping her through the emotions, and physical and mental pains from growing so fast. The formula controls every cell in your body and improves your body's strengths; accentuating and enhancing your natural gifts and desires. Eva's desires were attention; she craved it. She needed to be dominant and always in control. She was about receiving pleasure from any or all of her senses. She was just like Marci in that her sexual desires were strong. Combining that with their personality made these women a handful when it came to sexual desires.

Eva's mind developed even faster than mine at her age because we had trained her mind. Wolfgang and I forced Eva to learn, read and memorize as much subject matter as possible. I was never forced to learn like we pushed Eva. My adoptive parents treated me like a normal kid. They wanted to think I was normal, at least in some areas. It made them feel better about me and what they 'brought' into their lives. I didn't want Eva to struggle with who she was as a person. I wanted her to develop faster and better than I ever did growing up. I wanted her to always feel comfortable with herself, and to be fully and completely aware of what she was and what she was capable of being.

Eva's body was more advanced than any young human girl. When she was almost a decade old, her body was like an eighteen or twenty-year-old woman. She was almost completely developed physically.

Wolfgang believed that Eva might grow a few inches taller, thus her body would be most impressive for a woman, but for now, she was very advanced for her age. She was already five feet ten inches tall and her breasts were well developed. Her calves, thighs and buttocks were perfect in every way imaginable. Her long, golden blonde hair fell to the small of her back and was in perfect curl every second of the day. Not one blemish was on her skin and her eyes were so blue they almost glowed in the dark. Her lips and nose were of perfect size and were placed flawlessly on her face. Her mind was more advanced than anyone, her memory was unworldly, and her cognitive ability was unmatched. She had a highly dangerous confidence in her ability; she was cocky. She didn't run from her talents or hide them from anyone. She flaunted them for all to see.

All of Eva's combined traits made her a very dangerous woman for people to be around. Her personality dominated you. She knew how to control and manipulate people to get what she wanted.

Marci and I had a private conversation with Eva just before she went back to Juilliard to finish out her second semester. I said, "Eva, I understand you more than probably anyone in this household and especially in this world. I identify with you on all levels. I was once you, many years ago. So I know what you are feeling and thinking inside. But you have a strong sexual desire and I just want you to understand that it could get you into trouble. That is all I am saying."

Eva looked at me with a smirk and said, "Like you are preaching to me about sex?" Eva looked at Marci and smiled.

Marci smiled back and said, "I know, but please understand that we love you and we want you safe. We cannot protect you when you're so far away. We sense that you have done things already. We understand. That is your business, but just be careful. Okay?" Eva nodded. She understood and appreciated our candor.

The next day, Eva went back to Juilliard. I drove her to the airport but never brought up our conversation about sex again, and as I watched my sister walk toward her boarding flight, part of me envied her. I had loved my time at Harvard and I understood what she was feeling. The sense of freedom was exhilarating and intoxicating. Every new and exciting experience just heightened your senses and forced the formula to make every one of your senses on high alert. You would hear, smell, taste and see everything, and at times it could be overwhelming.

Chapter Five

*S*arah had made her peace with us and knew that she would never escape or be allowed to leave. Her main issue was her struggle with her so-called god. For the first time in her life, she had doubts about its existence because she was now allowed to think completely for herself. The formula changed her mind in many ways, and she was now void of having someone force-feed false information into her newly developed brain. She thought for hours on end, all during the day, about the concept of god. All she had was her mind. She thought how stupid she had been to believe that some entity from some world that no one had ever seen had so much control over so many lives.

As the days passed, Wolfgang called Marci and me to his lab. Marci and I immediately knew why. Wolfgang told us that Sarah was pregnant. Sarah sat on her bed looking down at the floor. She was scared because she knew what her job entailed. Wait, allow the babies to grow, and see if she survived the process. Marci was very excited. She looked at Sarah and for the first time, Marci started to care for her. Marci walked over to the cell and said, "This is so exciting. Don't worry. You will do fine." Sarah started to cry. Marci asked, "Why are you crying? Are you not happy?"

Sarah shouted, "Happy? What do I have to be happy about? I might die. Do you understand that? Then... then what is going to happen to my babies if I survive?"

Marci's smile and happiness were soon replaced with a frown and anger. I stepped up and put my arms around Marci and said, "Come on. Let's go upstairs." Sarah didn't have to hear Marci's thoughts, she sensed them. She knew that she had overstepped. She knew how much Marci wanted children with me. Now Sarah was carrying my children, not Marci. This made Marci jealous beyond all human comprehension. This was very difficult for my Marci to accept, but it was the only way to see if my love would survive a pregnancy in the future.

Marci quietly went upstairs and I came back to the cell. I told Sarah in a harsh voice, "Sarah, look. You need to act excited about this pregnancy. I do not want Marci feeling that you do not appreciate what we are doing here."

Sarah said, "What? How dare you preach to me about that monster! You had sex with me. I am carrying your children. Our children. I might die! You... you people are telling me that I might die before I give birth or they might fight their way out of me. Don't you understand what you did to me? Can you understand that? You people took my life away from me. I did nothing to you. Not once in my life have I sinned so great to cause this fate upon me! And now you want me to act happy for that monster you bed. You are just as sick as that freak wolf standing over there and your alien lover."

I quickly said, "Enough! Shut up! These freaks that you speak of are my father and my life companion. I will help you in every way possible, but never speak of them like that again. Do you understand?"

Sarah quickly looked down. She sensed the evil in my thoughts from the tone of my voice. She didn't want to suffer any more so she quickly said, "Yes, I understand."

As the weeks went by, Wolfgang and I took countless notes and videotaped Sarah every second of the day. We measured and weighed her multiple times throughout the day. We didn't know how fast the fetuses would grow. We assumed there would be more than one fetus, but again, this was all new territory for us. The formula always seemed to surprise us.

Marci and I kept Eva abreast of everything going on at home. We told her about Sarah's pregnancy, and Eva was beyond curious about whether Sarah would survive and what the babies would look like.

Over the next couple of weeks, Sarah had bouts of sickness and pain but as soon as the pain would hit her, it immediately passed as the formula corrected the pain sensors in her brain. With the numerous blood samples we took, not one of them were the same. Sarah's whole body was a working, functioning miracle. Her senses were very sensitive and she didn't have to increase her adrenalin levels much to have her senses heightened.

Wolfgang had Sarah tied up with chains around her ankles and wrists. He feared that she might hurt herself or worse, commit suicide. This didn't sit well with Sarah and scared her more than anything. On many occasions I attempted to calm her nerves. Marci was kind enough to leave her alone during this time. She, most of all, wanted this pregnancy to be a success.

Wolfgang taught himself how to work an ultrasound machine and found that Sarah was carrying four fetuses which grew at a fast pace. When a month had passed, Sarah's stomach had gotten larger. She felt tightness around her stomach and complained about the fetuses moving inside. After two months, the babies were as large as a normal human child. Sarah had some trouble walking because her stomach was so large. Her body changed during this process. She gained weight in all areas of her body and was in a constant state of hunger. For her meals, we fed her vegetables and freshly caught, raw meat.

The fetuses didn't show any signs of wanting to tear their way out of Sarah's uterus. This was a major success. Sarah did experience extreme discomfort, but the formula seemed to help her through some of her painful moments. When a shooting pain would develop, the formula seemed to attack that area and help relieve or at times remove the pain.

Wolfgang prepared the cell for the newborns. He set up the hospital bed with straps and bought a large stand for the newborns to lie in while under a heating lamp. He made sure we had plenty of washcloths and towels. He had also purchased other items that we needed for the delivery.

At exactly ninety days, Sarah's water broke. She was scared but excited at the same time. Wolfgang and I had convinced her that she was going to be fine and that she would have a normal delivery. Truth be told, we didn't know if that would be the case. Wolfgang recorded this entire event from many angles and made many notes on what was happening and what she was experiencing. He asked her many questions and Sarah tried her best to answer every question as precisely as she could.

We placed Sarah on the hospital bed. I held her large hand and tried to comfort her as best I could. Wolfgang sat on a stool at the foot of the bed. The fetuses in Sarah's belly were very active, moving around like dogs in a small kennel. After an hour, Sarah started the birthing process. It was painful for her and she was dripping wet with sweat. An incredible amount of liquid came gushing out of her vagina. Suddenly, Sarah took quick, short breaths then bore down and out popped the head of the first fetus. Wolfgang allowed the fetus to pull itself out of Sarah. The fetus moved its shoulders from side to side, trying to free its arms. One at a time, each arm made its way out of her as it took both of its hands and pushed itself out of the cavity. Wolfgang made sure it wouldn't fall onto the floor. He severed the umbilical cord and quickly moved the newborn to the stand with the heating lamp.

For the time being, I left Sarah and walked over to the stand to make sure the fetus would not crawl off the table. I sensed my Marci was watching everything. She stood ever so quietly outside of the cell, moving as slowly and quietly as she could. She had large, thick tears running down the sides of her adorable face. Her tears were dark brown in color which made them very apparent on her stark white skin.

I looked down at the newborn and saw a creature like I had never seen before. The newborn was a male and approximately thirty inches in length. Its eyes were almond shaped and pointed at a forty-five-degree angle on its face. The pointed corners of the eye didn't point to the nose like a human's eye does, they were pointed up to the middle of its forehead. The eyes were completely black, but the pupil was noticeable in direct light. Its forehead was rather normal in size and view. No eyelashes, eyebrows or hair were on any part of its body except for its head. The newborn's hair was jet black and straight. The hands and fingers were extremely long and thin. The arms and legs seemed to be slightly longer than a human baby, but the length of the torso was much longer. The skin color was a light shade of gray. The newborn already had large but squared off teeth in almost perfect squares, and there were rather large spaces between each tooth.

I lost my concentration when Wolfgang told me, "Here is the next one." He'd had to cut the umbilical cord on the second fetus, so we knew that each of the fetuses had a separate cord and didn't share a large cord with many offshoots. I walked over to my father and picked up another newborn. This newborn had the same features and length as the first one. I laid this one next to its brother. I looked over at Marci and caught her eye. She smiled at me and I whispered, "I love you" and said, "Everything is a success, my love." Marci cried hard. She was happy. I also felt her jealousy as well. She had watched me hold two of my sons from another woman. I said to my love, "Would you like to hold one of them?"

At that time, Sarah yelled said, "Don't touch my babies. Please don't hurt my babies."

Marci growled at Sarah and said, "Fuck you! They are not—"

Wolfgang quickly interrupted and said, "Marci! Shut up! Leave us! Now!" Marci was angry. She turned and stomped away, staring at Sarah as the third child made its way out. As Marci walked away, she heard

Wolfgang say, "This one is a girl." Marci threw back her head and cried out loud. She ran upstairs and Zelda met her at the top of the final step.

Zelda asked, "What's wrong, my dear?"

Marci tried to control herself and said, "It's a success. We can have children."

Zelda said, "So, that's a good thing, right? Why are you crying? You should be happy."

Marci said, "I am but... but... Garrison's first child was with another woman. I wanted to be the only women that he had a child with...you know? But I know what was done had to be done. It's just hard to watch your man holding his child from another woman."

Zelda said, "What else is bothering you, girl?"

Marci started to cry more. After she composed herself she said, "They are hideous looking. I cannot have children that look like that. They will never have a normal life."

Zelda reached out and in a rare show of affection, gave Marci a strong hug and patted her on the back. Zelda added to Marci's comfort by saying, "Don't worry, Wolfgang will not allow them to live for long. He will kill them when he is through experimenting on them. But Marci, you must understand that all of this was done for you. I know... he also did this in the name of science, but he does care for you." Marci shook her head in acknowledgment and made her way up to her room.

Wolfgang watched the fourth newborn escape Sarah's vagina and it was a girl as well. Two boys and two girls. All were under the heat lamp. Wolfgang cleaned up Sarah and I cleaned the newborns while Sarah was gasping for air. It was a painful delivery. The newborns pulled themselves out of her, which caused a strain on many of the muscles in and around her vagina. The inside of her uterus was damaged as well. The newborn's fingernails and toenails had scraped Sarah's insides.

Later that night, I went up to check on Marci. She was still crying. I comforted her the best way I knew. She knew that we had to continue with the experiment for her sake, and I understood this was difficult for her. The main issue she had was that she knew what our kids would look like. This bothered her in many regards. We talked about this all night long. I had to admit that I was somewhat bothered by the idea of our children being so different looking from humans. Did we want to bring this new species into the world? Marci's excitement went from the highest level of anticipation to total disappointment.

Marci said, "Oh, Garrison. I am so sorry, but I think I want to wait on having children."

I said, "I think that is a good idea. We need to monitor these children to see how they will develop over time."

Marci said emphatically to me, "I don't want them around the house for long. I want them dead."

I said, "I understand."

Marci said, "No, you don't understand. You couldn't possibly understand what I mean. I can't stand the fact that you had children with another woman. I don't want them living in the same house as us."

I understood her state of mind and shared the same feelings.

The newborns cried a few times during their first night of existence, but their crying was nothing like a human baby. During this time, Sarah got much needed rest as her body quickly recovered from the births. Wolfgang and I sensed an incredible bond between Sarah and her children. He monitored the four newborns closely and gave us daily reports on the newborns and Sarah. He even allowed Sarah to bond and nurture them. During the first week, the newborns grew quickly, so much so that they started to crawl around the floor. Sarah respectfully asked Wolfgang if she could name them. Wolfgang didn't care. In fact, he was in favor of it. He wanted to make sure the newborns had as much of a normal young life as possible. He believed it would help get better results in the experiment. Sarah named her girls Lucinda and Emma, and named her boys Eli and Simon.

When Marci heard about Sarah naming the newborns, she about lost control. Marci was still extremely jealous of Sarah's sexual experience with me, and having children with me didn't help the situation. When Sarah named the children, it pushed her over the edge. I tried to calm her, but it was of no use. Marci's emotions were driven by obsession and sex. Naming the children almost humanized the experiment for Marci. This was too much for her to bear.

I purposely stayed away from the newborns and Sarah. I didn't want to further upset Marci. She very much appreciated me not visiting them and that helped her remain somewhat controllable. Marci and I worked on our relationship, which was solid, but her jealously had to be addressed.

Wolfgang bought a bracelet for each, engraving their names in each one, and placed them around each of their wrists. Each bracelet monitored their heart rate, brainwaves, temperature, number of steps taken, and stress levels.

One day Eli made his way to the bars and pulled himself onto his feet. Amazingly, he walked down the front of the cell with the aid of the bars. The same day, the others followed his lead. During this time, the newborns were eating table food. By the third week, they learned how to run in the cell. They grunted if they wanted something and at times they seemed to speak to each other by way of their grunting sounds. By the fourth week, Eli started to form a word. Mom was the first word spoken. Sarah was delighted and encouraged the others to follow Eli's lead. Within a day, the others started to say the word Mom.

Wolfgang thought it was interesting that Eli was the first to walk, speak and eat table food. Wolfgang wanted to perform an experiment to find why this was the case. He took Emma out of the cell and out of sight of her brothers and sister. As Wolfgang was carrying Emma, Sarah shouted, "Where are you taking her? Please don't hurt my baby." She was very concerned.

Wolfgang taught Emma a few words then put her back into the cell with her sister and brothers. Within minutes, the others also spoke the new words she had been taught.

After numerous exams and mental tests, Wolfgang concluded that all the newborns' intellect was in line with their siblings. Eli seemed to be more intellectual, followed by Emma, Lucinda then Simon, but all would be classified as geniuses compared to humans. Obviously, the newborns, being a new species, were more advanced than any human ever at their age.

Over the next couple of months, the newborns' growth was nothing short of amazing. Wolfgang and I were amazed at their growth compared to Eva's and mine. The formula was so difficult to predict. It attacked certain DNA and cell structures that, without testing, any prediction was basically total guesswork. These newborns had more traits of the post transformation of Sarah than any of my traits. The lack of the wolf features, square teeth and no full body hair seemed to be the only traits of mine that they possessed.

Each newborn grew physically and mentally at the same rate, with their arms and legs growing faster than the rest of their bodies. Their torsos were thick and round while their arms and legs were rather thin and long. Their feet were wide and long, while their heads grew in a circular shape. Their necks were very short and their shoulders were narrow. The hair on the females grew faster and longer than on the boys.

Eli was the physical and intellectual leader of the group. The others seemed to be more followers and were completely satisfied with following Eli. Their personalities were different, but they acted very militaristic as a group. They were serious and curious in nature. They would smell all scents around them, like a dog or a deer.

As the weeks progressed, Eli learned how to speak a few more words. Wolfgang and I taught them how to speak, with the aid of Sarah. Sarah took on the role of a mother, which came naturally to her. She loved her children and was as protective of them as she could be. She knew down deep in her soul that she and her children would eventually be killed. She felt that her only hope was to keep us as calm as she could and hopefully she could keep herself and her children alive as long as possible.

Wolfgang continued his experiments. He would take a small ball and throw it toward the children. They would run from it and watch it bounce around until it stopped moving. They would then slowly walk up to the ball, smell it then touch it. Eli was the first to throw it to mimic Wolfgang's actions. Wolfgang tossed the ball again, but Eli stepped out of the way and another newborn would repeat the entire process with the same result. This process would continue until everyone had their turn at throwing the ball. Each one would stand there, and they would study how the ball moved, what it bounced off of, how many times it bounced, etc. They fed off each other's action. Wolfgang would take one of the newborns, isolate the chosen one from the others, and teach that offspring a different act with the ball. When Wolfgang returned them to the cell with the others, that offspring would immediately go to the others and teach them what they had learned.

Marci stayed clear of Wolfgang's lab and wouldn't have anything to do with the newborns. She didn't even want to hear about them over the dinner table. All she wanted to know about was their health. At this stage of the experiment, Wolfgang and I were highly confident that if Marci and I were to have children, they would be similar in size and structure as Sarah's.

The most important piece that came out of his experiment was Sarah's well-being after giving birth. At this point, Marci wanted to kill the newborns, but we talked her into giving us time to conduct more experiments on the children, although Marci thought the experiment was taking too long.

Sarah's offspring were ruining Marci's future pregnancy. Since Marci knew she wasn't going to die from giving birth, she found no reason for the additional experiments. If Marci decided to have children, she wanted to experience these first moments herself. She wanted that part to be sacred, for only us to experience.

She knew that Wolfgang's wishes were the law in the house. Marci knew her place, but her resentment toward Wolfgang was increasing and he knew it. This issue never came to a blow up; all she wanted was for the experiment to end.

Chapter Six

$\mathcal{E}$ va's life at Juilliard was flourishing. Everyone knew of Eva Seawick's brilliance. All the students wanted to meet her and either listen to her sing or play the violin. Her personality grew even larger than before she had first stepped foot on campus. Her professors tried to teach her some humility, but she never paid any attention to their guidance. Eva was at the happiest point in her young life.

She loved her busy daily schedule, between the long days of school and her singing and violin practices. She would routinely be a part of small groups of young artists that would display their talents for any interested campus onlookers at the weekly performances. Many of the music instructors would be in attendance, of which some were jealous of the young Eva while most were in awe of her multitude of talents. Everyone on campus knew the talent that she possessed for such a young lady, with the physical makeup of a twenty-something-year-old adult and the mentality of a clairvoyant, older genius.

Many young men at Juilliard would secretly talk sexually about young Eva. Her long, curly blonde hair flowed down her strong back while her large breasts would bounce in rhythm with every step she took. She looked down on everyone. In her eyes, no one was her equal. She was full of confidence and spoke the truth, which added to her cockiness. Many of her fellow students and professors envied her and begrudged her arrogance.

Wolfgang and I kept Eva apprised of all the developments at home, especially our latest experiment. We made sure no one else was around to see the newborns, but I would occasionally send her live videos of the children.

Eva was concerned that maybe one day her children would look like Sarah's. Wolfgang and I told her that would not be the case, but if the truth were told, we didn't have any basis on what my children with Eva would look like. Everything at that point was just an educated guess.

Marci told Eva all non-Sarah information. Marci was more concerned about any love interests that Eva might have had. Marci was very close to Eva and she missed her not being around the house. Eva understood Marci like few could. She understood her desires, her passions and her thinking.

Since Eva was busy at Juilliard from morning until night and only slept for a couple of hours a day, there were many times she found herself either reading a book or walking around campus while others slept. Eva was rarely alone, but from time to time when she found herself alone, her mind wondered about humanity, especially about boys and sex.

January was always a cold month in New York City. Eva had never experienced this kind of cold although she never wore a winter coat unless it was for show. She did wear a small sweater so people wouldn't talk, but of course they still did. Everyone thought it was amazing that Eva was the only one not wearing a winter coat and that she never complained about the weather. Eva quickly began to understand why Wolfgang and I were telling her to act as normal as possible, so she wouldn't draw attention to herself. But Eva loved and sought out the attention that was given to her.

Eva knew everyone on campus, especially the boys, and it didn't matter what age they were. She had a dominant personality that was difficult for the opposite sex to resist. She was not a bitch but demanding. Her beauty controlled them. Her young body mystified them. She was forbidden fruit. The boys couldn't taste, but they could look. She was the crown jewel of Juilliard and no male wanted to put themselves in a situation that could ruin their Juilliard experience and potential professional careers. Eva enjoyed the attention from the boys and she always played her sexuality to her advantage.

Eva's sex drive was peaking. She had been very sexual all her life, and had experimented with both boys and girls growing up, but she had never enjoyed intercourse. She pleasured herself and had allowed others to explore her body in her younger years. Even at her young age, her body and mind were far more advanced than her age. This was a common theme throughout Eva's young life. With all the attention she was receiving from the opposite sex, she was becoming more interested in exploring her vast array of options. As the days progressed, her sexual frustration increased by the hour. Eva wanted a guy, but she had to be careful who she picked.

Steve Callahan was a twenty-two-year-old bassoon and English major. He stood six-foot three and weighed about one hundred and seventy pounds. Steve had blond hair, deep blue eyes and large features. His hands, feet, arms, legs and torso were all long and thin. He was exceptionally brilliant but was painfully shy and quiet. He was a strict Christian and Eva could sense that he was still a virgin. Eva took a few classes with Steve in her first semester and the current semester they were together in two classes; violin theory and composition.

Most of her classmates were in awe of her being in the class. Her reputation more than preceded itself. Everyone knew of her and most wanted to befriend her, more out of curiosity than anything else. Every person was engaging with Eva except the person that she was most interested in meeting.

Whenever Eva had the chance, she would purposely sit next to Steve. She would flirt and ask him many questions to break his stubborn silence. Steve would smile and give short answers during his conversations with the young diva. Eva was careful not to draw too much attention to her interest in Steve, but dropped just enough clues to notify him of her interest. Steve thought it was cute, but he was very uncomfortable with the attention she was showing him. He found her very interesting and admired her mind and musical ability, and her obvious physical traits were hard not to notice.

Eva told Miriam about her sexual interest in Steve. Eva said, "Miriam, do you think Steve is hot? I mean, do you ever think about fucking him?"

At first Miriam thought it was cute but the more Eva talked about Steve, the more Miriam got concerned. Miriam said, "Eva! Steve will never go for it. He has too high of morals and he could get in big trouble if someone ever caught you two together. I mean, he is like an adult, a senior, Eva. You are sick, you know that?"

Eva said, "You are going to help me."

Miriam said, "No. No I will not."

Eva smiled and said, "Remember our little bet? It's time to pay up, little merry Miriam."

Miriam frowned at her and said, "Are you serious? This is some serious shit you are asking of me."

Eva smiled and said, "Whatever. Just do what I say. Okay?"

Miriam shook her head in disgust and said, "Whatever!"

Miriam knew Steve by way of some of her friends. He was a solid guy that wouldn't screw a first year student. Eva was frustrated with Miriam's beliefs. Eva knew that she could trick him and at some point, he couldn't refuse her. Miriam didn't want to be a part of any plot that could have Steve's reputation and career ruined if they were to get caught or if word got out about any sexual encounter.

As the days progressed, Eva didn't let up with the idea of having a sexual encounter with Steve. Eva wanted her first time to be special and, in her mind, Steve was that special man. Eva devised a plan for Miriam to ask Steve out. They would go out on a date and she wanted Miriam to play up to him and bring him back to the dorm room. Eva would be there waiting and would take it from there.

Miriam had no interest in men. She was a closet lesbian and only Eva knew her secret, but Miriam knew that if she didn't go along with the plan, Eva would probably out her. Even though Eva never said that she would, she couldn't take that chance. Miriam's father had major political aspirations, and many thought that someday he might make a run for the Presidency.

The next day, Miriam waited for Steve. Steve was walking down the hallway on his way to one of his classes when Miriam stepped out and started talking to him. Miriam said, "Hey, Steve. Which class are you headed to?"

Steve said, "Oh, I have English Literature."

Miriam laughed and said, "Interesting stuff, huh?" Steve lowered his head and snickered. Miriam looked around nervously and said, "Hey, if you're not doing anything this weekend, would you like to... you know... go out Saturday?"

Steve's face turned many shades of red. He looked away and said, "Yeah, I would like that."

Miriam said, "Good, is seven okay? In the lobby of my dorm?"

Steve said, "Yeah, that's fine. See you then."

As Steve walked away, Miriam sent Eva a text saying, "It's on for Saturday."

When Saturday came, Miriam got herself ready for her date with Steve. Miriam knew she had to play this date out or Eva might expose her secret and her family's reputation would be at stake. Steve met Miriam at their agreed upon spot and took her to the local movie theater then they went out to eat at a small family-owned pizza place near campus. They enjoyed their meal and had a great time together.

Eva impatiently waited in her room and cleaned up the best she could. Eva knew she had to be careful, and she couldn't allow herself to get pregnant. She couldn't take the pill because the formula would reverse the intended purpose of its use. She decided to trust her senses to determine when or if he would ejaculate. Eva read up on the sexual experience and had everything preplanned in her mind.

Toward the end of Miriam's date, she started to play up to Steve. She would touch his hand and arm, walk close to him, and walked arm in arm as often as she could. She knew that getting him to the room was going to be a challenge. Miriam tried her best to make over him and make sure he knew she found him interesting. Steve was a very shy young man and her actions were making him very nervous yet excited.

When they reached the dormitory entrance, Miriam invited him to come upstairs with her. He was nervous, but his excitement and curiosity got the best of him, therefore, he agreed that he would come up for a few minutes. While this was playing out, Eva made sure she was not in the room. Eva visited her friend Wanda a few doors down the hall.

Steve and Miriam entered the room, and Steve took off his coat and laid it on the bed. Miriam was as nervous as she had ever been. She'd had sexual relations with a man before but only a few times, and she hadn't enjoyed any of those experiences. Miriam tried to be as sexy as she could toward a person that she found repulsive simply because he was not a woman. She pushed Steve's coat off the bed and onto the floor then took his hands and looked at him. She moved to the bed and slowly sat down on the edge. She looked up at him while biting her lower lip. She glanced at his crotch then looked back up at him. Steve was nervous, and his first impulse was to look away while backing up slightly. Miriam held onto his wrists hard and pulled him toward her. She ran her hands up his forearms. Steve said, "I… I don't know about this."

Miriam smiled and said, "Shut up. Come on, just relax."

Miriam's hands made their way to his belt buckle. She nervously unbuckled his belt and awkwardly unzipped his pants. She quickly pulled his pants down to his knees. Steve said, "We shouldn't be doing this." Miriam swallowed hard, looked up at him and placed her hand on his penis. She gently squeezed and massaged his penis through his underwear. Miriam was totally grossed out, but she tried acting as if she was enjoying it. Miriam then pulled Steve's briefs down, exposing his penis to her. He was now totally into it.

Steve quickly got free from his pants and briefs then nervously took off his shirt. Meanwhile, Miriam stood up and removed her pants then her shirt. Steve moved in and placed his hands on her hips. Miriam looked down at his chest as, in one quick movement, she unlatched her bra and exposed her breasts. Steve immediately went for them, grabbing them in his hands. Miriam took some deep breaths, trying to fake enjoyment of his sweaty, nervous touch.

Miriam looked down, grabbed his cock, and pulled him toward her as she sat down on the bed. She maneuvered him so he was sitting next to her. Miriam took off her panties, held them in her hand then gently pushed Steve onto his back. Miriam swung her leg over his stomach, smiling and rubbing her panties along the sides of his face. Steve was very turned on. Miriam was trying not to enjoy her forced duties, but she was getting slightly aroused. Miriam was worried. She was thinking, *Where is Eva?*

Steve lustfully looked at Miriam and said, "I want you."

Miriam smiled and looked around the room as if Eva was about to appear suddenly. Miriam said, "I know you do, but I'd like to tease you a little more."

Steve said, "Oh no... please don't. I really want you right now."

Suddenly, the door opened and Eva walked into the room. Steve and Miriam's heads quickly turned to Eva. Miriam gave Eva a dirty look as if to say, *Where have you been?* Steve was trying to cover his hard-on by pulling his legs up. Miriam sat down on Steve's stomach and pushed down on his chest with all her might, trying to keep him down on the bed. Steve was shocked and said, "Miriam, let go of me. Eva is here. What are you doing?"

Miriam told him to shut up and Steve was mortified. So many thoughts were going through his head. As per Eva's prior instructions, Miriam clumsily reached behind her and grabbed his balls. She squeezed them hard and said, "Stop moving and do what we say."

Steve attempted to get up, but Miriam had other plans. She squeezed harder. Steve's voice rose as he said, "Get off me. What are you doing? That hurts."

Eva slowly walked over to the two and said to Steve, "Do you find me attractive, Steve? I find you rather hot. Very hot."

"What?"

Eva repeated, "Do you find me attractive?" and slowly removed her sweatshirt, exposing her large breasts that had been trapped in her very tight-fitting sweatshirt. She slowly and seductively snaked her sweatpants off her strong, muscular thighs. Miriam glanced over many times to ogle Eva's perfectly formed young body. Steve tried once again to get up, but Miriam applied so much pressure on his balls that he moaned in great discomfort.

Eva said, "Oh, don't hurt him, Miriam. I want that. I want to fuck him."

Steve said, "No. No. Absolutely not. You're a freshman and so young."

Eva looked at Steve and slowly ran her hands up to her breasts and held them. There stood one of the most beautiful bodies Steve had ever seen. The lust in Miriam's eyes was at an all-time high, and Steve couldn't take his eyes off Eva's breasts. Eva said, "Does this look like a young girl to you? I am very mature, and I find you very hot. I want to fuck you, Steve. I am going to screw you until you pop."

Eva removed her panties as Miriam's eyes were locked on Eva's body. Steve laid there watching every sultry move Eva's body was making. He allowed himself to look even though he knew it was wrong, so wrong that in his mind he shouldn't desire such a young, forbidden body. Steve's sexual desires were now at an unprecedented high. Her body looked like something out of a porn movie. Part of him attempted to rationalize what he was feeling, but his cock was now controlling his mind. He needed and wanted her badly. Thoughts of Sunday School, and lectures from preachers and parents were all being pushed away by his natural desires.

Eva moved slowly and confidently toward Miriam and Steve. Eva brushed her hair back off her shoulders and breasts as she reached down and replaced Miriam's hand on Steve's penis. Miriam moved off Steve and stood next to the bed. Eva said, "I wanted a bigger penis, but I guess this will have to do." Eva's other hand reached down and took hold of his balls. She squeezed them hard enough for Steve to moan. Eva took the head of Steve's manhood and rubbed it up and down her vagina. This felt so good to Eva, and after multiple strokes, she slid Steve inside of her.

Steve moaned hard. He knew this wasn't right but that only added to his enjoyment. He had never felt this much pleasure in his life. Eva was enjoying her ecstasy as much as Steve. He couldn't take his eyes off Eva's perfect breasts. He reached up to grab them, but Eva stopped him. She pinned his wrists down on the bed next to his head then moved her body which caused Steve to moan more. Eva pushed herself back up. Steve again went for her breasts. Eva blocked his hands again and before he knew it, Eva slapped his face hard. Steve's head jerked sideways and his cheek turned red.

Eva moved around on Steve's cock, pushing it deeper inside of her. She slapped his face again and quickly cupped his throat with a strong hand. Eva started pumping hard. She yelled at him, "Come on, fucker! Fuck me harder, you bastard. Give it to me. Harder!" Steve pumped his hips harder and faster. Eva continued to slap his face and kept saying, "Come on! Harder! Faster!"

Eva quickly looked over and saw Miriam playing with herself. Eva smiled at her, making Miriam very uncomfortable. Miriam looked away. She felt like she should move away from the bed, get her clothes on and leave the room, but she couldn't. She didn't want to.

Eva sensed that Steve was about to release his sperm. She pulled him out of her at his dismay. Eva sat on the base of his penis and slid her vagina up and down his shaft. Within seconds Steve lost control as he struggled to catch his breath. Thick loads of sperm were all over his stomach. Eva continued to slide across his penis and as she made her way to the tip of his manhood, she allowed him to enter her again. This time Eva braced herself on Steve's body. She pumped hard and fast. The most familiar, divine feeling developed in the pit of her stomach. Her thighs and vagina tensed up and started to spasm until she could hold out no longer. Eva came long and hard as she experienced her first orgasm with a boy.

When Eva was finished, she fell next to Steve who was almost in tears. He felt so guilty for his actions, yet he had just fucked the most popular freshman at Juilliard and, for that matter, in New York City. He laid there in guilt mixed with pleasure, thinking that he had just lost his virginity to her. He was afraid the news would get out and his family would find out. Would he be expelled from school? His mind wondered further, *What if this got out to the public? What if the news outlets ran with this story?* That is what he feared the most. Part of him was excited, but his mind was telling him that he had sinned and would be punished.

Meanwhile, Eva felt good, but she was not completely satisfied. Eva looked over at Steve and said, "Stop crying you piece of shit. You're not finished yet." Eva pushed Steve to sit up. She opened her legs and with both hands, she grabbed the sides of the hair on his head. Eva said, "Lick me clean, you fucking pervert." Eva forced Steve's face into her vagina. She moved his face around her lips from all angles. Steve cried from being humiliated by this freshman as well as his guilt.

Eva looked up at Miriam who was still touching herself. Miriam looked at Eva's shameless eyes watching her. She was so humiliated, but she didn't stop playing with herself. Eva lustfully said, "Come over here." Miriam walked over to Eva and Steve. Steve's face was still buried between Eva's legs, making slurping and heavy breathing sounds. Eva said to Miriam, "Suck on my tits... come on... suck them. Lick them." Steve moaned. Eva said to Steve, "Shut up. Make me come again."

Miriam sat down on the edge of the bed. She slowly reached out and held one of Eva's perfectly formed and hard breasts. Eva looked at her and said, "Suck it." Miriam started to cry as she moved forward and placed her lips around Eva's nipple. Miriam licked and sucked as her tears fell freely and often down her cheeks.

Eva looked down at Steve and said, "Eat it. Don't stop. Come on... make me come again." Steve licked, sucked, and moved his tongue around all her forbidden places. Eva continued to degrade him. She said, "You are pathetic. Look at you. Sucking off a beautiful girl like me. You probably don't even like it. I bet you wish you were sucking cock right now." Steve tried even harder and after several minutes, Eva lost control on Steve's face. Eva pushed him away from her with her feet saying, "You're such a faggot. You are terrible at sucking pussy. Get out of here before I call the police."

Steve clumsily fell out of bed. Eva laughed hard as Miriam continued to suck on Eva's breasts. Eva looked at Steve as he tried to get dressed as fast as he could. Eva said, "Look at her. She sucks so well. You could learn a thing or two from her. Maybe she can teach you to suck cocks tomorrow."

Steve was so ashamed, scared and nervous all at the same time. He heard every beat of his heart. Eva heard his heartbeat as well. Her eyes never left Steve's face.

Steve stammered, "Please. Please don't tell anyone about this. I didn't mean for this to happen."

Eva shouted, "Shut the fuck up and get out of here before I tell everyone you would rather suck cocks." Steve fumbled his way to the door and after several attempts to unlock it, he finally made his way out of the room. Eva had put another thought in his head now. He certainly didn't want people to think he was gay. He knew he wasn't, but if word got out that he was, his family would disown him for his grave sin against his religion.

Miriam didn't miss a beat with the attention she was giving Eva's breasts. Eva told Miriam, "Get on top of me and play with yourself." Miriam did as she was instructed. She straddled Eva's torso as she played with both of her breasts. Eva said, "Come on, I want to see you have an orgasm for me." Miriam looked up and started to cry. She moved her hand down and started to play with herself. Eva said, "That's right. You like that don't you? You love my body." Eva played with her breasts, licking her nipples and rubbing them over and over.

Eva said, "You want women don't you, Miriam? You're a lesbian, aren't you? That's okay. Your secret is safe with me. You don't tell anyone about my little fag boy, Steve, and I won't tell about your dirty little secret." Eva pulled herself up on her elbows, her breasts swaying with every movement. This added to the intense solo sex show Miriam was demonstrating to Eva.

Miriam ran her vagina across Eva's tight, muscular stomach. Back and forth she moved, and the longer it lasted, the closer she was to exploding. After a minute, Miriam needed release. She arched her head back and bore down hard on Eva, experiencing an orgasm like she had never experienced before. Miriam's entire body spasmed for what seemed like half a minute. Tears of shame mixed with tears of extreme pleasure rolled down her face and onto Eva's tight, young body. Miriam's saliva was dripping from her mouth as she was attempting to recover.

Suddenly, Eva started to laugh as she realized Miriam's fantasy quickly turned to the reality of what she had just done. So many thoughts were going through her head at that moment. The reality of the situation was that she had just masturbated on a woman. Miriam quickly got off Eva and sat at the foot of the bed.

Eva sat up, mirroring Miriam's actions. Eva smiled and said, "Did you like that, Miriam? Did you like getting off on me?"

Miriam's emotional scale was now one of anger and somewhat betrayal. She shouted back angrily, "What? Fuck you! You're a fucking slut!"

Eva busted out laughing saying, "I think you are the fucking slut, you dirty, perverted senior. Did you like me watching you?"

Miriam shouted louder, "Shut up! We shouldn't have done this. We... we... shouldn't have done that to Steve. I... I should not have done that to you. You... you... are too young for this. I've never done anything like this in my life. What are you, some sort of... evil bitch? Why did you do this to us?"

Eva got up slowly and said, "I did nothing to you. You agreed to everything. You acted on your own natural free will. I didn't force you or Steve to do anything. Oh... I might have tempted you guys, but that's okay. Nobody got hurt. Everyone got their pleasure. Right? I know you did." Eva winked at Miriam and said, "I need to get a shower. Would you want to watch me take my shower?"

Eva smiled widely. Miriam was mortified. All she said was, "Whaaaa—"

Eva continued, "It's okay. It's okay to be a lesbian and into girls."

Miriam quickly said with her voice rising, "I... IIIIII am not a lesbian... okay! I... I like boys... guys...I don't like women in... that way."

Eva reached out and took Miriam by the hand. She gently guided her off the bed. Miriam cried harder and said, "I... I am not a lesbian. Okay?" Eva started to walk toward the shower while holding Miriam's hand. Miriam said, "I am a good person. I... I—"

Eva said, "Shhhhhh. It's okay, Miriam. It's okay if you like women. I like men. I also like women's bodies. It's okay. Sex is for pleasure." Eva stepped into the shower and turned the water on. Cold water hit her sexy body, but she didn't move or have any reaction to the cold sensation, which puzzled Miriam. Eva stood there until the water heated up then asked Miriam to join her. Miriam slowly and reluctantly accepted the offer. Eva said, "It is okay to want me or another woman."

Miriam broke down crying again. It was as if the shower was a baptism of some sort for her. Eva reached for the soap and ran the soap across her body. Miriam said, "Ever since I could remember... I always liked other girls. I was never interested in boys. I mean... I fucked a few guys, but I always felt dirty. I never really enjoyed their touch or the penetration. But... you see, my dad... my dad wants to be President of the United States someday. He cannot have a dyke for a daughter."

Eva smiled and handed the soap to Miriam. She nervously took it and placed it on the top part of Eva's chest. Eva said, "Don't worry.

Your secret is safe with me. I will never tell anyone about your desire or about what happened tonight." Eva knew Miriam would make a powerful friend someday so she wanted to hold a secret over her head.

Eva said, "What else is bothering you?" Miriam looked down at Eva's perfect, wet breasts and shrugged her shoulders. Eva looked down at Miriam's body and said, "Do you feel guilty about what we did?"

Miriam looked up at Eva and nodded her head. She said, "Not that I am a religious person, but I feel so dirty, yet so satisfied."

Eva laughed and said, "I will let you in on a little secret, Miriam. God is overrated. In fact, he doesn't exist. Religion is a make-believe fantasy created by crusty old white men centuries ago. Do you feel good right now?" Miriam smiled. Eva said, "See... that's my girlfriend."

Miriam slowly started to feel better. She felt a wave of relief that engulfed her essence. Eva asked, "Would you wash my back for me?" Eva slowly turned her back to Miriam. Without hesitation she ran the bar of soap from Eva's chest to her strong and well developed back. She watched as the lines of soap traveled down her back. Some of the soap lines found their way down the crack of her ass, while others rolled across the muscular cheeks of her ass. Her mind raced, her ears rang, and her vagina dripped with her juices. The only thing on her mind was she so desperately wanted her tongue to replace those lines of soap. Eva spoke, "Why don't you rinse me off and lick my asshole." Miriam's head was about to explode. Her ears rang louder than before, all the while she wondered how lucky she was to have her first lesbian encounter with one of the most beautiful and desirable young girls in America. Miriam thought, *How did she know that's what I wanted?* As soon as the thought was completed, Miriam was in a place where she didn't care. She quickly bent her knees, making her face parallel to the most perfect ass she could ever imagine. Without hesitation, her tongue immediately found Eva's asshole and she licked it rapidly.

When Miriam brought Eva to another orgasm, she washed her again. After their shower, they retired for the night. Miriam went to sleep as Eva started to read a new book for the night.

The next morning, Miriam could barely look at Eva. Eva never brought up the event from last night and acted like nothing had happened. This bothered Miriam because she'd had a wonderful sexual experience with Eva. It seemed to Miriam that Eva treated the experience as a dinner date or a sleepover. It meant nothing to her. This was difficult for her to accept. She was also falling for Eva. This, among all the other odd twists to this relationship, was hard for Miriam to comprehend. Moreover, she still felt guilty about what had transpired that unholy night. She was struggling with acting on something that was against human nature. All her life she had been taught and told that homosexuality was a sin and was, therefore, wrong.

Miriam had always had sexual feelings for the same sex. It was natural for her but always made her feel guilty. Miriam's family members were religious people. Not overly religious but religious enough to make her hide her sexual preferences from not only her parents but her best friends. The only person that knew she was gay was this strange little girl that appeared in her life out of nowhere. Miriam was highly attracted to this mature freshman that appeared to her like a dark angel of the night. She admired her intellectually and sexually. To have her first lesbian experience with such a beautiful creature was the perfect confirmation of what she already knew from the moment she could remember. This was a powerful awakening for her, but what really bothered her was that at the end of his wonderful yet stressful moment, her partner treated it as a non-event. This significantly hurt her.

Miriam also had issues with how they treated Steve. Behind Miriam's outwardly rough and callous exterior was a good-hearted soul. She was a person that didn't like to hurt anyone but felt she had to in order to protect her own feelings. She was a young woman that was scared to admit who she was; a real person with extraordinary musical gifts that happened to be gay. But never had she ever set someone up like she did with Steve. She played him to have sex with her roommate. She felt dirty and responsible for creating this evil that would now haunt Steve as long as he lived. It took Miriam several weeks to mentally get over this.

Steve was embarrassed from the start. He was afraid he would get in trouble for having sex with a freshman. It was against Juilliard's rules to have sex with anyone on campus but for upper classman to have sex with an under classman was also against the code of ethics. Steve couldn't even look at Eva when they were together in class. A few days after their sexual encounter, Eva spoke to Steve before their first class started. Steve was so nervous he couldn't think straight. Eva had no feelings of emotion toward Steve or Miriam and took great amusement in her actions that unhallowed night. It was something she greatly enjoyed at Steve's and Miriam's expense. Eva loved to have been the one that changed both of these young adults' lives. It gave Eva the attention her soul craved.

What really bothered Steve was that he was turned on by what happened that night. He had never felt such intense sexual pleasure. To him, Eva was the most beautiful and sexual being he had ever seen. She was every boy and man's wet dream. The combination of her sexuality and her mental and verbal sexual abuse was so sexy that Steve struggled with the notion. It kept him up at nights. It dominated his thoughts and feelings every second he was awake. There was nothing he could do about the taboo desires that he had been taught all his life was a sin.

Throughout the semester, Steve never told a soul about his sexual encounter with Eva or Miriam. He couldn't breathe from all the stress he was under. That night dominated his thoughts. He thought that at anytime Eva or Miriam was going to tell people about his crime. What made matters even worse for Steve was that he was sexually aroused when he thought about that night. He would masturbate almost every night while reliving it in his head.

Eva didn't stop with her lustful desires and encounters with Steve. Steve was at the mercy of Eva's beck and call. While in class, Eva would whisper to Steve that she wanted him sexually on a chosen night. Steve couldn't refuse, but he told her that he wanted to stop seeing her. Eva didn't accept his wishes. She reminded him of the consequences if he didn't have sex with her.

Eva had no scruples. When she wanted sex she would call Steve. Steve would come to the room and they would have sex, many times while Miriam was in the room. Most of the time Miriam would leave, but sometimes she would stay and watch. Miriam never participated after her first sexual encounter with Steve. Eva spared Miriam from that action, which she was very grateful for. Steve was enjoying the sex, but in the back of his mind he still felt so guilty. He knew it was wrong. The counter-play between his feelings of immense pleasure then the guilt he was feeling made him a very confused and unsettled person. Throughout the remaining semester, his grades dropped and his musical talents suffered greatly.

Eva's sexual escapades with Steve grew in intensity. Eva became more forceful and dominant. She would degrade and humiliate him in numerous ways. She toyed with him and used him without any regard to his feelings or his pleasure. Many times, he would be forced to not have sexual release or he would have to play with himself in front of Miriam. At times, Miriam would even join in the humiliation. Eva would play mind games with him and have him constantly question his own sexuality and sexual preferences. Many times, she would threaten that she was going to have another man in the room waiting for him to perform oral sex on him. She toyed with the idea of watching him have sex with another man, all for her sadistic enjoyment at seeing Steve in mental distress. Steve would beg for mercy but had to endure some of most taboo sexual acts to prevent an encounter with another man or men.

Eva loved to see others in psychological anguish. That was her thing; sexual and non-sexual torment. She loved to dominate sexually, academically and musically. Any vehicle of control or dominance that made her superior to others gave her the most satisfaction. She was superior at reading people. She sensed others' feelings and traits then used that knowledge against others.

Steve wanted to drop out of Juilliard before the semester ended. Eva sensed that he was at the point of collapse. His nerves were gone and he couldn't control his hands from shaking. Eva didn't want the news to get out about them so she knew she needed to end their relationship. It would be in her best interest for him to leave Juilliard.

Eva told Steve she had one more task before she would release him. Eva had Miriam join them on a night on the town. Eva had him take them to a gay bar. The three stayed outside and waited for a couple of guys to come out. Two guys came out and Eva approached them. She said to the guys, "Hi. I have a friend that is gay and wants to have his first gay sexual experience. He wants to blow you guys." The guys were more than happy to take Eva up on her offer.

Eva forced Steve into the couple's car that was parked outside in the bar's small parking lot. Steve performed his service on the two men. Afterward, they pushed him out of the car. Eva stood there laughing while she showed him pictures of his performance on her phone. The three went back to Juilliard and, per Eva's instructions, Steve quit Juilliard and never returned. Steve was forced to accept the fact that the pictures Eva took would be held over his head for the rest of his life.

When they went back to the dorm Miriam said, "What you did to Steve this semester was very cruel."

Eva looked at Miriam and said, "So... what's your point? You enjoyed it, didn't you?" Eva smiled at Miriam. All Miriam could do was force a smile. She knew full well that she was no better off than her alias named Steve.

Chapter Seven

Eva came home after her spring semester courses were finished and stayed until her summer courses started in June. Eva loved Juilliard so much that she wanted to stay there year-round. I picked her up at the airport and took her home. I immediately knew she was having sex. Not a word was said between us because she could read what I was thinking. We both knew that our father was going to sense this, and it was not going to be pleasant.

When Eva first stepped into the house, she was greeted by our mother. Zelda hugged Eva and asked her if she was happy at her school. Zelda then sensed that Eva was experimenting with sex as she smelt her body scent. Zelda didn't say a word. Eva knew everyone would find out eventually, and when she first saw our father, she knew he was aware of her adventures. Eva waited for Wolfgang to make the first move. Wolfgang stood there, emotionless. He just stared at her then spoke, "Eva! You had sex. I sense, many times."

Eva smiled and said, "Yes. I had sex with only one man... well... if you count touching, I have been with only one woman as well." Eva laughed.

Zelda gasped loudly while Marci laughed out loud. Wolfgang screamed, "Enough laughter!" Everyone was silenced immediately. Wolfgang said, "This is why I didn't want her to go to this school."

Eva spoke, "But, Father, they won't say a word. They cannot prove anything. I was careful."

Wolfgang said, "That is not the point. The point is that you fucked a boy."

Eva smiled and said, "He was not a boy. He was twenty-two." Wolfgang stood there and said nothing. Eva continued, "I wanted to know how sex felt. I had a sexual need and I fulfilled that need. Also, it's none of your business anyway. If I want to fuck someone I can fuck someone."

Wolfgang was about to blow up from anger. Quickly, Zelda said, "Eva, we just don't want you to get hurt or expose our family."

Eva said, "I understand. But I have desires. Don't you guys have desires?"

Wolfgang said, "Desires need to be controlled. Especially desires that are dangerous."

Wolfgang knew he couldn't stop his daughter. He sensed that she knew what she was doing, but he was very concerned. All he could say was, "Remember, I made you, my daughter. It would not be wise for others to discover the secrets of this family." He turned away and walked toward the hallway on the way to his lab.

Eva said, "I understand, Father. I love and respect you. I also appreciate you sending me to Juilliard. Please believe me when I tell you that I'm very careful, and I have full control over my desires. I know what I'm doing."

Wolfgang stopped walking and looked over his shoulder and said, "Don't disappoint me."

Eva said, "I won't. So, how are the kids?"

Wolfgang said, "Follow me if you want to see them." Eva followed her father. Marci didn't want to go, but she wanted to see Eva's reaction to them so I went with them.

When we entered the lab, Eva saw Sarah's kids for the first time. At first, she was very concerned about their physical appearance and asked, "Is this what my children will look like?"

Wolfgang said, "I don't know, Eva. In all probability, no."

Eva looked at them and said, "I don't want my children to look like that." Marci lowered her head and started to cry. Eva went over to Marci and said, "Marci, I am so sorry. What's wrong? I... I didn't mean to hurt your feelings."

Marci said, "I understand. I don't know if I want this either." Marci cried hard as Eva did everything she could to comfort her the best way she knew how. I had known Marci was feeling this way, but I needed her to say it aloud to all.

I looked at Marci and said, "We do not have to rush anything. If you do not want children, then we do not have to have children. We have all the time in the world to make that decision."

Wolfgang nodded and said, "That is completely up to you guys. I have enough data on these specimen to keep me busy for a long time. It might be in everyone's best interest not to have children at this time."

Marci busted out crying. She said, "All I wanted was to have children with you, my love. My dreams have come true; I have eternal life. What I'm concerned with is how they will function in this world. They won't have any friends. They would have to be isolated from the rest of the world or they would be persecuted for the rest of their lives." Wolfgang and I agreed with Marci.

Suddenly, Sarah spoke. She said, "Please keep us alive. Please don't hurt us."

Marci immediately let out a horrific scream. Her large head reared back while her mouth was wide open, exposing her very long, sharp teeth. Marci screamed, "Fuck you and your kids. This is not about you. Fuck you! Nobody here cares about your fucking freaks! God... I hate you! I hate this fucking experiment. I want you dead! I want you tortured..." I quickly put my arms around my love's large body and tried to take her out of the lab. Marci was still screaming, "I am going to fucking kill you and your mutants. I am going to kill them in front of you and make you watch every god damn second of their death."

Eva stepped toward Marci and placed her hands on her. Marci seemed to calm down. Eva said, "Come on. Come on. Let's go upstairs." We took Marci to the great room and calmed her down.

Eva and I sat down with Marci and had a long discussion about her having kids. Marci wanted to share something special with me, and having kids was the ultimate adventure we wanted to share. The problem was what would happen to our kids. They would never have a normal upbringing. They would have to be sheltered from all human species so they would grow up lonely and would be isolated throughout their eternal years.

Eva started to feel that she was being ignored, so she quickly turned the conversation to her. She brought up the subject of her sex life. Marci wanted to know all the details of her sexual encounters so Eva talked about the many sexual acts she had performed, all the while promising to us that she would be careful. Eva told Marci that she didn't desire other women sexually, but she loved to control them. Marci laughed and said, "I understand. I have controlled some women in my life."

Eva said, "The way I look at it is if you can derive pleasure from them, then so be it. Use them for your pleasure. They are all worthless." Both ladies laughed uncontrollably.

Eva and Marci talked more about having children. Eva was scared about what her children would look like too. Marci said she would have beautiful children and not to worry about it. Eva had many concerns about her potential pregnancy, more along the lines of it killing her. Wolfgang and I had attempted to calm her nerves in the past and tried to make her understand that in all probability, her pregnancy wouldn't kill her.

At that point I left the ladies and went to visit my father in his lab. My father and I discussed Eva and the possibility of Marci and me not having children. Wolfgang understood that with Eva, the formula develops the strong parts of the host's personality. Obviously, for Eva, she craved attention through both music and sex. Eva was very independent, just as I was at her age.

A month went by then Eva went back to Juilliard. She had a full load of courses through the summer months. She wanted to take as many courses as possible and work on improving her voice. She didn't have that much to work on when it came to her voice, but she wanted to refine it to a point to where she was the best in the world. She also needed more vocal experience with a wider array of composer's works. As well, she needed to study languages other than German and Italian and their diverse pronunciations.

Miriam was going to take some summer courses as well. I saw to it that they would have the same dorm room the following semester. Both Miriam and Eva were happy. Miriam didn't want another roommate that she had to get used to and she knew it would be in her best interest to go along with what Eva wanted.

Sarah's children had all grown rapidly. They were about five months old and were developing according to Wolfgang's theoretical basis. Wolfgang believed that after a couple of years, the newborns would stop growing. Their height would top off at about four to four and a half feet. At this point, the four were talking, reading and writing thanks to Sarah who did a marvelous job teaching them. Wolfgang did his part in training them as well so he could properly test them in the future. He wanted to know their limits. From an intellectual point of view, they were at a genius level compared to a human, but not as intelligent as Eva, me, Marci or my parents. This confused Wolfgang to some degree. The formula corrected any mental or intellectual deformities, but it didn't improve the offspring's intellect level to surpass their parents.

One day, Marci approached me with a gleam in her eye. She said, "Love, I want to ask you for a favor. I really want to kill Sarah's freaks, at least one of them."

I said, "I know you do. I spoke with Wolfgang about this and he said it would be okay to eliminate one of them. He has plans for the other three. I think he wants the smartest, which is Eli, to stay alive, and he wants to experiment on the two females."

Marci was disappointed. She said, "I hate when you guys call them by name. They are horrible little monsters. They don't deserve names."

I assured her, "I understand your feelings."

Marci and I went to see Wolfgang in his lab. Wolfgang knew what Marci wanted. Before we could say anything, Wolfgang said, "You get Simon." Marci didn't say a word, just looked over at her prey. She walked toward the cell quietly, with great confidence. Sarah was the most guarded. She knew Wolfgang and Marci wanted Simon, but she didn't know exactly what they were going to do with him. Sarah paced in her cell like an angry tiger protecting her cubs. Her feet hit the tiled floor hard with every step. She puffed her chest out and bared her long teeth in anger. Marci was amused by her futile attempt at trying to show her toughness. Sarah moved Simon behind her and stared at Marci to the best of her ability. Marci's smile was too much for Sarah to handle. It angered her to a point where she leapt at Marci only to have the bars of the cell keep them separated. Marci laughed and walked toward Sarah. Sarah quickly reached between the bars, trying to get at Marci.

Marci stared at the outreached arm and watched the fingers move in an angry fashion. Marci looked at Sarah and said, "You don't want to attack me, bitch. I am very comfortable in my new body. You are not. You will certainly never take me at this point in your transformation."

Sarah shouted, "You will not hurt any of my children."

Marci angered quickly. She moved quickly to Sarah's hand, grabbing her wrist, and with her free hand she cupped her elbow. With one quick movement, she hyperextended Sarah's arm, causing it to bend in the opposite direction. Many pops and cracks were heard as the sound bounced from one bar to the next. Sarah screamed in pain while her children were yelling for Marci to stop.

Wolfgang ran over to prevent Marci from doing any more damage. Wolfgang held Sarah's broken arm as I went over to unlock the door of the cell. I had a long pole with a rope on the end of the shaft. As I walked inside, I went over to Simon. Marci was behind me as she closed the cell door to prevent anyone from escaping. Marci approached Simon, and I placed the rope around his neck and tightened the noose.

I walked Simon out of the cell while he held onto the shaft. Marci looked at Simon's siblings and said, "God damn it, you kids are disgusting."

Sarah turned her head around as best she could and yelled, "Leave my babies alone." Marci ran over to Sarah and applied her massive weight on her, pinning her against the bars.

Wolfgang said, "Stop it, Marci. Get out of here – now!" Marci took hold of Sarah's hair and pulled her head back as far as she could. Sarah was no longer scared of Marci, she was angry with her. Sarah felt feelings that she had never felt before. She felt hatred.

Marci's lips were inches from Sarah's ear. Marci shouted as loudly as she could, "They are not your children. They are freaks! Fucking freaks!"

Sarah did something she had never done before; she talked back to Marci. "These are your husband's babies, not yours. This upsets you, doesn't it?"

Marci had never felt so much anger in her soul. Marci got a better hold of Sarah's hair and slammed her face into the bars of the cell. She kept banging her head into the bars then, after several blows, Eli ran over and bit Marci on the leg. Marci screamed. She released her hold on Sarah and reached down and took hold of Eli. She picked him up with her hands on each side of his shoulders then threw him across the celled room. Wolfgang screamed, "No! Marci! No!"

Wolfgang went inside of the cell and grabbed Marci by the waist. Marci struggled to get out of his grip. Sarah quickly pulled her crooked arm out of the bars and went over to Eli who was lying on the floor trying to get up. Large, thick drops of blood dripped from Sarah's face. You could hear the drops of blood as they hit the tiled floor and onto Eli. Sarah said, "Are you okay, my dear?" Eli shook his head to say yes.

Marci did everything in her power to escape Wolfgang's hold. Sarah stood Eli up and quickly turned around and came after Marci. As she got close, Marci kicked her in the stomach, causing Sarah to bend over in pain. While Sarah was down on all fours, Marci managed to get one last kick into the side of Sarah's shoulder.

Wolfgang drug Marci out of the cell as I quickly opened the door then closed it behind them. Marci was screaming and kicking the entire time. Wolfgang let loose of his hold and Marci went after Sarah again, but this time Marci slammed her body into the bars of the cell, trying to get to Sarah. Marci reached inside the cell and grabbed her hair, and with one quick and swift movement, pulled Sarah's head into the bars. The back of Sarah's head was now bleeding. Marci pulled Sarah's hair as hard as she could until clumps of her long, black hair were ripped out of her scalp.

Sarah screamed and reached for the back of her head with her good arm. Wolfgang took Marci by the waist again and dragged her away from Sarah, but as he did, she pulled more hair out of Sarah's head. Wolfgang slammed Marci down onto the floor as she continued to kick and fight him. Wolfgang laid his massive frame on the lower part of her body as he pinned her wrists down on the floor.

Wolfgang continued to call her name. "Marci! Marci!" Finally, Marci stopped. Wolfgang said, "Enough! Calm down or I will kill you."

I pleaded with Marci to calm herself. "Damn it, Marci, calm down! He is going to kill you if you don't stop. Please stop... for me!"

Marci stopped fighting back. She laid there and started to cry. After several moments, Wolfgang got Marci up and took her out of his lab. Meanwhile, I placed Simon in the other cell.

The offspring were upset because they knew harm was coming to Simon, and their bodies were pressed up against the bars of the cell, trying to reach for Simon. Sarah remained sitting on the floor of her cell. She looked down at her arm that was bent in the wrong direction, reached down and forced her arm to go back into place, letting a loud scream escape while doing so. She then got up and attempted to calm down her children. She told Simon that he was going to be okay. She ended up making herself an arm sling after she cleaned herself up the best she could. A large clump of hair was missing from the back of her large head. She knew that in a short time the hair would grow back, and in less than a week her arm would heal itself. Her anger toward Marci grew to such an intense level that she was close to replacing that hatred for her over her own god.

Later that day, Marci had controlled her emotions, but when I took her down to the lab, she was still not in a pleasant mood. Wolfgang and my love eyed each other but didn't say a word. I told Marci not to pester Sarah, but she went over to her cage nonetheless. She saw where her head was bandaged up, along with her arm, and she began to laugh. Sarah rose from her bed as her three kids followed her. Sarah's attitude was calmer than it was during their last meeting. Sarah pleaded with

Marci saying, "Please don't hurt them. Please don't hurt Simon. He is an innocent boy. He has done nothing to you."

Sarah looked at me and said, "Please, Garrison. Don't let anything happen to your kids. They are..." Sarah stopped mid-sentence. She sensed Marci's anger swelling inside her. Sarah tried to backtrack what she had said. "I... I mean... they are innocent."

Marci let out a long, powerful breath and placed her large hand on my shoulder. She looked at me and said, "These are not your children. They are experiments that went horribly wrong. These animals are monsters."

I looked at my love. My heart ached for Marci. She knew they were my kids, but she didn't want to admit it. I loved her so much that I didn't have the heart to correct her, even though she knew she was wrong. They were my children, but I didn't have one ounce of feeling for any of them. Marci sensed that in me and that was all she needed to know. I never thought I would ever love her as much as I did at that moment. She was hurting inside and didn't want our future children to look like them. They would have to be sheltered all their lives and isolated from normal society.

The most damning part of our revelation was that we knew our kids together wouldn't come out normal. At that time it was more a fantasy for us, but at least we had each other. We knew I would have kids with Eva, and Marci was fine with that notion. Marci loved Eva and knew that if she couldn't have children, Eva's offspring would be the next best thing. This was a very difficult but important moment in our relationship. We grew closer to one another, something that I thought would have been impossible just hours prior.

Marci slowly walked over to Simon's cell without smiling or saying a word. She looked over at Sarah as large tears fell onto each side of Sarah's face. The children were holding onto Sarah's legs, and each one had great fear in their soul. Through the eyes of their mother, they viewed Marci as the devil.

Marci walked away from them, leaving the lab. I looked at Wolfgang and asked, "What was that about?"

Wolfgang said, "I don't know."

I stayed in the lab for a while. I sensed that Marci wanted to be alone. Little did I know, she had gone into the garage and took out an ax then went into the treed area of our property. She walked past the three enormous trees that were still feeding off Adam's cold blood that had contaminated the soil. The trees were tall, broad and thick, and most of the leaves were large and perfectly shaped.

I made my way out of the lab and followed her. I knew she could sense me watching her, but she made no attempt to acknowledge me. As I viewed this magnificent figure from afar, an overwhelming wave of pride overtook my soul. I said to myself under my breath, *I made her.* I had made her into what she was – a beautiful, perfect creature that no one would ever get to know. Her passion and love for me was something that only dreams were made of and I was most fortunate to have her in my life.

My love walked deep into our property. She didn't want to cut a large tree down so she found a dead, twenty foot tree that was lying on the ground. She made sure the tree was strong and not badly decomposed. She studied the dead tree from all angles then I watched as she took the ax as far back as she could and, with great force, slammed the sharp edge deep into the upper part of the tree. Every branch shook violently. Marci repeated her blows to the tree until she had severed the tree into halves. She then straddled the tree and hit it in the middle with the ax. She continued to swing her ax until she was at the base of the tree. She then cut the portion of the tree where it had snapped off of the trunk sticking out of the ground. Each half of the tree measured about six foot in length.

Marci picked up the detached tree halves in her arms, turned to me and said, "Hey, baby, would you get the ax for me?"

I walked over to the ax without saying a word. We walked back to the estate and went into the side walkout of the basement, into Wolfgang's lab. The offspring and Sarah looked at the long logs as Marci laid them down and walked over to the closet. She found some rope and walked over to the logs, placing the longest log with the cut side facing up. She took the smaller log and placed it across the top, with its cut side facing down to make the design of a cross.

Sarah gasped and said, "What are you doing? This is blasphemy."

Marci, without taking her eyes off what she was doing, said, "I am so sick of this fucking religious shit that spews out of that slutty mouth of yours."

Marci wrapped the rope around the two cut logs, tying the logs together as tightly as she could. Sarah was screaming, "Please! Please stop this, Garrison!" Marci calmly walked over to Simon's cell as Sarah ran over to the side of the cell that was closest to Simon. She was pleading with Marci, "Please! Please no! Please don't do this!" Marci smiled at Simon. Simon waddled back to the furthest part of his cell while Marci went to Wolfgang's large closet. She pulled out a large leather bag with several short pieces of rope then slid the pieces of rope across the tile floor as she watched them hit up next to the side of the cross.

Marci looked at Wolfgang and said, "Would you mind helping me, Wolfgang?"

Wolfgang nodded and smiled. My father and Marci had had some difficult moments in the past, but one thing they shared was their love of torture. Marci placed the leather bag next to the cross. Wolfgang and Marci walked over to the entrance of the cell and Wolfgang unlocked the door. Simon was nervous and started to run from one side of his cell to the other, trying to find a way out of his entrapment. Wolfgang quickly corralled him, grabbing him by the shoulders as quickly as he could. Simon fought back with all his might, but he was just not as strong as Wolfgang's powerful hands, arms and upper body.

Sarah was screaming, "Please! Please stop! Please leave my baby alone! Please don't hurt him!"

Wolfgang walked out of the cell holding Simon shoulder high with Simon's legs kicking in all directions and his arms holding onto Wolfgang's forearms. Wolfgang was so focused that he didn't react to Simon's fingernails repeatedly scratching his arms as he placed Simon down on his feet and quickly spun him around.

I went inside the cell, helping Marci with the cross she'd made. I quickly laid the cross down, went behind my father, and grabbed Simon's kicking legs by his ankles. Wolfgang and I worked as one as he pushed Simon down onto the cross as I pulled his legs out from under him. I placed most of my weight on his ankles while Wolfgang held his wrists down on the cross. He rocked the cross onto its side, raising the other side almost a foot in the air. Marci took a piece of rope, wrapped it around Simon's forearm twice and firmly tied a double knot. The same procedure was performed on Simon's other forearm.

Wolfgang replaced my hands with his around Simon's ankles. He raised the cross about a foot from the floor for Marci to fasten the rope for his legs. Simon was screaming, making loud, squeaky, pig-like noises. Marci wrapped the rope around his legs three times then placed his feet next to each other on the flat piece of the wooden plank. She again tied the extremities tightly but was careful not to cut off the blood flow.

Sarah was beside herself and her other children were all crying. They were not only upset at what Marci was about to do to their brother, they were upset over Sarah's reaction. Sarah ran her body up against the cell wall, making a loud sound. She reached out her good arm in a feeble attempt to save her son. Sarah pleaded with us not to harm him. She said everything she could think of, trying to stop this insanity from happening. She tried to bargain with us as best she could, but her pleas were ignored by all except Marci.

Marci looked over at Sarah and said, "Ask your god to save your son now! Plead with him to save him. Beg for a miracle, bitch!"

Sarah cried harder as she hid her face in her outstretched arm. There was nothing she could do to save him. Sarah started to pray. "Oh, God Almighty, all powerful and all knowing, please save my son from this most horrible fate. I ask my God in heaven for forgiveness for our past sins."

Marci enjoyed the show as much as anyone. She looked down at Simon and noticed the tears flowing from all corners of his large eyes. Marci bent down and pulled out six-inch metal nails that are used on railroad ties. Marci dropped one of the nails next to Simon's outstretched arm and dropped two next to his tied lower legs. Marci held one of the nails as she picked up a hammer.

Sarah cried even louder. She yelled, "Please... please, no. Please don't hurt him. Hurt me instead. Nail me to the cross, but please save my son!"

Marci smiled and said, "Is that the best you can do? Is that the miracle you request? So you will take these nails in order to save your son from his suffering?"

Sarah nodded and said, "Yes... please... please, strike your nails into me instead of Simon."

Marci walked over to Sarah's outstretched arm and ran the nail along the inside of Sarah's palm. She then ran the nail up Sarah's wrist and forearm. Marci knew that Sarah was weak. Even Sarah knew that she couldn't allow Marci to inflict that type of willing pain on her. Sweat was oozing from every pore of Sarah's body.

Marci said, "Keep your arm still while I drive this nail through your wrist."

Marci placed the sharp nail on Sarah's wrist and as she drew back the hammer, Sarah quickly pulled her arm back inside the cell. Sarah screamed as she looked at Marci. Marci stood there and smiled, which suddenly turned into laughter.

Marci said, "You pathetic bitch. You can't even take a little pain for your own child. How typical of a religious freak."

Marci walked toward the cross. She went down on her knees and placed the nail over Simon's wrist. Sarah screamed loudly, "Please... no! I am so sorry! I am so sorry, Simon!"

Simon yelled out, "Mommy! Why?"

Marci quickly drew the hammer to her shoulder and with great forced, slammed the nail into his wrist. The nail passed through the wrist and penetrated the wood behind it. Simon screamed in great horror and pain, sounding like a pig being slaughtered. His extremely high-pitched scream resonated throughout the lab's walls. Sarah matched each one of Simon's ghastly squeals with her own rendition of similar shrieks.

Without notice, Marci slammed the hammer onto the nail again, causing more pain, more screaming and more pleading from Sarah. A third and then a fourth blow followed until the nail was deeply buried into the tree. Blood was flowing out of the wrist and onto the wood. Splatters of blood were all over the floor next to the cross and Marci had small red dots all over the front of her dress. Simon was writhing from the pain. Within moments, Marci repeated the nailing procedure into his other wrist.

Sarah was filled with guilt. She allowed her body to slide down the bars of the cell, crying so hard that she couldn't see through the tears in her eyes. As the tears fell, there were moments that all she could see was Simon's little body squirming around on the cross.

Marci said to Sarah, "Oh Sarah, oh Sarah, why did you forsake your son?"

Marci and Wolfgang laughed hard. I smiled, thinking the commentary was funny as well. Sarah let out a horrifying scream in retaliation as Marci continued nailing Simon to the cross. She placed the last of the two nails just above the front top portion of Simon's large feet. Four fast blows of the hammer for each ankle was all it took to securely fasten Simon's ankles to the cross.

Simon had difficulty breathing from all his gasping for air due to his extreme pain. Saliva was flowing from the corners of his mouth and onto his neck, and every inch of his disgusting body was covered in sweat. All Sarah could do was watch this horrific scene unfold before her eyes. The rest of her children ran over to a cot, huddling together, hoping they wouldn't experience such torture.

Wolfgang picked up the cross while listening to Simon screaming his little heart out for mercy. The pain was so intense he could hardly comprehend what was happening to him, but Wolfgang was accustomed to hearing such screams throughout most of his life. He slid the cross toward Simon's cell. Wolfgang said, "Marci, get more rope."

Marci went into the closet and retrieved more rope as instructed. Wolfgang slid the cross to the opening of the cell and tilted it sideways. As he did, Simon screamed even louder as his body weight pulled on his wrist and ankles, causing more intense pain. Wolfgang pulled the cross onto the bars of the cell. All the movement caused more bleeding from Simon's wounds. Marci gave him the pieces of rope. He tied both ends of the cross to the bars of the cell to support it and keep it from falling over.

Marci went to Wolfgang's lab desk and pulled out a skinning knife, the one she had used on Carolyn before she died. Marci walked up to Simon and slammed the knife into his right side. Simon gasped, clinched his eyes, and attempted to yell. The pain from the stab was intense, and screaming was now even more difficult because the blade had penetrated his lung. Sarah was petrified from what she was witnessing. This was one of her own; her child was being crucified on a cross just like her Savior.

Sarah shouted, "Stop it! Stop it, you monster. Why are you doing this to him?"

Marci said, "Because I hate you. I hate this freak of nature and I hate your god!"

Sarah lowered her head as she pressed it against the metal bars. Sarah muttered, "You people are the most evil creatures I have ever known. How do you expect God to ever forgive you?"

Those words sent pinpricks down Marci's spine. She shouted, "Forgive what, you stupid sanctimonious bitch? Fuck you and your made-up god. He doesn't exist, you mother fucking bitch! If he is a god, then why doesn't he stop me from torturing your pathetic excuse of a son?"

Sarah cried loudly and said, "Why are you so evil? Why do you not believe in the son of God?"

Marci was so enraged with Sarah's talk about her god that she was now totally driven by anger. Her joy of torture was gone, and she needed her anger to be released. She walked quickly out of the cell, went to the laboratory's closet and again pulled out the ax.

Wolfgang and I stood back, allowing Marci to proceed. Sarah continued to plead with Marci to spare her son's life. Marci quickly looked at me as she walked by with the ax in her hand and said, "Turn the oven on." I did what I was told.

Sarah continued to scream, "No! Noooooo! Oh, please, God. No. For the Lord's sake, no!"

Marci walked over to Simon and stood in front of him. She looked at him and said, "You are a freak of nature. You should never have been born. Fuck you and your pathetic family."

She stepped off to the side, and with the ax in her hand, she pulled the instrument back, and with great force she sent the ax to its destination of Simon's right ankle. As the blade of the ax swiftly passed through the cartilage and bone, his right foot and ankle were severed from his lower leg. Simon, with all his might, screamed so loud that it hurt my ears.

Marci stood there smiling as the blood dripped from her ax. She tilted her head back, closed her eyes and said, "Isn't that the most beautiful music in the world? Just listen to those cries." In the background, Sarah was screaming, crying and pleading all at the same time.

Marci then proceeded with the other ankle. I watched as the ax glided with ease through the air then was abruptly stopped by a thud. More screams of pain and terror were unleashed from the boy's mouth. Amid this taboo auditory and visionary pleasure from many sources was my love's laughter. The enjoyment and need for punishment was pure ecstasy for her.

Simon's body slumped downward, pulling on his nailed wrists which in turn caused more suffering. Marci pulled her ax back behind her body and slammed it into Simon's left forearm. His body fell limp with only one nail holding his body from hitting the floor of his cell. Marci finished the final blow, dislodging the body from the cross. Simon's body hit the tile floor with a most interesting thud. His body lay limp on the floor with blood everywhere. Marci reached down and grabbed Simon by the hair, pulling him out of the cell and across the room.

Sarah was going out of her mind. Her other children ran under their cots, all scared out of their minds. Sarah was jumping around in place, slamming her body against the cell, trying to get to her son, but the bars wouldn't allow her the freedom that she demanded.

Marci pulled Simon across the floor of the basement and stopped in front of the crematory machine. The machine was hot enough to incinerate human flesh and bones. Simon's body was going into shock, with the formula inside his veins trying to repair what was injured, which is one of its most amazing traits. It can keep the body alive for long periods of time if the head is attached and is kept alive by the heart.

I opened the doors of the crematory machine. The pure heat that poured out of the machine took my breath away for a second. One could only imagine hearing the unpleasant popping and crackling sounds of the flames of the furnace. Marci reached down and picked up Simon while blood was dripping from all four of his extremities.

Marci shouted to Sarah, "Okay, bitch! I will give you a choice. I will spare this one in exchange for your other son!" Wolfgang was about to say something, but he sensed what Marci was doing so he kept his mouth shut.

Sarah cried out, "Please stop this madness. You are blaspheming all that is good about my religion and my God. What kind of monster are you?"

Marci shouted back, "Bitch! I am no monster. Fuck you then!"

Marci swung Simon's body back, and with great force threw his limp body into the flames of his fiery tomb. As his body hit the floor, his skin immediately started to slightly melt and then quickly turned black. Simon screamed so loud that his vocal cords almost snapped in two. Sarah's screams echoed her son's cries of pain and total desperation. Simon wanted to escape his tomb, but it was too late; the fire took the remaining oxygen from his lungs. Marci wanted the door to remain open so she could watch. In a matter of seconds, Simon's entire body was engulfed in flames. I quickly closed the door to protect us from any expulsion that might occur from the body.

Marci stood there laughing then without notice, she ran toward Sarah's cell and came just inches from the bars. She screamed, "Did you see that, bitch? I just burnt your fucking son after I mutilated him. I want you to feel hate, you fucking, god damned bitch! Feel it, you pathetic shithead! Feel the hate building inside of you."

I went over to Marci and attempted to pull her away from the cell. She was so big and strong I couldn't move her. Sarah had her back against the wall with tears flowing out of her large eyes like I had never seen before. After a few moments of staring at Marci and listening to her rant, her anger grew. This was a feeling Sarah had never experienced before. The pure hurt and mourning for the death of her child altered her feelings to hate. She finally lashed out at Marci and held nothing back. She shouted, "Fuck you! Fuck you! You are the daughter of the devil! You are truly Satan's daughter. You will rot in hell for what you did to my beautiful little boy… you bitch! I am going to kill you! Do you hear me? I am going to kill you!" Sarah suddenly stopped. She placed her hand on her mouth and regained control of her senses. She looked at Marci who was smiling and laughing at her harder than ever before. Sarah broke down, falling to her knees saying, "Oh, God! Oh, God… forgive me. Oh, please, God, forgive me. I have sinned against you. Please, God… forgive me."

Marci walked over to Wolfgang and said, "Is it normal for humans to act like this?"

Wolfgang nodded and said, "Yes, you should know that they are first scared, then they pray, then they turned angry. After that emotion is out of their system, they return to that god of theirs and they are back to where they started – being scared. All they have is hope. Take that away from them, they will eventually die."

Marci and Wolfgang walked upstairs together with the sobering cries of Sarah and her children ringing in their ears. I stayed back and turned off the machine when Simon's body turned to ashes. Sarah whispered to get my attention, but I ignored her. She raised her voice a few octaves in the hopes that I would listen. She pleaded with me to release her and her children. I quietly walked over to her and said, "Sarah, I will not release you. This is out of my control now."

I walked away from her and she said, "Please, please… come back… help me. Please help me. You must help me. In the name of God, please help me."

I stopped, turned toward her and said, "Please stop. Just please stop with the god crap. It only makes us angrier. It especially makes Marci very hostile. So, do yourself a favor and stop the god talk and all that fucking praying. It gets on our nerves." I turned away and went upstairs. As I left, I turned out the light. All I heard was crying. As I made my way up to the great room, Marci looked at me with that sexy look that only she could produce. We excused ourselves and went to my bedroom. That night we had incredible sex that lasted for hours.

Chapter Eight

The next morning, we ate breakfast together. Wolfgang wanted to speak to us about an experiment that he wanted to do on two of the children. We sensed what he wanted to do, but out of respect we heard him out. Wolfgang took us to his lab. He spoke loud enough for Sarah and her three remaining children to hear what he said. Wolfgang had us sit down and he began to tell us what was on his mind. He said, "Many decades ago when I was a member of the Nazi party, I met a man that was interested in genetic research on human subjects. He had heard about my work through Herr Hitler's conversations. My Fuhrer suggested that we meet and discuss our work. You have heard of him through your history books. This great man's name was Joséf Mengele. Joséf and I respected each other and became good friends. He was not a smart man, but he did have some interesting ideas regarding the human race. His goal, along with the rest of us, was to aid our Fuhrer in the development of our master race. Many thought we couldn't improve on the living but could improve on the next generation. Of course, I believed I could change the human condition while they were still alive. Many thought I was crazy, but not Joséf. Although our works were in opposite directions, our main goal was the same; to create the perfect master race."

"He worked with experimenting on many young kids in the concentration camps. He set up a kindergarten-type setting for these specimens. His people provided them with better food, living conditions and medical care, all to keep them as healthy as possible for his experiments. He was not a scientist like most of us, but he was very sadistic and he hated the Jews. He echoed many of our familiar sentiments that this race of people was dangerous to our father land and future way of life. He killed for the love of killing."

"Joséf liked to torture his specimens in a variety of ways. He would conduct a wide array of experiments on his samples, mostly for genetic research. He worked mostly with identical twins. He was trying to prove the supremacy of heredity over environment. He wanted to prove to the world that our cause was righteous, that our superiority of the Aryan race was due to our inherent factors, not just from people's natural environment that the Jews enjoyed and took from our people. Joséf thought if he could find a way to produce identical twins that were superior to others, that would rapidly improve the numbers of the desirable race of people having more preferred children. Over time, this would help aid the numbers of our master race of pure humans."

"Joséf also selected the people to go to the gas chambers at Auschwitz. There is where he did most of the genetic experiments on his identical twin specimens. Most of what he did was more for the pure enjoyment of seeing children suffer. He would unnecessarily amputate limbs or infect one twin with typhus or some other disease, then transfuse the blood from the infected twin to the non-infected twin. Many of his specimens died during these procedures. If one twin died, he would immediately kill the other twin and compare the postmortem reports."

"Joséf would also attempt to change the eye color by injecting chemicals into the eyes of living subjects. He experimented on dwarfs and people with a multitude of physical abnormalities. Any experiment that you could think of, he tried on his subjects, including sewing twins together back-to-back to create conjoined twins. Needless to say, these experiments were not really experiments, they were just torture techniques."

"Joséf shared all his techniques and findings with me although I shared very little of my research with him. When the Russians were invading Berlin, they destroyed most of his data and findings."

"After reading history books and articles that your media provides, I later found out that he fled to Argentina in 1949, went to Paraguay in 1959, and finally settled in Brazil in 1960. He died in 1979 off the Brazilian coast while swimming. I find it interesting that so many of the high-ranking officers and leaders of the party actually got out of Berlin when we did. This came as a great surprise to me."

No one could imagine how Marci and I felt while sitting there listening to a legend talk about a time that we had only read about, and neither had met anyone that was actually there. The people he met and associated with was something special. No matter what a person might think about the beliefs of some of those great men of that time, one must respect the pursuit of their main goal of perfection. I sensed great pride in my father that he had discovered something that could change the world forever. Few people had ever had that opportunity.

Wolfgang continued, "So I sense that you are wondering why I am telling you this. Well, part of me wants you to understand that not all of us were monsters. Most of my colleagues wanted to find cures for diseases and illnesses. We wanted to somehow slow the aging process or even stop it if that was possible. We wanted to create a society of physically and mentally superior people. We were small in number compared to the rest of the world, but if we could at least purify Germany, that was a start. It was a stepping stone to our ultimate goal."

Sarah rose up from her cot and walked over to the end of her cell that was closest to where we were seated. The look on her face was one of pure disgust. She said, "You people are just pure evil. I have never been around people like you. I have heard of these evil people from your country. How can you do these things to decent human beings?"

Wolfgang looked up and said, "Most of these decent human beings were not as decent as you think they were. Many of them were crooks and had stolen not only our money but rich, deep-seated traditions of our country. All the pure German people wanted was to have our country returned to its glorious past, a time when a German was a German and not diluted European or Middle Eastern scum."

Wolfgang rose from his chair and said, "Garrison, help me." I followed my father over to his closet where he pulled out two long steel poles with a rope on the end. These instruments were typically used to catch dogs. We each took one and walked toward Sarah's cell. Wolfgang said, "Bring your two daughters over to the entrance of the cell. You stay here." Wolfgang's long finger pointed at Sarah's position at the far end of the cell.

Sarah said, "What are you going to do?"

Wolfgang said, "If you want them to live, you will do as I say."

I walked over to the entrance of the cell holding both poles. Marci made her way behind me and took one of the poles as I opened the cell and we placed the ropes around each female's neck. Sarah's daughters, Lucinda and Emma, looked different but had the same basic characteristics as the rest of Sarah's children.

Sarah moved around a little and Wolfgang ordered her to stand still. Sarah knew that her daughters were in trouble and that she couldn't save them. She was at her wit's end. If she moved toward them, she knew we would kill them. If she allowed us to take the females, she knew we were probably still going to do harm to them. She had to play it safe. She did the only thing she could do and that was plead with Wolfgang.

Sarah said, "Please. Don't hurt them. You have already taken my son's life; please don't take my daughters.'"

Wolfgang said in a confronting voice, "We are not going to kill your daughters, we just want to observe them in a series of experiments."

Sarah demanded, "Experiments? What kind of experiments?"

Marci and I quickly took Lucinda and Emma out of the cell. Marci took both poles from me as I locked the cell door. Sarah moved toward her daughters, trying to reach out to them through the bars. The girls were also reaching out for their mother, but Marci made sure she kept them out of Sarah's grasp. Marci took the girls into the other cell and closed the door as instructed by Wolfgang. Sarah kept asking questions and pleading with Wolfgang not to harm them, but he just ignored her.

Marci and I knew what Wolfgang was going to do. It was exciting to witness my father in action. He said, "I want to see how much trauma a living being can take without dying." Wolfgang had reviewed all of Lewis's notes on the multitude of experiments that we had conducted in the past. He was especially interested in his notes on the execution of my brother, Adam. The body had still been alive after both the arms and legs were severed from its torso. Even though the body had lost a lot of blood, Formula L still produced enough blood to sustain life to the body. The question was how much physical abuse a specimen could take and still survive.

We had done experiments on many different types of animals and even humans, but rarely conducted an experiment on our subjects to see how close we could bring them to death. Only my torturing of Adam could fall into this category.

Wolfgang pulled us aside with the echo of Sarah's pleas bouncing off the walls of his laboratory. Wolfgang ordered Marci to be his assistant and to help restrain one of the twins, and told me to keep the other twin away from them. Wolfgang quickly left us and went to retrieve the other hospital bed that he had stored in his lab. He wheeled the large bed into the cell where we stood. He left the cell, went to his closet, and retrieved a large, worn, black leather bag. As he walked toward the cell, you could hear metal clanging inside the carrying case. He made his way to the cell and closed the door behind him. He said to Marci, "Hold Lucinda still." Wolfgang walked over to the four-foot creature who looked up at this massive, hairy deity that was standing before her.

Wolfgang took his powerful hands and started to rip and tear at Lucinda's clothes as she screamed for help. Sarah responded to her daughter's cries, only to be chastised by Marci saying, "Shut up, bitch!" Sarah could do nothing. She was confined by the bars of her current dwelling. Marci helped Wolfgang remove all of Lucinda's clothes. She stood there as naked as the day she was freed from Sarah's womb. Wolfgang ordered me to do the same to Emma. I followed my father's instructions, stripping her clothes from her. I then held her tight so she couldn't run around in the cell.

Wolfgang reached down and picked up Lucinda, roughly placing her on the hospital bed. He ordered Marci to hold her down on the bed, and ordered me to place Emma on the other hospital bed and hold her down, keeping her as still as possible. Wolfgang quickly reached into his leather bag and pulled out two instruments. One was a scalpel and the other was the old isolating saw that I had used on Adam years ago.

I said to my father, "Where did you find my saw?"

Wolfgang smiled and said, "It was stored back in a drawer in our lab." Wolfgang walked around to the left side of Lucinda, with Emma located on his other side. The girls were screaming, kicking, scratching, and doing anything they could to escape. Sarah was kneeling in her cell holding Eli. She was beside herself. Her voice was almost nonexistent from her crying and screaming for such long periods of time.

Sarah suddenly got up and pushed her large face into the bars of the cell, trying to get as close to her daughters as possible. So many thoughts went through her mind as she kept replaying the scene in her head. She knew she should have attempted to stop Wolfgang from taking her daughters. The guilt that she felt was unmerciful and unrelenting. She also knew she would have endangered her other son, Eli, if she had reached out and attempted to stop Wolfgang's abduction. She thought that to do nothing was her only choice. Now she knew she should have done something. These thoughts hurt Sarah more than her witnessing what was going to happen to her daughters.

Wolfgang said, "I am going to make many incisions, so I need to work fast. Please keep them as still as possible. They may pass out from the pain so please don't be alarmed and whatever you do, don't let loose of them." Wolfgang quickly went to work. He said, "I am videotaping this for our records. The purpose of this experiment is multifold. I want to see how much pain these subjects can endure without any anesthetic." Pointing to Lucinda, he continued, "I will amputate this subject's left arm and leg. I will remove the arm until the shoulder is square with the side of the body. I will then remove the skin and some tissue along the entire left side of the body. I will do the same with the right side of the other subject, Emma. I will then attach their sides together and sew them up. The intent is for the two bodies to grow together as one. Let's begin."

Lucinda screamed, "Mommy! Help me!"

Sarah mouthed the words repeatedly, "I can't" as large tears fell from her face.

Wolfgang proceeded to take the scalpel and without any hesitation, plunged the blade deep into Lucinda's shoulder socket. She screamed loudly. Wolfgang quickly but gently took the blade and made many jabbing movements around the socket of the arm. The blade from the scalpel cut through the many layers of skin, muscle, tendons and soft cartilage.

Blood poured from the wound. Wolfgang finished cutting around the entire circumference of the arm and shoulder socket then picked up the isolating saw. He turned it on and forced the blade into the cut area of the socket. He pressed the saw firmly with his hand as he waited patiently for the saw to do its job. The saw cut through the cartilage, deep-seeded tendons and muscles that the scalpel couldn't get to. Before we knew it, the arm was cleanly separated from the shoulder and the limp arm fell to the floor. Wolfgang, without missing a beat, kicked the severed arm out from under his feet. The arm slid toward the back of the cell, leaving a long trail of dark red blood. Every inch of Lucinda's body was in incredible pain. Every movement, every twitch she made caused her pain to intensify. Her wound felt as if it was on fire and she felt waves of continuous throbbing. Lucinda was powerless. Her pain was so intense that her body felt as if it was going to completely shut down.

Sarah screamed in her severely hoarse voice, "No! Please... no! Please stop. Oh, God in heaven, please make them stop this sinful act."

I held Emma as tight as I could. I looked down at this pathetic experimental specimen and noticed that she was about to vomit. I quickly pushed her face away from the right side of her body. Wolfgang screamed at me and said, "Don't let that crap infect my area and don't let it get on the right side of her body."

I said to Emma in a firm voice, "Come on now, we haven't even started on you yet. Don't be such a bad little girl."

Wolfgang quickly moved down to Lucinda's leg. Again, he took the scalpel and made a 360-degree incision around the top portion of her leg, trying to get as close to the leg socket as possible. He picked up the saw and placed it inside the cut area of the leg. He knew it would require more effort to remove than the arm. He held the leg with his left hand. He didn't want the weight, after he removed most of the leg, to tear the skin around the areas that might not have been cut thoroughly. Wolfgang guided the saw blade to cut through all the attached muscles, tendons and cartilage until the blade totally removed her leg. The specimen's body shook quickly, probably because it was going into shock. He told Marci to hold the specimen still.

Wolfgang stood there holding Lucinda's leg in the air. He took the saw and cut a large one square foot area out of the thigh area of the severed leg. He laid the detached flesh patch on Lucinda's stomach then quickly moved the saw onto its side and turned it on. He started the blade at the edge of her wounded leg area by her side, moving it up the entire left side of her body. The fleshy skin peeled away from her body. She was twitching so much that Marci had to lay her body on Lucinda to keep her still. Wolfgang worked quickly. He continued to cut a long, wide strip along the entire side of her body up to her arm socket. When he was finished, the long skin strip fell to the floor. He told Marci to turn her onto her uncut side, and Marci did as instructed.

Sarah sat there crying softly as her large body pressed against the bars. She recited prayer after prayer, none of which were making any sense. Her mind was not clear. She stared at this unholy act as if it was happening to someone else's daughters. She forced her mind to believe this was not happening to her loved ones. It was her only recourse.

From time to time Marci would disrupt her concentration by reminding her of the stark reality of the moment, giving her a detailed report on what Wolfgang was doing to her little girl. Sarah only heard about every other word that came from Marci's beautiful mouth. The others words she heard were her daughter's cries and shouts of unearthly pain.

Wolfgang turned to me and Emma. He told me to keep her as still as possible. Without hesitation he started on Emma's right arm. Emma screamed loudly before the blade even touched her arm. When the blade first penetrated her flesh, she shrieked like a baby. Before I knew it, Emma had passed out, but she was still alive.

Lucinda was lying on her uncut side, crying her little heart out. Marci repeatedly told her to stop crying, but Lucinda couldn't follow Marci's strong demands. Wolfgang repeated the same procedures that he had performed on Lucinda. He made his incision, and with the help of the isolating saw, he removed Emma's right arm. In less than a minute the leg was the next to be amputated. A large patch of skin, like Lucinda's, was removed from Emma's detached leg. It was placed on Lucinda's bed with the skin side down. Wolfgang quickly made the same cut along the entire right side of Emma's body, from her arm to her leg socket. I was ordered to move Emma onto her uncut side.

Wolfgang quickly stepped out from between the two beds. He ordered us to move the beds together then quickly tied the head and the foot of the two beds together with rope. He told us to lay the girls down on their backs. We slid them together so their cut sides were touching each other. Lucinda screamed even louder than before as Emma remained unconscious.

Wolfgang went to his bag and removed long pieces of thread and a long needle. He also got out a staple gun and a box of medical staples. With breakneck speed and precision, he started sewing the sisters together. Blood was everywhere on the beds, dripping down between the mattresses and onto the floor. Lucinda was weak from the excessive amount of lost blood, but the formula kept her alive longer than anyone without the formula in their system could.

My father finished sewing up the front side of the newly formed specimen. He then used the staple gun to reinforce the conjoined areas. Wolfgang applied liquid salve and a medical bonding liquid that would dry quickly onto the cut area. He then taped that area to stop the bleeding. We had to lift them up and turn them over onto their stomachs so Wolfgang could get the back area sewed and stapled shut as well. We repeated the procedure on the specimen's back side with the same materials. Wolfgang took the two large skin patches and placed them over the exposed area where the legs were once present. Again, he sewed, stapled and applied the medical supplies to that area to stop the bleeding.

When Wolfgang finished, he stepped back and looked at his work. He left the cell and went to retrieve a handful of long, adjustable straps, the type of straps you would use to anchor down a load in the back of a pickup truck. Marci and I secured the twins in the bed to the best of our ability then helped my father place the four straps across the body of the newly made specimen.

Wolfgang exited the cell once more and after several minutes returned with an IV for both halves. He needed to give the new body nourishment to help them not reject one another. For the moment, the bleeding had stopped although it was difficult to tell because there was so much blood everywhere. We cleaned the newly formed creature and wiped as much blood off the bed, floor, and from the bodies as possible while being extra careful not to break open the attached bodies.

Sarah was at her wits end. She couldn't believe what she had witnessed. Marci asked Wolfgang, "What should we call this new creature?" Wolfgang smiled and said nothing. She walked over to Sarah's cell and looked directly at her. Her large, black, lifeless eyes held no pity as she said, "How about LuEmma?" Marci stared at Sarah, waiting for a response. Marci said, "Or how about EmmaLu? Should we pray about it, Wolfgang? I wonder what 'god' would want. We certainly don't want to offend the almighty one."

Sarah whispered, "May God forgive you for your blasphemy and for all of your sins."

Marci said, "What did you say, bitch? May god do what to me? Fuck me? Is that what you said? You want your god to fuck me?" Marci leaned her head back and laughed. She continued, "I would break him and have him begging me not to stop. I could have him denying himself like I had you deny him. Remember that, my sinful little bitch?"

Sarah felt a rage inside her that she had never felt before as she was pushed too far. For what little human was still in her soul, she couldn't take Marci's condemnation any longer. Sarah screamed, "No! Shut up! Just shut up! Oh God, I pray to thee…"

Marci started to scream at her, interrupting her prayer. She said, "He is not listening because he doesn't exist! My Garrison created you. He was the one that brought you back from the dead. Just like he did for me! He is your god!"

Sarah shouted, "No! There is only one true God! His name is Jesus!"

Marci shouted back, "His name is Garrison and he stands there before you." Marci's long finger pointed to me as I sensed she was getting aroused. Marci continued, "He is your god, your creator, he is your almighty."

Sarah angrily rose to her feet and slammed her body into the bars of the cell. She reached out her good arm, attempting to grab Marci. She wanted to kill her. Marci stood just inches from her grasp. She looked at Sarah, smiled and said, "I sense your hatred. Do you feel it? I know you do. It's so fucking hot, isn't it? Do you want to worship my body? I know that you want to fuck me!"

Sarah yelled, "No! You bitch. You perverted bitch. What is wrong with you? The devil has full control over you and I hope someday you rot in hell. I hate you!"

Marci looked over at me and smiled. She said, "I think she just sinned again." Without looking, she quickly grabbed Sarah's wrist and bent the arm back against the metal bars, being careful not to break it. Marci reached inside the cell with her other hand as her long fingers wrapped around Sarah's throat. She pulled Sarah's head against two bars of the cell. Marci opened her mouth and extended her tongue, licking the side of Sarah's face. She moved her long, snake-like tongue over Sarah's lips, followed by her nose. Marci whispered, "You will someday be my pet and you will worship every inch of my body. You will adore every step I take, but you will suffer great pain to a point that you will not only wish you were dead, but you will beg every minute of your grueling life for me to end it. And guess what, my bitch? I will never grant you that wish." Marci looked down at Eli, Sarah's smartest and now only son. Marci said, "Hi there, little one."

Sarah yelled, "Leave him alone."

Marci said, "I am going to save the best for last, for you." Sarah struggled to get away from Marci's grasp. Marci said, "You are going to die soon." Sarah screamed loudly and spat in Marci's face. Marci stepped back and released Sarah, very surprised at Sarah's actions. Marci said, "You fucking shithead. You mother fucking cock sucker!"

I raced toward Marci and tried to pull her from the cell. She was so big and strong, I couldn't budge. Marci screamed at Sarah and for the first time Sarah was so angry she didn't back down. I somewhat controlled Marci and we left the lab. Sarah paced inside the cell. After she calmed down, she went back to praying. I kept Marci away from the lab for a week.

The concept of god, or some ultimate being, has always been a hot topic for everyone in our family. Through the years, my Marci had also grown to hate the concept of god. Wolfgang never truly believed in a god, per se. If he did, it would be rather difficult for him considering the vast number of people that he experimented on and killed throughout his lifetime.

Zelda is indifferent to the subject of religion. I would assume that even if she did believe, her husband wouldn't approve and that would have made it very difficult for her. My adoptive parents never went to any church, but they were not against any god concept either. The other people in my life have always believed in a god and had a religious belief.

I personally have always struggled with the concept of god and a religious affiliation with a certain genre of faith. I always wondered how someone could believe in a being they have never seen. I know there are species of animals that exist in this world that I haven't seen before, but others have seen them so, therefore, they exist. There are some species of animals that some talk about but scientists, and science in general, have not publicly acknowledged; like the concept of a Bigfoot or other strange creatures that roam our earth. Therefore, the question is: does that undiscovered or acknowledged species exist or not? Discovering the existence of my parents was certainly a shock to Lewis, me and others that have personally seen this type of species. If my parents can exist, who's to say that others like my parents don't exist?

That is the great dilemma that is presented to me. Maybe there is a god or some form of a spirit-like being. Maybe it is physical or spiritual. Either way, it is a difficult concept to accept without seeing or experiencing its existence.

I believe that most religions are created to keep the 'general population' under control. Simple minded people, which make up most humans, need hope for the future. Hope is what controls them and stops them from destroying each other in the present. Hope is the longing for a better future. If you knew that you were going to die and there was no afterlife, would you live your life differently than you do currently? Of course you would. Would that be better for mankind in general, for you and your friends to feel that way? Probably not. Why? Because there are a few people in that segment of a population sample that would have no remorse for hurting others or stealing others' personal property. Your more intellectual people would probably not steal, but the lesser minded people would be more inclined to take from others.

Humans are jealous of others. They want what they don't have. Even if they don't need what others possess, that desire of others' possessions is what drives many people. Most people don't want good things to happen to others. It makes them feel bad about themselves.

Animals in the wild don't have these feelings. They are indifferent. Animals take what they need and nothing more. Unless they feel threatened physically or they feel their hunting ground is being invaded, they move on with their lives and allow others to live theirs. It's an interesting concept.

Since Marci was abandoned as a baby, she grew up not having any knowledge of her parents. She never met them nor knows anything about them. They didn't want her. They dropped her off at a place that takes care of unwanted children. She grew up alone and didn't have anyone that truly cared for her. I partly understand the way she feels. My story is similar to hers, but in my case, I had adoptive parents. Of course, my father never really loved or wanted me. My mother feared me so she ended up killing herself in front of me. Thus, without proper guidance, it is challenging to accept a religious belief or a belief in some supreme being.

In my limited experience in religious matters, my main issue with any religion is the hypocritical nature of the model. First, humans created all religions, not a supreme being. Some religions might have been based on some man that was highly thought of a long time ago, and the people that knew of this man created a certain cult following that has lasted throughout time. I find it interesting that all religions seem to be based on a male human that is the divine one, but not a woman. I have difficulty understanding that status quo.

I see many faults in both the religious doctrine that any religion supports and the members of said religion's interpretation of the doctrine's beliefs. A religion preaches that it is a sin to have sex with another man's wife. The cult followers shake their heads in agreement and some even preach to others about the sin being committed by others. Then people find out later that these people are sleeping with other married people. These types of religious frauds are hypocrites.

I've read articles in magazines and newspapers or I see people on cable television talk about certain segments of our society that might prefer intimate relations with the same sex. Their religion or other religions say that God is all loving and forgiving, but is against physical intimacy with the same sex. These people who practice such activities are going to 'hell.' I don't understand that way of thinking. If God is all loving and forgiving, is that God going to condemn a person for having sex with a person of the same sex? Is that not a hypocritical belief? It cheapens that religion's view, does it not? It attacks the very core of those highly prized beliefs.

A religion should be a safe haven for all people to come together, help fill each other's needs, and support everyone in the group. But that's not how religion works. Religion is tainted by humans and their many inadequacies. Most people go through the motions and don't take time to reflect on the true purpose of the basis of their religion. Religious groups are more like cults or highly structured clubs. Even the basis of what any religion preaches is tainted by the hand of man. All these men are imperfect, impure, and unclean versions of a man who preached what they believe is their version of what a perfect human should resemble.

To dig even further into this falsehood of God or a supreme being, if this immortal exists, it is one sadistic aberration. Why would any god allow his own people to suffer? This has been my basic premise since the first day I can remember thinking independently. This leads me to believe that if this deity exists, it is envious of its own creations. Thus, he, she or it doesn't want any of his creations to achieve a high level of excellence. He frowns on any of his creations who might be flawless or superior in any way that might rival his abilities. That must be the answer, right? What father wouldn't want his son to be better than him in either mental or physical capabilities?

Accordingly, at the end of the day and after all the dust settles, Marci and I cannot believe there is such a thing as one invisible supreme being. It doesn't make sense. This issue upsets Marci on many levels. She had to change her physical appearance for us to be together forever. The way we have been treated throughout our lives proves the belief that the inferior one is just a fantasy for the weak minded.

Chapter Nine

The week after Marci's altercation with Sarah, we isolated her from the lab for everyone's best interest. Thanks to the formula's ability to heal rapidly, the twins started to heal and grow together. They would struggle and try to move away from each other, but each time one would move, it would cause extreme pain. After a solid day of figuring out that not moving would cause less pain, the attached parts started to grow together more efficiently. The formula from both twins worked in unison, expediting the healing process. After the second week, the wounds were basically closed. The areas were red and purple but clinically the wound was healed.

Wolfgang x-rayed the twins, and to his surprise some of the ribs were fusing together. There were places, on both twins, where Wolfgang cut too deeply, but the ribs that touched the other set took hold and started to grow as one. After the third week, Wolfgang had the twins standing on their own. In the beginning they lacked coordination. It took them several days to develop synchronization.

They started to walk on their own which was a difficult undertaking. One of the twins had to put their foot in front of them before the other twin could move their leg. To repeat this process continuously was hard for them. After a couple of days, they eventually mastered the task of being able to sit down and stand up together without falling over on one of their sides.

The twins had two separate and completely functioning brains so they were forced to adapt, to work together in order to accomplish even the simplest task, like going to the restroom and relieving themselves. They couldn't sit on a toilet so when they had to make a bowel movement, they had to crouch down somewhat and go on the floor. It was a humiliating task for them, especially when Wolfgang required the creature to clean up after itself.

At times they would have sharp pains in the attached areas. The two bodies kept pulling on each other and several times at those small areas, the skin would split open. The twins were not happy with their newly formed body, but since they didn't have a choice in the matter, they had to deal with the reality at hand.

Wolfgang needed to conduct a few experiments before he eliminated the twins' lives. He wanted to see if one twin could feel the other's pain. He tested out his theory by taking a push pin and sticking it into Emma's arm and seeing if Lucinda would feel it. He ran these tests on their ears, eyes, faces, heads, legs, feet and other areas.

The results came back that the pain was isolated to the individual's body. When one of the fused bodies saw the other half getting hurt, they would scream out in pain as much as the initial one receiving the pain. When one half of the body didn't see the pain coming, the other half didn't immediately cry out. The non-affected twin would eventually cry out when the other started to scream after feeling the pain.

Eli, the smartest of Sarah's children, had been locked away in another cell. Wolfgang had kept him isolated from the others. He gave him the best of the food, kept his cell cleaner than the others, and he kept Eli mentally stimulated, causing Eli to become more advanced than the others. This was no surprise to Wolfgang. If you alter one's environment, even slightly, that change affects the mindset of the person, thus changing their personality and development.

What confused my father was how far advanced Eli was over the others. From out the womb, Eli had a higher intellect than his siblings. In theory, the formula creates the fetuses, while in the womb, to have different traits from the others. Some traits in one fetus should be more enhanced than the others, but overall, their unique traits should equal out. Wolfgang couldn't understand why Eli was different from the others.

Meanwhile, Sarah was struggling with all that had happened to her. For the first time in her life, she was truly struggling with accepting what God had bestowed upon her and her children. Her internal struggle with her faith was very alarming to Sarah. She knew her surroundings were getting inside of her head and soul. Seeing her two daughters struggling to walk around the cell after being attached to each other tested her sanity.

Wolfgang was aware of this part of the physical transformation and how difficult it would be for the host, not to mention bearing mutated creatures. Transforming was the easy part. Dealing with the newly formed body was the most difficult part of the acceptance. The mind controls all your senses. It controls your heartrate, brainwaves, and any part of your body. Learning to control your feelings, your state of being and your emotions, is of utmost importance.

Wolfgang and I spoke with Marci about trying to control her emotions, especially when it came to Sarah. Marci said she would promise to do better, but we knew that would be difficult. Wolfgang told Marci that he was getting to a point where he had no use for Sarah and the conjoined twins. Marci was happy that Sarah and her children were going to be out of her life soon. They were a constant reminder of what Marci wanted more than anything else in this world, but she couldn't succumb to her desires. In the back of Marci's twisted mind, she toyed with the idea of keeping Sarah around as some sort of pet. Marci approached Wolfgang and I about this idea. Wolfgang was not for it one bit; I, on the other hand, didn't care. I was for whatever made my Marci happy.

The problem with Sarah was that she was so large. She weighed a little over four hundred pounds. The other issue was that we had to be careful not to have her bite anything and have that bit animal escape into the wild. Wolfgang hated the idea of Sarah being Eva's pet.

Marci was the only person in the house that took care of any pet while Eva was off at Juilliard. Wolfgang couldn't comprehend why Marci would want another pet creature around the house. It was just something else to take care of and a major potential problem.

Wolfgang was getting annoyed with Marci. Marci's obsession with Sarah wasn't healthy in his view, but he liked Marci. He had gone to great lengths to please her many times over the years.

Marci knew that this was her last chance with Sarah and thought about how she would murder Sarah's children. Marci needed to end this hatred for her own good and for the sake of everyone living in the house.

Sarah had never stopped praying throughout this entire experience. She knew her situation was bleak. She had no hope. Her situation was like the captive Jews' experienced in Nazi Germany. I often wondered what I would do if I was in her place. You can try to rationalize your situation to a point where you can make yourself temporarily comfortable then you ultimately come to the point of reality. You begin to understand that no matter how much time you spend trying to console yourself over a bad twist of fate, reality is always there to remind you of your destiny. You can give up, but you are still alive. Giving up might cause you more pain than if you had hope of surviving your fate.

Sarah was a lone voice in a wilderness filled with a vast amount of voices that despised everything she possessed to know to be good. She was in a world that hated what she stood for, worshipped and treasured, what she thought was important. It was a powerful juxtaposition of two opposite cultures and their different worlds, the contrast of the world of the pretend versus the world of realism. In this case, we had a person who was asking for forgiveness over an apparent sin that was not of their creation. She was taught to automatically assume that they were the root of a sin instead of the victim of a sin.

On the other hand, we had a group of people that were reaching out for answers to make their lives and the lives of many others better. This group was on the other end of a spectrum that sees the world differently, a world where people rely on themselves or others that are physically visible instead of relying on folktale of yesteryear. As a witness and participant in this marvelous ebb and flow of two completely different ideals, it was just fascinating to experience, especially when you knew the final outcome.

Life is a metaphor of classical opera with so many subtitles with various meanings and interpretations to digest and understand. In life, you will laugh and you will cry. You will fight and you will surrender. You will love and you will hate. You will live for a while then you will die. Therefore, you accept the lines that have been given to you because you have no choice but to do so. You must accept reality.

Sarah's constant praying aggravated Wolfgang. He constantly heard her prayers and would violently tell her to stop. He would physically hit her repeatedly to make her stop, but she just prayed louder. Marci would occasionally come downstairs unannounced, and as soon as Sarah saw Marci, she would get on her knees and pray out loud. Wolfgang was finally fed up with it and told Marci that he wanted it to end.

One night, Wolfgang and Marci decided they needed to take care of the Sarah situation. Marci wanted me to assist them. As in most cases, Zelda chose to stay upstairs. My mother always liked her quiet time. She would either listen to music or sing along to an aria from a German opera.

Marci and I walked hand in hand while we followed my father downstairs to his lab. As we made our entrance, Sarah immediately started praying. Marci quickly said, "Will you shut the fuck up! Damn, that is so annoying. Every time I get in your sight, you start that fucking praying. Doesn't that ever get tiresome?" Sarah continued to pray.

Wolfgang walked over to his desk and pulled out two tranquillizer darts. He went to his closet and located two short wrist chains and told Marci to take them from him. Wolfgang reached for a pair of long industrial pliers made especially for thick and heavy chains. He reached for his tranquillizer gun and loaded it without saying a word as he walked over to Sarah's cell. He pointed the gun at her, but she wasn't paying any attention to what was going on outside of her barred home. Wolfgang aimed and shot Sarah in the front part of her shoulder. She quickly yelled and pulled the dart out. As soon as she looked up, the second dart hit her other shoulder. The drug started to take effect. She fell forward, with her hands slowing her fall.

Wolfgang told Marci to open the cell door and go inside. Wolfgang and I followed her. Wolfgang pulled the neck and torso chains out of the wall and quickly placed them around Sarah's neck and waist areas. Marci attached the clasps around Sarah's wrist. She attached the wrist chain to the larger chain coming out of the wall then used the pliers to pry open the last chain and attach it to the large chain coming out of the wall. Marci secured the link with the pliers so Sarah's arm would be restricted from full movement.

Wolfgang left the cell and went back to his workstation. He opened a drawer and pulled out a drill. He searched around in another drawer and pulled out a roll of thick wire that was the size of a pencil. He measured by sight and cut three twelve-inch-long pieces. He picked up a large pair of pliers and wire cutters, as well as a large two-inch steel pipe that was about three feet long then made his way back inside the cell. He laid these items down on Sarah's bed. Sarah was starting to come out of her drowsiness. The formula was attacking the tranquillizer so Wolfgang only had a few minutes left.

Wolfgang walked out of the cell and over to the area where the wall chain was attached to the pulley. He hit the retracting button and the chains started to pull Sarah back toward the wall. Marci and I helped Sarah to her feet and tried to walk her back as far as we could. When she started to come out of her daze, we let her go and allowed the pulley to do all the work. When she started realizing what was happening, she started to fight the chains. The pulley drew her backward, and in a matter of moments, Sarah's head and back were against the wall. Her arms were around her waist, pulling and tugging in the attempt to free herself, but she couldn't move her arms above her waist.

Wolfgang calmly walked over and picked up his drill. He squeezed a few times on the trigger to see if the drill worked. Sarah's eyes were fixated on the spinning. Each tug on the drill caused Sarah's body to flinch violently. Wolfgang placed a bit inside his drill, tightened it in place, and walked over to Sarah. Sarah let out a blood-curdling scream.

Wolfgang said to Marci, "Hold your hand under her neck and your other hand on the top of the forehead. Press her head against the wall." Marci did as she was instructed. Wolfgang said, "Now move her head to the side."

As Marci moved Sarah's head she said, "This is so fun."

Wolfgang took the long steel pipe and placed it between Sarah's upper and lower teeth. Marci tried to keep the pipe in her mouth. Wolfgang took his large index and middle fingers and pushed them up inside Sarah's mouth. He moved his fingers up to expose the light pink flesh of her gums. Wolfgang said, "Hold her head steady." Wolfgang placed his other fingers around her jaw for more support. He took his drill and held it near Sarah's face. He calmly placed the drill bit on the side of Sarah's upper gum line, turned it on, and as quickly as he could, pressed the drill bit into her gum. Every inch of her body tightened. It took all of Marci's strength to keep her as still as possible. Sarah bit down on the pipe, causing a few of her teeth to crack. Wolfgang quickly moved his drill to Sarah's upper front gum line. He moved his two fingers across her gums, pulling back her lips so he could see his predetermined targets. Without hesitation, he drilled a hole into the front of her gums. Wolfgang repeated the same drilling procedure for the side and front of Sarah's lower gums.

Sarah's mouth felt like it was on fire. Her teeth loosen their grip on the steel bar because biting it hurt even more. Marci was still struggling to keep Sarah's head still. Through her tussles, the iron bar slid out of Sarah's mouth and fell onto the tiled floor. Wolfgang moved the drill around to the other side of Sarah's mouth as Marci moved Sarah's head toward her so Wolfgang could get a better look. Wolfgang again put two of his long fingers into Sarah's mouth and drilled one hole in the upper gum and one in the lower gum. He backed away and placed the drill down on the cot beside them. He picked up the steel rod and wires. My father didn't want her to bite his fingers so he placed the steel rod back between Sarah's teeth.

Marci repositioned her long fingers and hands over Sarah's head, cupping Sarah's chin with the palm of her right hand while holding the steel rod with her thumb and first two fingers. Wolfgang proceeded to take one of the wires and thread it through the new holes in the back, upper portion of Sarah's gum. He then took the threaded end and looped it through the back opening of the lower gum. Sarah was in great pain each time the wire moved and touched the wounded holes in her gums. Wolfgang continued to thread the wire through the top and bottom holes of her front gums. He proceeded to thread the other side as well, making sure to have both ends of each of the three wires come out of Sarah's upper and lower gums.

My father quickly pulled the steel rod out of Sarah's teeth and told Marci to close Sarah's mouth as rapidly as she could. Marci held Sarah's mouth shut as Wolfgang twisted the wires together. Sarah moaned and struggled mightily while in a great deal of pain. He went back with his pliers and twisted each of the three wires together even tighter. Each twist sent a shocking pain throughout Sarah's body. Her entire body was again drenched in sweat. I watched her wrist bleed from struggling for release. She was powerless to stop his perverse yet delightful plan.

When Wolfgang was finished, he stepped back and ordered Marci to release her hold on Sarah. We all stood in amusement, watching Sarah's head move from side to side, up and down, trying to relieve her pain in any way she could. Her neck chain cut deeply into the front part of her neck, causing the skin to break. We heard a snap and when I looked down, Sarah had broken her wrist while trying to escape. Sarah was writhing in pain. She was writhing like a trapped snake under a large rock. She pounded her feet on the hard tile floor, trying anything she could to escape her torture and agony.

Wolfgang walked out of the cell and retrieved a spool of thick thread and a sewing needle. He walked back into the cell as Sarah started screaming even louder through her closed mouth. She started to kick with all her might, but her kicks were limited by the chains that bound her. Again, Marci assisted without being asked. She held Sarah's massive head as still as possible while Wolfgang threaded his needle with the thick, yarn-like thread. He tied the end of the long piece of thread, reached over and pinched Sarah's upper and lower lips together with his forefinger and thumb then took the needle and expertly ran it through her lips. Sarah had to endure the warm, stinging sensation of the needle passing through her lips then she sensed the thick thread as it slid through the thin layers of her skin. Wolfgang continued to sew Sarah's lips together in six separate places. When he was finished, he cut the thick yarn and left several inches of it dangling from Sarah's bloodied lips.

I watched Sarah closely. She cried so hard that her blood pressure must have been at an all-time high. She sobbed as tears streamed down her face, mixing with the blood streaming from her mouth. Hordes of thick drops of blood seeped from her tightened lips. Sarah couldn't spit out the amount of blood that she wanted so she had to swallow most of the red liquid. Suddenly, her body just stopped and she went into shock. She was fully aware of her surroundings, but her body needed a break from the pain. I remembered Adam's body doing the same after prolonged torture. The body can only take so much damage then it has to shut down. We all knew what the formula was doing inside of Sarah's mouth. It repairing what was damaged.

Wolfgang collected his tools and walked out of the cell. Marci and I followed his lead. I asked, "So, what are you going to do with her?"

Marci quickly stated, "Starve her to death."

Wolfgang smiled and said, "We used to sew up some of the Jews' lips in our concentration camps. Some would die a slow death from malnutrition but some of them would break their lips free from the thread. They would pull and slowly separate their lips from one another. In cases where the subjects didn't have the constitution to do this, we would document how long they could survive. So, in her case I would assume this process will be much longer than our previous subjects." I looked over toward Sarah and her large eyes just blinked in utter terror. She wanted to die. It was the only way out of her situation, but Wolfgang and Marci were not going to grant her that wish anytime soon.

I often pondered the concept of the very essence of pain. What is pain? Obviously, you have two different forms; one is emotional and the other is physical. Emotional pain tortures the very core of what you perceive as meaningful in your life. It is the hardest to overcome. Physical pain is typically temporary but is the most feared.

For the well-educated species, emotional pain is the greater evil. A subject will eventually overcome the physical torment that might plague their life. To overthrow a pain that you cannot see, touch or treat with any medicine is an extremely difficult feat. Sometimes these pains marry and mutate into a much different type of pain. This realm of suffering is a combination of constant pain from both the imagination and the physical worlds. It is at this point that the subject loses the most important element to survival. That element is hope, a desire or a will to live. At this stage is where a creature, either human or animal, is at the crossroads of their existence, being at their most vulnerable or most dangerous point.

Wolfgang had taught us many things including how, in his experience with torturing and killing thousands of people, a tortured subject is at their most dangerous point when they are close to the end of their life. I find this also true with killing animals for my food. When they are attacked or captured, their instincts will cause them to strike out at their predator. Humans are no different.

Instinct is what all living animals have in common. Instinct is having the innate ability to detect and predict, with some relative certainty, of how an animal or human will react. It might be immediate or prolonged, but that ability to foresee the impending act could be the difference between death and life for the observer.

Wolfgang warned us that Sarah was now at her most dangerous. He warned us to be careful and to anticipate her attacking at any moment. Sarah was still scared but not as much as she was from the start of her abduction.

As I watched Sarah in such pain, I could sense her hatred mixed with feelings of self-pity. She had never experienced such feelings, emotions and despair. She wondered why her God was allowing this to happen to her. She had time to reflect, even through the monumental pain she was experiencing. Waves of hatred mixed with waves of forgiveness came at her from every angle. Her emotions were so conflicted. All her life she had been taught that God was good, and that He was a forgiving and healing God. He was someone in which a person could find refuge in time of great need.

Sarah sat on her cot, reflecting on what had happened to her over the past few months. She felt blood dripping down the back of her throat with her pounding mouth and gums that felt as if they were on fire. Every inch of her body ached and her mind was tired of pain. She was trapped in a world that wasn't allowing her any rest. This was the time of epic despair that she would never have dreamt of undergoing. She prayed, begged and wished for her experience to end. She had witnessed the death of her son, the torture of her two daughters and herself, and she knew the end was not going to be any better. She knew she was going to witness the death of her remaining children. Sarah was face to face with reality, and called upon her God for help, but her God was not answering her needs.

I noticed Sarah occasionally looking down at her new body and shaking her head in disgust. Her impure thoughts of questioning her God made her internal soul quiver at its core. Thoughts of knowing she could never return to her former way of life were slowly eroding her constitution. She would look down and see a strange new body that, in her mind, was so grotesque it made her sick to her stomach. The thought of God abandoning her made for some horrifying thoughts in her incarcerated and self-perceived evil world.

We left Sarah to lament all her feelings for a day or so. She spent most of this time crying, praying, and loathing her situation and all who caused this evil to happen. The sight of her conjoined twins reaching out to their mother was too much for Sarah to take. Her heart felt like it was being ripped apart. She was helpless and could do nothing for them. The twins didn't understand why their mother was not coming to their rescue and they verbally wondered why she had allowed this to happen to them.

Marci and my father loved to play with people's emotions. My father enjoyed torturing Sarah and her children. He had forgotten how much he enjoyed this unique form of entertainment. What made this even more enjoyable was seeing the pleasure Marci derived from these acts of ungodliness. I had taken an inventory of my internal emotions during this time as well, and I must admit that I enjoyed seeing the suffering of others also. I especially enjoyed the punishment of the people that deserved to be chastised.

I believe it is more difficult to punish a group than it is to punish an individual from that group. For my father and my love, Sarah and her children represented a group, a section of people that they loathed. To torture a few was like torturing the group to them. It gave them pleasure and a sense of redemption. That is what many don't understand. It's not always about the individual, it's what that individual represents.

We gave Sarah several days to recover. I walked behind my love as we made our way to Wolfgang's lab. Marci's scent was heavy. Her beautiful body excreted a wonderful, gamey scent whenever she became excited. That scent was an aphrodisiac for me.

Marci hurried her stride to enter the laboratory and greeted my father. She looked at Sarah who was now free to roam half of her cell in chains. I noticed that she had lost several pounds.

The formula was working on repairing her gums and lips. The areas where the yarn was imbedded in her lips were reddish-pink in color. I looked down at her broken wrist and saw a bone that was misplaced under her skin.

The 'twins' were in the other cell. They looked at Marci and me, immediately becoming restless, sensing something was going to happen. Marci unlocked the cell and walked inside. The twins moved backward as fast as they could but suddenly one of them tripped and they fell backward. Marci laughed at the comical sight. I heard Sarah moan and her motherly instinct caused her to lunge toward them. The chains made an eerie but interestingly musical sound. The shackles stopped her, causing pain.

Sarah temporarily forgot about her mouth being wired shut. She attempted to yell which further increased her pain. Marci went over to the twins and picked them up. She roughly pulled on Lucinda's half, causing the twins extreme pain. Their halves were almost completely healed but they were still sore. The twin's heads were moving from side to side as they were following Marci, who they didn't like and were afraid of.

Marci took her large hands and held the twins by their shoulders then bent down between their heads. It was a long way down for my Marci since the twins were almost half Marci's height. Marci said, "Now be still, my pretties." Marci rose up quickly and moved to the side of the twins. She looked down and with her right foot, kicked Emma's leg out about a foot from her body. Marci's firm grip on the twins' shoulders held them in place. She quickly raised her perfectly formed foot in the air. Without any hesitation, Marci's foot came down with colossal force on the lower portion of Emma's leg. I heard a crunching sound and as I looked down I saw where Marci had caused a compound fracture on Emma's leg. The tibia and fibula were completely broken in two. Marci let the twins' body fall to the floor.

Emma was screaming in pain. Marci looked down and saw Emma's leg bent in the shape of an L. Lucinda didn't feel the pain but when she fell with Emma, she hit her chin on the hard tile floor, causing a laceration.

Sarah was moaning and attempting to scream through her wire-closed mouth and sewn-closed lips. Marci looked back at Sarah and smiled. She said, "Oh, my. I bet that hurt like a bitch."

Marci laughed and walked over to Lucinda's side of the intertwined body. Marci seductively looked at Sarah as she placed her right foot in the middle of Lucinda's leg. She bent down and with her right hand took hold of Lucinda's ankle. Marci said to Sarah, "Now beg for me not to break its other leg."

Sarah's screams were muffled, trying with all her might. Sarah was so distraught that every inch of her body was struggling to free itself from the chains. Marci smiled and said, "I'm sorry, I can't hear you. What did you say?"

Sarah tried to scream louder but the muffled sound couldn't be any louder. Marci's facial expression changed. A serious look formed on her face. She screamed at Sarah, "I cannot hear you!! Again! Beg for me not to break this leg in two. I want to hear you say it and I want it to be clear."

Sarah's body was pulling hard on the chains. She tried to be as clear as she could. She started to grunt the words, "I... beg... you... please... don't... break... her... leg."

Marci said, "I can't understand you. Say it again!"

Sarah moved her large head from side to side, struggling with grief, pain and frustration.

Marci looked down at Lucinda and said, "You. Freak. Look at me."

Lucinda looked up at Marci and said, "Please don't. Please."

Marci smiled and said, "Fuck you."

Without warning, Marci pulled Lucinda's leg up, breaking it in two. The cracking sound was intense. Lucinda let out an incredible scream. Her cries were much different from Emma's, who was screaming in her own distinct tone next to her.

Sarah's body was pulled to the max. She tried with all her might to free herself from her chains. She backed up a little and rushed forward, attempting to bust the chains in two.

Marci walked toward the far end of the twins' cell near Sarah's chained imprisonment. Marci said, "How does it feel to be in so much pain? Hmm? It gets me very horny."

Sarah started to feel rage, and her hatred for Marci increased. She felt pure, unadulterated hate. Marci sensed this feeling and loved it. She said, "I feel your hate toward me. If you think you hate me now, just wait until you see what I'm going to do to your little freaks."

Marci walked toward the twins, bent down, grabbed and extended Lucinda's right arm high above her head. Marci turned Lucinda to face her mother. She interlocked Lucinda's elbow with hers, and with Marci's free hand, she grasped Lucinda's wrist and started to pull it downward. The pressure of Marci's grip and the bending of the wrist in an unnatural direction was too much on Lucinda's forearm. Within seconds the bones cracked and the arm was unnaturally bent. Lucinda cried harder than ever before.

Sarah's hate for Marci was growing stronger by the minute. Marci quickly moved on to Emma's arm. She applied enough pressure and at the last moment, she jerked her arm in one direction while she pulled in the other. Crack! Emma's arm was broken in a similar fashion to Lucinda's.

The lab was filled with sounds of the twins screaming, mixed with Sarah's moaning and grunting. Sarah's rage was beyond a motherly love for her children. She was beyond angry and filled with hatred. She wanted a piece of Marci. She wanted her dead. Everything that Sarah had been taught throughout her life was now questioned. She had completely turned her back on her God. Multiple impure and evil thoughts raced through her shattered soul. This was the first time she had ever willfully wanted to commit a mortal sin. The commandment, "Thy shalt not kill" was forgotten.

Marci stepped away from the entwined human pretzel. She looked down and saw legs and arms pointing in strange but humorous directions. Lucinda and Emma's heads were thrashing around, screaming while in great pain. Every time one would move, it would cause the other more pain.

Sarah motioned with her hands as if to say, *Don't move and lay still.* Lucinda and Emma didn't pay attention to their mother's gestures. Sarah pulled even harder on her chains, trying to get closer to her children. Each pull caused more pain to Sarah's waist, neck, ankles and wrists. Sarah looked at Marci and mumbled, "You evil twisted... bitch! I am going to kill you for this!" Even though her gums were wired shut and her mouth sewn up, the words could still be deciphered.

Marci laughed at Sarah's mumbled words. She said, "So you do get angry and you have the ability to say bad things. I was beginning to wonder. So... are you going to pray to your pretend god or have you finally reached the conclusion that the fraud just doesn't exist?"

Sarah couldn't shout back. She thought, *God is all powerful. Vengeance is mine says the Lord*, but not this time. Sarah knew that this time God would understand. She knew Marci was the devil and that she must be defeated in the name of God.

Marci looked at Sarah and quickly said, "Oh shut up. Just shut the fuck up, you piece of shit. You are like a broken record. I know what you are saying. You are trying to say something about that fucking god shit. Just give in to the hate, bitch. I know you want to kill me because I hurt the people you love. You don't hate me because you think I am some fucking devil. I mean, really? You hate me because I have hurt you and the ones that you hold so dear to your fucking, pathetic little heart. Damn you and your god."

Sarah moaned loudly and tried to utter the words, "God is an ever-loving God..."

Marci interrupted her saying, "Oh fuck off!" She stormed out of the cell and went directly to Wolfgang's closet where he housed numerous tools and other items of torture. She picked up an ax and ran back to the cell.

Sarah was moaning even louder, "No! No! For the love of God, no!!!"

Marci stood next to Emma's side of the twins' body. Both girls turned their heads toward Marci with a look of sheer terror. Marci looked over her shoulder and smiled at Sarah. She said, "Watch this, you fucking cunt."

Marci turned her head toward Emma then pulled the ax over her head. Without saying a word, she dropped the ax in a downward motion. The blade of the ax went directly into the back of Emma's neck. Lucinda started to scream. The ax hit the tile floor and bounced back a foot. Emma's screams were silenced quickly. The ax separated most of the neck from the torso. Only a few muscles were attached at the back portion of the head. Marci bent down toward the pool of blood. Blood splatters were everywhere, especially over Lucinda's head and facial area. Marci grabbed Emma's lifeless head in her left hand, took the ax, and slammed it a couple times on the tissue that was still attached. Marci gave one last forceful tug, the remaining muscles snapped and the head was completely severed.

Marci rose to her feet to the sound of Sarah screaming. She saw the lifeless body lying in a pool of blood pouring out of Emma's severed head area. Lucinda was terrified; she wanted to get away not only from Marci but also from Emma's now dead body that was attached to her. Marci looked over at me and smiled. She said, "Listen to these two. What beautiful music they make."

Marci laughed so loud that it almost hurt my ears. Her mighty, roaring laugh was beautiful but haunting at the same time. The juxtaposition of Marci's pure, twisted joy and the immense suffering that was evidenced in the voices of both Lucinda and her mother was inebriating. Marci turned her sexily-shaped body and walked out of the cell, holding Emma's head by her hair.

Sarah fell to her knees and was a slobbering mess as large tears poured out of her eyes. Marci opened Sarah's cell door and stepped inside, quickly tossing Emma's head toward her. Sarah's reaction was priceless. At first she reached out for the head coming at her, but at the last moment she pulled her hands away. Emma's head hit and bounced off her chest. Sarah attempted to catch her daughter's head, but it was too late. The head hit the floor and rolled out of the reach of Sarah's outstretched arms. Sarah tried to let out a scream, but forgot that her gums were wired together. The wire pulled on the gums, causing Sarah to quickly reach for her mouth. She was in great physical pain and every nerve in her gums ached.

Marci violently laughed so hard that she had to bend over to catch her breath. After she recovered, she walked toward Emma's head and kicked it with her bare foot. The head rolled toward Sarah who was kneeling on the floor in pain. Emma's head bounced off Sarah's legs and rolled a few feet in front of her. Sarah instinctually reached for her daughter's head. As her long fingers reached out, one of her index fingers brushed against part of the broken bone that was protruding from her neck. Sarah jerked her hand back and almost touched her sewn mouth with the finger that was covered in blood from her daughter's head. Sarah sobbed as she couldn't bear to look at it resting on the floor. After several moments, she looked up at Marci. Another great wave of anger filled her heart. Marci's eyes didn't leave Sarah's. She stood there smiling with all her long, sharp teeth showing. The moment was broken by a loud gasp from Lucinda.

Marci quickly turned and ran out of the cell. As she passed my father and I she said, "This is so much fucking fun." She went inside of the cell that housed Lucinda. Marci reached down and with both hands took hold of Lucinda's hair and pulled her to the entrance of the cell. Lucinda's body wouldn't fit through the entrance so Marci had to turn the body over on its side. Marci then drug Lucinda's wounded body to Sarah's cell.

When Marci finally got Lucinda's body into the cell, she released it, allowing it to hit the floor. Marci made sure Lucinda was just out of Sarah's reach. Lucinda was lying on the floor and wouldn't stop crying. She had just witnessed her sister's beheading from the same torso as hers. Although she didn't feel Emma's pain, mentally she was losing control of her wits. Lucinda's arm and leg hurt badly, but just knowing that her sister's beheaded body was still attached to hers revolted her, causing her to dry heave multiple times.

Marci walked toward Sarah as she watched and studied every inch of Marci's walk. Marci knew exactly how far Sarah's chains would reach from the wall and got dangerously close to that threshold. Sarah swiftly lunged toward Marci only to be stopped just a few inches from her. Sarah struggled with all her might, trying to get a finger on Marci. Marci stared at Sarah as she swung her large head from one side of her body to the other. Marci said, "You are so filled with hate... aren't you?"

Their eyes met and locked. Without warning, Marci hit Sarah in the mouth, causing Sarah to hit the floor, holding her mouth. Marci's punch was so hard that every pain sensor in Sarah's mouth lit up. The pain was so intense that Sarah looked as if she was going to pass out. Marci reached down and picked up Emma's head, bringing it over to Lucinda and placing it next to her face. Lucinda turned the other way, screaming. Marci grabbed Lucinda's head and held it in place while again moving Emma's head next to Lucinda's. Lucinda was so scared and grossed out at the same time that she started to have convulsions. Marci took Emma's head and acted like it was kissing Lucinda. Marci got the biggest kick out of the torment. After several moments, Marci got up and rolled Emma's head over to Sarah as if it was a bowling ball. Sarah was in so much pain that she could hardly react.

As Marci left the cell, I quickly closed and locked the cell door. Sarah was still in such excruciating pain that she could hardly move. Lucinda continued to cry as she lay helplessly on the floor. Her sister's blood was all over her face, but she couldn't wipe her face clean because of her badly bent and damaged arm. I stood there thinking how helpless these creatures must feel. You must admit that at least once in everyone's life, the thought of suicide had entered the thoughts of the depressed. Just imagine if you were in so much pain that suicide would be a gift of mercy or a vehicle of relief, then to have that taken from you because you just couldn't physically kill yourself. Imagine how helpless you would feel. Every waking moment you felt that everlasting pain. It just kept pulsating through your body, wave after wave of incredible agony. Imagine being so completely helpless that no one would come to your rescue because they were getting too much pleasure out of watching you in pain. That must be the worst situation a person could find themselves in; hopeless, powerless, and in constant suffering without end.

Marci walked toward Wolfgang and said, "I wonder how long that thing will live with that attached, rotting corpse."

Wolfgang smiled and said, "In her situation, probably forever."

Sarah was slowly recovering. As she began to get control of her senses, she tried to reach for Lucinda, but she was again out of her reach. Lucinda was in so much pain that she didn't want to make any attempt to move toward her mother. Sarah couldn't speak but her grunting out the words were somewhat understandable to Lucinda. She tried a few times to move, but the pain was too great. Both mom and daughter wanted and needed each other. They wanted to hold each other, thinking that would help with the pain as well as their situation. But the several feet of space that kept them apart was like miles to them. Sarah tried many times to get to her daughter, but her struggles further hurt her.

The next morning, Marci went inside the cell. She gently and slowly pushed Lucinda toward Sarah's outstretched arms. Marci made sure Sarah's first touch was Emma's dead body. Lucinda was screaming in pain. Every inch that she was pushed on the floor caused more intense pain. After several long, agonizing moments, Sarah finally got to her daughter. Sarah quickly pulled Lucinda toward her and attempted to calm and soothe Lucinda's pain. Sarah felt so helpless in her attempt to console her daughter.

Several days passed as we left Sarah and her daughter alone. Both were very hungry. Wolfgang finally threw an apple and a banana into the cell. Sarah quickly grabbed the fruit and helped Lucinda eat. Sarah, of course, couldn't partake in any food rations because of her sewn-closed mouth.

As the days passed, Lucinda's crooked bones started healing. Sarah was very concerned. She knew the bones would grow crooked. Sarah knew that she had to at least attempt to reset the bones to the best of her ability. Sarah swallowed hard and started to bend Lucinda's arm back into the correct position. Lucinda screamed loudly and begged for her mother to stop the torturous act. This was one of the most difficult challenges Sarah had ever had to endure. To cause pain on your own daughter had to be torture for her.

After she straightened the arm, Sarah moved on to Lucinda's leg. Lucinda was screaming, "No, Momma, No. It hurts. Please don't."

Tears were falling from Sarah's large eyes. She could only grunt out the words, "I'm sorry. I'm so sorry, my dear."

Sarah adjusted the leg as Lucinda cried out even louder. Lucinda screamed at her mother, "Oh, God... it hurts so... bad, Momma. Please... kill me! Please kill... me! For the... love of God, kill me."

Marci ran down the stairs to get inside the lab. She looked at Lucinda's adjusted arm and leg. Lucinda cried so hard she vomited and her chest was heaving. Sarah sat there with her hand on Lucinda's chest, trying to console her. She felt so powerless. Suddenly, Lucinda's breathing slowed and she passed out.

Sarah rocked back and forth as her large hands covered her face. Her cries were sorrowful as if she was asking her God to forgive what she had just done. Marci could hear Sarah talking to herself through her gritted teeth. "Oh, my God... please forgive me... oh please forgive me. Oh, God... help me."

After Sarah was finished, she looked over and saw Marci, whose large, dominant body was pressed against the bars of her cell. Marci didn't say a word, she just smiled. Sarah's hatred for Marci grew even stronger, but at this point her thoughts were on her daughter and her own life. Sarah was getting hungrier. It had been a while since she had eaten anything. All the stress from witnessing the death of her daughter and son, and the endless pain from her gums and lips were taking their toll on her body.

A few days passed, and Lucinda's arm and leg were improving as the formula was rapidly working at repairing the broken bones. She was still in a great deal of pain, but she was improving each day. Emma's decaying carcass was still attached to Lucinda's body. The flesh was turning in color and was now looking leathery in appearance. Liquids were coming out of the dead portion of the body, especially in the anus area. The smell was horrific and Lucinda was beside herself. She pleaded with her mother to help her.

Sarah was powerless and didn't feel well at all. Her body was lacking nourishment, causing her to become weaker by the hour. She had lost a considerable amount of weight and body mass. At times, she looked delusional but suddenly the formula would correct that symptom and Sarah would come back to her right state of mind. This constant juxtaposition between feeling horrible one minute and then having her body repair it the next was confusing for Sarah's emotional state. Waves of pain followed by waves of fleeting relief was almost more painful to endure than experiencing normal stages of suffering.

Wolfgang was particularly interested in how long Sarah would last. He had never starved any of his experiments who had the formula inside them. In theory, Formula L should keep the subject alive, but the mystery was for how long. Also unknown was the physical state of the subject over this period. The formula could only repair what isn't correct to the body. At what point would the formula still be effective when extreme and constant malnourishment became an issue?

Wolfgang continued to monitor Sarah and Lucinda, who were one of the most interesting experiments my father had been a part of. Marci was getting annoyed with Wolfgang treating this situation as an experiment and taking over her enjoyment. He wanted to keep the two specimens alive for as long as they would live. He wanted to test the formula to see just how far its boundaries were in trying to repair tissue that was dead. He was extremely interested in how the formula would react to a body that was not getting any nourishment. These were areas that neither Wolfgang nor I had explored.

Another week passed, and Lucinda's extremities had almost healed, but she was sick. Lucinda was not in her right state of mind. The toxins that were inside Emma's decaying body were making Lucinda sick. When Emma died, her body temperature fell, causing the formula to die. The formula in Emma body was dead and could never be regenerated to its previous state. Lucinda's formula had to work harder to stave off both Emma's toxins and the repairing of the arm and leg. Lucinda had a yellowish tint to her skin tone. She felt bad and looked worse. She begged everyone to kill her.

Sarah was on the verge of losing her mind. She was starving, had lost a lot of weight, was weak, and began hallucinating often. You could tell that every time her daughter begged for someone to kill her, it bothered Sarah terribly. Seeing Lucinda move around the floor like a snake was hard for her to accept. Her arms weren't strong enough to pick up the living half of her body, so for her to move, Lucinda taught herself to slither across the floor.

Sarah heard everything that we talked about. We didn't keep any information from our two specimens. Lucinda was trapped inside of her own body and Sarah couldn't communicate with her daughter. Her lips were now starting to grow together. She knew that her jaw muscles were adjusting to their new position. It had been so long since she had opened her mouth, even if she'd had the opportunity to do so, she didn't know if she could because of atrophy.

Many thoughts come to mind when you're in a desperate situation. So many ideas are configured inside your brain about what to do to change your fate. I knew it was hard for Sarah to balance the hatred verses the forgiveness that she had been taught all her life. Her emotions were in a constant battle with one another; good versus evil.

I noticed Sarah looking down at her daughter struggling to slither across the floor. Marci placed Lucinda's food at the far end of the cell, far out of Sarah's reach. Thus, for Lucinda to get her food, she had to retrieve it herself. Many times she would just eat the food off the plate. She would attempt to move her only arm, but it was too painful for her to move it toward her mouth, much less grab ahold of food. The atrophy that set in made her movements even more limited.

On other occasions, Lucinda would bite the plate of food and drag it across the floor toward her mother. Sarah would then help feed her, which made Sarah fall further into depression. Tears, which had become her familiar friend, appeared in her large eyes. As she looked around the lab, her eyes caught mine. She moved toward me until her chains stopped her movement. She reached her arms out to me, muttering words that I couldn't understand. She quickly looked over at Wolfgang and started to plead with him. She closed her right hand to make a weak attempt at a fist. She moved her hand up and down in quick motions. She was saying, "aaaaaacccc…aaaaaccccc."

Marci looked over and said, "What the fuck is she saying now?"

Sarah continued to repeat her movements. She brought her forearm up and pointed her other hand out and was signaling a chopping motion.

Marci stated to laugh. She said, "The bitch wants an ax." Marci moved over to the cell and said, "Is that what you want? An ax?"

Sarah vigorously nodded yes. Wolfgang said, "Be careful, she might throw that at one of us."

Marci said, "We can't give you an ax, my dear. You might kill yourself and we don't want that, now do we?"

Sarah pleaded with Marci. Lucinda looked up and said, "Momma, please kill me. Please."

Marci looked at Wolfgang and said, "You're not going to allow this, are you? Your experiment is not over, Wolfgang."

Wolfgang looked at my Marci and nodded. He said, "It's not time."

Another week passed, and Sarah had lost almost half of her body weight and her head looked half as wide. Her skin was wrinkled and her eyes looked to have contracted into her head an inch. Emma's deceased body continued to rot, and the smell was pungent. Zelda started to complain to Wolfgang about the smell. Even he was bothered by the stench.

Sarah could barely move. She had little to no strength. Lucinda was so sick and not able to recover from Emma's toxins. Sarah looked around and suddenly a wave of energy passed through her. She shook her skinny but long head as if to say she couldn't do what she was thinking.

Lucinda sensed her mother was going to act. She hoped beyond all hope that this was finally going to be the end of her life. Sarah struggled to get up. She made her way to Lucinda who was within her reach. Sarah placed her hands on the rotting flesh of her dead daughter. Her body was starting to fall away from Lucinda's. Sarah closed her large eyes and took a deep breath. When she opened her eyes, she felt as if she had her old strength back. She reached and took hold of her dead daughter's flesh and started to pull the skin from the bones. At first nothing was coming off so Sarah had to dig her fingers down into the rotting flesh. She pulled gently at first, and her sorrow could be heard from one end of the lab to the other.

Wolfgang looked over and saw what was happening but did nothing to stop Sarah's actions. Wolfgang quickly called Marci and me on our intercom system. We were in the kitchen when we heard Wolfgang say, "Hurry up and come down to the lab. You don't want to miss what is happening."

Marci moved as fast as she could. Her body knocked one of the large kitchen chairs over onto its side. I raced behind my love, but I struggled to keep up with her. As we made our way down to the basement, Marci saw a wonderful sight. At this stage, Sarah had removed the arm from Emma's body. Marci said, "Oh this is wonderful." She looked over toward me and said, "Don't say a word." She moved her long and sexy finger to her pouting lips. She looked at Wolfgang and motioned for him to do nothing.

Lucinda was crying but not because of pain. She was mortified by her mother's actions. She was numb to the fact that her mother had dug her fingers and ripped the decaying flesh from Emma's body. This went on for several minutes. Sarah had this crazed look on her pathetic face. Lucinda continued to scream saying, "Momma... stop it. Just kill me instead. You can't get her off me!"

Sarah looked up toward the ceiling and made two fists. She was saying something that we couldn't understand. Suddenly, she looked down at her daughter and went for her head but stopped and pulled her hands back. Lucinda screamed, "Do it, Momma! Just do it." Sarah's hands went for Lucinda's head again. She grabbed it as tight as she could. She didn't want to kill her only surviving daughter, but she needed to put her out of her misery.

Marci raced to the front of the cell saying, "No. Don't."

Sarah closed her eyes and with what little strength she could muster, she twisted Lucinda's neck as hard as she could. Sarah made sure she twisted the neck enough to kill her. Everyone in the lab heard the crack and the small choking sound Lucinda made. Sarah quickly let go of Lucinda's head, and the sound of her head hitting the tile caused Sarah to cringe. She was sad, but this time she didn't cry.

Suddenly, Marci started to laugh. Sarah raised her head and looked at Marci. She was so tired. Her eyes were heavy, she felt so weak, and her stomach hurt badly from starvation. Marci continued to laugh. Sarah got up and turned her body to face Marci. Sarah wasn't happy. She raised her arms in the air and grunted, "Shut up! Stop laughing! I killed her. Isn't that what you wanted?" Every word was audible.

Marci continued to snicker saying, "Oh, this is just too good to be true."

Sarah stood there looking defeated in every way. She was at a point where she no longer cared about what was going to happen to her. She was growing immune to Marci's attitude and twisted personality.

Marci said, "Oh, you stupid, fucking cunt. You didn't kill your freak of a daughter. It's still alive."

Sarah looked up at Marci and saw her point her long index finger toward Lucinda. She was confused. She slowly looked down and saw Lucinda's motionless body lying on the floor. Her eyes cascaded across the body and there were no signs of life. As her eyes lifted, she quickly noticed the head. The head was faced toward Sarah. Suddenly she noticed an eye looking at her. She was still alive. Sarah grunted, "Ohhh, no!!"

Marci laughed even harder. She said, "You can't kill what can't be killed. You and I will live forever. That means your daughter will live forever as well. All you did was just paralyze your little deformed monster. It is still alive. It can hear you, see you. It knows what you did, it just can't move now. Congratulations, bitch, you just paralyzed your own flesh and blood."

Sarah continued to scream through her gritted teeth. "No! No! I am so sorry! I didn't mean to hurt you like this!!"

Marci said, "The only way to kill her is to cut the head off. But... now let me see. How are you going to do that?"

Sarah stood up and placed her hand over her mouth. She paced back and forth, not knowing what to do. She looked down at her daughter and Lucinda's eye just looked at her. Her eyes moved down her daughter's body. It was a haunting image. Sarah looked around and walked toward Marci. She again extended her arms toward her, pleading her to help Lucinda. Sarah pointed at her daughter, and for the second time asked Marci for help by using her hands. Sarah grunted out the words through her gritted teeth, "Help me... please!"

Marci smiled and walked toward Wolfgang's closet. She pulled something from it, but I couldn't see what it was. Marci hid the tool behind her back and walked slowly to the cell. Sarah was down on her knees, trying to console her daughter. She didn't want to move her.

Suddenly, Sarah was startled by a pair of tin snips that Marci had thrown into the cell, which made an ear-piercing sound as they hit and slid across the floor, stopping by Sarah's leg. Lucinda's eye was twitching, moving in all directions, trying to see what had made that noise. Sarah looked down and slowly picked up the heavy tool. She was so weak from not eating in weeks that she could barely pick it up.

Marci said, "Now you have a choice. You could use the tin snips on that thing lying on the floor. It might be a little painful for it to handle or maybe it won't feel a thing. I don't know or really care. You could smash its brains in with it, but I don't know if that would be a good idea; it might still live through the trauma. What you could do is cut your lips and wires free and… well… let me see… you have powerful jaws there, you ugly bitch. It wouldn't take too long for you to rip that thing's head off. So, what will your decision be? Kind of a tough one, isn't it? I just love this kind of conundrum because it's so much fun."

Sarah closed her eyes and shook her head, thinking that this nightmare would never end. Her first thought was to do nothing. The problem was that she couldn't eat and would eventually end up being closer to death than ever before. She couldn't beat the tin snips into her daughter's head because she didn't want to inflict that much pain, and she worried about the possibility of her surviving the attack. She couldn't use the tool on Lucinda's neck. It would take too long to completely remove the head from the neck, putting her through a prolonged agony. Her only option was to use the tool on herself.

Sarah turned from her daughter and her audience. She took her hand and felt her sewn lips. She glanced around and looked at the mirror over the sink in her cell and stood in front of it. She was getting weaker by the second. She wanted to lie down and rest. Rest usually helped her regain strength, but she couldn't rest. She had to continue. She couldn't allow herself that time. If she did, she might not go through with what she felt was her duty. With tears streaming down her face, she brought the tin snips up to her mouth. They were long, about two feet in length, with very sharp blades. She opened up the shears as wide as they could go. The sharp edge made for a decent type of knife.

Marci was so excited. She looked over at me and smiled. She then smiled at Wolfgang who didn't show any type of emotion. Marci stuck her snake-like tongue out at him and wiggled it. Wolfgang smiled and tried not to laugh.

Suddenly, Sarah let out a painful moan. She took one of the blades and ran it between her sealed lips that had grown together. She had to stop because the pain was too great. She had made a one-inch incision on the right side of her fused lips then took the blade and pressed it against her bonded lips. With a sawing motion, she moved the blade between them. The pain was intense, but she couldn't stop. She tried to cut her lips until she got to the other side of her mouth. About two-thirds of the way, she had to stop. Blood was flowing down her chin and into the sink. She could hear the large drops of blood hitting the porcelain. She collected herself and finished cutting the remaining portion of her merged lips.

The pain was difficult for Sarah to endure. She let go of the tin snips as she brought her hands up to her cheeks and held them tight. The blood-coated tool made a loud clang as it hit the sink. Sarah felt as if her lips were on fire. She wanted to touch them, but she knew it would cause more pain. She stood there, trying to calm her pain the best way she knew how. She tilted her head up to ease the throbbing then slowly adjusted herself and looked in the mirror. Through all the blood, she saw the thick piece of wire in the front portion of her mouth. The wire was twisted many times and was bent back, and the holes in the upper and lower gums had closed around the wire. Without looking down, she reached for the tin snips in the blood-filled sink. When she found them, she picked them up with both hands, holding the middle part of the handles. Her salty tears continued to flow, some of them touching the open wounds of her lips which caused more stinging pain.

Marci moved around to the other side of the cell to get a better look. Sarah was beyond caring about what Marci was doing or saying. Her full attention was on the task at hand. She positioned the open blades over the twisted part of the wire in front of her teeth. She thought this was the best solution. She didn't want to cut the wire close to the closed opening of her gums. The wire was so tight that skin from the gums had grown around the wire. The only part of the wire that was exposed was over her teeth. She gently closed the handles so the tips of the blades were touching the wire then fully closed the tin snips. The pain was horrific as all the nerves were activated. She looked at the wire in the mirror and noticed that she had only cut part of the wire. She had to repeat the technique until the wire was completely severed.

Sarah took her left hand and painfully moved her bleeding lips so she could see the wire on the left side of her gums. Again, she repeated the same procedure as before. She brought the tin snips up to her mouth and rested the slightly open blades on both sides of the wire. She had to let her wounded lips rest on the tin snips as she cut the wire in two. Just like before, this caused more pain. The movement of the wire being cut awoke the gum's nerves.

Sarah was mentally distraught and physically exhausted. She knew the last wire to be cut was going to be the toughest. Pain resonated from every place in her body. With all that she could muster, she repeated this process on the last wire located on the right side of her mouth. As the blades slid across the wounded lips, tears swelled in her eyes and a thousand beads of sweat oozed out of her pores. She thought to herself that she only had one last wire to cut. She hurried to set the blades on each side of the wire, and with a deep breath she made the cut. As with the last two wires, the pain shooting throughout her face was unbearable. She slammed the tin snips down on the porcelain sink, cracking it. Sarah moaned as she held both sides of her head.

Marci thought it was so entertaining. She mocked her every step of the way, but Sarah didn't care. She was so focused on her pain that she paid no attention to Marci. Sarah moved around her confined cell. She looked at Lucinda who was still lying motionless on the floor. Sarah paced back and forth, trying everything she could to subdue the pain.

Wolfgang stepped closer to the cell and shouted, "Can you open your mouth?"

Marci said, "Yes! Oh yes. Can you open your mouth? You know, you just cut the wires, but they are still in your gums, right?" She laughed hard and continued, "And here you thought you were through. Hell, honey. Your pain has just begun. Come on, you ugly bitch. Open your mouth."

At that moment, Sarah felt as if her heart had hit the pit of her stomach. They were all correct. The wires were still embedded in her gums at six different places and they were not cut in the back of her closed teeth. She knew that if she opened her mouth she was going to feel pain like she had never felt before.

Marci continued, "Come on, bitch. Open your mouth. Do it for your fucking child."

Sarah moaned louder. She first tried to separate her teeth from one another, but the pain was too intense. Her hands went to her face again. She hopped around in place while in intense pain.

Marci and Wolfgang laughed and mimicked her. Marci said, "Come on, cunt. You have to do it. Or do you want to take those shears and cut your little freak of nature inch by inch until you finally get that fucking head off? It would hurt like a bitch, cunt. But at least you won't be in any pain. You big pussy. What's it going to be? You or it?"

Sarah clinched her fists and lunged toward Marci, but as usual, the chains stopped her. Sarah was extremely angry. She had never felt this much anger in her soul. She hated Marci and was telling her how much she hated her through her gritted teeth. Sarah said, "I hate you. You are the devil and one day your time will come. You will spend eternity in hell with Lucifer, your god. I pray that it happens soon."

Marci laughed at her and said, "Lucifer doesn't exist. My maker is my love. My Garrison. He is the one that created me. He brought me back to life. Don't you understand this yet? Garrison has the power to bring people back to life. They all have the power. Even I possess this power now."

Marci pointed to Wolfgang and continued, "And this man standing right here invented this wonderful formula. If it wasn't for him, none of us would be standing here... watching you entertain us. You are the very essence of what I hate. I wanted children so bad with my Garrison but you, you ruined that for me. I don't want my kids turning out like your freaks. They are horrible looking. You and your kids are such a disappointment to me."

Sarah went after Marci again, only to be stopped by her chains. She screamed through her clinched teeth, "I never asked for this. You people kidnapped me. You forced this on me. I never wanted to be a part of your sadistic and evil experiments, as you crazy people call it. I hope you never have kids. You don't deserve them. You are evil. You are the devil. God should never bless you with kids. There is a reason you were never wanted as a child. No one wanted to have a devil for a child. They were all afraid of you."

Marci's rage rose to a level that I had never seen. She screamed loudly in a powerful roar. Every part of her wonderful body tensed up. She ran past the cell and pushed Wolfgang away in the process, fumbling around to find the key to the cell. When she found it, she raced back, but Wolfgang stopped her. She raised her hand in pure anger and hit him across his face. He stumbled back. I quickly moved over toward him. I was afraid he might attack my love. I shouted, "Dad... No! Let her go!" Wolfgang growled loudly. His long, pearly white teeth glistened from his saliva.

I looked over and saw Marci opening the cell door. Sarah still had her hands made into fists, ready to fight her demon. Marci opened the cell door with great force. The door slammed into the side of the cell, making a loud crash. Marci ran toward Sarah, and as soon as she was close enough, she threw a punch at Sarah. Sarah blocked it with her arm. Marci threw another punch with her other fist and Sarah blocked that attempt as well. At the same time, Marci kicked Sarah in the stomach. Sarah screamed loudly. The force of the kick forced her to slightly open her mouth which sent thousands of nerve endings spasming with pain. The pain was so great it immobilized her. She fell to her knees, holding her jaws as she rocked back and forth.

Marci walked over and picked up Lucinda by the hair and drug her in front of Sarah. Marci grabbed Sarah's long, matted hair and held Lucinda close to her face. Marci said, "Now you are going to put this miserable thing out of its misery and I want to see it. You are going to chew the fucking head off with your own teeth, you pathetic cunt." Marci threw Lucinda's head down onto the hard tile floor. Lucinda couldn't feel a thing from her neck down nor could she speak or move a muscle. She could only move her eyes. She fell onto her back with her head away from Sarah. Marci let go of Sarah's hair and quickly moved Lucinda's head around saying, "I want you to see this, freak!"

Without hesitation, Marci's hands went for Sarah's head. She pulled Sarah's head up as she took her right hand and placed it just above her upper lip, covering her nose with her large hand. She took the other hand and placed it on her chin, making sure she had a solid grip on Sarah's head. Sarah grabbed Marci's forearms, but before she could react, Marci pulled her hands in opposite directions. As Sarah screamed, the wires were pulling loose from the gums. Marci pulled harder the second time and forced Sarah's mouth open as wide as it could go. Marci didn't want to pull the wires out in fear of Sarah biting off some of her fingers.

Marci released Sarah and pushed her down onto the floor. Sarah hit the tiled floor with great force. All she could do was hold her mouth and attempt to somehow deal with her intensified pain. Marci ordered me to get a pair of pliers. I raced like a bat out of hell to find a pair. I ran over to the cell entrance and tossed them to her. Marci smiled and winked at me saying, "Thanks, lover." Marci bent down and placed her large and beautifully shaped leg on Sarah's chest, holding Sarah's head down on the floor as she forced the pliers inside of Sarah's mouth. She pulled out the wires, one by one. Sarah was in so much pain that she was beyond the point of trying to fight back. The pain coupled with being so physically weak from starvation caused Sarah to just lie there, wishing the intense throbbing pain would stop. She felt as if her face was going to explode.

Marci got up and looked at Sarah rolling around in pain. Marci said, "Listen to me! Hey... cunt! Are you listening to me? Unless you want your freak of a daughter to live like a vegetable all its life, you need to kill it. You know what you must do. Just do it, bitch!"

Marci walked out of the cell, closed the door, and locked it. Marci walked over to Wolfgang and handed him the key. My father was still upset that she had hit him. Marci showed no signs of remorse as she stared back at him for an uncomfortable moment. Marci then walked over to the end of the lab to cool down.

I spoke with Wolfgang and tried to convince him that Marci was upset and to have patience. He was upset and had always had trouble forgiving people causing him physical harm. I broke the awkwardness by directing my father's attention to Sarah. She was trying to get up. Most of her body, as well as the floor, were covered in splotches of blood. She looked down at Lucinda but couldn't talk because of the pain. She reached out as if to say she was sorry.

All of us sensed that Sarah was appalled at the idea of killing her own daughter in such a barbaric way, but it was the quickest and most efficient way to behead her. She knew she had to put her daughter out of her misery. She again paced back and forth, her body exhausted and beyond the brink of starvation. She'd had no food or water for over a month now. Her muscles ached, especially where Marci's hands and leg had been. Her jaws, gums and mouth felt as if they were on fire. Her lips would crack every time she moved them, causing more bleeding and, of course, pain.

Sarah walked up to Lucinda's motionless body. Only her eyes were moving. The eyes are the windows to any creature's innermost thoughts, and not a word needed to be said. She knew what Lucinda was thinking. She knew what had to be done. Lucinda wanted to die. Sarah slowly bent her knees as she closed her eyes, praying silently to her God. As her knees suddenly hit the floor, large tears fell from the deep recessed corners of her massive eyes. Sarah looked Lucinda in the eye and saw the terror that was present in them. She couldn't help but cry loudly. Sarah said, "I love you, my dear Lucinda. Please forgive me for what I am about to do. I do this in the name of God, for his mercy is endless and ever forgiving." She gently turned her daughter's head to the other side of her body so she couldn't see her looking at her.

Sarah moved backward a couple of feet and bent down with her hands in front of Lucinda's body, moving her head closer to Lucinda's neck. She knew this was the only way to put her only living daughter out of her misery. Sarah gathered all the inner strength she could muster then jerked her head toward the heavens and screamed as loudly as she could. "Oh God, forgive me! Give me the strength… please forgive me, my dear Lucinda!"

Suddenly, Sarah opened her mouth as wide as she could. The stinging pains were quick reminders of the punishment that she had endured from Wolfgang and Marci. This time Sarah didn't give in to the pain. She kept her mouth open, bent her neck, and quickly moved her head toward Lucinda's neck. She paused for a few seconds when she got a couple of feet from her target. Tears were flowing freely as she watched several hit the floor next to Lucinda and onto the back of Lucinda's neck. Sarah closed her eyes for a moment and when she opened them, she quickly placed her large mouth around the back of Lucinda's neck.

Sarah closed her eyes and bit down as hard as she could, her razor-sharp teeth penetrating Lucinda's flesh. Sarah was only halfway into her bite when she heard her daughter make a sound. It was the sound of pain. Sarah's mind was racing, but she knew she had to complete her task to end her daughter's suffering. Sarah repositioned her mouth and this time she bit harder. Her teeth went in deeper as Lucinda made another sound of pain. Sarah bit down harder for the third bite. This time she felt her teeth on Lucinda's spine. Sarah ripped the skin and muscles from Lucinda's body and spat portions of Lucinda's neck out next to her. Sarah didn't stop biting. She continued to keep her bites rapid and sharp. She felt the warm, musky smell of her daughter's blood on both sides of her cheeks. Sarah had no time to notice her daughter's lifeless body that swam in a pool of blood, nor Lucinda's body jerking sadistically as each bite went deeper into her neck.

During this, Eli sat in his cell without moving or uttering a sound. He was scared and felt great pity for his sister. Watching her and his mother suffer was unbearable for him, but he was too shocked and frightened to react. With the surreal events that played out before him, all his attention was focused on the situation. He thought any action would only make the pain worse for them.

Marci watched and enjoyed every moment. Wolfgang and I stood there amazed at the notion that an animal would go to any lengths for their offspring. Sarah gagged through most of her dutiful deed. When Sarah got to the neck bone, she bit down harder than ever and finally, after a couple of tries, Lucinda's head was only attached to her body by a small portion of muscle and tissue. Sarah cried deeply as she pulled her daughter's head from her mutilated body. Lucinda's head rolled a couple of feet and as it came to a rest, the face was pointed toward Sarah. A look of tremendous pain, suffering and horror adorned her face. It was a haunting image. Sarah knelt by Lucinda's torso crying, and suddenly she started to gag for several moments. When she recovered, she said, "Oh, my Lord in heaven. Why are you doing this to me? Oh God, please forgive me for questioning you, but why?! Oh, my Lucinda... I am so sorry I hurt you."

Suddenly, Marci started to clap her massive hands together, which created an overwhelming sound that reverberated throughout the laboratory. Sarah closed her eyes and said, "Shut up! Just shut up! I did what you wanted."

Marci walked over to the cell and said, "Your god did this to you. You know that, right? He brought all of this upon you. He brought us into your life. I wonder why he did this to you." Marci laughed, and it continued for what seemed like an eternity.

Sarah said, "Why are you doing this to me? I have done nothing to you. I didn't even know you. Why are you doing this to me?"

Marci said to Sarah, "Condemn your god before me and I will end this miserable life that possesses you."

Sarah said, "I cannot condemn my Savior, my Lord, my God."

Marci screamed, "Condemn him before us!"

Sarah shouted, "No!"

Marci, growing more angry shouted, "Condemn him, you stupid cunt! I will take all of this suffering away from you!" Marci motioned for me to stand next to her. I stood next to my love as she held me tightly and said, "This is your god. He created you. Condemn your false god and pray to your real creator."

Sarah shouted even louder, "Why? Why are you doing this to me?"

Marci shook her head. She took my hand and walked me out of the laboratory. Sarah knelt by her daughter's corpse and cried for hours.

Marci and I made wild and passionate love that night. I asked my love what she wanted to do with Sarah and she told me that she wanted her as a pet. I asked her if that would be a good idea and she said, "If Eva can have a pet, why not me?" Marci had never had a pet while growing up in the orphanage and she wanted one, something to play with, not necessarily to love. We talked throughout the night about how to make this possible for my Marci.

The next morning at the breakfast table, we discussed what we were going to do with Eli. We didn't know what to do with him. Wolfgang had finished running all his tests on him and had no further use for him.

Marci said to Wolfgang, "I'll take care of it. You want it dead, right?"

Wolfgang nodded and smiled. Marci immediately got up and walked toward the basement steps. I followed my love with great interest, wondering how she was going to accomplish ending this little freak of nature's life. When Marci got to the lab, she went to retrieve a machete. The machete was the same tool that she'd used to kill herself on that terrible night. It brought back so many painful memories for me. Just seeing that knife brought a severe feeling of how much I hated that instrument of death.

Sarah watched Marci's every move as she unlocked Eli's cell door. Suddenly, she started shouting, "Leave my baby alone, you monster!"

Marci looked at her and said, "This is your god's son." Marci turned her head toward me and asked, "What do you want, my Lord?"

I said to my love, "Kill it."

Marci laughed and said, "Of course I will."

Eli was scared and ran to the far end of the cell. Marci started to chase the little freak. Because of her long arms, she was able to trap Eli into a corner. He panicked and without thinking, lowered his head and tried to run under Marci's legs. As he did, she allowed him to run past her then she cut his back with the tip of the machete. Eli screamed as he abruptly stopped and attempted to assess the damage on his back.

Marci quickly ran after him again, only this time he ran to his left. Marci reach out and nipped his arm. Eli was running for his life in the limited cell space as Marci repeatedly cut him on his arms and legs, and again on his back. He was crying and screaming as he looked over to his mother for help. Sarah was powerless to do anything.

Eli, in great pain, tried to escape Marci's flying machete, but this time, the top portion of the blade went deep into his thigh. Eli fell to the tile floor and Marci quickly jumped toward Eli and impaled her blade into his spinal cord, rendering him motionless.

Marci pulled the blade out of his back. She walked around toward his head and sliced his face with her knife. The blade entered Eli's left eye and went into part of his brain. Eli remained motionless. Marci calmly pulled her machete out of his head. Eli made a slight and sudden groan. Marci raised the blade over her shoulder then lowered it with great force. The blade passed through Eli's neck, and within seconds his head was free from his body.

Sarah shouted out for Marci to stop, but all her pleas were ignored. Marci went over to Eli's head and stuck the blade of the machete into the side of Eli's skull then calmly walked out of the cell carrying Eli's head on the long steel blade.

I stood calmly and watched my love walk toward me. I heard nothing but her heavy footsteps and Sarah's familiar and uncontrollable sobbing. Marci asked me to open Sarah's cell for her. I opened the cell door and as Marci passed me, she stopped and kissed me with the most passionate kiss. As her lips left mine, her long forked tongue snaked out of her mouth and made its way up my chin and lips. She walked inside of the cell and lowered the machete with Eli's head on the tip. Sarah loudly screamed, "No!" Marci placed the head on the tile floor then put her foot on the head removing the machete. She turned and walked away, leaving Eli's head just out of Sarah's reach. As Marci turned to walk out of the cell, she stopped herself and said to Sarah, "Are you hungry, my dear?" Marci pointed to Lucinda's body and said, "Well, enjoy your dinner." Marci laughed as she left the cell. She gave me a wink as she watched me closely while locking the cell door.

Meanwhile, Wolfgang picked up Eli's headless body and placed it in the crematory machine. Sarah went into shock. She stared at Eli's head lying on the floor and watched the blood pour out of the skull. Her eyes made their way to Wolfgang as she watched him turn knobs on this large, foreign machine that had captured Sarah's attention since the first day she had laid eyes on it. The flames grew inside of the machine and without any notice, Sarah let out a vicious and long scream. Marci and I left the laboratory while Wolfgang watched Eli's body go up in flames.

Chapter Ten

*E*va had dramatically improved both physically and mentally since her first day at Juilliard. Her voice and violin skills were at a point of total perfection. Eva was getting job offers every day to either perform in an opera or for a permanent position from the major orchestras around the world. Her skills had now entered the realm of legendary status. Her ability was a direct result of the formula but also intense training and practice. The training she received helped her skills, but the attention she was getting was the main driver to her success. Eva loved attention, and the more she received, the better she excelled in everything she set her mind to accomplish.

During the summer, Eva and Miriam were still in the same dorm room. I had arranged for the two to remain roommates until one of them graduated. Eva now had full control over Miriam. She was completely in lust with Eva to a point where part of her even loved her. Miriam was filled with guilt because she felt that what she was doing and feeling was wrong. Not so much in her eyes; she was more concerned what others thought. She had never told her parents that she was a lesbian out of fear of how they might treat her and because of her dad's political career.

Just before the spring semester ended, Eva received a call from the lead production manager, Stephanie Thompson, from New York City's Metropolitan Opera House. The main part of her job was to contract singers for their operas. Eva had always dreamed of performing on the Met's stage in a full-scale opera. Eva told Stephanie that she would be delighted to show up and audition for any part.

Later that week, Eva arrived at the Met. She was taken back to the production room where Eva had to sit and wait with over one hundred or so other singers. Eva was a bit perturbed over having to audition, but she knew she had to play the game by their rules. The opera was Verdi's *Macbeth*. The positions were small sections of cameo appearances.

When it came time for Eva to sing, Stephanie and four others were sitting in attendance. They knew of Eva's ability and wanted her in the opera to draw ticket sales, knowing she was one of the best young sopranos in the world. Eva performed her small lines and her voice was pitch perfect, her pronunciation was spot on perfection, and her limited acting for the role had no flaws.

When Eva finished with her audition, she knew she had gotten the part. A few moments later, Stephanie announced the five that got the parts. Eva was one of the five. They told the young performers to meet back at the same spot in a couple of days for the start of rehearsal. Eva filled out her paperwork for the job and quickly notified me of her most recent success.

On the morning of the first rehearsal, Eva was wired and Miriam was so happy for her. She helped her get dressed and pick out the perfect outfit. Miriam accompanied Eva to the Opera House. Miriam had always wanted to perform under the lights of the New York Philharmonic so the Opera House was just as exciting for her. The two ladies made their way to the entrance of the building and Eva persuaded security to allow Miriam to come with her. As Eva stood there with the other four performers, they started to talk. Eva remained silent.

One of the girls named Julie asked Eva, "Isn't this exciting?"

Eva smirked and said, "I have experienced better."

The four girls stopped what they were doing and nothing was said for a while. Stephanie entered and started barking out orders of where to stand and when they should come in and sing.

After hours on end, the rehearsal was over. Eva kept her eye on the main soprano of the opera. Her name was Theresa Morgan. Theresa was a long-time opera singer that had grown up in California. She spent many years in Italy studying and singing all forms of opera. Theresa had the lead role of Lady Macbeth in Verdi's opera, *Macbeth*. This was a role that Eva wanted badly. Over the past few nights, Eva had committed to memory all the lines for Lady Macbeth's role.

Eva waited for the right moment and when Theresa was talking to Stephanie and the conductor of the opera, Eva walked their way. She interrupted them during their conversation.

Eva said to Theresa, "Excuse me! Hello. My name is Eva Seawick. I am singing in this opera with you."

Theresa looked at her and said to Stephanie, "What a rude little girl."

Eva quickly said, "I am not a little girl, thank you. I am a beautiful woman." Eva quickly turned to Stephanie and said, "Her voice is off for this role, you know that don't you?" Theresa gasped in disbelief.

Stephanie said, "I'm sorry, what did you just say?"

Eva repeated herself and continued, "I could sing this part better. I would like to have an opportunity to land the role of Lady Macbeth. I memorized and have total command of every line in this opera."

Theresa just laughed and said, "Right... who are you?"

Eva looked at her with the most evil glare. "You know who I am. I am the one that is going to take your part from you."

Stephanie quickly moved in and said, "Now look here. I know you're a very famous singer and performer, but that doesn't give you the right to come in here and demand roles. How dare you!"

Eva said, "Then let's compare voices." Eva looked at the conductor, Sir Colin Duckworth. Colin Duckworth was from London, England, had a vast reputation for Verdi opera, and had conducted over one hundred operas. Eva seductively said to Duckworth, "You want to have the best singers for this wonderful opera, don't you, Sir Duckworth?"

Colin smiled and said, "Maybe next time, young lady."

Eva said, "There might not be a next time. This might be your only shot at landing me for this role."

Theresa was beside herself and Stephanie had to restrain her. Colin said, "So you know all of her lines?"

Eva said, "Yes, test me."

Colin laughed and said, "Okay. Tomorrow I will give you one minute to prove yourself. If you don't live up to the billing, you will go back to your role."

Eva smiled and said, "Perfect."

The next morning, Eva arrived at the Opera House and Theresa was the first to meet her. Theresa said, "Look here, you little bitch. This is my role and how dare you try to take this from me."

Eva, without pausing for a moment said, "You were upset last night, weren't you? So, how many shots of vodka did it take for you to calm down last night? You need to be able to control your emotions, dear. Hard to fight for what you think is yours on only a few hours of sleep. Why don't you take another upper and starting studying your lines, cunt."

Theresa stood there speechless. Over ten people heard the exchange. Theresa couldn't believe what she had just heard Eva say. She thought to herself, *What a cocky girl!*

Stephanie took Eva and Theresa to the stage. They stood there waiting for a few moments until Colin entered the pit area. Colin said, "Okay, let's get this little issue over with, shall we?" Colin knew of Eva's talents but was fully confident that Theresa was the better singer and that she had command of her lines. Colin looked up at Eva and said, "Now, you said you know all of Lady Macbeth's lines, correct?"

Eva said, "Yes, I did."

Colin smiled and said, "We are going to start Act 3 in the witches' cave where Macbeth is shown the ghost of Banco—"

Eva interrupted and said, "Yes, yes, let's get on with it."

Colin's smile turned, for he didn't like to be interrupted. Colin cleared his throat as the orchestra adjusted their instruments and the music started. Eva started to sing on queue. Her voice was flawless. Even Theresa was bothered by her beautifully breathtaking voice. Colin stopped the orchestra after several minutes. He then had Theresa sing the part. Her rendition was excellent but many listening thought Eva's rendition was better.

Colin went on to a different section of the opera. This time he didn't ask if Eva knew where her lines were in the opera. Without saying a word, the orchestra started and Eva picked right up with the orchestra again. When the aria was finished, not a sound could be heard in the auditorium.

Theresa's part of the competition was up next. She again sang beautifully. For the third time, Colin started at a different section of the opera. Again, Eva went first and, like the last two arias, Eva performed flawlessly. After the aria was concluded, he slowly put his baton down on the podium. He said, "Never in all my years of conducting have I ever seen such an impressive display and mastery of an opera. How did you do that, Eva?"

Eva smiled and shrugged her shoulders and said, "It just comes natural to me."

Theresa was noticeably upset and didn't know what to do. Everyone was looking at Eva, not at her. She knew for certain that Eva had a better, more powerful voice than her, causing Theresa to want to run away and hide. She had to leave so she briskly walked off the stage. Everyone noticed and their whispers grew louder as they watched Theresa walk toward her dressing room. Of the multitude of performers in the opera, over half of them supported Eva and thought she should have the starring role.

Later that night, Miriam drove Eva back to their dorm. On their way, Eva wanted this boy that she'd had her eye on meet her when they arrived. His name was Tim Loster. Tim was a shy boy of twenty with a nicely shaped face and a very thin body. Eva started talking to Tim, who was also a piano major, during the many classes they shared. Tim had a major crush on Eva, but since she was so talented and popular, he never entertained the thought of really dating her.

Eva had asked him out many times but he always declined. He came from a very strict Baptist, faith-based family. Many times, Tim would ogle Eva's curves and the way she moved. Eva had a sexual way about her that forced the opposite sex to take notice. It was as if her every movement was a premeditated reason to intentionally cause awareness to her sexuality.

As the weeks passed, Tim slowly became more interested in Eva's subtle advances. He knew he could never relieve his pent up sexual urges with her, but he did like sitting with her in class and the attention that it brought upon him. Tim, like every other male at Juilliard, found it amazing that this young freshman had the look and physical shape of a mature woman. Everyone that looked at Eva was intoxicated by her unearthly beauty. What was really amazing was the number of people that were attracted to her skills as not only a singer but as a violinist as well. To add to all these powerful assets was her intelligence. No subject was even the slightest bit difficult for her to master.

Eva wanted to celebrate, in her own special way, her successful debut in the operatic world. Eva sent Tim a text and told him to meet her at the entrance of her dorm. When Tim received the text, he was nervous at first, but he still wanted to see her. Meanwhile, Miriam was not pleased. She was visibility upset while driving Eva to the dorm. She had been hoping to spend some alone time with Eva. Eva knew Miriam was upset but acted like she didn't notice.

Miriam parked the car and the two ladies got out. Eva said, "This is such a wonderful night. The whole world is fascinated with me, Miriam. Isn't that just wonderful?" Miriam smirked but before she could say a word, Eva ran toward the dorms. Within minutes, Tim appeared and Eva took his hand and they started to walk inside. Miriam hurried to keep up with them. After a short elevator ride up several floors, Eva let Tim and Miriam get off the elevator first. Eva floated across the hallway and made her way to their door. When Eva opened the door, she let

Tim go first and Miriam followed. When Eva closed the door, she immediately barked out orders.

She said sternly, "Tim… take off your clothes."

Tim stood still. He felt all his blood racing to his head. At first he wondered if he had heard Eva correctly.

Tim said, "What — now?"

Eva said, "Miriam… take off his clothes."

Miriam reluctantly followed Eva's instructions. She walked over to Tim without emotion and started to unbuckle his pants. At first, Tim was pushing Miriam's hands away, but she slapped them hard so Tim allowed her to unzip his fly.

Tim was excited but knew that having a sexual relationship with Eva was wrong and against his religion. He kept looking at her and when she caught his eye, he immediately looked at Miriam. Miriam started to get rough with him, which bothered him a little. Panicking, he helped Miriam as he hurried to get out of his clothes. After several moments, he stood in front of the girls as naked as the day he was born.

Eva walked over to Tim and said, "You dirty little fucker. You know I am a sinful vixen. I can get you in so much trouble, little boy."

Eva reached down and grabbed his manhood. Tim didn't have time to react. Eva immediately raised her knee and jammed it into his scrotum area. Tim fell straight to the floor, kneeling in pain. He screamed a little but tried not to make a lot of noise. He knew what they were doing was wrong. It was against the policies of Juilliard as well as his religious views.

Tim knelt there holding his balls while in noticeable pain. Eva turned to Miriam and laughed. For the first time since the car ride, Miriam smiled.

Eva said, "I'm going to punish the fuck out of you, you piece of shit."

Eva pushed him onto his back with her foot and stood there looking at him. She quickly got down onto her hands and knees then took hold of his penis and placed it in her mouth. She sucked hard at first and then soft. She licked him from the base to the tip of his penis. Eric was moaning, trying not to enjoy this forbidden pleasure. Suddenly Eva bit down rather hard on the head of his penis and wouldn't let go. Eric tried not to scream too loud. He grabbed and held Eva's face.

Eva released her grip on him and said. "You do understand that I am about to make history, don't you? The youngest to ever play Lady

Macbeth. And just think, you perverted asshole, you are going to have sex with this famous bitch. Or... I should say...some form of sex."

Eva took off her jeans and lifted her shirt over her head, exposing her large breasts and enforcing the fact that she hated to wear any kind of underwear. She crawled up Tim's body until her knees were on each side of Tim's head, and knelt there for a moment as she looked at him seductively.

She started to rub herself as she said, "You're a faggot, aren't you?" Before Tim could respond, Eva said, "Come on, admit it. You are a faggot and guess what? Tomorrow everyone is going to know about it."

Tim panicked and tried to get up but Eva quickly turned her body and took her fist and hit him in the scrotum. Tim was gasping for air.

Eva continued, "Come on, admit it to me." She said loudly, "You're a faggot!" Eva continued to play with herself just inches from his mouth.

Tim started to cry and said, "Please don't tell anyone, it would ruin me."

Eva said, "Are you a faggot?"

Tim said, "Yes... yes I am."

Eva said, "Come on. Say it. You are what?"

Tim said, "I am a faggot, you demented... sinner."

Eva smiled and fingered herself furiously. She was moaning, which in a twisted way was turning Tim on. Miriam was about to lose it as she stood motionless, watching Eva's little show. Eva continued to play with herself until she had fingered herself into a powerful orgasm. Just before her release, she pushed herself onto Tim's mouth, forcing him to take in all of her sexual essence.

Eva said breathlessly, "Come on, faggot, lick it. Lick it harder." Miriam was about to lose control herself. She was touching herself through her clothes as she watched Tim's sexual denigration.

As Eva finished her orgasm, she got up and said, "Don't worry. I won't tell, but from now on you are my little orgasm buddy. Whenever I need sexual release, I am going to call on you. If you ever refuse, I will tell the world about you, and you will be ruined. Understand, my little limp dick faggot?"

Tim nodded as he started to cry. Eva told him to get up, get his clothes on and leave the dorm. Tim did as he was instructed.

When Tim left, Eva looked over at Miriam and said, "Now you need some release, my favorite little lesbian." Eva turned and laid the lower portion of her body on her pillow and gently hiked her ass up ever so slightly. Eva said, "Now come over here and eat out my asshole."

Miriam hurried to do what was instructed of her as she eagerly performed her service for over thirty minutes while she rubbed herself into two orgasms. Eva laid there and enjoyed her domination of her friend as thoughts of her new little boyfriend bounced around in her head.

The next day, the cable and newspaper feeds were bustling over such a young teenager taking the lead role in Macbeth. The potential of upsetting Theresa Morgan from her top spot in the opera even made headlines in Europe.

The praise that was unleashed on Eva made her more tolerable to be around. That was something we had worked on before Eva set foot onto Juilliard's campus. She had to control her attitude. She was very cocky and condescending, especially if she needed attention. I told her that she needed to change, but like Marci, she was a little headstrong. Eva's personality was similar to Marci's. Their personalities required attention and praise, and when they don't get that responsiveness or admiration from others, they lash out at their peers in order to achieve attention. They must not and cannot allow other people to control their emotions. I tried to train them, but this was an individual characteristic the formula enhanced.

The next day, Eva learned that she didn't get the lead role at the first performance of Macbeth, but she was going to perform in the second performance. This didn't sit well with her so she stormed out of the theater. Most of the cast members were in awe while a few snickered. She called me the moment she learned this. I told her that they couldn't make this change so quickly. After many minutes of lecturing Eva, she finally accepted the fact that she had to sit out this opera.

The world was now on notice; a new star had been born in the operatic world. Eva would have her first major operatic role as a teenager, all in a week.

Eva and Theresa had strong words for each other before the first run of the Macbeth opera. When Theresa was off stage, Eva would tell her every mistake she had made. She criticized her pronunciation, her acting, and sometimes even the way she walked. The confrontation showed in Theresa's performance.

After the Met's second performance of Macbeth, Eva's pretrial as Lady Macbeth had the world buzzing. She had perfect diction, acting and vocal command of all aspects of her part in the opera. Live feeds were sent to all public television stations throughout America. Our parents watched Eva's performance with great pride and anticipation. Eva's fellow singers were supportive of her during the opera's run.

Eva's success in Macbeth paved the way for other leading roles although many conductors and producers weren't as taken by her youth. They thought she wasn't mature enough for many of those leading roles, but the attention an opera house got by way of ticket sales forced many to change their minds on such short-sighted views. The administrators at Juilliard were most pleased with their latest prodigy.

Theresa, meanwhile, was transferred to an opera in a different state. She wasn't thrilled over being ousted by a little girl, but down deep in her soul, she knew Eva was a better singer and actress than her.

Theresa never fully recovered professionally, even years after Eva took her leading role from her. Theresa went on to have a marvelous but short career in the world of opera, but time was not good to her voice. Approximately five years later, Theresa suffered and died of throat cancer.

The next couple of months after the Macbeth opera, Eva starred in the leading soprano role in two other operas, Wagner's *Tannhauser* and Verdi's *Stiffelio*. Cast members from all three of the opera's Eva performed in were shocked by her ability to learn her lines so quickly. They were also impressed with her innate command of the Italian and German languages. At her youthful age, Eva posed a presence on the stage of an opera diva in her prime. Every major opera house was after her to star in their latest opera for the upcoming season.

Eva felt so desirable and it made her so happy and sexually aroused. Eva and I again spoke about her being careful in her love affairs. We didn't want her sexual promiscuity to get out in the public light. We didn't want anything to derail her career.

Chapter Eleven

*D*uring the past twenty to thirty years, the United States Government had become so large and expensive to keep running that, over time, it had become extremely unsuccessful. The government was cumbersome and hurt more people than it helped. More than any other time in American politics, the majority of Americans wanted something new and they were tired of career politicians. Miriam's father, Eric Staples, was on the cusp of making a run as the Presidential candidate of the United American Party.

The United American Party was a newly developed political party created by five former senators; James Henry of Oklahoma, Joshua Finny of Texas, Don Hart of Florida, David Dennerson of Nevada, and Eric Staples of Indiana. These ex-senators had decided a while back that the traditional Democratic and Republican parties were too heavily involved in corporate endorsements, corrupt special interest groups, receiving illegal donations from foreign countries' special interest groups, and other illegal activities. Throughout American political history, these complaints had been voiced. Other non-traditional political parties had developed over the years, but they could never conquer the Democratic and Republican platforms. The UAP was created to be the exception.

The members of the UAP were well organized and politically shrewd. They made it a point to make sure every member was on the same page. In other words, every person preached on the same issues so their message was clear and concise. The five former senators banned together and created a constituent of basic, middle of the road, common sense ideals on all issues.

Eric Staples was appointed the leader of the UAP as soon as the party started to take form. The party's slogan stated, 'We Stand United as One.' The symbol of the UAP was the American Bald Eagle with its wings extended in full flight.

Eric had graduated from the University of Nebraska where he received his undergraduate degree in Chemical Engineering. Eric continued his education at Purdue University where he received his Masters and Doctorate degrees in Chemical Engineering.

Eric was an intelligent man who longed for his name to be known well past his death. He was driven, worked hard, and was well liked by his peers. Soon after he graduated from Purdue, he partnered with his lifelong friend, Jerry Tharp. They started a company called S&T Communications in Indianapolis, Indiana. The company's primary objective was creating and perfecting transmitting microchips and other communicative devices. These chip-like devices were primarily used on farm animals. The chips were able to track where an animal was located by a simple GPS program inside the chip. The chip also had other beneficial uses for farmers, like tracking the animal's vital signs.

The chips were injected into animal's skin, similar to how a dog or a cat would be microchipped. The company was an instant success. Within a few years, the company was a multimillion dollar producing public company. After several years of continued success, Eric bought out Jerry's portion of the company.

Over the years, S&T grew into a billion-dollar empire. Eric's microchips were all over America. Many of the larger farms located through the States were using his microchips in their livestock. The way the process worked was a small microchip would be inserted into a live animal. What made Eric's invention so special was that his chips could also monitor a livestock's heartrate, food and nutrition intake. The chips were so advanced that they could even detect flaws in the livestock's DNA. Over time, a farmer could track the health, eating, and even the mating habits of their livestock. The farmers would then be able to adjust their livestock's food intake to produce a better grade of milk, eggs or meat. They could also adjust the environment of the livestock proportionally to help aid farmers in producing a better product.

The microchip process spilled over to other areas where the optimum level of physical growth and individual egg or milk production levels would be tracked. The chips also had the ability to control the smaller animals by allowing the farmer to send shocks to the animals to control their temperament and allow them to corral animals to precise areas.

The chips became so advanced that the government was interested in his ideas on artificial intelligence. The United States had been experimenting with AI for decades before the U.S. government's discovery of Eric's company. Neither the CIA nor the FBI had seen a company so technologically advanced as S&T. As the government became more involved with Eric's company, it became even more prosperous.

Meanwhile, as Eric's company was growing rapidly, so was his social and romantic life. Eric was invited to all the influential parties and social events. Eric was careful not to make enemies or offend anyone, nor participate in any kind of self-destructive behavior. He was very discrete in all his activities, and never drank too much or had one-night stands.

During one of these social events, Eric met his future wife, Joyce. Joyce was a lawyer in Indianapolis. They dated for about six months then quickly married. Just a few months into their marriage, Joyce was pregnant and they had their only child, Miriam.

As the years progressed, Eric decided to run for Senator of the State of Indiana. The first time he ran for public office, he lost the nomination. The next election, he refined his strategy and won the State Senator's race. He served two terms then decided to run for the position of Governor on the Republican ticket. After a long, hard, and nasty battle, he won by a slight margin of votes. After serving a couple of years as Governor, the President at that time, Donna Esposito, appointed him as her Secretary of State. Eric served in that capacity for four years. When he stepped down as Secretary of State, Eric and four current serving Senators started to show interest in creating a manifesto of their vision of a new government party in America. This is when they created the UAP.

The UAP was created during a time in American politics where the people were more disconnected from the federal and state governments than at any other time in the Republic's history. Over the past century and a half, the vast majority of American citizens voted for the party their parents and grandparents had aligned themselves with.

Over the decades, the Democratic and Republican parties were becoming similar. The Republican Party had almost given up because so many young people and minorities were voting Democratic. In fact, the Democrats dominated the political landscape. When the economy fell into a depression, the first since 1929, many people found themselves in dire financial straits.

Over half of the country depended on some form of financial assistance. After decades of government abuse and misuse of funds, the government could no longer afford to continue their free handouts; therefore, the government abruptly stopped giving money to the people that had been living off the taxpayer's money. Because these people didn't work or care to improve themselves, many of the poor and uneducated lacked the necessary work skills and experience to be a viable candidate for the limited job openings that were available. This caused companies not to expand their businesses, thus not creating non-skilled jobs.

America was looking for new leadership. Each election they were sold the same bill of goods, with people saying they were different, but in the long run they turned out to be the same part of the old establishment. The country was split, more than ever, into a two-class system; the haves and the have nots.

Race wars were covered on television on a daily basis. The media was so one-sided that it caused the race wars to get higher viewership. The poorer people tended to gravitate toward the inner cities while the richer people left for the outer areas of the city, with the exception of the top five or ten most populace cities in America. The police departments were merging with the National Guard, and parts of the United States Army were permanently established in every major city across the country to keep control of the poorer population.

The poor didn't like what was happening in their neighborhoods and how they were viewed. They felt like outsiders. They increasingly hated the 'other half' as each decade passed, thus the successful people wanted to be segregated from the poor. The successful citizens made it impossible for the poor to be wanted in their areas across each town. The discrimination laws of the past were all but ignored, and parts of the constitution were no longer followed because the Supreme Court was more interested in keeping peace than enacting or enforcing the proper laws in society.

America was ready for an unprecedented change. The poor also acknowledged that something had to be done. There were many different parties that had been developed during this time, but none lasted long term, especially during an election year. The people were becoming hopeless and desperate. Everyone wanted some form of change. The biggest worry was that the country would fall under the rule of another country.

All this chaos was destroying the United States stock market. Interest rates were high, municipal bonds were almost worthless, and the banks were doing well just to stay in business. One area that was extremely financially successful was the commodities market.

Trevor and his parents built their fortune on real estate and gold mining companies. Throughout my first ten years, Carolyn had run the Seawick companies with an iron hand. Seawick Enterprises continued to grow exponentially through my first thirty or so years. Gold was the most precious commodity throughout the world. We, or should I say I, owned vast amounts of gold and gold mining companies throughout the world. I bought up every gold mining company that I could find. It was rumored at one time that I was one of the top five wealthiest people on earth.

I had always been too busy to follow politics. I knew many people and all the politicians of that time wanted me to throw my money at them, but I never paid any attention to them. Throughout the years, I did notice that the UAP never contacted me for any form of endorsement or political contribution. When I first met Eric, I walked away very impressed. Not once did he mention his party or the office he held within the UAP, and he never asked me for a donation.

Eric and I got to know each other better throughout Eva's time at Juilliard. He first helped me with Eva by forcing his daughter to share the same dorm room. He could have easily asked for something from me, but he asked for nothing. While Eva was studying at Juilliard, Eric and I conversed many times via video chat and phone. We considered ourselves to be good friends.

As the months went by and our friendship grew stronger, I took it upon myself to further research Eric and his colleagues. They had many ideas that I found very interesting. He trusted me and told me many things that he didn't share with others. Eric had two distinct personalities; political and personal. He was a hard man to read, but I could sense what his agenda was after just being in his company for a short period of time. His political side, of which he made public to all, was like a Libertarian's outlook although he had slightly more controlled and less radical views than the pedestrian Libertarian.

Eric wanted lower taxes for both individuals and corporations. He wanted to tax companies that took jobs out of America and into foreign countries. He wanted to build larger jails, lift extreme regulation on businesses, and reconstruct the tax code for all wage earners. Eric wanted to increase funding for space exploration and the military, and he wanted to open our borders to all people who legally wanted to become American citizens. He wanted to eliminate the IRS. He wanted local governments to govern their areas and to force the Federal government to be a tenth of its current power.

Eric's personal side was somewhat different from his political side. He wasn't an evil man and had everyone's best interests at heart except for certain races of people. He didn't look kindly on the Black race nor did he care much for any religion. In fact, he wanted to take all religion out of the government, schools, and any public arenas. He didn't believe in public education and believed that all families should pay for their children's education in their local neighborhoods. He didn't believe it was the government's responsibility to educate people; it was the individual's responsibility. If people couldn't pay for their children's education then, in his opinion, they didn't deserve an education.

Eric was against any form of government aide to the unemployed. He wanted to abolish all forms of welfare, including free public housing and food stamps. Eric believed these areas shouldn't be part of the government but a part of private funding. Eric believed in building bigger jails and forcing debtors into prison if they were chronically behind on their bills. He believed that babies and young children would be better off being fostered or adopted into more successful family homes, taking them out of their dangerous, self-destructive environments.

In the many cases where these lower-class babies and young children were not adopted or fostered, Eric thought they needed to be forced out of these situations. He believed their parents, and in many situations it was only one parent, was the main reason for their ultimate downfall later in life. Many of these kids had single mothers that were on drugs or were just having multiple babies to increase their government welfare payments, so many of them would grow up with no parental guidance or positive role model. This is where gangs get their strength. They prey upon these young children and offer them a seemly better life. They offer brotherhood and protection from rival gangs.

Eric's solution to these issues was to form another branch of the country's military. He even named it The Restructured American. This new branch would be divided into two separate parts and would be responsible for two completely different functions. One of the divisions would be called The Phoenix. Its function would be taking in kids whose parents could not or would not be willing to take care of them. This branch would be responsible for developing young people. They would physically take these kids from the parents that couldn't afford them, place them in a military setting, and take care of them until they reached the age of eighteen. During this time, the new branch of our military would feed, clothe, educate and house these lesser, unfortunate kids. He felt that poverty was an endless cycle and became generational. With poverty comes a bad and unsafe area of town. This environment doesn't foster educational or economic advancement of any kind. In fact, the opposite has taken place since social welfare programs first developed.

Eric felt that our government was paying out our tax dollars to these kinds of people since the 1960s but the money never really fell into the right areas. The money that was supposed to go for the support of these children was being intercepted by their parents or guardians. The kids never saw the money, thus never could receive financial help. Also, their environment made it nearly impossible for them to grow and prosper. The other lesser people they were associating with wanted to keep them down in order to profit off them by way of drug money. The lesser people also viewed strength in numbers. The greater the number of people with the same agenda or issues, the harder they are to control.

The second division of this military branch would be called The Laborers. This division would take the younger and abled people, mostly inner-city minorities and poor people living in the country, into the military. They would be forced to serve the country in some capacity. The more violent members of society would be forced to serve in overseas operations or do physical labor along highways. These people wouldn't receive an education but would be given food and a place to sleep. The more hardened criminals who had committed felonies would be placed in federal prisons throughout the country. Eric even contemplated that some would be transferred to Mexico in exchange for their more productive people.

Eric wanted and believed in making America great again but it was impossible through the decades because the lesser Americans were feeding too much off others' tax dollars. So, the only way to correct the situation was to at least get something out of these people or to trade them to other countries for their people that were just better. All of this was in the name of creating a better America.

Eric wanted to be President of the United States. He wanted this position more than anything and would do anything to achieve his goal.

Eric was a good man and was still a very clean, honest type of person. He was faithful to his marriage and a good father.

The problem for Eric was that he knew he couldn't run on his personal issues. He knew he had to keep these issues private if he ever wanted to win the Presidency. He knew he had to win the nation's highest-level job then he would have an opportunity to address these issues.

I gathered this information not only from Eric himself but from Eric's most private thoughts through my senses and through Eva's friendship with Miriam. Miriam shared everything with Eva. She told Eva all her father's thoughts, plans and goals.

Eva was so much like me, always thinking ahead and looking around corners. Eva floated out the idea to me that she thought I ought to 'buddy up' with Eric and that someday I could run for political office myself. The thought was intriguing but I would never want to draw attention to my Marci and my parents. I would be so vetted that someone would dig up the true story of my parents and Eva. We also had to do everything we could do to keep the press from asking too many questions about Eva and her newfound operatic success. So this thought, as fascinating as it was, could never materialize. At least I didn't see how it could at that point.

Eric was always concerned about Miriam. She had always been a rebel and very sassy. In his mind, the only area where the media would attack him would be through his daughter's potentially harmful actions. The moment he first met Eva, he believed Eva would be a good influence on his daughter. Eric also knew Miriam was a lesbian, although Miriam didn't realize that he knew. This wouldn't have made much of a difference in any electoral campaign, although it would be for the best that it never leaked out. Eva and I knew this upfront.

Miriam was inherently embarrassed and ashamed of her lesbian desires. Eva used this knowledge to her advantage and played on her fears to manipulate her. During the past year of rooming together, Miriam had become very close to Eva. She wanted her sexually, and admired her intellect and her ability to not only sing but also play the violin.

Miriam didn't want to do anything that would derail her father's political aspirations. Even though she could be a hateful bitch to anyone she met, she had always respected her father.

This was an awkward time for Miriam. Just a short year ago, she was looked upon as the most gifted student at Juilliard. Now Eva had shown up and stolen that honor from her, but her sexual attraction and rapidly growing feelings for Eva softened the blow. Miriam had never felt this way about anyone outside of her parents. She was falling in love with Eva and the fact that she knew Eva was not sexually interested in her made her desire for Eva even greater.

Chapter Twelve

While Eva was at Juilliard, she kept Marci up-to-date with every detail of her life. Marci so loved Eva and wanted nothing but the best for her. They viewed each other as sisters and had never uttered harsh words toward the other. They shared all their innermost thoughts and secrets. At times, they would be on the phone for hours just laughing and enjoying each other's company, talking about everything, including Eva's latest sexual experience.

While on video chat, Eva would often explain to Marci what Miriam was doing to her sexually. Marci would even tell Miriam how to please Eva. Miriam hated when these sessions took place, but somewhere in that troubled soul of hers, it aroused her sexually, even though Eva showed her no mercy.

Eva usually denied Miriam an orgasmic release and wouldn't allow her to touch herself or Eva for long periods of time. Eva would mentally dominate her with verbal abuse, shaming her with guilt for being a lesbian or telling her how pathetic she was for letting herself be dominated by a better female. Many times she would have Miriam lick and suck on her toes. Eva would force Miriam to give her back massages and have her tell Eva what she would love to do to her. Miriam loved the games, and Eva knew just how far to push Miriam – to the point where she became frustrated and was begging for some sort of sexual release.

Eva thoroughly enjoyed physically abusing Miriam. She would slap her face, pinch her nipples, or knee her in the vagina. Eva would spank her so hard with one of her expensive belts or shoes that she would draw blood.

Eva would take clothespins and clamp them on Miriam's nipples, playing with them while watching Miriam in her blissful agony. She would sit on Miriam's face and smother her for long periods of time. Every now and then, Eva would force Miriam to perform oral sex on her little boy toy, Tim. Miriam hated to administer oral sex on men, but she loved to make Eva happy.

Eva would eventually reward her with either a taste of her vagina or a large nipple to suckle on to heighten her sexual experience. On sporadic occasions, Eva would allow Miriam to finger herself. During these special moments, Miriam would have multiple orgasms in a short timeframe.

Eva had Miriam buy a large dildo at the beginning of their sexual relationship and on special occasions, Eva would use the instrument on her. She would scream so loud, as if she was out of her mind, that Eva would have to muffle her screams by placing her dirty panties in Miriam's mouth.

Miriam was not only in love with Eva, she was obsessed with her sexually and emotionally. This was the result Eva wanted. Eva was careful not to let this relationship get out into the public. In fact, many times Eva would verbally degrade Miriam in public. Most of Eva's friends and fellow students thought she was a major bitch to Miriam, and many knew Miriam was Eva's largest threat, thus the tension that Eva had toward her was somewhat justified.

Eva told Marci everything. During their normal nonsexual conversations, Eva talked about her schoolwork and how easy her classes were. She would laugh about how everyone had to study long hours and how they were worried about their grades. She would publicly chastise the students that struggled academically or onstage. Eva told her fellow violin and opera students about their many flaws after their performances so many students disliked her honesty although a few appreciated her candor.

Marci would laugh along with her, but down deep it hurt her. Marci had been one of the many types of students that Eva made fun of — those struggling to achieve perfection. Eva knew it hurt Marci but continued to degrade and dismiss the struggling students. Eva rarely told Marci about anyone that she was impressed with; she was too busy talking about herself and how she was so much better than the others. Eva needed this self-aggrandizement. It was part of her personality and she required the attention. She always needed to feel more important than others.

Eva told Marci about her third starring lead role in as many operas. Marci was very excited but again, it unsettled her because she was a bit jealous of Eva. Eva was everything that Marci wanted to be; beautiful, successful and talented. Everything came easy for her and she flaunted her abilities to all.

During these conversations, Marci was forced to look back on her past life and the many struggles that she had encountered. Those struggles had now been mastered, but she could never demonstrate her talents to the general public although Marci never regretted the decision that she'd made in transforming her body. I tried to prevent the transformation, but that was the only way to make her perfect and for her to live forever. The chemical structure of the formula couldn't be changed to prevent the host from being absent of any physical transformation. That was the price my love had to pay for perfection and everlasting life.

One day, Eva asked Marci what she had in mind for Sarah's future. Marci told her what she was going to attempt. Marci didn't want to tell me or Wolfgang although she knew we would sense her plans. A couple days later, Marci took me to Wolfgang's lab. As we entered, I saw Sarah sitting in the middle of her cell floor. She was depressed and just sat there staring at a spot in front of her on the tiled floor.

Wolfgang told us that she rarely made eye contact, probably in fear of upsetting him. He knew she didn't want to go through being tortured again. Her mind was fragile and she was depressed like no other time in her life. It had been a couple of months since we had killed all her children, and her body, including her gums, had healed from all the abuse.

Sarah knew the moment Marci stepped inside the lab that she was on a mission. Her large head rose with a lifeless expression tattooed on her face. Marci had tortured the life out of her. She had taken everything from her, including her comfortable and simple life. Marci forced her to have children that she didn't want, only to discover that she had fallen in love with her unwanted and deformed children.

Sarah felt responsible for the deaths of each of her children, especially Eli who Marci killed. Sarah felt so guilty and evil. To add to her inner strife was the fact that she had denied her God before everyone. In her own words, she had succumbed to the devil's ways.

When Marci and I made our way to the lab, she seductively walked over to Sarah's cell. Without looking away, Marci said, "So, I have an idea of what I want to do with you." Sarah sat there without moving a muscle or saying a word. In her mind, she was beyond being upset. She didn't care what was going to happen to her. In fact, she wanted Marci to kill her, but she knew that wasn't a probability. She knew Marci was not through torturing her. This was Sarah's ultimate torture.

Sarah couldn't figure out why Marci hated her so much. She couldn't even comprehend or entertain that kind of hatred. She thought, *How could anyone hate that much? How could anyone be so evil to another person? How could anyone possess that much pent up rage inside of one's soul?*

Marci asked Wolfgang for assistance and his blowtorch. As Wolfgang gathered his equipment, Marci retrieved an ax and a large saw. I asked Marci what she had in mind and she just smiled and said, "I have always wanted a pet. Eva has a pet. You know, I never had a pet of my own at any time in my life. I did have this stray little dog once. It was so cute, curly fur and had the most adorable face that you had ever seen on a dog. I wanted to keep the dog but, of course, the headmistress of the orphanage didn't allow anyone to have pets. I remember looking down at the little doggie and said, "Goodbye, little one, I will see you tomorrow." The doggie just looked at me and cocked his head to one side. I swear to this day that he understood what I was saying to him. Well, the next day my doggie was gone and I was so upset. I cried so hard. When the headmistress asked me what the problem was, I asked her, *Where is my dog? Where did he go?* The bitch told me some other cunt that worked at the orphanage had picked up the dog and took him to the original owners. She also told me there was a reward out for the lost dog. The cunt took my dog. The owners paid the cunt to take my dog! I explained to the headmistress that I had told my little dog that I would see him tomorrow, but she didn't care. She laughed at me. Since then, I've always said I never wanted a pet. However, down deep in my heart, I knew that was a lie. I always wanted one. The cunts took my dog, Garrison!" Marci was very upset. My heart wept for my love.

Sarah listened to every word Marci said. She had stared at Marci the entire time as she told her sad story. She had horrid feelings falling on her in waves. Suddenly Wolfgang asked, "Are you ready or do you want to do this later?"

Marci smiled and said, "I want to do this now. Do you have everything ready?"

Wolfgang walked toward the wall socket, plugged in the blowtorch and said, "Yes," then opened the cell door. Sarah quickly rose to her feet and retreated to the back wall. She was getting increasingly nervous. Marci slowly walked inside with the ax in one hand and the saw in the other. She said, "Wolfgang, I need your help. I want her face down on the floor."

Sarah screamed, "No! Oh, please don't do this to me! Not again! I did everything you wanted from me. I even denied God for you."

As Marci's eyes met Wolfgang's, they rolled their eyes. Wolfgang went for Sarah. She fought back, but Wolfgang was too large and strong for her. He wrapped his large arms around her and forced her to the hard tile floor per Marci's wishes. Marci took Sarah's left arm and pulled it away from her side then put her lovely foot on the arm to hold it in place. Marci took her saw and gently threw it on Sarah's back while Sarah was screaming, "No! Oh please, God... no... not again. Oh please no... I beg you. Have mercy on me!"

Marci said, "I always wanted a pet and I couldn't think of any pet that would be better than you. We have so much history together and I want you to be my special little companion. How blessed are you to be able to entertain me for years... decades... or even centuries."

Marci laughed loudly. Her laughter was as beautiful as a Mozart piano concerto, especially when it was mixed with my father's snickering and Sarah's woeful cries of despair.

Marci quickly took the ax and swung down hard on the arm, just an inch from the top of the shoulder. Sarah's scream was muffled because of the shock of what was happening to her. The pain caused her large body to go into a state of semi-shock. Sarah felt the combination of the cold ax penetrating her arm mixed with an extreme burning sensation.

Marci swung the ax again and this time the large, thick arm was mostly separated from the shoulder. Sarah finally discovered a way to release the massive pain from her lungs. She let out small yet forceful screams. Marci had to use her saw to cut away the remaining tissue that the ax had missed. Blood was pouring and squirting out of the wounded area. Sarah suddenly found herself back to her all too familiar state of pain and suffering, the type of suffering where the endless pain just cripples a person. Sarah knew all too well these familiar feelings, where all your thoughts are just focused on one pain source. She found herself violently screaming and uncontrollably crying. Sarah was experiencing the type of indescribable pain that forces a person to agree to anything just to make the pain go away.

Marci backed away and stared at her handiwork. She walked over to the severed arm, picked it up, and threw it over to the other side of the cell. Marci said, "Wolfgang, would you be a dear and sear the bitch's cut?"

Wolfgang smiled and said, "My pleasure." He picked up the blowtorch and lit it while Marci knelt on the floor on Sarah's unharmed side, holding her tightly to the floor. Wolfgang took the torch and seared the massive wound. Sarah screamed so loud that her sounds of pain echoed throughout the lab, her screams louder than the torch itself, causing my ears great discomfort.

When Wolfgang finished cauterizing the bloody area, Marci rose to her feet. She walked around to the other side of Sarah and repeated the procedure on Sarah's right arm. This time when she lowered the ax on Sarah, she gently slid the ax a little when it first hit Sarah's fleshy arm. This made for a longer but shallower cut. After a couple of blows, the right arm was separated. Marci again had to use the saw to detach the remaining tissue that was clinging to the separated limb.

During this process, I witnessed the same amount of screaming and pain from Sarah. I also witnessed that same blank expression on my father's face. Wolfgang had this lifeless and almost bored expression that seemed to be more about business and less about pleasure. For my Marci, the juxtaposition couldn't have been different. The torture she was unleashing on Sarah was pure and extreme pleasure for her.

Wolfgang again seared the second wound as Marci held her in place. The armless victim was again in constant pain, just as she had felt just a couple of months ago. She prayed, as best she could, for this nightmare to stop. Yet again, Sarah had to endure this unfair torture. She couldn't understand why her God kept allowing this unrelenting pain to be forced on her. She wanted to get up and run away but she couldn't even if they would have let her.

Wolfgang and Marci looked at the blood seared wounds where the arms used to exist. Some spots were bleeding, but most of the blood had stopped.

Wolfgang said, "I think we ought to wrap the areas."

Marci said, "With what?"

Wolfgang told me, "Go find me some rope and four towels."

I did what my father instructed. Wolfgang took the towels and placed them on each side of the injured areas then wrapped the rope around her shoulder a few times to secure them. This process caused additional pain for Sarah. The movement broke open many of the scabs that were formed by the torch.

After they bandaged Sarah's upper torso, Marci was ready to continue to work on reshaping Sarah's body to her liking. She again had Wolfgang restrain Sarah on the floor. Marci took her hand and ran her fingers down to locate Sarah's hipbone. When Marci found the location, she stood up, raised her ax, and made a very precise chop just above the hipbone. The blade of the ax went cleanly into Sarah, causing a massive cracking sound of broken bones mixed with Sarah's increasingly painful cries. Marci pulled the ax out and again came down with it, making the wound larger. Blood was dripping from the ax and splattering everywhere as a large pool of blood formed under Sarah. After a few repeated swipes with the ax, the leg and part of the hip were almost separated from the body.

Marci gently laid down the ax and as she picked up the saw, she asked Wolfgang, "Would you mind rolling it over on its side for me?" Wolfgang roughly moved Sarah onto her side. Her body was going into shock, shaking and twitching on the floor. Wolfgang had to hold her down as Marci took the saw in her hand. She started to saw through the muscles and skin that the ax had missed. Sarah began to scream louder. After the leg and hip area were totally removed from the body, Wolfgang seared the cut area with the blowtorch.

Wolfgang told Marci to move fast on the other side of the body. Marci quickly picked up the ax and proceeded to work on the other side. Again, the ax plunged deep inside Sarah's lower back area. The sound of bones breaking, mixed with the bloody flesh being penetrated, was majestic. Sarah's screams were becoming softer as the continued shock of reshaping her body was just too much for her vocal cords to endure.

After a handful of swings, Marci again used the saw to remove the leg and hip cleanly from the body. Marci tapered off any remaining skin, muscles and tendons that persisted. Marci threw the detached limb with the others on the other side of the cell. Wolfgang cauterized the wound just like he had on the other side. As he had done with the arms, he quickly placed two towels on the sealed areas then wrapped them in rope.

Marci and Wolfgang stepped back from Sarah's deformed body. The formula was working to keep her body alive. We watched her lying there on her back as she tried to remain as still as possible, but the pain was so great that she had to occasionally move. Each movement sent massive waves of pain throughout her body. I looked down at this newly formed creature and noticed that it was shaped like a cigar. Where the legs used to be, Marci had trimmed from the hip area down to the lower torso into a point that resembled the head of a cigar.

I said to my love, "This is an interesting shape."

Marci smiled at me and said, "I was going for a snake-like shape. My new pet will use its stubby little shoulders to help crawl its body across the floor."

Marci looked at Sarah and noticed something that could affect Sarah's movement as a snake. Marci said, "Oh fuck! I forgot about the tits. You can't be a snake with tits, now can you?"

Sarah moaned and said, "Oh please, no! Have mercy."

Marci said, "Shut the fuck up. Snakes can't talk. They only hiss."

Marci picked up the saw and knelt on the bloody floor. Marci said, "God damn it, you are a mess. You sure bleed a lot, bitch."

Marci took her large hand and cupped the top of Sarah's right breast. Marci moved her hand around the breast, making sure she was stimulating the nipple and that area. Marci smiled and said, "Enjoy this pleasure, my pet, because this is the last time you will ever feel your tits."

Sarah screamed, "No! Oh, God, no!!"

Marci placed the saw on the ribcage and started to move the saw into the lower part of the breast. Sarah screamed in agony, her body squirming violently on the floor. She couldn't keep from moving, but each time she did, Marci's saw would rip and tear more flesh.

Marci yelled, "Stop moving around, cunt." After a minute or so the breast was removed. Sarah laid there screaming so loud that it was again hurting my ears. Marci took the breast in her hands and offered the front part to Sarah saying, "Do you want to suck on your breast for the last time?" Sarah moved her head away and continued to scream.

Marci tossed the breast into the pile of arms and legs as she moved toward the other breast. This time, my love worked quicker and within a half-minute, the breast was removed. Without a word spoken, Wolfgang stopped the bleeding with the blowtorch. I handed my father two additional towels and he placed them over the sawed areas as he wrapped the entire upper torso with rope.

She was in so much pain then suddenly her body started to shake as she gasped for air. Marci said, "What is happening to my pet?" She noticed it was vomiting then after several moments, the entire body stopped moving. Marci screamed, "What the fuck!"

Wolfgang raised his hand to signal for her to stay calm. Wolfgang said, "I think she had a heart attack."

Marci said, "Well, son of a bitch. Is it dead?"

Wolfgang said, "Wait a moment."

As soon as he said those words, Sarah opened her eyes and took a huge gasp of air. She coughed hard and as she did, more chunks of vomit shot out of her mouth.

Marci looked at me and said, "What the fuck happened?"

Wolfgang said, "I assume she had a heart attack. The formula adjusted accordingly and repaired the heart. Now it's probably repairing the brain, if any damage was done from a loss of oxygen. She will be fine in a few minutes."

Sarah breathed heavily as tears flew from her large eyes. For a brief instant she was pain free and couldn't even recall the moment.

Marci sighed, "Fuck, I thought for a second that my pet had died on me."

Wolfgang said, "She will only die if the head is separated from the body. The formula will keep the body alive even in the most extreme state."

I added, "This is so true. I basically butchered my brother into multiple pieces. He would not die on me. He was hanging on by a thread, but he was still alive. I had to cut his head off for him to die."

Without warning, Sarah started to talk. Marci shouted, "Shut up. Pets aren't supposed to talk! I need a leash. A big one!"

Wolfgang said, "There are some chains with metal collars that we used on her before. That will obviously work."

Marci said, "Good idea, Wolfgang."

Marci walked out of the cell and headed toward the closet that housed a multitude of supplies. She found a smaller yet thick chain with a large metal collar. She walked past me and blew me a kiss. I returned the motion. She entered the cell and quickly placed the collar around her pet's throat. Marci said, "Damn, my pet is a mess. I need to clean it up."

Wolfgang said, "Let the wounds heal and then we can clean her up."

Marci said, "How long is that going to take?"

Wolfgang said, "A week to a week and a half. She needs to heal."

Marci quickly turned around and stormed out of the cell, pouting like a little school girl. She quickly ran out of the lab. I followed her up the stairs. She was upset about having to wait, but after I talked to her for a while she calmed down and was fine for the rest of the day.

Wolfgang gathered the limbs and burnt them. Sarah was in such great pain that she didn't care what happened to them, she just wanted the pain to stop. No other thoughts entered her mind, not even prayer. This time all she could think about was her pain. Every part of her body throbbed.

As the days passed, Sarah began to heal but never slept. The pain was still present, but her body was getting used to the pain. After five days had passed, Wolfgang removed the ropes. As he took the towels off her wounds, it pulled away many scabs of dried blood, causing more pain on Sarah's body. Wolfgang, who was never known for a great sense of humor, said, "This probably reminds you of your god when they supposedly stripped him of his clothes after being whipped. It must make you feel connected." As Wolfgang laughed, Sarah stared at him with a painful and disapproving look.

Over the next few days, the injured areas made from the removal of the towels started to heal. Two weeks after the dismemberment, her wounds were completely sealed.

During this time, Marci stopped by and checked on the progress. After Sarah was healed, Marci and Wolfgang gave her a shower, cleaning her from her head to her bottom area. Wolfgang kept Sarah nourished by placing food in a dog bowl. Sarah ate, which was extremely painful for her. Each time she moved, a scabbed wound ripped. The weight of her body where her breasts used to be caused her additional pain.

Wolfgang attempted to train her to move her body a certain way so she was able to get from point A to point B. She had to move and bend her shoulders so they hit the floor. To do this, she had to move her head to the side so her chin wouldn't hit the floor. She had to push off the floor with that shoulder and bounce on her other shoulder then repeat the process.

At first, she didn't want to crawl on her shoulders, but Wolfgang had many ways of forcing her to do what he wanted. Wolfgang would take a bullwhip and roughly smack her back or her ass. After leaving a few deep cuts in her skin, she was inclined to do as instructed.

After another week passed, Wolfgang told Marci to meet him in the lab. He showed her a device that he had made for Sarah. This device was a thick metal pipe with chains attached to both ends. The chains looped around the head and were anchored to a metal neck brace. He told Marci that he wanted Sarah to wear a device in her mouth whenever she wasn't eating. This was to protect everyone in the house in case Sarah wanted to bite one of us.

When it was time for Marci to receive her new pet, the family went down into the lab. Eva wasn't present, but I Facetimed her on my phone. She watched because she was still on tour and couldn't come home for Marci's special moment. As we entered the lab, we saw Wolfgang holding the chained leash in his large hand. Obviously, the leash was around Sarah's neck. Sarah had the large, round metal pipe between her teeth. They were waiting for us. Marci was so excited she went over to Wolfgang and hugged him. Wolfgang offered the leash to Marci as she gladly accepted the gracious gesture. She said to her new pet, "We are going to have so much fun together." Marci gently pulled on the chain to move Sarah's large head around. As Sarah looked at my love, tears formed in her eyes. Marci said, "Now, now. No crying from my little pet."

As I watched my love correcting her pet, I heard Eva laughing on the other end of my phone. Zelda and Wolfgang stood together and proudly smiled as if they had just witnessed their child's first spoken word. Marci said, "Okay, let's go upstairs." Marci walked slowly as she pulled on the chain. Sarah pushed her body up with her shoulders. She had been practicing long hours with Wolfgang, trying to perfect her movements. At first, she developed so many blisters on her underside, especially where her arms were severed, but over time they developed into hard calluses.

There was about half an inch of Sarah's upper arm that was coming from the shoulder. Sarah used these stubs to lift her shoulders, neck and head off the floor. It took a while for Sarah to move, but once she started, she moved swiftly. She would bounce from one side to the other. As she moved her shoulders, she would then move the lower part of her body, which pushed her forward.

Sarah had to contort her body like a snake. When the lower part moved to her left, she had to bend her upper body to the right. She moved like a lizard when she crawled. After some time, her head would get too heavy for her to keep raised, so it was easier for her to move her head from one side to the other. When she moved her right shoulder up, her right ear would face the ground. When she moved her left shoulder, she would rotate her head to the other side.

When we made it to the steps, Sarah had a very difficult time, which caused Marci to become impatient to a point where she picked Sarah up and carried her to the top of the stairs. She let her down rather gently then took her pet into the great room.

Down deep in my soul, I found this amazing as well. I thought deeper about what Sarah must be going through. What thoughts were going through her pathetic mind? Just imagine what she was experiencing, not only at that moment, her being passed off as a pet, but her entire experience since being abducted. What was going through her mind and how was she able to cope with everything that had happened to her?

I kept asking myself, *Why did she keep her faith in that god of hers?* Obviously he had failed her beyond any reasonable expectation. Not once during her capture had he saved or helped her. She never received any form of mercy from her god, but she continued to pray to it. Obviously, praying was her only ability to reach out for anything that, in her mind, could help her, even if it was something that didn't exist. I was the one that created her – I brought her back from the dead. She knew that but outside of a couple of times, she rarely called on me and pleaded for my mercy. Instead, she pleaded with an entity that she had never even seen. I found that amazingly perplexing.

Imagine waking up one day, going about your daily life, when suddenly you're kidnapped. You're tortured, killed, and brought back to life by way of a formula unknown to man. Your physical body changes into your worst nightmare and you consider yourself a monster. Your faith is questioned to a point where you deny the very god you had worshipped all your life – twice. Your only solace is that you have advanced mental abilities. You are more intelligent than you have ever dreamed of being and your only payment for using the formula is your physical body change.

Of course, it is difficult adjusting to the physical change, but you have advantages, such as the increased level of intellect and the ability to live forever. These advantages alone would confirm the choice that the transformation was worth the effort. But down deep, you still feel as if you've been cheated by your god. You're not supposed to possess such power – intellectually or physically. You're not supposed to sense what others feel and think, or to live forever. This is mostly against your god's will. This fortune or evil, depending on how you look at it, was forced on you. You feel violated by a power greater than you. Down deep in your most private thoughts, you wonder if there really is a god. Then you question god, which in your world is another sin. Why did he allow this to happen to you? You begin to question everything that you had been taught since birth and that's when your mind wanders to forbidden places.

Religious people are entertaining. They are controlled by an invisible and silent being that was fabricated in the imagination of humans. This made-up story that has been passed down from generation to generation was probably created for the sake of churches getting money from people. I sometimes think this story was created to keep the humans in order. Fear drives them, over logic. They fear the unknown. They are more concerned about what might happen instead of controlling what can be altered for their future betterment.

I know some very smart people that believe that this being created the world in six days and rested on the seventh. Are people that gullible or just that senseless? You have science in one corner that has proof that our earth has been around for billions of years. It developed into its current state through evolution. By contrast, you have these religious people that think some god just whipped up the mountains, seas and animals in a week. I often wonder how these people get through life.

Chapter Thirteen

When Eva had a small break from classes at Juilliard as well as the opera season, she came home to visit. When I picked her up from the airport she gave me a big hug. It was amazing how much she had grown in just the few months since I had last seen her. She had grown a few inches, gotten broader in the shoulders, and added muscle. She was perfect, as always. A small crowd gathered as we made our way out of the airport. Eva was a superstar in our state and she loved every second of the attention. When we got into the car I sensed that she was very happy. We drove home and I could tell she loved our home. She loved it because it brought peace and calm to her being.

Over the past few years, Eva had grown more distant from our parents. I think part of this was a phase she was going through in her life. It never really bothered Wolfgang, but it did disturb Zelda. Zelda had always wanted a daughter, a daughter to do things with, share life experiences with, and just have as a friend.

My mother was very lonely during this time. She'd had no one to relate to over the past one hundred or so years. Zelda wanted desperately to bond with a fellow female. She grew close to Marci over the years, but Marci always seemed to be occupied with her own life. Zelda admired the fact that Eva was an opera singer. She herself had always wanted to sing on a national stage. To see her own daughter singing at the Met gave Zelda an incredible sense of pride.

One of Eva's many life issues was her relationship with her parents. As the years progressed, Eva understood why she was the only one of her sisters that was allowed to live; her father only kept her alive to mate with me, her only living brother. Eva couldn't get past the idea of why she was chosen and not her sisters. The fact that her own mom would step back and let her father kill her other three daughters was difficult for Eva to understand. With age comes wisdom, but it's often accompanied with revolt. This was Eva's relationship with our parents.

The formula has multiple effects on various people. It enhances your innate abilities and exaggerates some of your lesser qualities. For me, I am a hopeless romantic when it comes to my Marci. I have a great desire to be wanted. Marci is a nymphomaniac who also derives pleasure from someone else's pain. Eva's desires are total and complete acceptance and attention from others. She not only desires it but demands to be treated like royalty.

As Eva entered the house, Zelda greeted her first. Eva was rather cold toward our mom. She just smiled and said hello after our mom held her arms open for a hug. I sensed the hurt in Mom's heart. I looked at her and she just shook her head as if to say, *It's no big deal* and just let her go. It was obvious that Eva's personality had changed over these months while she was away. She didn't treat me or Marci any differently, but she did our parents.

As Eva entered the great room, she saw Marci with Sarah on her leash. Eva laughed hard and said, "Why, Marci, I love your pet."

Eva bent down with her hands on her knees saying, "Hi there, little Sarah. Do you like your new body?" Laughter filled the room.

Wolfgang sat in his chair without saying a word. Eva didn't even acknowledge him. Eva went over to Marci and they hugged. Marci said, "I've missed you so much, Eva. Look at you. You have grown so much."

Eva said, "I've missed you as well."

Eva looked around the room with a bewildered look on her face. She said in a rather sarcastic voice, "Hey, where is Midnight?" Her transformed cat was always closely guarded since we didn't want the mutant cat to get out of the house. We couldn't allow Midnight to bite another animal and have that animal carry the formula to others. That situation could get out of control quickly and mankind would never be the same. Since the first time Wolfgang discovered the cat, he'd had the animal under lock and key. We could only bring it out on its leash. Since Eva had been gone, Wolfgang had had the cat in his crate for months, only letting him out at times for bodily elimination, and those times were limited.

Wolfgang spoke up and said, "That cat of yours is downstairs."

Eva looked over at our father and said in a condescending tone, "I expected Midnight to be waiting for me. Why is he still downstairs?"

Wolfgang jumped out of his chair and rushed over to Eva. Eva didn't move a muscle, she just stared at him. Wolfgang got inches from her face and said, "Look! While you're in this house you will be respectful to me. Is that understood?"

Eva, without blinking said, "It is understood. Now can I see my cat?"

Wolfgang quickly turned around and grunted as he walked away. I immediately stepped in and said, "I am sorry, Eva. We tend to forget about Midnight. With all that has been going on here, it is a little difficult to keep up with everything."

Eva looked at me and said, "You mean you haven't been playing with my cat?"

Marci interrupted and said, "I have, Eva. When I got the chance."

Wolfgang snorted and said, "She is always playing with the thing."

Eva said, "I can't believe that I have to go downstairs to see my cat. I thought you people would have him waiting for me."

Wolfgang said, "Eva! Shut up. Watch your tone!"

Eva just stared at our father. She closed her eyes and whipped her head around. A massive wave of perfectly formed blonde curls followed her as she raced toward the basement. I followed her. As we walked down the stairs I said, "Eva, what is wrong? Why are you acting like this?"

Eva said, "Acting like what?"

I said, "You need to show people more respect. I know you have had a lot of people kissing your ass lately, but you need to find a center. Remember, your only enemy is yourself. Do not self-destruct."

Eva shook her head and said, "You're right. Sometimes I expect too much from others. Ever since I've been at Juilliard, everyone just gives me what I want. It's been awesome. Everyone is so far up my tight little ass, and I love it. They all love me and are jealous of me. It's incredible. Did you ever feel this way?"

I said, "Yes I did. But your vice is attention. My vice is obsession, especially when it comes to love. Your personality is constructed differently from mine, even though we are created the same. You have to be more mindful of your personality than I do, at least to some degree."

Eva said, "I understand."

We walked toward Midnight's crate and there it was sleeping. Eva knelt and tapped on the door of the crate. Midnight awoke and was very happy to see Eva.

Midnight was a very evil cat. Even when Eva first discovered the cat before its transformation, it was evil. It would walk around the estate, stalking everything in its sight. She'd kept it hidden for a while until Marci discovered that Eva had a secret pet. The cat grew to like Eva after its transformation. All other animals ran from her and they still do. Animals can sense that we are predators and they sense danger when we're around them. When Eva bit the cat, she transferred the formula. In a matter of a week, the cat mutated. Since the mutation, Midnight had only been warm toward Eva and Marci and doesn't like anyone else.

Eva opened the crate. Wolfgang always kept the leash around his neck even when it was secure in the crate. When Eva opened the door, she held the leash firmly in her hand. Midnight jumped out and onto Eva's chest. Midnight's ultra-white, bare skin rubbed against Eva's large breasts. Large blue veins were visibly running all over Midnight's body. Midnight was very clean; in fact, he constantly licked himself throughout the day and didn't possess any cat-like odor.

Eva held Midnight and the leash tightly as we made our way upstairs. When we walked into the great room, Midnight quickly noticed Sarah lying on the floor and started to hiss. Marci thought it was funny. Eva petted Midnight and he quickly calmed down. Eva walked over to Wolfgang and sat next to him. Eva said, "Dad... I want to apologize for my behavior. You know how I am and how I can be at times. Thank you so much for letting me go to Juilliard and to perform in all those wonderful operas. Have you seen any of them?"

Wolfgang smiled at this daughter. He said, "I know you are putting on a show for me. You're not sorry, are you?"

Eva smiled and said, "No, I'm not sorry, but I'm working on it."

Wolfgang nodded, "Yes, I have seen them. All of them. Your voice is as beautiful as your mother's."

Zelda was standing motionless at the entrance of the great room. She hadn't heard many compliments from her husband come her way in a long time. She was shocked that he would praise her.

Eva looked up and said, "Thank you, and thank you, Mother, for letting me experience the world of music and opera." Zelda started to cry. She just nodded her head then turned toward the kitchen. Marci looked at me and rolled her eyes. Wolfgang sat there with a slightly confused look on his face. He couldn't understand why she was crying.

Sarah was lying on the floor next to Marci's large but erotic feet. She couldn't take her eyes off Midnight. Midnight didn't like being in the same room with the freak. He was hissing and snorting at Sarah. Eva had to stroke Midnight many times to calm him down. Sarah tried to hide herself the best she could, but every time she moved, Marci would pull her back into Midnight's line of sight. Sarah started to say something but as soon as the first word came out of her mouth, Marci roughly yanked the chained leash. Sarah's head bent so far backward that half of her body was off the floor. Marci would just say, "Stop it. Lay still." This scene played out most of the time whenever Eva and Marci would sit together with their pets.

During Eva's short visit, Marci and Eva talked constantly. They did everything together, including playing music. Marci played the violin while Eva sang. At times I would join in and play the violin or piano. Even Zelda would participate from time to time, but Eva didn't like when our mother would sing with her. When it was time for Eva to leave for school, we all said our goodbyes. Like an old habit, I took Eva to the airport, we said our goodbyes, and I sent her back to New York.

When Eva was gone, Wolfgang wanted Marci to keep Sarah in her cell when she wasn't playing with her. My father was always cautious not to make careless mistakes. His worst nightmare was Sarah getting out and running away. Marci would take Sarah out on her leash from time to time but as the weeks went by, she grew tired of her. She would keep her chained up in her cell, only having enough room to eat and eliminate her body waste. Wolfgang made Marci clean up Sarah's waste and to clean her occasionally. Marci was vigilant in her duties but she grew tired of her chores. Having a pet was not as fun as what Marci had first thought.

There was something bothering my love. I had sensed it for a few weeks. Marci had a strong mind and was able to keep little secrets tucked away deep inside her brain although she knew everyone in the house could usually sense what she was thinking and feeling.

Although we can sense what others are feeling, we also have strong minds and are able to block our thoughts on certain subjects, which makes sensing what you're thinking extremely difficult. Marci was an expert at this. Over time, she developed the skill not to think about things that bothered her, especially important thoughts that she wanted to keep to herself. It was difficult for me to sense what it was, but I knew the subject was weighing heavily on her mind. I asked her about it on numerous occasions but she always deflected my questions. After several weeks, I finally got Marci to tell me what was bothering her.

From the moment I saw my Marci, I knew there was something special about her. When we first met, she was a very guarded and private person who wouldn't let anyone inside her private world. I knew that she'd had a difficult life growing up as an orphan, so anything related to this issue wouldn't be a surprise to me. Marci took her time coming around and telling me what was on her mind. When she finally got up the courage to express her feelings, I had sensed what was on her mind.

Marci said to me, "I assume you know what has been bothering me of late?"

I said, "Yes. Do you want to talk about it?"

Marci went on to explain, "Garrison, I want to find my parents. I sense that they are still alive, but I don't know for sure. I have always felt that they were still alive. I just want to know why they gave me up. I don't even know how old I was when they dropped me off at the adoption agency. All I know is that I was born here in Kentucky. Growing up at the agency, I never wanted to know who they were. I wanted nothing from them. I hated them. The people at the adoption agency told me my birthday when I got older and threw small birthday parties for all the kids there. Many didn't even get to celebrate their birthdays because they had already been adopted. But not me. I just sat there, waiting for some family to adopt me, but no one came. I spent a few nights at people's houses, but they quickly returned me to the agency. I never understood why no one adopted me as a little girl. When I was older, I finally had one of our caregivers tell me that some kids just get left behind for no reason. I do remember this one little fat bitch told me that I had an attitude and that I gave off bad vibes. She told me that was the reason I was never adopted. You just don't know how that feels. I have no clue of my past." Marci broke down in tears.

I listened to what my love was saying. I hated to see her break down emotionally and feeling bad about herself. Her story was all too familiar. My story was somewhat like hers. I wasn't wanted by my birth parents, wasn't even wanted by my adoptive father, and my own mother feared me. My brother hated my guts and I didn't know of my birth parents until I was older.

Marci asked me, "How did you feel when you found out you were adopted?"

I said, "From what I can remember, Travis and Adelle were dishonest with me from the start. It was a long time before they told me I was adopted. They had no clue how I came into this world. They did not know much about my story. All they knew was some local villager had found me near that small creek area that I showed you when we went into the forest. They picked me up and placed me in an orphanage.

I was fortunate to have Sonja make a call to my adoptive mother. Trevor pulled some strings with the local officials and my adoption was legal. It is amazing what money can buy. When I came home, I started to do odd stuff and my adoptive parents got doctors involved. That is when Lewis came into the picture. After I bit Trevor and he changed, Lewis went to Germany, to the place where I was first found. He discovered Wolfgang and Zelda. At that moment, they kept that part of my life a secret from me. It was not until I was in college or so that Lewis told me about my parents. At first I was pissed that they did not tell me sooner, but Trevor had told Lewis not to tell me about my birth parents. So, I guess I could not get too upset with Lewis. He was just carrying out orders."

"At first, when I found out I had parents, I was hurt. Then I felt angry. As time went by, I wanted to meet them. To some degree, my situation is very different from yours. I knew what my parents were like before I met them. Of course, look at them today. They are intimidating as hell."

"When I first met my father, any anger I had toward him disappeared for obvious reasons. I was more concerned about my life than being angry at him. I think in your case it would be the opposite. Of course, my love, I do not think it would be wise to show yourself to either of your parents; that is if they are even alive today."

Marci agreed, "Oh, I know I cannot show my face to them. That will be difficult though."

I said, "I do not know if this is a good idea. We might want to try to keep this from Wolfgang, but would you like to talk to one or both of them?"

Marci's eyes lit up and she said, "Yes, I would love to talk to them and… give them a piece of my mind."

I said, "I understand, but you cannot tip them to where we are located. You also cannot lead them to any suspicious behavior that might force them to act, like contacting the police or the FBI." Marci shook her head in agreement. I said, "Well, with your permission I could hire someone, but Marci, it seems it may be a little difficult to find them."

Marci said, "I know. I have nothing to go on except for what little information they gave to the agency."

I said, "So is it just your gut feeling that they are alive?"

Marci shrugged her shoulders and said, "I just don't know, Garrison. I think they are. What little I do know is that they were young when they abandoned me."

I asked Marci, "If you do not mind me asking, why now? Why did you not try to find them in the past?"

Marci looked down and said softly, "Well, I could never afford a private investigator and I didn't know the value of having a family or someone that cared for me until I met you."

Later that day I asked some of my contacts and the next day I got some names of private investigators. I called one of the names on the list and set up an appointment with him later that day to meet at his office. The gentleman's name was Myron Keens. Myron was a tall, thin, middle-aged guy. He had many years of experience finding people. I told him Marci's story and that she didn't know I was trying to find her parents. I couldn't have Myron meet with Marci so in essence, I became her. I gave him the address of Marci's adoption agency and since Marci was a ward of the state, all her records had public access. We agreed upon a price and after a firm handshake, I went home.

A week went by before Myron called me. He told me he had found some information. We met for lunch and he handed me a package. Inside the package was all the information he'd found on Marci's parents. They were both alive. He gave me a rundown on their stories. After lunch I came home and as I pulled up the driveway, I saw Marci looking at me through the window. I got out of my car and went inside with the package. Thankfully, my parents were nowhere to be seen. As I entered the house, Marci stood there, motionless. I smiled and said, "Hi. Well... he founded them. They are alive. I have all their information in this package."

I sat down in the kitchen chair and Marci followed my lead. I placed my hand on the package and gently slid it in front of her. Marci put one hand on mine and moved it back toward me. She said, "You open it."

I grabbed the large envelope, opened it, and slid out the papers. My mind was racing and I sensed Marci's was racing faster. Marci asked, "So, what does all of this say?"

As I was reading, I said, "Well, it looks like your mother's name is Julie Effington." I looked up and saw tears streaming down my lover's cheek. I could somewhat sympathize with how difficult this was for her. I continued, "She is from Virginia Beach, Virginia and is now living in Madison, Wisconsin. She has been an elementary school teacher for over twenty years. She has been married twice. She is currently in her second marriage which has lasted about nine years. She has three sons, all from her first marriage."

Marci interrupted me and said, "She has three fucking sons?" More tears poured from her eyes. Her large hand covered her mouth as she was shaking her head.

I paused for several seconds, not knowing what to say. For the first time in a while, my Marci cried. She said, "How... how can a mother... give up her child... then go out and have three more and keep them?" I understood what Marci was saying. I don't understand it either. Marci said, "Virginia? How did I end up in Louisville?"

I scanned through the large stack of papers. I noticed her age and doing some quick math in my head I slowly stated, "It looks like she had you at sixteen." As I looked through the information, something wasn't adding up. I noticed there were several months of lag between Marci's birthdate and when she was turned in for adoption. As I continued to read, it made more sense. It was difficult for me to tell Marci. I didn't want to hurt her further, but I had to tell her what the papers said. I continued, "Okay, this is going to upset you. It looks like she kept you for a few months, 88 days. It looks like her father accepted a job with UPS. He was a pilot. They moved here to Louisville and after a couple of weeks here, they dropped you off at the adoption agency." Marci let out a gasp. She closed her eyes and cried harder. I just sat there scanning the report that was in front of me. I continued, "All of her sons are currently living in Wisconsin."

Marci sat up straight in her chair. She wiped her eyes and said, "What about my father?"

I shuffled through the papers and said, "Your father's name is Scott Ironhill. He is from Brokenbow, Nebraska. It looks like his father was in the Navy. He had lived in numerous states. California, Texas, Louisiana, Virginia... including Virginia Beach, and... yes... at the same time your birth mother was in Virginia Beach." I scanned down the many papers that were in front of me and said, "Yes, they attended the same high school. So it seems that your father got your mother pregnant, she took you home, her father got a job here in Louisville, they brought you here and after a couple of weeks, she... dropped you off at the adoption agency."

Large tears ran down her porcelain white cheeks as she listened to every word I said. I continued, "It would seem they were high school sweethearts and he got her pregnant during the time she knew she was going to leave."

I looked through the paperwork and came upon additional information. "It looks like your birth father is a mechanical engineer living in Sacramento, California. He is currently divorced, for about four years, and is now in a serious relationship. According to these records, neither your mother nor your father ever attempted to contact you at any time since your birth."

Marci shouted out, "Does he have children?"

I scanned down and said, "Yes. From his first marriage. Had a girl and a boy. One lives near him just north of Sacramento and the oldest lives in Seattle. He didn't have any children from his second marriage."

No sooner than I had finished, Marci stood up and shoved her chair backward with the back of her legs. The chair flew halfway across the kitchen. Marci shouted, "Fuck this! Fuck them! What the hell gave them the right to dump me and both of those god damn motherfuckers went on and had more children! They kept them, but they didn't keep me! What... the... fuck, Garrison!"

I got up and went over to her. Marci pushed my arms away. She was so upset. She said, "I... I am sorry, but I just need time." She ran out of the kitchen and went upstairs. I went over and picked up her chair.

Suddenly, Zelda came in the kitchen and asked, "What happened?"

At that point, I decided to tell her the story. When I finished, I noticed Wolfgang standing in the great room listening to our conversation. I just shrugged my shoulders and said, "We need to give her some time to process all of this."

Later that night, I went to our bedroom. Marci had not been out of the room all day. She was lying on the bed crying. I entered the room and said, "Marci, I am so sorry. I do not know what to say. I am here for you. I love you. Take all the time you need. If you need me, I am here for you."

Marci just cried harder as she buried her face in her pillow. I asked, "Do you want to be left alone tonight or do you want some company?"

Marci paused for a moment then quickly pushed her head up from the pillow. She turned to me and said angrily, "You know what I want!" She got up from the bed and stormed over to me. For the first time, I was frightened of Marci. She said with incredible passion, "I want to meet them! I want to fucking meet them. Both of them, so I can torture the fuck out of them and wish that they never did that to me! I want to kill them, Garrison. I want to kill them!"

I stood there nervously and said, "But Marci, you…we cannot do that. You would be exposed to the world. You would expose all of us to the world."

Marci interrupted me and said, "Fuck you!! Fuck that!!"

I said, "Marci! Calm down! If you bring them here and kill them, you will have the whole fucking world snooping around this place!"

Marci moved closer to me until her large breasts hit my shoulders. She kept pushing me backward with her body as she seemed to attempt to walk through me. Suddenly, my back hit the wall. I heard my parents running up the stairs. When Wolfgang got to the entrance of our bedroom, Marci look at me and said, "Stay." She walked over to the entrance.

Wolfgang said, "What's going on in here? Are you okay?"

Marci looked at Wolfgang and said, "Do you mind?" With that said she moved her long tail to the middle edge of the door. As she turned her body, she quickly slammed the door in Wolfgang's face with her tail.

Wolfgang sensed what was going to happen. All I heard was my father saying to my mother, "Let's go."

My heart was beating so fast, but I now sensed I wasn't in any danger. Marci walked over to me and I felt her tail on my ass. She moved closer to me as her long, snake-like tongue came out. She used it to lick the side of my face. She said, "I know how to get to you, my dear! You are so turned on right now, aren't you?"

I had to admit it. It had been a while since we'd made love and all the excitement was getting to me. She suddenly ripped off her shirt and lowered her shorts. Her tail went inside of her vagina and she said, "Oh… just imagine this could be your dick inside of me. That can happen if you just agree to set up a meeting with them."

It was very difficult to think but I said, "Marci, with all due respect, I cannot let you meet with them face to face."

Marci seductively said, "Ooooooh!"

I said, "But I can arrange, maybe, a telephone conversation with them. That is really the only option."

Marci knew it was the only way she could ever converse with her parents, but she never let her guard down for a moment. Her anger was beyond any reason. She thought she would have an outside shot at meeting her parents in person so she had to take that shot.

When I look back on this moment, I fully understood my Marci's desires. I had those same desires with my brother, Adam. I was going to torture then murder him. It was just a matter of time. I didn't care about any consequences that would result from my actions, I just wanted him to suffer then eventually die. I told myself I would worry about the consequences later. This is where Marci's mind was at that moment. I stood there feeling my body shaking and my mind racing. I was worried about my Marci. She was so obsessed and hurt. Decades of wounds had been reopened for my love. She felt vulnerable and she hated the way that felt.

I knew my father would never allow Marci to physically meet her birth parents. I doubted he would like her talking to them over the phone. Marci knew she was going to have a major issue with Wolfgang as well, but she was ready for the fight.

What a cruel ultimatum Marci had bestowed upon me, but I loved her with all my heart. For the second time since we had met, she played with my emotions to get what she wanted. The first time she killed herself before me so I was forced to bring her back to life. She wanted to go through the transformation so she could be perfect and be with me forever.

Marci knew I would have done anything for her. In her mind, she made the ultimate sacrifice by giving up her physical appearance for perfection and everlasting life. So, it was my turn to show my love for her. I believe she wanted to test my love and see just how far I would go for her. At that time, she knew I would have risked anything for her and that turned her on sexually more than anything.

Marci never loved me more than the day she momentarily tricked me. Marci stood there pouting, trying to change my mind about physically meeting her parents. She slowly undressed me. Her long tail was wet from being inside her vagina. As she smiled, she moved her tail around my manhood and started to gently massage me. She led me to the bed while holding onto my penis. She laid down on her back and quickly pulled me toward her. She rubbed the head of my penis across her vagina. After several tantalizing minutes of coaxing, she forced me inside her. I could barely stand it – I needed release.

Marci anticipated that I was about to ejaculate. She grabbed me under my arms, pulled me out of her, and put me on her chest. I quickly noticed those beautiful breasts. I placed my penis between them as she squeezed them together, tonguing the end of my penis with her forked tongue. The feeling was so intense. I couldn't last any longer, I had to release. I held my breath and focused on my cock until I exploded all over her. She took her tongue and lapped up every drop. Marci didn't allow me to recover. She threw me off her, I landed on my back, and before I could react, she mounted me. I was still hard as she forced herself on me. All I could think about was what an incredible woman I had fallen in love with.

That night we continued to make wild, passionate love. Our lovemaking went on for hours on end. I knew she was hurt, but she was getting over the initial shock of what had happened to her nearly forty years ago. This was her way of dealing with the news of her past. As the night passed, Marci began to think that just maybe she could pull off this charade. She would love to meet either one or both of her parents, especially her mother. I believe that if she had been standing before her that night, Marci would have killed her on the spot.

The next morning I was sitting at the kitchen table, thinking about how I should make contact without going to prison. How could I get them, or just one of them, to the estate? Marci would have her way with them but I knew the authorities would be knocking at my door. I couldn't just kidnap someone that had so many ties to their community. Their entire family, children, and friends would be out looking for them. How could I put everything and everyone in jeopardy? All the lives that I would be affecting and everything that I had worked for all my life would be gone. With all this knowledge, my only thought that remained was that I couldn't disappoint my Marci.

Wolfgang entered the kitchen and immediately sensed my desperation. Without even asking me he shouted, "What is going on here? What are you thinking about doing? Don't do anything that you will regret, boy!"

I was scared. For the second time after so many encounters, I was scared. I about jumped out of my skin when Marci entered the room. She was confident and cocky. She said, "Oh, Garrison hasn't spoken to you yet about my parents coming to visit me?"

Wolfgang was speechless for a moment. His anger grew into rage. He bellowed, "You will not bring those humans into this house! You will not endanger the many lives in this house!"

Marci and Wolfgang stared at each other. Marci was now getting upset. Wolfgang snarled, "Listen to me. I have put up with a lot with your fucking tantrums and ideas. I have bent over backward for you. I even let you torture four kids and made their mother into a pet for you. But this time you ask too much!"

Marci was seething. She shouted back at my father, "You don't know how it is to be abandoned and have that haunt you every day for forty fucking years, you prick!" Wolfgang growled. He bared his pearly white teeth at my love as she continued, "Garrison is going to set something up for me."

Wolfgang interrupted, "He is only helping you because you tricked him with your sex. You're a fucking whore."

Marci then bared her teeth at Wolfgang. I had to step into the argument – and fast. I said, "Look, Marci is not a whore. She did not trick me into anything. Let us talk about this. This issue cannot come between us."

Wolfgang said, "No human is stepping into this house. It is too dangerous."

Marci said, "All I want is to get to know them. I have never met them."

Wolfgang laughed and said, "Do you take me for a fool? I know what you want. I sense it, woman. You want to kill them. Then what? Where are you going to hide? Most importantly, where I am going to hide? What about Eva or your fuck partner, Garrison?"

Marci said, "That fuck partner is your son, you fucking bastard!"

Wolfgang said, "Don't raise your fucking voice at me!"

Marci shouted, "Don't fucking tell me what to do, you piece of shit. You killed most of your offspring. Fuck! You are no better than my fucking parents. In fact, you are worse than them."

Wolfgang was getting angrier and roared, "Shut the fuck up, Marci!"

Marci continued, "You don't love anyone. You are just like them. The only difference is they didn't kill me. I despise people like you. You even killed your own."

Wolfgang stepped toward Marci only to be slightly held back by Zelda. I quickly moved in front of Marci only to be gently pushed aside by her large and powerful hand. Wolfgang shouted, "You are no better than me, woman! You killed your husband's children… four of them! Only for your own selfish desires!"

Marci had never felt so much anger in her life. She couldn't think or see straight. To have Wolfgang push that in her face brought her to the brink of insanity. Those four children were my children from another woman. That had been the most difficult part of her life. Marci wanted children so badly, but she didn't want to endanger her life. Seeing those four little freaks forced Marci into accepting the fact that she didn't want her children to look or act the way Sarah's children did. The cold hard had facts hit her square in the face. She was never going to be a mother. To hear those words coming out of Wolfgang's mouth was too much for her to bear.

Marci's rage was out of control. Wolfgang and I sensed it. Before I could react, Marci went after Wolfgang. Her large hands went for his throat. Wolfgang quickly batted them away and immediately grabbed Marci's throat with his right hand. His long fingers wrapped around the sides and most of the back of her neck. Marci immediately took her left hand and wrapped it around the side of Wolfgang's neck then moved her strong and powerful thumb just under Wolfgang's Adam's apple. The harder he squeezed, the harder she squeezed. Both were in physical pain.

Zelda ran over and hung on Wolfgang's arm, screaming, "Wolfgang! No! Stop it! Let her go!"

I pleaded with Marci and my father. "Stop it! You are going to kill each other! Stop it!"

Wolfgang took his left arm, made a fist, and quickly punched Marci in her side. All her air came out at once. Without any warning, he punched her in the face. She released her grip and stumbled backward, falling onto the floor. I immediately ran over and stood between her and my father. I held up my hand saying, "Stop it! Just stop it! I have had enough of this, god damn it!"

Wolfgang stopped and allowed Zelda to hold him back from attacking her more. Marci was hurt. Her right cheek was bleeding, her side was hurting, and she was having trouble breathing. I again shouted, "Stop! Just stop it! I have had enough of this shit. I have seen my adoptive father get killed by my brother, my own mother and even my girlfriend killed themselves before me. I have had enough!! Understand? Do you understand me?!"

Marci placed her hand on my leg to acknowledge me. Her large eyes looked up at Wolfgang in a haunting gaze. Wolfgang matched her glare and said, "Don't attack me. Don't ever do that again. Do you understand, Marci?"

Marci looked at my father with no expression. Wolfgang repeated, "Do you understand?"

Marci grunted, "Yes, I understand. Whatever."

I had to take control of the situation. I said, "Okay, Marci, we cannot invite your parents here to the estate." I looked at Wolfgang and said, "But we can call them on the phone. We are untraceable so they cannot find out where we live. I did not bring you guys here from Germany to have you discovered. So, are we in agreement that we can talk to them on the phone?"

Wolfgang looked at me with a gleam in his eyes. I knew he was proud of me for standing up to him and taking control of the situation. I began to understand this was his goal from the start. He said, "I don't like it, but as long as I am in the room while the phone call is made, then so be it."

I looked at Marci and she gave me a disapproving look and said, "Fine. Whatever."

Later that night, Marci was on the phone with Eva. She told her about the whole incident with Wolfgang. Eva was very upset with her father, but Marci calmed her down and told her not to tell her father about their conversation. Eva told Marci that she wanted to help her out with anything that she needed, although Marci understood that Eva couldn't really help her. Marci knew, even before Wolfgang 'setting her straight,' that the best she could hope for was a telephone conversation. Marci told Eva that her career was the most important goal for Eva right now and to concentrate on that and her schoolwork.

The next day, the tensions were less. I sat down with Marci and my parents. I reviewed the entire file that the private investigator had given me. Marci hadn't seen everything in the package so I looked at Marci and asked, "Do you want to see what your parents look like?"

Marci held her massive hands up to her face. Zelda, who was sitting between her husband and Marci, leaned over and placed her large arm around Marci. I dug out many photos of both Julie and Scott and laid them down in front of Marci. As soon as she saw them, she cried. For the first time she had seen her parents' faces. The first picture that she saw was of Julie. Julie was an overweight lady with relatively short, dirty-blonde hair that stopped just before her pale jawline.

Marci then picked up a picture of her father. Scott was a large man, about six feet three inches tall. He had a barrel-type chest and was in excellent shape. He had a full head of hair and looked overly tan for his age.

I covered every document that was in the package then reviewed the information that I'd told Marci the previous day. This was a very emotional time in Marci's life, but she wanted to find her parents. Not a word needed to be said because we all understood what Marci had and continued to go through emotionally. It was a difficult moment for all of us, especially for Marci and me. Both of our parents had abandoned us and then had more children after they gave us up. Even with all of that out there for us to contemplate, Marci didn't completely blame Wolfgang and Zelda. She maintained her composure.

Marci broke the awkward silence and said, "You know, this is very hard for me because of what they did to me years ago, but also because of your history with Garrison. You guys gave up Garrison although I understand why you did. You know, because of your circumstances and all. But for me, my situation was very different. I understand that I cannot meet them. I should have met them before I transformed, huh?" Marci laughed while she looked at me from across the table.

I said, "Well, I think it is a good thing for all of us that you did not." Everyone in the kitchen laughed, which helped break the tension.

Marci said, "I'm sorry, Wolfgang. I truly am sorry. You have done so much for me and Garrison. I was wrong to attack you. I hope that you can somehow understand why this is so emotional for me."

Wolfgang sat thinking deeply. He said, "I understand. What happened, happened. We need to move on. I'm not the emotional type, but I must admit that I am very glad Zelda kept you alive, Garrison. To this day I still can't believe she was able to keep that from me all of those years."

Zelda spoke up and said, "I didn't think you would survive the night, but it was my only choice. When I got pregnant it was something that shouldn't have happened. Wolfgang... well... it happened. We had always been so careful that he not ejaculate inside me. But it happened."

Wolfgang said, "I was angry at the time for getting Zelda pregnant. I didn't want to take the lives while they were inside of her; that cave was not sterile. So, we waited until she gave birth. When she gave birth, I had to kill them. I couldn't control all those kids. I couldn't let them get out in the world and affect other living things. The whole process of a naturally living species in this world could have been affected. Imagine if one of those offspring would infect a small animal, then they in turn would bite another living organism. The consequences could have been catastrophic."

I laughed a little and said, "You are correct. That is exactly what happened. I bit Trevor and he changed."

Wolfgang said, "I knew something wasn't right the moment I saw that doctor guy walking in my forest. At that moment, I knew something was not right."

Zelda said, "I know. When I first saw him, I sensed that the baby that I had left at the small stream had lived. What was confusing me was how he ended up as an American."

I said, "Well, as you can see, Marci, we have an awesome responsibility to not only mankind but most importantly to all species that roam this planet."

Marci nodded to say she understood. Wolfgang said, "This is why I worry about Eva. I hope she understands the gravity of the potential situation that she could unleash on the world. All it would take is just one bite, to break the skin of another and inject the formula."

I said, "I know. We have spoken at great lengths about it and I am very confident that she will not misuse the formula."

Later that day, I went to my office and closed the door. I picked up the phone and called Julie. As the phone rang, my mind was racing as fast as my heart. The phone went into her voicemail. I left a message saying, "Hello, my name is Garrison Seawick. I was hoping you would return my call. I have high confidence that my fiancé might be your daughter. This is not a prank call. Your daughter and I have been dating for many years and she wanted to reach out to her birth parents. She would like to talk to you at your convenience." I left her my number and asked her to please call back.

I looked through the files and found Scott's phone number. With a deep breath I called his cell number. Again, I experienced the same emotions when the phone was ringing as I did during my call to Julie. I was shaken a bit when a voice answered. I said, "Hello, my name is Garrison. I am calling from Kentucky. I would like to speak with Scott Ironhill."

The voice said, "Speaking."

I said, "Good afternoon, Mr. Ironhill. This is a difficult phone call to make, but my fiancé wanted me to call you. Please don't hang up, this is not a prank. She believes that you are her father. We hired a private investigator and after some digging, we discovered that you and Julie Effington had a daughter in Virginia Beach, Virginia. We are not looking for financial support or even to meet with you. She just wanted to talk to you and Julie for some kind of closure. I know this is hard to believe, so I apologize that I am dropping this on you. I know you need some time to process all of this so please take your time. If you need to call me back, please feel free to do so."

When I stopped talking, I sat there and listened. The reception was very clear. I could hear his heartbeat through the phone. He cleared his voice and said, "Wow. I was not expecting this." He laughed and I chuckled, mimicking his actions.

I said, "I understand this is a shock. I can send you all the papers that the investigator gave us. I know this is an invasion of your privacy, but all of the information we gathered on you was through public records."

Scott said, "No. No, I understand... I just... well... it has been what... twenty something... twenty-eight or twenty-nine years?"

I said, "Over forty years."

Scott said, "Yeah... forty years, yeah that is about right. Well... man... what a shock. Yeah, I would love to speak with her. You know, I think about that day a lot. We were just teenagers at the time. We were so scared. I was a Navy brat back then. We moved so many places then Julie's dad got a job out of state and there was no chance that I could have custody of my daughter. Well... I would love to speak with her. Is she... there?"

I said, "No, not at the moment. She does not know that I have called. I think she would like to speak with you and Julie at the same time."

Scott said, "Sure... sure just... call me whenever. Thanks for calling. Wow, I cannot believe this is happening."

When I hung up the phone, I just sat back in my chair. I turned myself around and looked outside. I was thinking about the best way to handle this news before I confronted Marci. Suddenly, my concentration was broken by the ringing sound of my phone. I quickly looked at the caller ID and it was Julie's number. I answered the call. I said, "Hello, this is Garrison speaking."

The women on the other line said nervously, "Yes… this is Julie. You called? What is this about again?"

I said, "This is about the daughter that you gave to the adoption agency, New Beginnings in Louisville, Kentucky, about forty years ago. My fiancé is your daughter and she wanted me to reach out to see if you would like to speak with her on the phone. I have already contacted Scott Ironhill and he agreed to speak with her. I would like for you to join him on a conference call. Your daughter would love to hear your voice."

Julie said, "Who is this? Who are you?"

I said, "My name is Garrison. My fiancé and I have been dating for many years. We hired a private investigator to explore her past. We believe that you are her mother. We are not looking for money or even to physically meet with you, she just wanted to talk. You are Julie Effington, correct? From Virginia Beach, Virginia? You went to Eastern High School where you met Scott Ironhill, a Navy brat. You two had a daughter. Your father got a job transfer to Louisville, Kentucky so you brought your daughter here for a couple of weeks then gave her up for adoption."

"Okay!" Julie said. I gave her some time to collect her thoughts. Julie asked, "Is she… on the line with us?"

I said, "No. Would you be interested in a conference call with your daughter?"

A long, awkward silence followed. Julie said, "Yes. How is she?"

I said, "She is fine. She turned out wonderfully. She is the most beautiful woman you could ever imagine." I heard Julie becoming very emotional and said, "So let me inform her that you guys are interested and I will set up a time for the conference call. Is that satisfactory to you?"

Julie said, "Yes. Thank you."

With that I said goodbye. As I hung up the phone, I heard a knock on my door. It was Marci. She knew I had spoken with her parents. I looked at her and smiled. I got up and raised my arms in the air. She ran over to me and we hugged. Marci said, "I am ready to talk to them."

I said, "Let me get Wolfgang and let us do this."

I went downstairs and told Wolfgang and Zelda about Marci's parents. They followed me into my study. I saw Marci sitting in my chair, holding the phone while she moved her large thumb gently over the screen. I asked, "Are you okay?" Marci nodded her head. I sat down in the chair in front of the desk as my parents stood. I gently took the phone from my Marci's hand as she gave it up willingly.

I dialed Scott's number first. After several rings, Scott answered, "Hello."

For the first time in Marci's life, she heard her father's voice. I said, "Scott, this Garrison. Is this a good time?"

He said, "Why... yes. Yes it is."

I said, "Hold on, let me get Julie on the other line."

I placed Scott on hold and called Julie's number. She quickly answered the phone after the first ring. She said, "Hello! This is Julie."

I said, "Julie, this is Garrison. Is this a good time for you?"

She said, "Yes. Is my daughter there?" Marci moved around in the chair, trying to stay calm. She had her large hand over her mouth with tears forming in her eyes. She sat there, closing her eyes from time to time, trying to remain calm.

I said, "Yes she is——."

Julie interrupted and said, "Hello... this is Julie... your mother."

I quickly said, "Hold on, Julie, let me bring Scott back on the line. Hello, Scott?"

Scott said, "Yeah, I'm here."

I said, "Julie, are you there?"

She said, "Yes... hello, Scott. It's been a long time."

Scott said, "Yes it has. How are you and the family?"

Julie said, "Good, yours?"

The conversation was a haunting reminder of Marci's past, a past that she was constantly forgotten and ignored, time after time.

I quickly sensed that they might be more interested in talking to each other than speaking with their daughter. Not once did her parents seem like they wanted to talk to her first; they wanted to talk to each other instead.

I saw Marci looking down at the table. Her eyes were fixed on the paperwork that I had on her parents. She was looking at her mother's file. After a moment, Marci closed her mouth tightly after she heard Julie said, "Good, yours?" I knew all of this was coming to a head soon. I didn't know how to manage the consequences of where this conversation started. I quickly said, "I have your daughter here on the line. That is the purpose of this phone call."

I waited for a response. Finally, Julie said, "Hello. My name is Julie." A long pause ensued. I looked at my Marci. She was just sitting there, looking at me, staring a hole through me with a lifeless expression on her face.

I said, "Your daughter is here with me. I think the shock of hearing your voices for the first time might be more difficult than what we first thought." I looked a Marci and whispered, "Do you want to continue or do you need for us to call them back at a later date?" Moments passed as she just sat there, staring at me. I was having trouble sensing what was wrong. She was in full control of her emotions, or at least I thought that at the time.

Scott broke the awkward silence, he said, "Uhhhh, this is Scott, your father. Are you okay? Is everything good with you?"

Marci moved her head toward the phone and slightly opened her mouth. Saliva started to drip from her lips and run down the side of her chin.

Julie said, "Yes, how have you been?"

Marci continued to stare at the phone and after several uncomfortable moments Marci yelled, "Marci!"

Julie, on the other line, let out a small yip. She said, "Oh! I'm sorry. Is that your name?" Marci looked at me and I closed my eyes as soon as her eyes met mine. I could immediately sense what Marci was feeling.

Marci moved her hands out across the table as if she was searching for something to hold or grab onto. Four decades of frustration, pain, and mental anguish were all coming to the forefront at that moment. Marci yelled, "My name is Marci! Are you fucking kidding me! Not once did you ask my name! My name is Marci! I don't even fucking know if that was the name you picked out for me or if some bitch at the adoption agency gave me that name!" Marci waited for a response. They didn't say a word. Marci said again, even louder, "I said, was it you that gave me that name? Answer me!"

Julie quickly and nervously said, "It was me. I named you. I have an aunt named Marci."

Marci said, "Did you ever once think about me? How I looked growing up, what I was doing, what I sounded like, did someone adopt that piece of shit child that I gave up?" Julie started to cry on the phone. Marci said, "What? Are you crying? What the fuck! Do you feel sorry for yourself? Why are you crying? I should be the one crying! Why are you crying?"

Julie shouted, "This is all so difficult for me..."

Marci interrupted, "Difficult for you? Fuck you! Did you ever once think about me? Why have you not even tried to contact me?"

Julie was crying hard over the phone and asked the rudest question I could imagine, "Why did it take you so long to contact me?"

Marci was outraged. She said, "Because it is not my place to contact you, bitch! You gave me up! I never asked to be born! You abandoned me!"

Suddenly Scott wanted to say something, which was a mistake on his part. He said, "Now, Marci, let's calm down…"

Marci quickly interrupted and said, "Calm down? Fuck you! Why did you let her take me from you? Why didn't you want me?"

Scott cleared his voice and said, "Okay, please let me explain. This is what happened. We were both in our junior year in high school. Julie and I dated throughout our junior year. We made a mistake and Julie got pregnant."

Marci interrupted, "So I was a mistake."

Scott said, "No! I don't mean it like that. I should have worn protection, but I didn't. It… just happened. Then while she was pregnant, her father got a job out of town. It was a very difficult time in our lives. No court was going to award me custody of you and my parents were very upset with me. When Julie told us that she was going to leave, it was a relief to my parents, but not to me. After you and Julie left, I thought it would be better to stay out of contact with everyone. I was living in Virginia and you guys were in Kentucky. Then Julie called me and she was hysterical. I will never forget that phone call. She called me right after she sent you to the adoption agency. I was very upset with her at the time, but I understood. Having a child at seventeen would have been very difficult. We thought you would end up in a loving home, a home that you deserved."

Marci said, "But no one adopted me, asshole! I grew up alone. Alone! I had no one! I was all alone. I had no one in my fucking life. No one wanted me. I missed out on all those Father-Daughter dances. I missed my proms because I couldn't afford a dress. I still, to this day, don't know what it's like to go out and shop with my mother. It took me years before I wore something new. I always wore hand-me-downs because that's all I got from anyone. I never had a steady friend in my life. No one at school wanted to come and visit me like their other friends did. I couldn't go over to other girls' houses because I wasn't allowed to by the fucking bitches that ran the agency. I was a good kid. I was beautiful. I was smart. But time after time, no one wanted me. I would go through interview after interview. The older I got, the less people wanted me. I have no idea why no one wanted me when I was a baby. Maybe I gave off some evil scent or something. Some of the bitches at the center told me years afterward that people would say there was just an air about me. That is what I was told about me. I had an air about me. I mean to this day, I still cannot fucking figure that out. So what is your side of the story... Mother?"

Julie started to sob but pulled herself together. She said, "I am so sorry! I never wanted to hurt you. I was young and scared. I was living with my parents in a strange new city. I didn't have a friend to rely on. My parents had just uprooted me and I had this baby. You were so beautiful and you were a good baby. But after a couple of weeks living in our apartment, my parents told me that it would be in everyone's best interest to give you away. It was a terrible decision to have to make and follow through with. As I handed you over to the child care services lady, I wouldn't let you go. I almost dropped you when she tried to take you from my arms. My mother forced you out of my arms and gave you to them. She literally dragged me out of that place. I didn't speak to her for the longest time and I hated myself for years. When I turned eighteen I went on to college and moved into a dorm. I never went back home. It took me years before I could look at my mother without thinking of doing harm to her. While I was in college, I majored in Education. I studied to be a teacher because I wanted to help young children."

Marci said, "Did you not once think about coming to visit me? You never made any attempt to contact me. Why?"

Julie started crying again. She said, "Because I was scared. I was scared because I wanted to take you back and they wouldn't let me. I didn't want to relive that pain all over again."

Marci started to laugh in a rather evil way. She said, "What about the pain that you put me through? Did you ever once think about that, you fucking bitch!"

Scott interrupted and said, "Here now, there's no need—"

Marci shouted, "Shut up! Just shut the fuck up! You fucked her, she left you and you were off the god damn hook! You never once owned up to your responsibilities. You had it easy! Not once did you ever try to contact me! Not one fucking time! And... you know what really is just fucking amazing is that you stupid piles of shit went on with your lives, fucked other people and had more god damned kids! Multiple kids! I am surprised you didn't give them up for adoption. Which begs the question. Why did you not give them up?"

A long period of silence dominated the call. Marci said, "Well? Hello!" Not a word was uttered. Marci said, "Are you there?" Both of her parents started to say something and Marci continued, "Maybe because it was convenient for you to have kids at that time in your miserable, pathetic lives. You were ready to have kids! Oh, to hell with Marci! She wasn't part of the plan. She was a mistake! Well fuck you both! I hope you rot in hell. I wish I could come over to your fucking houses and break every god damned bone in your pathetic bodies. I wish I could rip the fucking arms off you pieces of shit. I wish to fucking god I could cut your little fucking limp dick off and shove it up your god damn asshole, you mother fucking cocksucker! And you, 'Mother,' three fucking kids? You had three of them? Let me tell you something, you god damned cunt lover. I am better than any of them. I am fucking perfect now. I am perfect! Fucking perfect! God damn you, your children, and everyone associated with you people. You people disgust me. I hate you both and I hope to see you in hell someday, you cocksuckers."

Marci was screaming at the top of her lungs. I wanted to say something, but I just sat there looking at the phone. I could hear both Scott and Julie moving around on the other end of the line. I could feel their tension. Scott was pissed and wanted to tell her off. Julie was beyond upset. She was about to totally lose control over her emotions. They never thought this phone call was going to be filled with this much intense hatred. I had never experienced that much hate in one person. I felt so sorry for my love. She was truly a tortured woman.

Scott said, "I really don't have to put up with this—"

Marci yelled, "So what are you going to do? Run off again? Leave me again like you did years ago? Go on, mother fucker, leave. Leave now before I come over to your fucking little house and shave every inch of skin off your fat, faggot body, you fucking pervert. Go fuck yourself!"

Scott slammed the phone down. I was worried about my Marci. She was getting more and more out of control. I didn't want to say anything to her because that would have aggravated her more. I was sure glad that our location was untraceable, and I knew Wolfgang was worried about Scott calling the authorities, but having the scrambler on our phone soothed his fears.

Julie was still on the phone, crying even harder. Marci said, "Oh shut up! Stop your fucking crying. If anyone should be crying it's me. How could you leave me at that center? What was going through your mind, bitch? All I have ever wanted was to have a boyfriend and a family. I only have one of those. I am so thankful each and every day that passes that I have a man, a real man, that loves me for who I am. A man that will not give me up for someone else. But what really galls my ass is that you had three, not one but three other kids. How can you live with yourself?"

Julie was hysterical. Her voice quivered. She said, "I know! I know! It was the hardest thing I have ever done. Not a day goes by that I don't think about it. You have every right to be upset at me. I don't blame you. I would be upset too if I were you. It's unforgivable what I did to you. Never in my wildest dreams did I think you wouldn't be adopted by a nice family."

Marci's tears were running down her face as she said, "I was not even close to being adopted! What was wrong with me? But the thing that I most have trouble dealing with is that you never called me. How can you live with that guilt of just abandoning a little baby? You and that limp dicked boyfriend of yours never wrote or called me. Why? How could you do that? Did you not once wonder about how I turned out or what happened to me?"

Julie tried to compose herself. She said, "I know this is wrong, but it was the only way of dealing with this issue."

Marci interrupted and screamed, "Issue! Oh, I am so sorry that I was such an issue for you!"

Julie said, "I shouldn't have said issue. I don't know what to say. In my situation, that event... that took place in my life, I had to deal with it the best way I knew how. For me, at that time, was to try to forget it. I know it was the wrong thing to do, but it was my only option. I couldn't allow myself to think about you because that would make me want to come back to you. You wouldn't have wanted me as a mom then. Then time got away from me, I met a nice man, we fell in love and I got married. Naturally, we had children. I am so sorry but what is done is done. I cannot control the past. I can only hope that someday you can forgive me."

Marci was getting angrier. She yelled, "Forgive you?" She leaned toward the phone and in the most disturbing voice I have ever heard said, "I will never forgive you. You are dead to me. I wish I could kill you, but I can't. I wish you nothing but death. A very painful death. I hope you rot in hell, bitch!" Marci backed away from the phone and tilted her head back. As she bent forward she let out the most impressive and haunting roar. Her voice was so strong my desk was vibrating from her sound.

Julie screamed on the other end of the phone. She said, "What was that? Are you even human?"

Marci screamed, "Fuck you! Fuck you!" She rose up from her chair and raised her large hand in the air. She made a fist and swung down with all her might, and as her hand hit the phone, it broke instantly as her fist drove through Trevor's old and expensive desk. When Marci pulled her hand out of the hole, large splinters of wood embedded themselves into her hand and wrist, causing deep cuts in her flesh.

As my parents watched everything, I quickly stood up and got out of her way. Wolfgang walked toward Marci in a non-confrontational manner. Marci tilted her head back as she screamed loudly. My whole office seemed to quiver from her haunting growl. She stepped away from her chair, picked the right side up and pushed it out of her way. Wolfgang stepped back as Marci yelled, "Get out of my way!" She stormed out of the office and ran down the hallway. Wolfgang and Zelda followed her. I tried to keep up, but their strides were much longer than mine. Wolfgang was worried that Marci might do something crazy. He wanted to keep her in the house because he was worried about where she might go or what she might do.

I raced downstairs as fast as I could. I ended up tripping on the last step and fell hard on my side. As I laid there trying to recover, I heard Marci and my parents in the great room. I struggled to get up, but my ankle was very sore and started to swell immediately. I limped into the great room. Marci seemed to be experiencing a panic attack as she was pacing back and forth. Wolfgang and Zelda were trying to calm her but to no avail.

Marci's eyes caught mine. She knew I was hurt. She started to cry harder. Her large hands covered her mouth as she held back her scream. I raised my hand to say I was fine. I said, "I just twisted my ankle. I am fine. Marci, I am so sorry. I know that upset you and I am so sorry. This is all my fault."

Marci stood there shaking her head back and forth. She struggled to say, "It's not your fault, my love. You did what I asked you to do. Thank you for finding them. It's just... so hard to accept. So many bad memories came back to me from my past. I have been so happy since I met you, but talking to them upset me so much."

I said, "I know. At least you got some of the frustration off your chest, but I understand what you are saying. It reopened some old, buried wounds."

My love stood there wiping the tears that were pouring from her eyes. Wolfgang sensed that she was regaining control of her emotions. Zelda came over and put her arm around Marci. Marci said, "I'm sorry for acting this way. I just can't understand why they would dump me like that."

Wolfgang turned away and headed to the kitchen. Marci turned her head and sensed what Wolfgang was thinking. Wolfgang stopped in his tracks and looked over his shoulder at her. He showed his teeth with a low sounding growl. Marci wasn't intimidated as she stared at him. Suddenly, Marci stepped away from Zelda. Zelda now sensed the coldness from Marci. Marci said to Zelda, "You gave up Garrison. How could you do that? All he wanted was a family."

Wolfgang interrupted and said, "No, Marci. This is not the time for this discussion."

Marci looked at Wolfgang and stuck her head out toward him. Suddenly she opened her mouth and a horrifying sound came pouring out. I saw her mouth open wide as she made this hissing sound. Saliva was dripping from most of the exposed teeth. Wolfgang returned the gesture. He stood square and mimicked Marci's growl but replaced her hissing with his deep, earth-shattering roar.

Marci's breathing was heavy. Her massive lungs were expanding and deflating at a maddening pace as she clinched her hands into fists. She looked at Wolfgang then quickly looked at Zelda. Marci let out a loud hissing sound at Zelda, which my mother returned with a quick growl. Everything was happening so quick, I didn't have time to react. Marci said, "You left him to die!"

Zelda said, "You don't understand."

Marci interrupted as she glared at Wolfgang. Marci said, "Oh yes I do. I understand what happened."

Wolfgang returned the same evil glare toward Marci, who tried to calm herself the best she could. She said, "I get it that you didn't want children." Her eyes then shifted toward Zelda and said, "But did you not feel anything when you left Garrison at that stream of water?"

Zelda was just staring a hole through my love. My mother's eyes found mine and suddenly a wave of calmness developed on her face. She said, "I knew you were going to die, but I gave you a small chance. I ran as fast as I could that night through the forest. I am surprised Wolfgang didn't follow me. In fact, I always wondered about that."

As Zelda looked over at Wolfgang, he said, "At first I had no clue. But as the years went on, I knew he was alive. I had heard some of the stories about a baby being discovered in the forest. I knew it was our son."

Zelda said, "I also knew he was alive. I just sensed it, but I never allowed myself to entertain the thought of him actually being alive. But to answer your question, I never wanted to have kids after my transformation. It wouldn't have been fair to them to be raised in the forest and away from their kind. It wasn't hard for me to leave Garrison." Zelda looked up at me and said, "I love you, my son and I am so happy you're alive. I cannot say why I wanted you to live and not the others. I witnessed Wolfgang killing your siblings, but something inside of me wanted you to live. I cannot explain it."

Marci slowly turned and walked over to me. She reached out her hand and caressed my face. I remained emotionless. Marci thought that was strange and I could see it in her eyes. Suddenly, she knew that being unwanted at that time didn't bother me like it used to. She understood, she knew, she sensed that I had come to peace with the terrible fact that my own parents didn't want me. I was somehow saved that day by the hiker that discovered me. He had no business being that deep in the forest. How is it that at that exact time, someone could discover a small infant lying on the ground near a stream of water? All the numerous events had to line up just so at the same exact time and place. It was amazing to ponder that if that person would have turned around a second sooner or went left instead of right, I wouldn't be here at this moment.

Marci sensed all my feelings. Not a word needed to be exchanged between us. She was feeling better. She was accepting what had happened to her. For the first time in her life, she was finally at a place in her mind where acceptance, as small as it might have been, was slowly entering her mind. It was taking root in her very being. I was an honored witness to the beginning stages of her acceptance of what her parents had done to her decades prior. Forgiveness was not in Marci's nature; therefore, this feeling was rarely explored and experienced by her. Marci was at a point where she had to let it go. It was eating her up and driving a wedge between her and my parents. Marci looked over her shoulder at Wolfgang with an open and accepting face.

My father stood there showing more of his teeth. My love slowly moved her large head in an up and down motion. Wolfgang's eyes squinted as he was surprised by her forgiving gesture. Wolfgang didn't care either way, but he was impressed by Marci's maturity. He was again surprised at how quickly she regained control over her emotions.

Marci slowly walked out of the great room and headed for the basement. I quickly followed her. I was concerned that what had happened upstairs was a charade. I watched every step she took and while she walked down the steps, I sensed the anger starting to rekindle within her. I gave her room to gather her thoughts, but suddenly her pace increased and she was already in the lab. I ran as fast as I could, and out of the corner of my eye I saw Marci with a large iron pipe, heading for Sarah's cell. I didn't know why the pipe was there or for what purpose, but I knew she wanted to do harm.

Sarah was flopping around in the cell, trying to get away or hide, but there was no place for her to go. The chain around her neck prevented her from going anywhere.

Marci quickly went into the cell and closed the door behind her, locking herself in with her pet. At first she just stood there holding the pipe with a glazed look on her face. She slowly turned her head and looked at me. Her haunting gaze slowly turned into an evil smile. She gently pulled her pants away from the lower part of her stomach as her eyes never left mine. To my surprise, she dropped the key inside her pants. My mind raced, knowing the key had come to rest at the lips of her vagina, and at that moment, I knew Marci was going to be fine. I nodded my head at her, acknowledging the fact that she was in her right mind. I quietly walked to the far end of the lab.

Wolfgang and Zelda abruptly appeared. I had to stop them from going any further. Wolfgang looked over at Marci and said, "That woman of yours is unstable."

I said, "No. No, she is not. She is perfect. She just deals with her emotions in a different way than you or I."

Marci glanced at the tiled floor and adjusted the pipe in her large and powerful hand. Sarah finally spoke, saying, "I know something is bothering you. I am sorry. Forgiveness is God's greatest gift."

I laughed a little to myself, knowing that was the worst mistake the pet could have made. Marci closed her eyes and gripped the pipe as tight as she could. Sarah started to back pedal on her comment. She said, "I am sorry. I didn't mean to say that."

Marci said, "Yes. Yes you did." Marci got very angry and changed her voice to mimic Sarah's in a condescending way. She said, "Yes, you did mean to say that!" Suddenly, Marci took the pipe and backhanded the instrument against Sarah's face. She hit her so hard that I saw a few fragments of her teeth fly out of her mouth. Marci was still mimicking Sarah's voice saying, "Forgiveness is god's greatest gift!" Marci's voice was almost shockingly similar to Sarah's. She said, "Just look at you. You are a freak! Look at what we have done to you, and you still pray to that folklore legend? I mean, for the ever-loving sake of satan." Marci raised the iron pipe over her head and struck the middle of Sarah's back. Marci screamed, "Come on! Repeat after me!" Marci again hit Sarah in the same spot on her back. "I deny there is a god called jesus christ!"

Sarah was in so much pain. Every inch of her back was hurting. She couldn't concentrate on what Marci was saying while she continued hitting her back with the iron pipe.

Marci continued, "I deny there is a god called jesus christ! Come on, bitch, say it! I will stop hitting you if you just will fucking deny it."

After multiple blows to her back, Sarah started to say something. She was finding it difficult to talk because many of her ribs were now broken and she was having trouble catching her breath.

Momentarily, Marci stopped hitting her. She knelt on the floor and got uncomfortably close to Sarah who was trying to get air into her lungs. After several long and agonizing moments Sarah uttered, "I... I... deeee... deny god... called jesus christ."

Marci smiled and patted her on her shoulder. She got up and said, "You have denied your god three times. Doesn't that sound familiar? You are a good little pet."

Sarah couldn't cry any longer. She was so tired of the pain and she couldn't handle any additional discomfort. She was at a place where she would do anything to be at peace. Of course, she knew she had denied her God, not once but three times. As I stood there watching the entertainment, I had to think how much I loved the irony in all of this.

Marci walked out of the cell and went toward Midnight's cage. She put on her thick gloves to protect her from Midnight's sharp teeth and claws. Marci also always kept Midnight on his leash, even when he was in his cage. After Midnight had been out for a while, he tended to calm down and became more controllable. As Marci walked Midnight toward Sarah's cell, it was hissing, biting and scratching. He even hissed at me while I stood there watching what my love was up to. Marci brought Midnight inside the cell and loosened Sarah's leash a couple more feet in length. Sarah was scared. She tried to get away but her chains wouldn't allow her to move more than a foot in either direction. The pain she experienced resonated throughout her body. Not only was she having trouble breathing, but her back felt as if it was on fire.

We knew her spine was broken when she told us she couldn't feel her lower torso. Marci allowed Midnight to jump around just a foot in front of Sarah's face. He was hissing and trying to scratch her, but Marci kept him at bay. Marci looked at Sarah and said, "I hate you, my pet. I hate you so much."

Sarah looked up at her and said, "No! Please..."

Marci moved her arms toward Sarah so Midnight was within reach of Sarah's head. Midnight took his large, powerful paw and scraped his long claws across Sarah's face. Marci encouraged Midnight to ravish Sarah.

Marci said, "Come on, Midnight, rip her to shreds."

Midnight let loose. For the first time in the creature's young life, it was allowed to experience its natural instincts, such as clawing, scratching and nipping. Midnight showed great passion toward his newfound freedom. He jumped on Sarah's face with all four paws. Sarah tried to get away but she was too limited in her movement.

Sarah was trapped inside her forced, private hell. Imagine something horrible, with sharp claws and teeth, on your face. Visualize being so helpless that you are powerless to stop the attack.

Midnight took his claws and dug them into Sarah's face. Midnight would sink his claws into the flesh then with a rapid motion, rip his buried claws out of her skin. Midnight repeated this multiple times.

At one point, one of his claws dug into Sarah's right eye. He poked and scratched at it until Sarah was blind then continued to scratch at it until it was out of Sarah's head. Midnight took the eye and bit into it, pulling on it until the optic nerve was detached. He sat and chewed on the eyeball until it was completely consumed. Midnight then went back to work and this time he attacked Sarah's left eye. After several moments, that eye was blinded as well but was still in its socket. Not one inch of Sarah's face was spared from Midnight's claws. He then jumped on the back of Sarah's head and crawled halfway down her back. Sarah's body tensed up, not able to scream because her lungs couldn't find air.

Marci continued to encourage Midnight to play with Sarah. After a few minutes, the upper half of Sarah's body was completely covered in blood, as was Midnight's. His stark white skin was now covered in Sarah's rich, thick, red blood. Midnight made some of the weirdest sounds during his attack and didn't rest for a moment.

I recorded the scene for Eva. Eva would enjoy this and would be so proud of her Midnight for getting the best of Marci's pet.

Marci told Midnight to get off her pet, but he didn't listen. Marci repeated the order, but he again ignored the instruction. Marci had never had trouble controlling Midnight, but when she pulled hard on Midnight's leash, he violently resisted, immediately digging his claws about an inch into Sarah's back. When Marci pulled him off the subservient pet, chunks of flesh fell to the floor by Sarah's side. She moaned loudly and strange sounds of pain filled the room. The formula was again preventing her from dying.

This was Sarah's situation. There is no death, or no natural death, meaning I had seen people momentarily die then seconds later they were back to life. This was the case with my brother many years ago. I can't tell you the number of times I thought he was dead, or should have been dead, only to have the formula work its magic and bring him back to life.

I sensed Marci was growing tired of Sarah. Maybe Sarah's wish would come true, which was for Marci to end her life so she could escape from this constant suffering.

Marci took Midnight over to a large washbasin that we had in Sarah's cell then cleaned the blood from his body. Midnight was making some strange sounds that were between a growl and a purr. After Midnight's bath, Marci lead him back to his cage. After locking the cage door, Marci focused on Sarah's moans for help. Marci went to Wolfgang's closet and picked out a long, thick rope. She walked over to the cell and stood next to her pet, quietly wrapping the rope around Sarah's neck then tightening the rope in a few knots. She then released the chains keeping Sarah on the floor.

Marci dragged Sarah across the floor by the rope. When her body was to the bars of the cell, Marci took the rope and placed it on the second highest bar. She looked at me, smiled and said, "Garrison, would you help me?"

I said, "Of course! What do you need?"

Marci said, "Take the end of this rope and thread it through to your side of the bars." I followed Marci's instructions. Marci picked up Sarah and said, "Now tie it as tight as you can on the bar below and wrap it around the bar a few times."

I took the rope and did as I was told. I tightened the rope to the bar just below Sarah's lower body as Marci continued to hold her pet. She smiled at her the entire time and didn't look away. Sarah was trying to speak, but nothing was coming out.

When I was finished tying the knot, Marci told me to step away and to get a knife and a long tube. I retrieved the supplies and rushed back to the cell. Marci told me, "I need for you to trach her. Cut a slit just up from her collarbone." She pointed to where I needed to cut. I took the point of the knife and sliced into her throat, making an incision of approximately two inches. Marci said, "Good. Now put the tube in there." I placed the tube into the incision. Sarah moved around and whimpered in pain.

Marci roughly let loose of her pet. Sarah was dangling on her rope and had no way to relieve the choking sensation because she had no arms or legs. She just dangled there like a helpless fish on a hook.

Sarah could still breathe, although not very well, through her trach. Marci said, "Now please step out of the cell, this might be messy." As I walked out of the cell, Marci picked up her iron pipe. She pulled the pipe back as if she was in a baseball stance. The pipe whistled through the air and I suddenly heard a thump mixed with the cracking of bones. The pipe had hit Sarah in the middle of her ribs. Marci then hit Sarah the same way on her other side.

As Sarah struggled to breathe, Marci continued to hit her repeatedly. After so long, each hit caused blood and chunks of flesh to splatter everywhere, which was causing quite a mess in Wolfgang's lab. Sarah's sides, from her armpits to the lower part of her belly, were bright red. She was barely alive. After every swing of the pipe, Marci was screaming, "Fuck you, Scottie. This is for you, bitch. Fuck you, cocksucker."

Marci continued to swing until both sides were completely gone. I saw Sarah hanging by the rope with her entire middle section gone, only being supported by her spine. Marci took one last swing with all her might. As the pipe hit the spine, it severed in two. The lower part of Sarah's body fell hard onto the floor. Marci looked up and noticed that Sarah was still alive. Marci said, "Can you fucking believe this? It's still alive. Amazing."

I said, "I had a similar situation with my evil brother, Adam. I had to cut his head off."

Marci looked at me and shook her head in amazement. She asked me to untie the rope. As I did, Marci let what was left of Sarah's body hit the floor. Marci picked up the rope and dragged her over to the crematory machine.

Without warning, Wolfgang entered his lab. He said, "What the fuck happened in here?" He looked around and saw blood splatter everywhere, and he was furious. He said, "You two... clean this shit up — now! I want this to be spotless before morning!"

Marci said, "Yes, sir."

Marci threw Sarah's barely alive body into the chamber of the machine. Marci knew she could still hear her. Marci said, "Okay, bitch. Your time is up. Now you are going to burn in hell." Marci went to pick up Sarah's other half. When all of Sarah was inside, the last thing she said to Sarah was, "Fuck you. Your family is next." Marci then closed the chamber door.

I knew Marci wasn't going after Sarah's family, she just wanted that to be the last few words Sarah ever heard. I turned the machine on and, like a tradition, I waited for Marci to hit the button that would start the fire. When she did, the chamber warmed up and after several moments, everything inside was on fire. Sarah had finally received her wish.

As for as Sarah, I couldn't imagine the pain she had felt during the last few moments of her horrible life. I would like to think that for her, she came to peace with her pain. Denying pain only makes it hurt more. One must accept pain and embrace it so the body can get adjusted to the suffering.

Marci and I spent the entire night cleaning up the mess we'd made. Marci wasn't as happy as I thought she would be, but her mind was still on her parents. She was having major trouble getting past her parents' rejection. I felt so sorry for her. She wasn't accepting their rejection and I wished I could have taken away her pain, but this was, unfortunately, out of my control.

Chapter Fourteen

Eva was doing well in her academic and musical careers, and enjoying her time away from the family. When Eva was at the estate, she was rarely the center of attention. In fact, she was pushed aside more often than not. Either I, Marci or one of our experiments took center stage, and the estate was not a stimulating environment for her. When she was on her own, the world bowed at her feet; when she was at home, she just blended in with her surroundings.

I spent a fortune on Eva during this time in her life. She wanted for nothing. I wanted her to appreciate the money we had, but she had a mind of her own. Many times we would get into arguments over the way she spent money, but I knew she wasn't going to change her ways.

When the opera houses throughout the world contacted her to perform, she started to become self-supporting, especially when it came to her travels. They told her upfront they would pay for her travel expenses, but Eva wanted the most luxurious things that were available. She wanted the best hotels, service and food that money could buy. Food was a key issue with her.

Like the rest of the family, cooked meat made her sick to her stomach, and most restaurants wouldn't serve her raw meat. One way around this was with sushi. Eva loved raw fish and usually ate large portions. She again was always the talk of the afterhours at the opera set. Many times she would be found sitting in the finest sushi restaurants eating alone.

Juilliard was very accommodating to Eva's travel. She was producing so much attention to the school that they overlooked her attendance. Eva's grades were all high; she carried perfect grades throughout her short career at the school. She took so many classes and tested out of some that she was in line to graduate in two years. Julliard also allowed her to participate in video conferences in many of her classes. This option was not afforded to just anyone, but in Eva's case, they made an exception. This fact was not looked upon kindly by many of her fellow students, mostly because Eva bragged about it to everyone.

Eva's skills in both violin and voice showed her to be in complete mastery in both disciplines. Going to class was a waste of time to her and her teachers. Many times, she was too much of a distraction to the other students, and some professors uncharacteristically told Eva not to attend their class. This was when Eva would do special exercises on her violin. I remember when she sent me a video of her playing a complicated violin sonata by Beethoven backward, from memory, a feat that is still being talked about on campus. Over seven minutes of playing an intricate piece completely backward even hit the New York Times. They couldn't believe this to be true so they sent several reporters to Juilliard to observe the feat in person. After the reporters witnessed the phenomenon, the media outlet ran a feature on Eva. This made my sister very proud and satisfied.

On a few occasions I would receive a call from the Met, begging me to perform with my assumed daughter. Eva and I would only perform onstage together if the conductor played what we demanded. We could play any piece of music, but we preferred Mozart.

When we played, we either played the violin together then followed up with the next piece where I played the piano and Eva played the violin, or on some occasions I would play piano while Eva sang. This particular musical genre was the most popular. We would set the world on fire when we took the stage together. Thunderous applause would shower down upon us. We would look at each other and talk back and forth with our minds. Even the music critics said that at times it looked as if we could read each other's minds. My name in the musical world had somewhat faded because I had rarely made an appearance over the past decade or so. Most of the classical music observers and professionals believed that Eva had slightly surpassed my skills on the violin.

So many questions were asked of us before and after our performances. The most common question was how such a young girl could have so much talent. Occasionally we would come across a reporter, someone in the orchestra or a fan that would say crazy things to us, like we were possessed by the devil or that our performances were fake. Of course, these instances were far and few between but it greatly upset Eva. She would always fire back with a quick, hurtful retort.

Eva would get sexually aroused after every performance. The attention that she received was the sexual release that she needed. On many occasions, Eva would converse with Marci about her sexual adventures. She was always careful not to ruin her name in some sex tape or to be caught having a public sexual adventure. Her ability to anticipate, hear, and see things that others don't perceive helped her greatly in this regard.

This was an especially wonderful time in Miriam's life as well. Eva was becoming good friends with Miriam, who was very accommodating to Eva and her demands. She knew that Eva was not gay, but if she did the things that were asked of her, she would at least get a sexual taste of Eva.

The most erotic of these events would take place with Tim, who had experienced many sexual adventures with the women. He was ashamed that he was being sexually dominated, but he was captivated by Eva's beauty and was being blackmailed by the vixens.

One night, Eva told Marci that she was bored so Eva had Miriam text her boy toy. Tim begrudgingly showed up at their doom. He was always nervous due to their threats of exposing him as a sexual slave and having rumors spread around campus that he was gay. They got into his head so much that his grades fell from straight As to Ds and Fs. He was so concerned that everyone at Juilliard was going to find out about his sexual encounters.

Tim's family was very poor and his father did everything he could to send him to this most prestigious institution. Tim had received a scholarship, but it didn't cover everything. Eva knew this and used it against him. She would repeatedly threaten that she was going to his father and tell him that he was raping her; therefore, he had to do what she wanted.

This night was one of the most erotic but stressful nights of his life. When Tim entered the room, Eva and Miriam were standing in the middle, completely naked. Miriam was standing behind Eva, playing with her large breasts. Tim felt as if all his blood had raced to his head and penis. What really got to Tim was the teasing. He was just waiting to dive into something sexually taboo. He knew he was doing something wrong, but he couldn't help himself. The two women had trained his mind to love feeling guilty. Eva sensed this in him and used his desires against her prey.

Tim was ordered to take off his clothes. Eva then walked up to him while Miriam put his own dirty sock in his mouth. Without

Eva walked toward her drawer and pulled out an object which she had kept hidden from Miriam and Tim. Eva told Miriam to get up and retrieve Tim's sock. The way Miriam was feeling, she would have done anything Eva had asked, no matter what she wanted. She had yet to climax and she had never been this horny in her life.

Tim allowed Miriam to remove the dildo and replace it with his worn sock. Eva told Miriam to sit on his chest, put his arms under her legs, and hold his wrists down on the floor. Tim was paralyzed with fear and knew this was not going to end well for him. In the meantime, Eva interlocked her powerfully strong legs with Tim's. She twisted his legs around hers then sat down on his stomach in an interlocking position. Tim's penis, scrotum and ass were exposed. She then opened the secret instrument that she'd pulled from the drawer. It was a pair of pliers. Eva quickly grabbed his scrotum and squeezed so both testicles were exposed. Without any warning, Eva took the pliers, opened them up, and placed them over his right nut.

Tim was now screaming and trying to get away. Eva said to Miriam, "Hold onto him, sugar." Miriam held him down as best she could. Eva took the pliers and squeezed his testicle. He screamed like he had never screamed before. His back and shoulders popped and cracked. He felt that he had broken his legs that were trapped by Eva's gorgeous and powerful legs. He had never felt so much pain in his life. The pain went from his balls to his stomach. Eva fought to control his legs so she tightened her leg muscles and pulled back an inch or so, causing more pain for her victim.

Tim screamed and moaned louder, which was music to Eva's ears. She was really enjoying this form of torture. She then went to work on the other testicle. She quickly squeezed it with her pliers until it popped. Tim was bucking up and down like a horse with his whole body covered in sweat. Eva sat there admiring his pain.

Eva told Miriam to let him go and shortly thereafter, Eva released her hold. Tim rolled himself into a ball, trying to catch his breath. His legs were cramping from the awkward position Eva had placed them in.

Miriam was concerned. She said, "Did you cut off his balls?"

Eva laughed and said, "No, I just pinched them a little."

Eva got up, walked over, and turned off the phone's video. Tim crawled around on the floor, moaning and trembling. His whole body was shaking from pain and the shock of what had just happened. He would have given anything in the world to reverse what he'd just gone through.

Eva was so turned on that her vagina was swollen and dripping wet. She got on the edge of her bed and told Miriam to rub her vagina. Miriam raced to the edge of the bed and sat down next to Eva. She slowly slid her hand down Eva's perfectly formed stomach. When the tips of Miriam's fingers touched Eva's vagina, Miriam started to rub slowly. The longer her fingers moved, the faster she picked up her pace. It didn't take long until Eva experienced a powerful release. Her orgasm took over her tight, perfect body. After her orgasm, Eva told Miriam to lick her fingers clean. Miriam was more than happy to follow her orders.

After several long moments, Tim struggled to get on his feet. He had witnessed Eva's pleasure, which made him feel even worse than before. He painfully got dressed. He was so angry with Eva, but he knew not to say a word to her. When he was dressed, he limped out of her dorm room. Eva closed the door and laughed hard. Miriam said, "You really hurt him. You know that, right?"

Eva said, "So what? Fuck him. He is so fucked up now!" Eva kept laughing. Miriam was sexually satisfied but after a few minutes of letting her mind absorb what had just taken place, she was mortified by what she had experienced. Moments like this caused Miriam to worry about the kind of relationship she had gotten herself into with Eva.

Tim struggled to walk down the hallway. Some of the girls in the dorm wondered aloud what was wrong with him. Tim just wanted to get to his dorm. He was so confused, hurt and sick to his stomach. His legs felt as if they were fractured and his wrists were starting to swell from Miriam's legs sitting on them.

Tim knew he couldn't go the hospital. What would he say and what would the people at the hospital think? His balls were completely crushed. He wondered if he was going to be okay. After what seemed to be hours, he finally made it to his dorm room. As he entered, he saw his roommate, Joshua, sitting at his desk studying. Joshua knew immediately that something was wrong although Tim denied that he was hurt. He tried to go to sleep, but the pain caused him to stay awake all night. When he first used the restroom to urinate, he didn't inspect his scrotum, but as the fluid passed through his penis, the piss felt like thousands upon thousands of microscopic knives were slicing the inside of his cock.

The next morning, he felt as if he was having a panic attack. He felt so alone. Waves of terror came over him, thinking about what Eva would do with that video of them. He couldn't ever go home if that were to get out. He would have to quit Juilliard. He couldn't face everyone's reaction.

So many thoughts went through his mind. He started thinking, *Did I like getting it up my ass?* At some point of the experience, he had liked the feeling. He liked when Eva dominated him and called him a fag. It turned him on. Tim thought long and hard all day about what had happened to him over the past couple of months. Of course, this added to the continued stress of his bad grades since he'd met Eva and Miriam. His mind was dominated by those two. He knew he was a horrible person by fucking such a young girl. What made it worse for him was that at first he enjoyed his sexual adventures, but as time passed, he liked those encounters less and less.

Two days after the incident, Tim's scrotum was black and blue. He was so depressed. As the days passed, he couldn't focus on anything but that video and how he had fucked up his life. His roommate, Joshua, was very concerned about him.

Unlike Tim, Joshua came from a wealthy family. He could afford many things, so out of pure generosity, he offered Tim a line of heroin. Tim had never used drugs before. Tim's heart was pounding hard as he watched Joshua dig out a bag of heroin from behind his dresser. As Tim watched, Joshua prepared the drug before him as he thought, *What do I have to lose?*

Tim reluctantly bent over and snorted the line. First, he coughed and sneezed then he experienced a sensation that he'd never felt before. After several moments, he started to feel different. The pain and stress were leaving his body.

After several days of going without his newfound love, Tim wanted more of this incredible drug. He was beginning to feel nervous and upset, and worried about everything. One day as he was walking down the hallway on his way to class, he saw Eva walking his way. She looked at him while she was walking with many of her classmates. Eva always led the way when she entered her class. As she walked by Tim, Eva pointed at his penis and laughed. Eva's classmates started to laugh along like mindless puppets.

Tim thought they all knew. Out of complete fear and embarrassment, he ran down the hallway, mortified. He heard the laughter increase as he ran away. He knew at that moment that he had to get out of the school. Eva shouted, "What's wrong with him? Come on, let's go after him." They chased Tim until he got to his dormitory. He ran up to his room, slammed the door, and started to cry. He wondered if she had streamed the video. He nervously got on his phone to check but saw nothing, leaving him wondering why they were laughing at him.

The entire day he sat in his room and never came out. He was sweating, his stomach hurt, and his heart was racing a mile a minute. He was being bullied by a young, famous girl, a powerful young girl-child, the most powerful person at Juilliard who was loved and admired all over the world. Everyone was going to hate him and no one was going to believe his side of the story. Eva was going to be the victim, not him.

The next day, Tim waited for Joshua to leave for his class. As soon as Joshua left the room, Tim immediately went to Joshua's hiding place and picked up the small bag that he'd hid. Tim nervously picked up some of the white power with his thumb and forefinger. He snorted that small pinch and started to feel better. Tim knew that he shouldn't have taken the drug, especially stealing it from his roommate, but at that time in his life, he didn't care. Tim needed some form of relief from his life, even if the relief was a small refuge. He decided to pinch another portion then repeated it for the third time. He felt his heart racing as if he'd just run a marathon. He needed to get out of his dorm. He had to run for some strange reason. The world seemed weird to him as the items in the room seemed to come to life. He thought he heard voices and that freaked him out. He was scared.

Tim raced out of the room, down the hallway, and flew down the flight of steps like a bat out of hell. He ran as fast as his legs would allow him, racing toward a large building. His heart was beating at a rhythm so fast he thought it was going to explode.

Tim franticly ran around the side of the building. He didn't want to run in the front because he didn't want to cause a scene. The voices in his head were getting louder, his vision was blurred, and objects looked strange to him in size, shape and color. Suddenly, he noticed people were looking at him and covering their mouths. He believed over a thousand eyes were watching him. He panicked and decided to run toward the back end of the structure, and as he got several feet from the door, it suddenly opened. He raced inside, pushing the people that were coming out. They screamed and started yelling. More voices, more attention was being placed on him. He had to hide. He needed to get away, to a safe, dark and cold area.

When Tim was inside, he founded himself in a corridor. He stopped and the only sound he heard was the pounding of his heart and his heavy breathing. He noticed that no one was around. He saw no one then suddenly an immense feeling of abandonment came over him. He started walking, and with each step he took, the walls were getting closer to each other. He stretched out his arms, trying to prevent them from closing in on him, but he was perplexed when his hands didn't feel the walls moving. The abandonment sensation quickly turned into paranoia. He felt that the voices were after him and he had to escape. He needed to get out of this place. He ran down a long, unoccupied hallway then finally saw an opening to the left. As he turned a corner, he tripped over his own foot and fell. He slid several feet on his side.

Tim's heart was racing so fast that he could barely distinguish his heartbeat. All he felt and heard was a rapid thumping, as pain started in the middle of his chest. He looked up and saw the ceiling starting to fall on him. His arms covered his head and after several seconds, he felt nothing coming down on him. For some unexplainable reason, he couldn't understand why he was disappointed that the ceiling hadn't fallen on him. He noticed the floor was shaking and starting to move in a wave-like motion. He braced his hands and knees on the floor in an attempt to stabilize himself.

Tim was trying to comprehend why the walls, ceiling and floor were moving. Suddenly, he heard a violin playing, but he couldn't figure out where the music was coming from. He knew the voices were getting closer when he heard the high-pitched violin music. Now in a complete panic, he stumbled to get up and started running down this familiar hallway. The faster he ran, the louder the music got. He wanted to turn around and go back to where he came from, but he heard footsteps behind him.

The cream-colored hallway suddenly turned darker. Air rushed over his face, which caused additional concern. He felt streams of sweat snaking down most of his body. The music was very loud, as if someone was playing above him. He quickly looked up and saw a bright light. He looked away and before him he saw the figures of people who were hissing at him while others were trying to talk to him. Out of the corner of his eye, he saw a ladder. That was his only way out. He raced toward the ladder but felt someone grab him. He awkwardly jerked his arm and freed himself from their grip.

Tim focused on the ladder, but it was also moving. He had trouble putting his right foot on the first rung. When he correctly positioned his foot on the rung he started climbing, but each step was met with difficulty because the ladder kept bending. One side would get larger then quickly get smaller. He knew he had to keep climbing, but the further he climbed, the louder the voices were getting, and they were all talking at the same time. They were getting closer.

The combination of the voices and the violin music was too much for Tim to handle – emotionally and mentally. Tim struggled getting up the ladder. He slipped multiple times, but after what seemed like an hour, he got to the top. There was a small landing at the top. It was dark and the air had a still, musty scent. He carefully stepped onto the landing, which seemed to move under his feet. He heard the voices talking, but this time he could make out what they were saying. It seemed to him that the voices were at his feet saying, "Hey, what are you doing up there? Get down from there! Watch out!"

Tim's mind was overflowing with horrible thoughts. He just knew that Eva had told everyone about their sexual adventures. He knew the entire world was after him because of his most grievous acts.

Tim screamed, "Why are you after me? I didn't mean to have sex with her. She came on to me! I was a virgin! She took advantage of me!" Suddenly, Tim heard thunderous amount of laugher and it was coming up from his feet. He was freaking out. He said, "Stop laughing at me. I am not a fag! She forced it in me. That does not make me a fag, god damn it!" The laughter got even stronger and louder. Tim felt a hot feeling that quickly hit him and again, sweat was pouring out of his pores. He attempted to focus on what the voices were saying. Finally, he could hear several words but the rest were muffled under the laughter. He wanted this nightmare to end. His only desire was to run away.

The voices continued to laugh at him. He was embarrassed and his heart was racing. The voices got louder and suddenly the music had stopped. Why had the music stopped? Why were the voices getting louder? He looked around and saw lights, large canister lights, shining down on him. He was so high on his heroin trip that he had trouble processing everything that he encountered. He turned around to see where he had come from but all he saw were wires hanging everywhere.

Why were there wire hanging from the ceiling? The voices continued to haunt him. His mind was in a fever pitch and he had to get out of there.

Tim looked around and saw these beams of light all around him. His eyes fixated on one of the lights in the distance, but he couldn't comprehend why the light was shining in a downward direction. He was confused. He thought, *Down to where?* His eyes followed the light and suddenly, there was a person. Finally, he saw something that made him feel better. He was not alone. As he stared at this woman, he noticed she was holding a violin. Could this be the person playing the violin? He shouted, "Please don't hurt me. I didn't want to have sex with that girl. Please don't tell anyone. I didn't want it up my ass."

The laughter started up again, mixed with screams. The voices with no faces knew, they all knew. At this moment, Tim knew his life was never going to be the same. He was convinced that Eva had posted the video on the Internet.

More voices, more laughter and more screams filled Tim's ears. He started to plead with the figure holding the violin and he thought to himself, *Oh my god. It's Eva.*

Eva turned her lovely head and stood there smiling directly at him. Tim desperately wanted to talk to her, but he was afraid of what she might say or do to him. He quickly made his decision. He felt the need to talk to her so he started to run, but an iron bar caught him just above his knees. It scared him, causing him to scream, "Get off me!" The voices were now blaring at him. Tim bent down and used his hands to grip what seemed like a bar. He thought, *It's not a person, it's a hard pipe.*

Tim swung his legs over the pipe, but as his legs passed over the bar, his left foot caught on the pipe. He braced for a fall by placing his hand out in front of him, but for some reason he kept falling. He felt the musty air blowing past his face as he felt weightless. He screamed for help as he couldn't control any of his reflexes. He was in a total freefall.

Eva stood there watching in pure delight. She saw Tim's body falling out of control from over thirty feet in the air. She momentarily laughed to herself as she thought that Tim was falling head over heels for her. When Eva was at her apex of enjoyment, Tim's body hit the stage floor, headfirst. His body followed and quickly made a cracking sound. His back was bent in two as his legs hit in front of his head. Tim's body fell awkwardly to the side.

Total silence filled the theater. Eva closed her eyes as she thought she could hear everyone's breath and thoughts at the same time. When

Eva opened her eyes she said, "What just fucking happened?" Everyone in the theater started screaming. Eva slowly walked off the stage toward Miriam, who was standing with her hands over her mouth and tears in her eyes. Eva looked at the horror in Miriam's eyes and said to her, "Oh, fuck!" Eva started to snicker, followed by a large, beautiful smile on her face. Eva said, "I can't believe he would actually do it. The fucker really fucked himself up, didn't he?"

Miriam slowly turned to Eva with a shocked look on her face. She couldn't believe that Eva was saying this. She had no feeling whatsoever about what had just happened. She thought it was funny and was laughing. Miriam felt the guilt of both her and Eva. Eva sensed this and said, "It's not your fault, Miriam. He was weak and foolish."

Eva started walking out of the theater. She was leaving her violin class because the professor was eventually going to cancel the class anyway. When Eva was walking out, people were looking at her in amazement. Eva was the only one in the theater that didn't show any emotion. Everyone was shocked by Eva's reaction. She had so much self-control.

Miriam followed Eva as she left the theater. Miriam noticed that everyone was watching her and Eva walk out. All eyes were on them. This made her even more nervous and upset. Miriam hurried to catch up with Eva. When she finally caught up to her, Miriam asked, "Did you really post that video of us?"

Eva laughed loudly and said, "Fuck no. I had no intention of posting it."

Chapter Fifteen

A year had passed and our young Eva's time at Juilliard was ending. She had completed her four-year degree in just over two years. There had been many talented prodigies that entered Juilliard but no one had seen the likes of Eva Seawick. She was one of the few at the Juilliard School to graduate Egregia Cum Laude in Violin, Voice and Chemistry. Egregia Cum Laude is the rarest honor that can be given to any student. Eva's personality had grown into a dominating diva who had little time for anyone. Although many of her classmates viewed her as a mega bitch, most respected her and many envied her talents both in the classroom and on the stage.

Throughout the world, Eva was known as one of the top singers on the operatic stage. She was demanding and knew everyone's role and lines in the opera she was performing. The older actors and actresses needed time to except her attitude, but after they witnessed the beauty of her voice, they all looked past her perceived personality flaws.

Eva's physical growth was amazing to watch over the past decade, especially since I experienced the same growth patterns. Eva had grown into a towering six-foot, one-inch woman with a perfect hourglass figure sporting large, firm breasts and rear. She exercised a few times a week by running and kickboxing. She was a powerful woman with extremely strong abdominal muscles, arms and legs, but those attributes never took away from her femininity. Eva's long, curly, blonde hair grew so long that it reached the small of her back. Her hair grew so fast that within several days after her hair trim, it would grow back to its previous length. Her complexion was perfect and pure in every way; free from moles, blotches, or any other foreign marks. She was beyond perfect – she was the perfect image of how a woman should look to a man's eye. If there was a god, it would stand back in total wonder and admiration of this creation that possessed all the characteristics of a perfect being.

Eva's violin and voice skills had improved to a degree that she never made an error in thousands of played notes and her voice was perfection at its finest. When she sang, there was never a quiver in her voice. In fact, when Juilliard and other opera houses tested her voice for recording purposes, the people that tested her said no other human being had come that close to such perfect pitch and tension.

When I look into Eva's eyes, I see myself. I see a flawless, impeccable human being that has been misplaced in a world of physical and intellectual imperfectness. I only wished that I could have given my Marci this gift. This will haunt me for the rest of eternity, but I can only do so much. I am not a mythical god that can wave his hand and change something physically.

I now understand that my parents can create perfect beings, but it must start at the moment of conception. I have come to the realization that even though I am perfect physically and mentally, I am still not a so-called god. God – what an idiotic concept. The absolute absurdity of the idea of someone creating something out of nothing is beyond my understanding or patience. Nothing could be further from the truth. No man or woman should ever allow themselves such folly.

Miriam was having the time of her life. She always had feelings for her love, Eva, who was her wet dream come to life. After the very rocky start in their relationship, the two girls had grown very close. Miriam knew that Eva was not in love with her and she came to accept that fact. She even knew Eva was using her at times, but as long as Miriam had access to Eva, she was happy with their arrangement. She worked hard to make her relationship with Eva work. Eva pushed Miriam in the classroom, on stage, and in life. Eva taught her little secrets about how to properly play the violin, and not the way she was taught at Juilliard.

They would stay up late at night and practice for hours on end. Eva was not easily impressed and certainly had no patience at all with imperfection. Miriam was extremely jealous and envious of Eva's ability in voice and violin. At times, Eva would recognize this and would let up on her criticism. Miriam reminded Eva so much of Marci, which is one of the reasons why Eva took such an interest in her. Eva felt sorry for Miriam and that rarely happened. Eva only cared about one thing and that was herself.

Miriam ended up graduating with Eva. They wanted to go out together and make Juilliard very proud. Miriam was widely thought of as one of the best prodigies that Juilliard had seen in some time. Miriam had wonderful control of the violin, as well as complete command of diction in the Italian and German languages. Miriam was a brilliant student who had never taken a back seat to anyone in her young life. Miriam graduated Summa Cum Laude in her academic disciplines. As great and as talented as she was, Miriam was still considered the second-best student at Juilliard, behind Eva.

Eric Staples was very proud of his daughter's accomplishments, but down deep he was jealous of the fact that Eva came in and took the spotlight away from his daughter. To make matters even worse for the Staples family, Eva was chosen to be valedictorian for the graduating class, an honor that Miriam thought was hers. After knowing Eva the past two years, Miriam fully understood just how special Eva was during their complicated friendship.

Our parents were extremely proud of the young diva although Wolfgang rarely showed any type of emotion to anyone, especially his daughter. Their relationship had always been strained.

Marci was ecstatic for Eva's accomplishments and for the highest awards she received from an institution that Marci had only dreamed of attending. There is a fine line between jealousy and envy. Marci so loved Eva and thought of her as her daughter, a daughter like she would never have of her own. She admired her effortless ability to excel and dominate any task that she set her mind on achieving.

Eva was very proud of herself and all that she had attained. Even though Eva expected many things, she was always happiest when she was given praise. She loved to be praised and worshipped. She not only loved the attention, she demanded people treat her like a goddess. That vanity made Eva into the person she had become. She fed off the desire for people's admiration, jealousy and pure adoration of lavish attention.

Being valedictorian was one of the biggest events in Eva's life. It was her chance to speak to her classmates, their parents, and supporters in the audience. She wanted her voice and opinions to be heard all through the Juilliard community – the past, present and future participants. Of course, I was the first person that my sister invited. I had to play the role of the proud father.

Eva worked on her speech with Miriam's help. Eva was pleasantly surprised at Miriam's gift for writing, something Eva didn't know Miriam possessed. The days progressed and the day of commencement was upon them. This was a big moment in Eva's life and everyone of importance was present. Many of the Juilliard alumni of the past were there to meet and greet the great Eva Seawick. Eva made herself available to all as she shook many hands, exchanged smiles, and accepted lots of praise.

I attempted to stay in the background because I didn't want to take any attention away from Eva, but that proved to be a difficult task. I saw many people that I knew through business contacts and met other influential people as well. Truth be told, many people showed up at the event not only to have a chance to mingle with Eva but to meet me as well. Eva didn't seem to mind since she didn't have a moment to herself. She was kept busy with the numerous people that wanted to speak with her. So many questions were thrown at me; when did you know Eva was a prodigy? Is she more talented than you? Did you have a hand in any of her training in her younger life and if so, how much?

The time was getting closer to Eva's speech. She allowed her long hair to flow freely down her back. Everything about her was flawless and perfect. When the commencement began, Eva was called up for many awards. Surprisingly, she was greeted with a very warm round of applause from her fellow students, some of which were students that Eva publicly berated either in voice, violin or academic classes. She was the most outspoken student at Juilliard and the fact that she was granted that privilege by the administrators didn't sit well with her classmates.

Eva received countless standing ovations when she received numerous accommodations in the fields of voice and violin. Many of the people in the audience that showed support were former students. These individuals didn't know Eva's personality so their opinions were not as jaded as many of her current classmate's sentiments.

When all the honors were given out, Eva was asked to speak for the graduating class. When Eva was introduced by Jim Callen, the President of Juilliard, Eva slightly bowed her head and rose from her seat. She walked to the podium wearing a tight black dress that accentuated every one of her perfectly formed curves. Her long, flawlessly curled, blonde hair bounced with every step, and her four-inch heels clacked on the floor with just the right precision. You could have heard a pin drop in the audience. As Eva walked up the steps, not one male in attendance had their eyes anywhere but on Eva's backside. I sensed that half in the room felt guilty about even looking and thinking all kinds of impure thoughts.

The President of Juilliard stood by the podium and quietly waited for Eva's arrival. When Eva reached the podium, she extended her hand to Jim. She expected him to gently kiss the back of her hand. When Eva offered her hand to him, Jim was a little surprised. He awkwardly took her hand and quickly kissed the back of it while Eva smiled and giggled.

A wave of coughing and whispers filled the auditorium. I heard one lady in front of me say, "What a bitch." Her husband was sitting next to her and he elbowed her in her side. She looked at him with a surprised look. He whispered that her father was sitting behind them. She quickly looked at me out of impulse. When our eyes meant, I winked at her. She quickly turned around as the blood rushed to her face. After several moments of adjusting herself in her seat, she felt the urge to get up and leave. The nervous husband turned around to me and said, "I am so sorry for that. I apologize."

I quickly said, "It is a shame that you have to apologize for your own wife." He gave me a dirty look. I continued to say, "Let's see what the bitch has to say."

The people around me laughed under their breath. Eva stood tall at the podium as she looked down at the microphone. It was too low. She smiled and slowly closed her eyes as if she was making love. She looked at Jim as she adjusted the microphone, acting as if she was put out at having to adjust it herself. Eva looked around the room and smiled. All eyes were on her. She felt her adrenaline pumping hard through her body as she began to speak in the most eloquent yet commanding voice.

"Good afternoon, ladies and gentlemen. It is with great honor and respect that I carry the responsibility of delivering this commencement speech. Although it has been a short time for me at Juilliard, I have developed magnificent and hopefully lifelong friends during my stay at the most prestigious performing arts school in the world." Eva looked directly at Miriam. Miriam smiled as a tear formed in her eye.

"I recognize that I am not liked by all. In fact, I am hated by many, but I could care less, for I am only interested in perfecting my skills on the violin, my voice and acting. Like every one of my fellow classmates, we have walked the halls of this great institution like so many before us. They didn't care about people's opinions or their condescending words either; they were only interested in learning, experiencing and creating music."

"We have all wondered, at one time or another when it will be our turn at greatness. When will it be our turn to get our shot at immortality? For some, these goals are not important, for others they are of the upmost significance. It really doesn't matter which side you fall on, just make sure you are a part of the main goal. The goal that we all strive to be – perfect. Whether it be a violin, piano, oboe, cello, clarinet, or voice major, we all have one thing in common; we practice long, non-stop, grueling hours. We never stop practicing. We practice for hours on end for achieving only one goal – the goal of being perfect. Perfecting notes that were written hundreds of years ago by men that created music for their pleasure as well as the satisfaction of others. That very purpose makes our lives better."

"For many of us to have the ability to recreate these perfectly placed notes in the exact order for which they were intended to be placed down on paper, is truly an honor. I think about the infinite number of hours of practice that it took most of us to work on our respective instruments of wind, wood or percussion. For some of us it might even be our voice." Eva stopped and smiled. Most members of the audience laughed.

"The highest compliment we could give to those musical creators is our extreme sacrifice for striving and putting forth our greatest efforts, our dedication to performing their colossal works to the best of our abilities. It is our responsibility to reproduce what our great masters wanted us to perfectly complete, note by note, so their thoughts could be permanently etched into our own DNA."

"These Master of Music understood when they started to create their masterpieces that the responsibility would be ours, the listener, to complete our serviceable dedication to the music that was created. That no music will make sense to even the most educated ear unless it is played to the intent to which it was envisioned. These works, written by men whose talents dwarf us all, are a constant reminder that some may never fall into the glorious abyss of the perfect musical mind of such greats as Beethoven, Mozart, Vivaldi, Bach, Puccini, Verdi, or whomever, the list goes on and on. It is our responsibility to carry on their musical works as well as their traditions of style – counterpoint, juxtaposition, and tension – so those messages will reach the listener of any century. We must keep their message and internal thoughts alive throughout time. We must venerate their ideas and pass on the very essences of the eternal greatness and immortality of these music creators. They and only they are the creators of this sublime mixture of sounds that even supreme beings are forced to listen to."

"For a few of us, there will be moments where we will reproduce those perfect moments. Some of us either have or will create those composers' envisioned moments of sublime and glorious perfection. Those of us that have attained such glory, even on a regular basis, should be honored and not scorned for having the ability to create music on a perfect level. People should be in awe of others that can accomplish this feat."

"As we embark on our journey through the real world, hopefully we will all experience that transcendent moment of perfection. For that is the goal of humans, all humans. I have experienced many of these moments and I will tell you this – it is a beautiful thing."

"My dear Juilliard, I will miss you. We all will miss you. From the most talented to the most average student and to anyone that is not worthy to enter your halls, thank you for the pleasure. May you live forever, my sweet queen."

The crowd erupted into a thunderous applause although some of the students sat there without participating in the praise for Eva's speech. I was so proud of her because she had poured her heart out and explained to everyone what music meant to her and thus what it should mean to all of us.

Eva slowly stepped away from the podium and waved to the audience like she was running for office. She continued to acknowledge the crowd as she made her way down the steps and to her seat in front of the stage. Eva's heart was pounding away. She was so proud of herself. She knew that she loved attention, but she had now discovered that she loved to speak in front of people. The power that she felt standing in front of those people was almost as exciting to her as singing in front of an audience. What she loved about speaking was that she had more freedom. She was not restricted in what she had to say or when to say something.

As the day fell on the commencement awards, everyone was invited to mingle outside of the auditorium. Large groups of people waited for Eva's entrance as she was still inside the auditorium waving and shaking hands with people. She finally caught up with Miriam. The two hugged and jumped around screaming. They were so happy. Eva and Miriam's complicated relationship had changed so much over the past couple of years, but they felt as if they had known each other since childhood.

Miriam made Eva feel special, which fed Eva's ego. Eva made Miriam feel special when she gave her the attention that she so craved. Miriam was in love with Eva and if it was up to her, she would marry her. Of course, since Miriam knew Eva wasn't gay, that dream was just that – a dream. Also, Miriam's father wouldn't approve and he would make her life a living hell if they were to marry.

Everyone was so excited to see Eva. One must understand that during this time, Eva was the most sought-after opera singer in the world. This was a special time for her most loyal fans. Even if some didn't want to admit it, to even be in the same room with her was an honor that they would tell their children about with great reverence.

A Juilliard woman is forever, and here, one of their own kind was not only famous but might be regarded as one of the all-time greats by the time Eva's opera career was finished. Of course, I was sure Eva hadn't put too much thought into this; the biggest issue for Eva was going to be her pending retirement from opera. That would be very difficult for her to accept, if she even accepted the fact. Eva was no different than me. We will live forever, thus we will never age like other humans. I believe I stopped aging around thirty years of age. So, how long can I play the violin on stage? At some point people are going to figure out that I hadn't aged a day since I turned thirty, so how long could I present myself to the public? Thirty years from now they would be expecting a sixty-year-old man, not the same thirty-year-old.

A few days after Eva's graduation, I presented this issue to her. I knew from the empty expression on her face that I had brought up an unpleasant subject to her. She loved performing in front of a star-struck audience, and the very thought of leaving the stage at any time in the future was not acceptable to her. She knew I was right, but at the time she wanted to think that she could do this forever.

Throughout all the self-denial, Eva knew this was an issue that we had to address. Therefore, the question before us was, *How do we deal with the time issue?* Everyone we knew would age and look older, but not us. Because we were so well-known, we couldn't up and move to another state or country and start our lives or careers over. Of course, we had many years to worry about this, but we needed to figure out what our backup plan would be – and soon.

Eva wanted to stay at Juilliard for the summer months until she found a place of her own, and Miriam desperately wanted to stay with Eva as long as she could. She didn't want to go back home because she felt there was no future for her in Indiana. Miriam didn't attend a school like Juilliard only to go back home to Indianapolis four short years later. Miriam wanted New York, the musical capital of America, as her home.

Eva asked me if I could arrange a deal with the President of Juilliard to have the two ladies on campus for the summer. After only one phone call, he was more than willing to accommodate my request. Later that afternoon, I received a video call from Eric who wanted to speak with me about our daughters' relationship.

Since Eric was so concerned about his image and what people thought about him because he would soon be making a run for the country's highest office, Eric started the conversation by saying, "Garrison, I don't know how to approach this, but I feel it is important to address this potentially sensitive subject. I feel that Eva and Miriam have a very close relationship and I am very happy that they get along so well. I know at first their relationship was a little rocky, but over the past year or so they seem to be inseparable. Not that this is a bad thing, but I am just a little concerned about where this might be headed."

I asked, "What do you mean, 'by where this might be headed?'" I could sense his nervousness and could see the sweat around his lips and on his forehead. Eric was in a very stressful place. He needed my financial support for his run for President, and we also had some financial deals in the works that he didn't want disrupted.

Eric said nervously, "Well, I don't mean that in a negative way; what I'm saying is that... well... do they have other friends? I never hear Miriam talk about other friends. Does Eva talk about friends other than Miriam?"

I said, "Eva does not have many friends. People tend to be very jealous of her. I, for one, am very happy that at least they have each other as friends, aren't you?"

Eric fidgeted in his chair while he cleared his throat and said, "Well... yes. Yes, I am glad they are friends, but... well, I guess you have a point. Miriam never had many friends because most of her classmates were jealous of her as well. I know she can be very difficult to be around. Is it that way with Eva and her classmates?"

I said, "Oh yes. In fact, Eva does not have any other friends that she is close to at Juilliard. She had a few friends in Louisville during grade school, but they were few and far between. So, what is your issue? What is your concern, Eric?"

Eric said, "Okay, I will be just come out with it. Do you think our daughters are gay? I mean, I have no personal issue with them being gay if that's the case, but I am concerned about, you know, what the potential voters might think."

I said, "Eric, this is not the early 2000s, you know. People do not care about that anymore."

Eric said, "I know, I know, but I just want to have all my bases covered."

I said, "You just do not want a scandal. You also do not want a gay daughter. Just admit it."

Eric said, "Well, I mean, I love Miriam and I want the best for her. You know... I know you feel the same about Eva."

I sat there toying with Eric. He knew that no one really cared outside of a handful of his friends; he just didn't want a lesbian for a daughter. It was just a twisted pride thing for him. Silly humans. I said to Eric, "I feel confident that Eva is not a lesbian. She is a free spirit, and I support that about her persona. I do not possess any concern whatsoever if Eva wanted to marry another woman. That is up to her, but I know my daughter and I feel that she has no romantic interest in your daughter or any women that I know of. Now, Eva is a very passionate individual and she may give off that impression at first, but to my knowledge, Eva is not the one that is gay."

Eric looked at me and suddenly his perfect Presidential face developed a horrified look. His eyes grew large, his mouth closed, and he felt lightheaded as his pulse was going wild. I had just confirmed his worst nightmare – that his daughter was gay. Eric said, "Do you think Miriam is actually gay?"

I said, "Have you asked her?"

Eric said, "Well, no, that's not something you just ask someone, much less your daughter."

I quickly interjected, "Yes, it is. If you truly care about her or how it might affect you, just ask her. That is the only way you will know for sure." Eric looked dumbfounded. I continued, "Well, Eric, it has been a pleasure talking and seeing you, but I have to go. Please remember you have my continued support. I hope it stays that way."

Eric looked nervous and said, "Yes. Thank you. It will. Don't worry. Thank you for your insight and, of course, your time. Goodbye."

I quickly called Eva and told her about my conversation with Eric. Eva wasn't pleased. Miriam was her friend and in a twisted way, Eva felt that she was the only one that could play with Miriam's feelings, no one else. After our conversation was over, Eva immediately went to see Miriam. Eva said, "Miriam, I have to tell you something. Your dad called my father and asked him if we were gay. My father told him that I was not. He never said you were, but I think your dad is going to ask you. I just thought you ought to know."

Miriam was very upset. She didn't want her dad or anyone else for that matter to know she was gay. It was now beyond hurting or embarrassing her father or potentially hurting his political future. She was mostly concerned about her musical career and how hirable she would be to potential employers. A part of her was embarrassed to admit that she was afraid to tell her small group of friends, fearing she might lose them as well. Eva sensed that she just didn't want to put up with people's attitudes about it.

The nation's sentiment toward being gay had changed over recent decades, but there had been some issues arising that had not been too favorable to the gay community. All minority groups had come under fire over the last decade. As the economy worsened during this time, people's acceptance had lessened. Racial tensions that had been dormant for a couple of decades had increased over the last several years. American citizens were afraid of the economy going into another depression, and the majority of Americans blamed the millennial depression on minorities that had made a socialist movement right before the depression.

Miriam said, "What the fuck am I going to do? What should I say? I can't admit to him that I'm gay. It really isn't his fucking business."

Eva said, "Then tell the bastard that, but you need to act surprised when you tell him. What do you want from me?"

Miriam said, "He will want to meet with me in person. That's just the way he is. He's so fucking guarded and paranoid. Please come with me. Please be there for me."

Eva said, "If it works into my schedule, I will be there for you."

As expected, Miriam received a video call from her dad, wanting her to fly home. At first Miriam refused, but her dad said it was very important. He told her that he wanted to tell her about his strategy to test the waters on running for the President of the United States. Miriam agreed but unbeknownst to Eric, Miriam was bringing Eva. Eva had an open window in her appointment book so she was able to go. Truth be told, Eva wanted to go on a trip and get away from New York for a while before she began her search for a permanent home in the city.

Eva and Miriam flew into Indianapolis. Eric arranged for his driver to pick up Miriam from the airport. Much to the driver, Greg's, surprise, Eva came along. As Greg took them to the Staples estate, Eva was looking forward to meeting the entire family on their home turf. When the driver pulled into the long, winding road that lead up the estate, Eva noticed the large trees that surrounded the house. The house was older than she thought it would be and it was easily the largest house in the small but very affluent neighborhood. As the car came to a rest, Miriam was the first to get out. Eva stayed in the car for a moment because she wanted to make an entrance. Eva saw some movement in the house and as Eric opened the large, dark oak door with a large wreath firmly attached, he walked out to greet his only daughter. Joyce followed and it was her turn to give out hugs. Miriam kept looking back for Eva then suddenly Eva gave the signal for Greg to open the door for her.

Eva had waited for the perfect time to make her exit from the limousine, to be as dramatic as possible. Meanwhile, Miriam continuously looking over her shoulder was soon noticed by her parents. As they looked at the limousine, Greg opened the door for Eva. Just like in the movies, Eva placed her left foot out of the car and firmly planted it on the hard concrete. Eva wore her four-inch-tall white, Italian, handmade shoes.

Eva would rarely be seen anywhere without wearing some form of heels on her feet, and her extremely tight fitting, all-white dress with a plunging V-neck more than complimented her curves. Seldom did she wear a bra, saying bras were too confining and uncomfortable. Her large, perfectly shaped nipples were tastefully protruding through her silky dress.

Eva wore a thin but ultra-expensive diamond-laced necklace with complimentary diamond studded earrings. One of Eva's most cherished trademarks was her hair, which seemed to represent an extension of her body. Eva's powerfully built leg pushed her perfectly formed body out of the back seat as her mini sunglasses, which looked like reading glasses, sat firmly on the middle of her nose. For some time now, Eva had loved the look and it was becoming another trademark for her. Her fans loved the look as did the people covering her in the media.

While Eva emerged from the limo, her eyes looked around while she carefully placed her steps. As she walked toward the Staples family, her eyes looked deeply into each family member's eyes. Eric said, "Well, I was not expecting you, Ms. Seawick." Joyce looked up at her husband then cast her questioning eyes at Miriam.

Miriam said nervously, "I asked Eva if she could come along with me."

When Eva approached, she raised her right hand toward Eric. Eric gingerly accepted her offering and gently kissed the back of her hand. Eva looked over at Joyce and offered her hand to her. Joyce said, "Well, it certainly is an honor to have you in our home."

Eva laughed and said, "The honor is actually all mine."

Eric said, "That was one inspiring Valedictorian speech that you gave, Ms. Seawick."

Eva said, "Thank you so much and please, call me Eva."

Eva strongly sensed every one of Eric's thoughts and feelings. She always knew what people were thinking, some more than others. She knew he was in lust with her, but he felt bad about his feelings because of Eva's age. Eva had grown used to having older men ogle at her figure even before her teenage years. Since she was eight she'd possessed a strong, young and powerful body that looked more than the legal age for sex.

When Eric first saw pictures of Eva's preteen years, he thought there was no way this beautiful creature wasn't older. Nothing tipped off her age, certainly not the way she carried or expressed herself. Now that Eva was barely legal, her sexuality intoxicated all men and even some women, to a point of shameful embarrassment for those captive slaves of her aura.

Eva looked at Miriam and placed her hand on Miriam's upper arm, a movement that caused a reaction from Eric. Eric cleared his throat and he said, "Why don't we come inside? Greg, please take Eva's luggage up to the spare bedroom." Eric looked at Eva and said, "I wish I knew you were coming. I would have been more prepared."

Eva said, "That is perfectly fine, Eric. Don't worry, I don't require much sleep."

Miriam laughed and said, "She is a strange one, Dad. She only sleeps a couple of hours a night, if that."

Joyce chimed in, "Oh dear, you need more sleep than that, especially with your busy schedule."

The Staples family gathered in the kitchen, and Eva and Miriam accepted beverages to refresh themselves. Eva sparked up a conversation by saying, "Eric, I have been following your UAP party and I must say that I like what I see. I think if you play your cards correctly, you can win the Presidential election."

Eric said, "I think I have a good shot, but I hope that nothing..." Eric cleared his throat and thought carefully, "unexpected will derail my mission." Eric looked at Eva then at Miriam, which caused her to lower her head.

Eva said, "As long as you keep yourself in good standing with America, you shouldn't have issues, right?"

Eric said, "I am not worried about me; it's other people that I'm worried about."

Eric continued to look at Miriam, making her more uncomfortable. Eva quickly said, "Surely you don't think you will have any issues with Miriam. She is one of the finest young women that I know. She is an asset to you and certainly will never cause any embarrassment for you."

Miriam said in a low voice, "Eva..."

Eric's nervous brow was sweating. He didn't want to have this conversation with an outsider the likes of Eva Seawick. Eric said, "And I hope Miriam will stay that way."

Miriam quickly said, "Okay, guys. Like, I'm standing right here!"

Eva and Miriam went to their rooms to change their clothes for dinner. The Staples' served cooked meat with vegetables which, for Eva, like her family, couldn't digest. Eva politely refused to eat. Eric and Joyce felt bad about serving a meal that Eva couldn't partake in. Eric said, "Are you a vegetarian?"

Eva said, "No, I prefer uncooked meat, but the vegetables are a splendid accompaniment."

Joyce said, "Oh. So, you prefer sushi?"

Eva drew up a smirky smile and said, "Yes."

The end of the day came quickly and the girls went to their respective bedrooms. The next day, Miriam took Eva out on the town and they visited a few of the major attractions Indianapolis had to offer. Eva was only stopped a handful of times to sign autographs.

When the ladies came back, Miriam asked if Eva would like to take a swim. Eva was an excellent swimmer and she loved the feel of the water as it hit every inch of her body. Miriam gave Eva a bikini and a robe to wear and they went to their rooms to change. Miriam quickly changed into her bikini. Meanwhile, Eva slipped out of her clothes and into the robe that Miriam gave her. They walked down the stairs, out through the kitchen area, and onto the porch. Miriam rushed to the pool and swan-dived into the water. Eva walked toward the pool as if she was on a catwalk at a European fashion show as her four-inch heels hit the pavement with confidence and assurance.

Eric was in his first floor study overlooking the pool and the back portion of the estate. He was on the phone talking to one of his close friends and business partners as he heard noise outside and naturally looked up. Out of the corner of his eye, he saw Eva walking slowly toward the pool.

Miriam was already swimming to the other side of the pool before Eva got halfway to the pool area. Eva slowly untied her robe and allowed it to slide off her body as she literally walked out of the garment. When the robe fell to the ground, Miriam came up from the water, turned around and saw that Eva was completely naked and was walking toward her. Meanwhile, Eric couldn't believe his eyes. He almost dropped the phone. He cut his conversation short as he got up from his desk and stood at the window watching Eva seductively walk to the edge of the pool. Eva could sense that someone was watching and guessed that it was Eric, but she didn't care. All she wanted was to feel the sensation of having the water caressing every inch of her body.

Eva stopped at the edge of the pool and slipped out of her heels. She looked at Miriam and smiled. Miriam said, "No, Eva, not here. My parents might be watching." Eva raised her arms toward the sky, tilted her head back, and gently swayed her head from one side to the other. Her long blonde hair moved like a snake as the tips of her perfectly groomed hair was now below her perfectly shaped rear. Eva bent her powerful legs and dove into the pool, making the most beautiful sound. She stayed under the water for a moment then appeared next to Miriam.

Eric, who had been watching the whole scene, didn't want to be caught watching the young vixen skinny-dipping so he quickly moved away from the window and raced out of his office. Eva heard him moving around inside of the house, but she didn't let on that she knew it was Eric. Miriam was completely unaware that her father had seen Eva's flawless body.

Eric went to the kitchen to get a beverage from the refrigerator. He didn't want to look out but he did; he couldn't help himself. He inched closer to the window to get a better look. From a distance he saw Eva's perfectly formed breasts bobbing in and out of the water. Eva let herself go for a moment. She wanted to have fun with her friend's father. She allowed herself to be happy, and from time to time let out little squeals of excitement. Miriam told her to be quiet but Eva paid no attention to her pleas.

Suddenly, Joyce stepped into the kitchen and said, "They sound like they're having lots of fun out there."

Eric felt as if his heart had fallen to the pit of his stomach. He didn't want his wife to know that he had seen Eva naked. He tried his best to stay calm as he quickly walked over to his wife and started to kiss her. He smiled at her and after several moments, he guided her to their bedroom. Eric had always had an active sex life with Joyce, but even this was highly unusual, although she didn't care. Eric took Joyce up to their room and they made love. Eric couldn't get Eva and her body out of his mind. As he made passionate love to wife, he fantasized that she was Eva.

Miriam and Eva swam in the pool for a while then retired to the lounge chairs to lie in the sun. Miriam was so turned on seeing Eva lying there without any clothes covering her body, having the sun kiss every inch of her gorgeous body, which drove Miriam to take her bikini off. At this point, Miriam was beyond caring if her father saw her or not.

Eva lifted her legs up in the air and spread them out, demonstrating her extreme flexibility. She reached over for the suntan lotion and covered every inch of her legs and private area with the lotion even though Eva never had to use suntan lotion because the formula would never allow her skin to burn or permanently change color for that matter.

Miriam was dripping with anticipation but she knew Eva was playing with her. It was moments like this that made Miriam sometimes dislike Eva, but the teasing was such a turn on for her that these things had triggered orgasms for her in the past. This was one of those times. Miriam tried desperately to hold back, but she had an orgasm while watching Eva spread lotion on herself. Miriam's orgasm was so intense that she bit her lower lip as she squeezed her legs together while holding onto the sides of her lounge chair.

Eva looked at Miriam's body shaking and said, "You are so fucked up."

Eric, who had just finished making love to his wife, saw the show that Eva put on. He quickly walked away so as not to draw any attention to his viewing pleasure. Eric felt so guilty that he was thinking of this young girl, but she didn't have the body of a young, innocent girl. Eric knew she was a vixen, a temptress, a wild girl that was nothing but potential trouble.

After supper, Eric and Joyce asked Miriam if they could talk with her privately. Eva left the room and went upstairs although both Eva and Miriam knew what the conversation was going to entail. Eva even prepped Miriam on what to say since she didn't want to admit to her parents that she was gay. Miriam had known all along that the only reason her parents wanted her to come home was because they wanted to ask her if she was a lesbian.

Miriam and her parents went into the family room. Eric poured himself a very expensive glass of Kentucky bourbon that, ironically, he'd received as a present from me. Joyce had a concerned look on her face and she knew Miriam was nervous as she noticed her fidgeting with the end of her dress. She kept looking at the clock on the wall, just wanting this conversation to be over.

Eric said, "Miriam, you know that I'm going to be running for President of the United States. Now I would like to keep this a secret so please don't tell anyone, especially your friend, Eva. I want to make sure that nothing personal would derail that goal. I only have one shot at this run and that is now, not in the future or the next decade, but now. Now is the time to run if my party is going to win this election. So, this is very difficult for me to ask because, well, to be perfectly blunt, the Seawick's are very supportive of our party. Obviously, we did a lot for him, thanks to you, in helping to acclimate his daughter to Juilliard. So, as you can see, this is a very sensitive subject matter, but I have to ask. Are you in love with Eva?"

Miriam sat there and immediately began to perspire. Eva had coached her on trying not to sweat or show emotion, but controlling these emotions is very difficult for humans. Miriam's mind was racing and she could only muster, "What?"

Eva was listening in the other room, unbeknownst to Miriam's parents. Eva rounded her eyes and said to herself, *What a stupid cunt.*

Eric said, "I said—"

Miriam interrupted and said, "No! I am not in love with Eva or any other woman for that matter."

Eric said, "So you're saying that you're not gay?"

Miriam got up, threw her hands out to her sides and said, "What? Why are you asking me these questions?"

Joyce said, "We are not judging you, Miriam, we just don't want to be caught off guard."

Miriam said, "I... I can't believe this."

Eric said, "Miriam, will you please answer the question. Are you gay?"

Miriam walked over to the window at the far end of the room. She felt so alone. She wanted Eva to come running into the room to rescue her, but she knew Eva would never do that. She understood that Eva wasn't gay but she wished she was. It would make everything less complicated. Miriam was forced to keep her sexual preferences to herself.

Eric asked again, "Miriam, are you gay? Do you prefer women over men? I mean, I wish you liked men, but it's okay if you like women. I just want—"

Miriam turned around and screamed, "All you fucking care about is yourself! You don't care about me. I was always a trophy daughter for you. You just wanted me there to make you look good in front of your friends. Both of you."

Eric and Joyce looked at each other. Joyce immediately said, "That's not true."

Miriam started crying as she said, "Yes, it is. Look, I am a graduate of Juilliard and I am damn proud of what I am. I have worked hard to make you two proud of me. I just wish you would, just once in your lives, tell me how special I am or how proud you are to have me as your daughter."

Joyce arose from her chair and ran over to Miriam. She said, "We love you so very much and we are – we are so very proud of you."

Eric came over and said, "Of course we are. We are very proud of you! Where did you get the idea that we aren't? All we want to know is if you're gay."

Miriam shouted, "I am not fucking gay, all right! God, would you please put it to rest? I fuck men, Daddy! I fuck men!"

Eric said, "Well, it just seems that you are always around that Eva woman."

Miriam interrupted and said, "Eva is my friend. My best friend and really the only fucking friend that I have. You leave her alone. If you fuck up my friendship with Eva, I will never speak to you again! Understand? Eva makes me feel special, that is all. She is not interested in me sexually. She likes men. She fucks men too."

Eric raised his hands up in the air and said, "Okay, okay, I believe you. I just wanted to have a conversation with you about this subject because I don't want something coming up in the future that might surprise me. I hope you understand."

Miriam said, "Eva is my friend and as long as we are friends we are going to be seen together."

Eric said, "Okay, that's fine. I'm sorry to upset you."

Miriam said, "I have to go. I have to get out of here."

Miriam stormed out of the room with Joyce shouting, "Miriam! Please don't go." Joyce turned around and said to Eric, "Why were you so hard on her?"

As Miriam left the room, Eva acted as if she had just run down the steps. As they met each other, Miriam hugged Eva. Miriam said, "I have to get out of here." Eva let her go as she watched her friend exit the front door. Eva looked at Joyce and Eric as they ran into the foyer. They were afraid Eva might have heard everything. Eric thought to himself that those two were keeping something from him. He just knew something was being kept from him.

As Eva looked at the two standing there, she acted concerned and went upstairs to her room. She actually *was* worried about her friend. This new emotion was something Eva had never felt about anyone in her life and it caught her off guard. She wanted to run after Miriam but she thought it would be best not to leave or say anything to Miriam's parents.

Later that night, Miriam came home and Eva consoled her. Eva told her not to be surprised if her father apologized. Eva went over to Miriam and embraced her with a caring hug. Eva said, "Don't worry, Miriam, I will take care of your father. Don't worry. I won't hurt him, but I will make sure he leaves you alone."

Miriam whispered, "Thank you, but please don't hurt him."

Eva kissed the top of Miriam's head and whispered back, "I won't hurt him."

Eva put Miriam to bed after she'd taken a few downers to calm herself. Miriam rarely took drugs of any kind but did on special occasions, and this moment in her life was one of those special occasions. Eva went to her room and plotted out a plan to help Miriam.

As the night grew long, Eva stepped out of her bedroom. She had previously walked the entire house during the nights of their stay. She rarely stayed the night over at her girlfriends' houses but when she did, she always explored late at night. Eva never slept more than an hour or two so the rest of the time she found herself bored out of her mind.

Usually Eva would read a book or two during the night but sometimes, if the family was interesting, she would explore both the inside and outside of their house. She especially had an interesting time at night inside the Staples home. As she walked through the large house, she studied every room. She snooped around and looked in desks, end tables and kitchen drawers. She looked through the shelves on bookcases and on mantel tops. She quickly started to gather more information on the family and, to a small extent, even their nightly habits.

Eva knew Joyce always went to bed several hours before Eric retired for the night. Eric was a night owl and didn't require a lot of sleep, usually going to bed well past midnight. Eva quietly held her heels in her hand and walked out of her room. As she walked down the hallway, she heard Joyce lightly snoring in her room.

Eva wore very little clothing at night, even when she was not sleeping. This night was no exception. She had on a short, silky white nightgown with a thin rope tie that just covered her backside. Like so many of her clothes, she had bought this gown during one of her opera performances in Rome. As Eva was quietly walking down the stairs, she heard sounds coming from the kitchen. Eva knew it was Eric because of the way he cleared his throat. She knew this was her chance to speak with him alone.

Since Miriam was out like a light from her drugs and Joyce was in a deep sleep, Eva slipped into her four-inch white heels that exposed most of her feet and walked down the large foyer area that lead to a hallway. She had her phone in her hand. As she was walking, she turned on the video feature of her camera. When Eva got to hallway, she turned her perfectly formed body to the right. As she entered the kitchen, she quickly placed the camera up against the backsplash.

A startled Eric turned around with a half glass of bourbon in his hand. He wasn't expecting anyone to be up this late at night. Eva said, "Hello. I'm sorry to have startled you." Eric was amazed at what he saw. There was this beautiful young girl that looked to be at least ten years older than she was. Her blonde hair was almost as long as the night gown that she was wearing. Her perfectly taut breasts were halfway covered by the softest looking piece of cloth Eric had ever seen. The light coming from the pendant lights hanging over the large granite island were dimmed just enough to cast shadows in the most unique areas of Eva's body. Each step she took made a loud clacking sound that cascaded throughout the kitchen. Eric so desperately wanted her to stop walking so that sound would stop. He was afraid it would wake up Joyce and Miriam.

Eva didn't attempt to accelerate her seductive allure. In fact, she did the opposite. She carried herself with a youthful, innocent fervor mixed with the self-confidence of a prima donna that she was famously known to possess. Eric was sweating, knowing he shouldn't be in her presence, not with the way she was dressed. Eva said, "I'm having trouble sleeping." Eva walked to the refrigerator and opened the door. Her back was to Eric, whose guilty eyes couldn't stop ogling her highlighted silhouette that was accentuated by the light coming from the refrigerator. Eric's eyes were still on Eva, and he tried not to look at her ass that would poke out at him every time she leaned slightly forward. She found nothing that she liked so she closed the door.

Eva noticed a wine refrigerator that was down toward the end of the long stretch of cabinets. She walked over and opened the small door. She looked inside as she gingerly bent forward. The back of her garment rose up, exposing her perfectly formed ass. Eric wanted to say something but couldn't. Part of him liked what he saw, but the other part knew he was staring at a barely legal eighteen-year-old girl. Eva sensed that she had his full attention. Eva said, "Oh look, this looks like a good bottle." Eva bent all the way down as she totally exposed her private area to Eric. Eva gently moved her ass ever so slightly from one side to the other.

Eric coughed louder than normal and said, "Now... aaaaa... Eva, I don't think you should be drinking wine so late at night." Eva pulled the bottle out, stood up and ever so slowly turned to him. Her breasts were almost coming out of the tight-fitting nighty. Each side of the nighty was widening through all of Eva's movements. Eric could now see a hint of her well-developed stomach. He also glanced down and saw a glimpse of her bald private area. Eva shaved her pubic area daily.

Eric quickly turned around and said, "Eva, you need to wear something besides what you have on. It's very revealing."

Eva said, "I'm sorry to embarrass you, Eric, but I'm sure I don't have anything that you haven't seen before. Right?" Eric didn't answer. Eva walked over to the island and placed the bottle on the granite. She said, "Do you have a bottle opener around here?"

Eric turned around and said, "Eva, I don't think it's a good idea to drink that wine so late at night. I think it's time for you to leave and go to bed."

Eva said, "Do you really want me to go to bed? I'm all alone."

Eric quickly said, "Now, Eva. I know your father and he wouldn't approve of this type of behavior and..."

Eva started to walk over toward Eric. She turned on more of her seductive charm and sensuality. She untied her nighty and expertly demonstrated a little trick that she had developed. She walked out of her nighty as she allowed it to hit the floor. Eric was sweating as he tried to walk away from her quickly, but Eva grabbed his whiskey glass, causing a portion of the whiskey to spill out onto the floor. Eva took the glass from Eric, brought it to her pouting lips, and took a drink.

Eva slowly turned her back to Eric. He glanced at Eva's breasts as she turned. Eva placed the glass of bourbon down on the island as Eric looked at Eva's perfectly formed and muscular upper back. His eyes trailed downward to the small of her back then he stared at her perky ass that was just aching to be touched. He knew he shouldn't be looking at this forbidden vixen. There before him was the daughter of the latest donor in his campaign, the world's most beautiful woman, and one of the most popular women in the world, bending over for him in his kitchen. To add to the difficulty of the situation, she was his daughter's best friend. He had to do what was right so he quickly looked away.

Eric said, "I think it's time to get your clothes on, Eva."

Eva smiled to herself. She flung her flowing hair back and shook her head as if to mock him with her hair. Long, perfectly formed, natural curls gently and softly touched a large portion of her back. Eva knew this was the time to make her move. Eva immediately moved backward with all her might, leaving Eric no time to react. Her naked body collided with Eric, causing him to stumble backward as his ass hit the front of the farm-style sink behind him. As Eva pushed her body into him, her ass was on his groin area. Eva shouted loudly, "Oh! Mmmmm!"

Eric almost had a heart attack. He was not only caught off guard but he certainly didn't want to wake up his wife or daughter. Eric's natural impulse was to grab Eva. His hands touched the sides of her shoulders when she backed into him. When she screamed, one of his hands went to her mouth while the other went toward her neck area. Eva quickly grabbed his hands and moved them down over each of her nipples then forced him to squeeze his hands over them. As Eva was directing Eric's hands, she pressed her ass further into Eric's groin and started to grind her rear into him.

Eva stood an imposing six-foot one inches in height, even without heels, making her taller than Eric so he was a little easy to manipulate. Eva pressed her back onto his chest as she turned her head toward his then quickly moved his right hand down toward her vagina. Eric stopped her by trying to pull his hand away but as he did, she rammed her ass into his private area with a hard thrust as she forced his hand onto her vagina. Eva kept rubbing Eric's hand over her entire left breast and kept his right hand busy on her vagina, all the while grinding her ass hard into his privates.

Eric looked down at the most erotic sight he had ever seen. He looked at the most sensually suggestive face looking back him with her mouth open and couldn't resist any longer. He moved his head to the side and inserted his tongue into Eva's mouth. He kissed her as passionately as he had ever kissed any women before. He was now at a point where he didn't care what was happening; all he could think about was this young, sexual dynamo. Eva could sense that he was about to ejaculate so she quickly stepped away. Eric moaned rather loudly, not wanting her to stop. Eva walked away slowly as she looked over her shoulder at him. She went in front of the island, turned around to face him and jumped, sitting on top of the granite.

Eric's mind was racing as he stepped toward her. As soon as he got a few feet from the island, Eva lifted her right leg up and placed it on his chest. Eric stopped abruptly. Eva moved her foot over his left pectoral muscle and said, "Worship my foot." Eric was very much taken aback and looked confused. Eva said, "Worship my foot and you will get into my pussy." Eric looked down at her vagina as if he was in a trance. Eva said, "You want my pussy, don't you? Well, don't you?" Eric's natural impulse was to nod his head, automatically answering her question with a confident yes. Eric took Eva's foot by the ankle and began to lick the sole of her foot. Eva commanded, "Now get your cock out." Without any hesitation, Eric used his free hand and unzipped his pants. Eva said, "Take your pants off so I can see your cock." Eric unbuckled his belt, unhooked his pants and let his trousers hit the floor. Eva continued to instruct him by saying, "Now get out of your underwear. Good god, man, is this like your first time?"

Eric nervously and awkwardly pulled his underwear down with his one hand and finally he was free from his elastic imprisonment. Eva took her foot away from Eric's mouth. Eric moved toward her as if he were going to mount her right there. Eva quickly and harshly slapped him across his cheek. The slap was so hard that it caused his head to spin to the side. Eric was very surprised and instantly lost some of the hardness between his legs. Eva said angrily, "No one takes me. I take them." She instantly reached down and grabbed his penis. Eric about jumped out of his skin. She roughly pulled him toward her as she placed her other hand over the head of his penis. Eva circled the end of his cock on the palm of her hand. Eric was moaning, but he dared not say a word. Eva then took his penis and rubbed it across her vagina, and took his head and traced the outline of her cunt with his penis. Eva suddenly pushed Eric back by his control knob.

Eva turned around on top of the granite and got on her knees. She bent down on all fours and hiked her ass up toward Eric. Eva said, "Lick me. Start with my asshole and lick all the way down." Eric quickly walked over to the most beautiful piece of ass he had ever seen. His mind was now racing even faster than before. He started with her asshole as instructed. He was careful not to do anything she hadn't instructed him to do. Eva was now in full control. After several minutes, Eva said, "Now get your tongue inside me. Come on... lick it. Eat it out." Eric's tongue exploded every angle of the inside of her vagina. He couldn't get enough of her.

Eva quickly moved her ass down, and the look on Eric's face was priceless. He looked like he'd lost everything he owned. He didn't want to stop licking her, but she'd made him stop. Eva moved down from the island and walked behind him. She reached around and took hold of his penis as her other hand cupped his scrotum. Eva said, "See your drink over there?"

Eric muttered, "Yes."

Eva said, "Yes, my mistress!"

Eric repeated, "Yes, my mistress."

"Slide the glass in front of you."

"Yes, mistress." Eric did as instructed. Eva was now sliding her hand over his penis as she squeezed his testicles.

Eva said, "I want you to come in that glass. Then you are going to drink it all up for me."

Eric said, "Oh... okay... but..." Eva squeezed his balls hard with her hand. Eric bent forward and said, "Okay... okay... please don't hurt me."

Eva said, "Come for me, you little bitch. Come on. Pretend I am your little girl. I want to see daddy come for me."

Eric said, "Please don't do that. This is so wrong. You are making it worse."

Eva again squeezed his testicles hard, but this time Eric raised himself up on his toes. Eva said, "Come on, do what you are told because if you don't come and drink it up, I am going scream like a motherfucker and fuck your whole life up like you have done with Miriam. You know Miriam, right?" Eva's pace was now picking up and she was stroking Eric hard, fast and rough. Her hand would slam into his balls as she slid her hand back. Repeatedly, Eva continued to jerk him hard. Eric was in that state of blissful pleasure with just enough pain to heighten his sexual experience. Eva knew just how coarse she could be with him to cause him to teeter on the edge of sexual release.

Eva continued to taunt, "Come for me, daddy. Come for your little girl. I want to see you pop. Come on. Come for me."

Eric couldn't last any longer. He nervously slid the glass in front of his penis and started to explode. One pulsating spasm after another unleashed his semen into his watered down, expensive bourbon. Eva told him, "Good daddy. That's a good daddy." Eva gently kissed his neck and said, "Now drink it all up for me." Eric took the glass in his hand and nervously brought it near his mouth. Meanwhile, Eva took the palm of her hand and roughly rubbed her hand over the top of his extra sensitive penis. Eric was now actually in pain. Eva said, "Drink it or I will pull this little thing off right here." Eric quickly moved the glass to his lips and first took a sip then started to gulp his drink down in large swallows.

Eva said, "Good. That's a good daddy. Now you will continue to be a good daddy by leaving Miriam alone, right?" Eric didn't say a word. Eva took her open hand and pounded it on the tip of his penis.

Eric moaned and shouted, "Please stop!"

Eva said, "Shhhh, you don't want wake everyone, now do you? Okay, so here's the deal." Eva continued to rub the head of his penis. "You are going to let Miriam live her life the way she wants, right?"

Eric said, "Yes."

Eva said, "So if she wants to lick pussy, that is just fine with you, right?"

"Yes. It's fine with me... no problem."

"Promise?"

Eric said, "I promise."

Eva let go of Eric's penis, placed her foot in between his legs, and forced them apart. Eva said, "Now, I taped all of this and if you ever get out of line, a copy of this tape will find its way to every cable outlet in the world. Got it?" Eva moved her right knee up with great force into Eric's scrotum. Eric immediately fell to his knees, gasping for air. He tried to hold himself up by holding onto the island but he needed both of his hands on his dick. He fell onto his side and continued to gasp for air.

Eva moved her leg over his head and aggressively straddled him. She moved her vagina just inches from his red face that was so desperately trying to get air. Eva said, "And also, don't forget about my real Daddy. He might want to help you with your campaign. See, all you have to do is leave your daughter alone and let her live her life as a free woman. Let her make her own decisions and just be proud and supportive of her. And give my dad anything he wants. You do that and you will be so successful. Is this all understood?" Eric nodded. Eva said, "That's a good daddy." As Eva got up, she patted Eric on the top of his head as if he were a dog.

Eva walked over Eric, picked up her nighty, walked toward her phone and said, "Remember… I have everything recorded and this little session has been saved." Eva picked up her phone and walked out. A panic came over Eric. He struggled to get up and quickly started to clean up the mess he and Eva had made. At times, he would spit out the taste of the bourbon and his manhood that lingered in his mouth. He nervously cleaned up everything so as to not leave any evidence behind that would raise questions about his unfaithful endeavor.

When Eric had cleaned up everything, he looked at the clock in the kitchen which read 4:13 in the morning. He was too nervous to go to sleep and his testicles hurt him every time he moved. He couldn't get Eva's voice or body out of his mind. He knew he had sinned gravely and he only prayed that she wouldn't tell anyone about what had happen. If she were to ever tell or release that video, his life would be ruined. It would absolutely mortify Joyce and especially Miriam. He was caught on tape doing something that would never or could never be forgiven. He was so ashamed and nervous that he thought his heart would jump out of his chest because it was beating so fast. He was now controlled by an evil and seductive temptress.

The next morning, Eva made sure she was the last to come down for breakfast. Eric didn't want to be there, but he had to show his face. His heart about jumped out of his chest again when he first heard those loud, commanding clicks from Eva's shoes. As Eva walked into the kitchen, she acted as if she was in full control, but he never let on that she had done anything wrong during the night. Eva was a master at hiding her emotions – that was one of the many reasons why she was so good at acting in the operas she performed.

As everyone ate breakfast, Miriam said, "I think we ought to go back to New York soon."

Eva said, "Whatever you want. That's up to you."

Eva looked over at Eric and he immediately said, "Yes, whatever you want. Although I hate to see you go." Miriam looked over at her father with a bewildered look. He said, "Miriam, I have to apologize to you. I am sorry about last night. I beg for your forgiveness. It's your life and you do what you want. I trust you. You are so smart and responsible. I am just so controlling at times, especially with the election coming up. I hope I still have your vote."

Miriam just sat there with her mouth open. She looked over at Eva, but Eva was busy drinking a glass of milk. Eva looked at Miriam and all she did was raise her eyebrows. Miriam said, "Okay. Thank you."

The entire day, Eric avoided everyone in the house until later when Eva walked up to him while he was standing in the garden. Eva said, "Your garden looks to be doing well. That's good. Thank you for your hospitality. It looks as if everything might turn out well for you."

Eric said, "Thank… thank you for keeping our secret."

Eva smiled and said, "What secret?"

Eric nervously laughed and said, "And I will not forget about your dad."

Eva's smile grew larger. "Of course you won't. Goodbye, Eric Staples… or should I say, Mr. President?"

Eric forced a small laugh as he watched Eva walk back to the house. Eric knew that last night would haunt him forever and that he would have a hard time living with it, but he had no choice. A part of Eric died that night, and his self-respect and dignity were tarnished forever. He doubted that he could ever rest peacefully as long he lived. Having something like that hanging over your head would make any man slowly go insane from guilt and concern of their taboo past.

Later that day, Miriam confronted Eva and said, "Okay, Eva, what's going on? What did you say to him to change his mind? Did you… tell me…"

Eva said, "Miriam, we did have a small talk. That's all. Your father is a great man. He is an understanding man and father. Don't worry. He will never give you any shit about being gay or anything for that matter. Okay? So that is all."

Miriam said, "But Eva..."

Eva quickly said, "Everything is fine. Leave it. You are free."

Miriam knew Eva had done something to her father, but she didn't want to know what. All she knew was that her father accepted her and would now leave her alone. Miriam knew how lucky she was to have such a great friend as Eva. She also knew Eva would never love her as much as she loved Eva. She understood that they would never be married or have a union, and Miriam knew that not many times in life does one come across such a caring and thoughtful friend. Miriam was happier after this trip home than she had ever been.

Eva and Miriam flew out of Indianapolis the next day and back to New York. While on the plane, Eva told Miriam, "Now I have to find a home for us in the city."

Miriam's head was about to explode from surprise and excitement. Miriam said, "What did you say? A home for... us."

Eva said, "Well yes, silly. We can't live in a dorm all our lives. I mean... you do want to live in the same house as me, right?"

Miriam said, "Yes! I mean... of course... yes... yes I do. I just didn't think you wanted me to live with you."

Eva said, "Look, we are best friends, right?"

Miriam said, "Yes, I hope so."

Eva said, "Well, we are. Just don't forget how lucky you are." After a short pause, the two ladies looked at each other and laughed.

Miriam settled back in her seat as she felt the plane lift off. She looked over at Eva who was on her phone reading the daily news. For the first time in Miriam's life, she was completely free and it was all because of the ultimate diva, Eva Seawick.

As the plane soared through the air, Miriam thought about what her new life would encompass and which direction she was headed. Little did she know that Eva was in total control of those future plans and if truth were told, I don't think Miriam would object to Eva's plans for her. Eva knew what Miriam desired. She knew what made her happy.

Meanwhile, back home in Indiana, Eric sat down in his office chair and took a sip of his bourdon-filled glass. He lamented at the numerous events that he had experienced over the past few days. Those events plagued and dominated his thoughts. He wanted Miriam to live in Indianapolis with him. He loved his daughter and wanted her near him. He was also a control freak that at times feared his own shadow. Eric wanted desperately to run the country and he didn't want anything to derail him from his plans. He loved America and wanted to get the country back on the right track. Of course, he was also very vain and loved the spotlight, so this potential position of having almost absolute power was something that he desired greatly.

Now he sat and wondered if he had just destroyed his entire career, family and life by having sex with a younger woman. But he knew what was done, was done and couldn't be changed. He had to move forward like nothing had happened and he hoped that the truth would never come out.

Eric felt that if he kept Miriam close to home, she would stay out of trouble since she had been a somewhat difficult child growing up. Like most prodigies, she always felt and acted like she was entitled, but since she was introduced to Eva, her cockiness had subsided. Eric also wanted her to be independent from Eva. He knew that Eva had control over him because of their sexual encounter. He thought that the more he kept the two away from each other, the better it would be for him. On the flip side, Miriam had improved her attitude since she'd met Eva. Eva, in a twisted way, had been beneficial for Miriam. Eric knew that he had to play his cards right and keep Eva happy because he didn't want me to know about their wild night of lovemaking. Thus, Eric's hand was forced and he had to let Miriam make her own decision on where to live.

So here was our beautiful and lovely Eva who, at a very young age, had managed to set the stage for her future wishes. Eva had been in complete control of her life since she was a very young age. Her passion and drive were unlike anything I had ever seen. She had the uncanny ability to anticipate and sense what others wanted and desired, and she used that gift to her advantage in every way to control and manipulate people. She was in complete command of the direction of her plans regarding her future. Unbeknownst to me, buried within those plans, involved my future as well.

About the Author

Kevin C. Popp was born and raised in Louisville, Kentucky, graduating in the early 1990's from Bellarmine University with degrees in Business Administration and Accounting. After working a couple of jobs after college, in 1997 he found a great company in the Financial Securities market, working in the finance department.

Kevin grew up as an only child, living modestly. His parents saved every dime they made, but when it came to Kevin's basic needs, he wanted for very little. His parents were much older than most of his friends' parents, thus his grandparents were older as well. His mom and dad spent the majority of his youth taking care of their parents, so his entire youth was surrounded by grandparents' illnesses, hospitals, nursing homes and eventual pending deaths.

One of Kevin's childhood memories was a struggle to find time to be alone. He felt strongly that he needed that time to himself, even for short time spans. He would regularly take long bike rides through the neighborhood, ultimately taking him through a park that his neighborhood bordered on. At times he would think to himself about money, politics or the concept of God.

Kevin took up golf at an early age and played the game well, but not to the level that he desired. He always admired people that were great at something, venerating intelligent, athletic, wealthy and attractive people, both young and old.

Kevin had many obsessions growing up, including golf, stamp collecting, money, stock market and numbers. He grew up thinking he was poor, but actually the opposite was true. He always saved more than others. At the impressionable age of twelve, he invested in the stock market and quickly enjoyed making money.

Although very intelligent, Kevin never liked school, and constantly daydreamed, thinking about things that never occurred to others. His mind, even to this day, continuously ponders and worries about everything, planning out numerous courses of action for every situation that he attempts or is forced into doing.

As an adolescent, Kevin was starved for attention so he attempted to be the class clown, only to find himself a colossal failure in that role. One area of his mind that was not a failure was his imagination. His mind worked continuously, exploring many subject matters. The one motif that kept his attention was horror. He loved watching 'monster' movies, and found that he could stomach the most ghastly scenes that included demonic possession, dismemberment, and torture at a young age. His mind was fascinated with the macabre, both real and imaginary, trying to understand the complicated relationship between life and death and how God played His part between the two.

As the years passed, Kevin could no longer find any outlet to whet his appetite for this strange, dark world resting in the innermost parts of his brain. One day at work, he decided to write a book, and began creating an outline. Before he knew it, he had over five typed pages of notes. Creation, he loved that word! So he began creating a story, not about anyone in particular, but a story that he created from his imagination alone. He quickly found that he could create something by writing down what was in his mind.

Although certainly not the twisted, heartless monster you see in his books, Kevin says he sometimes has a dual personality, especially when he writes. While busy typing away, he loses himself in an imaginary world of a multitude of sadistic renderings, and his hope is that he is talented enough to bring his imaginary world into focus for all to see and enjoy. It is his goal, as the writer of this series, to disrupt not only your cognizant state of mind, but also your unconscious realm simultaneously. Like any great composer of music, artistry or writing, as you read his books, he wants you to experience what is in his mind and soul. He wants you to understand his repulsion and loathing for a portion of the human race, as well as the pursuit of perfection that is inside his being. He doesn't want to just scare you, he wants to firmly implant horrific torture scenes in your memories that will haunt you daily. He wants you to question the human race and the many gods they pray to. He wants to dominate your thoughts and force you to feel others' pain.